See

I was already moving, but I wasn't fast enough. By the time I'd gotten the little marble out of my pocket the gun had gone *clack* three more times. The suppressor muffled the shot so that the loudest noise was the metallic sound of the action cycling and the *thud* of bullets chewing through flesh. The man shot Anne a final time as I threw the marble, and the man watching their backs had only time to flinch before it shattered against the wall.

The marble was a one-shot—effectively a single spell with an activation trigger. This particular one was a condenser spell, and as the crystal shell holding the magic in stasis broke, mist rushed out to blanket the area in fog. The cloud was only about forty feet across and it wouldn't last long, but for a minute or two anyone in that area was blind.

Except me.

Praise for
FATED

"Harry Dresden would like Alex Verus tremendously—and be a little nervous around him. I just added Benedict Jacka to my must-read list. *Fated* is an excellent novel, a gorgeously realized world with a uniquely powerful, vulnerable protagonist. Books this good remind me why I got into the story-telling business in the first place."
    —Jim Butcher, #1 *New York Times* bestselling author

"Benedict Jacka writes a deft thrill ride of an urban fantasy—a stay-up-all-night read. Alex Verus is a very smart man surviving in a very dangerous world."
    —Patricia Briggs, #1 *New York Times* bestselling author

"Jacka deftly invents the rules of magic as he goes along, creating an emotionally satisfying story arc and a protagonist who will keep readers coming back."
    —*Publishers Weekly*

Ace Books by Benedict Jacka

FATED
CURSED
TAKEN

taken

BENEDICT JACKA

ACE BOOKS, NEW YORK

THE BERKLEY PUBLISHING GROUP
Published by the Penguin Group
Penguin Group (USA) Inc.
375 Hudson Street, New York, New York 10014, USA
Penguin Group (Canada), 90 Eglinton Avenue East, Suite 700, Toronto, Ontario M4P 2Y3, Canada
(a division of Pearson Penguin Canada Inc.) • Penguin Books Ltd., 80 Strand, London WC2R 0RL,
England • Penguin Group Ireland, 25 St. Stephen's Green, Dublin 2, Ireland (a division of Penguin
Books Ltd.) • Penguin Group (Australia), 250 Camberwell Road, Camberwell, Victoria 3124, Australia
(a division of Pearson Australia Group Pty. Ltd.) • Penguin Books India Pvt. Ltd., 11 Community
Centre, Panchsheel Park, New Delhi—110 017, India • Penguin Group (NZ), 67 Apollo Drive,
Rosedale, Auckland 0632, New Zealand (a division of Pearson New Zealand Ltd.) • Penguin Books
(South Africa) (Pty.) Ltd., 24 Sturdee Avenue, Rosebank, Johannesburg 2196, South Africa

Penguin Books Ltd., Registered Offices: 80 Strand, London WC2R 0RL, England

This is a work of fiction. Names, characters, places, and incidents either are the product of the author's imagination or are used fictitiously, and any resemblance to actual persons, living or dead, business establishments, events, or locales is entirely coincidental. The publisher does not have any control over and does not assume any responsibility for author or third-party websites or their content.

TAKEN

An Ace Book / published by arrangement with the author

PUBLISHING HISTORY
Ace mass-market edition / September 2012

ISBN: 978-1-937007-72-0

ACE
Ace Books are published by The Berkley Publishing Group,
a division of Penguin Group (USA) Inc.,
375 Hudson Street, New York, New York 10014.
ACE and the "A" design are trademarks of Penguin Group (USA) Inc.

PRINTED IN THE UNITED STATES OF AMERICA

10 9 8 7 6 5 4 3 2 1

ALWAYS LEARNING   PEARSON

taken

chapter 1

The Starbucks in Angel is on the corner of the busy intersection of Pentonville Road and Upper Street, set deep
into the offices around it with a glass front that lets in the
light. The counter's at ground level, but climbing to the second floor gives a view down onto the high street and the
crowds streaming in and out of Angel station. Opposite the
Starbucks is Angel Square, a huge, sprawling, weirdly
designed building checkered in orange and yellow and
topped with a clock tower. The clock tower looks down onto
City Road, a long downhill highway linking Kings Cross
and the City. It was eleven A.M. and the morning rush was
long past, but the roads and sidewalks were still crowded,
the steady growl of engines muffled through the glass.

Inside, the shop was peaceful. Two women in work
clothes chatted over their lattes and muffins, while a stolid-
looking man with greying hair hid behind his *Times*. A

student sat absorbed in his laptop while three men in business suits were bent over a table full of spreadsheets, their drinks forgotten. Music played quietly over the speakers, and the clatter of cups and coffee machines drifted up from the floor below. And near the window, chair turned to watch both the street and anyone coming in, was me.

I like the Angel Starbucks for meetings. It's easy to reach, there's a nice view, and it's just the right balance between public and private. Usually it's quiet—most of the trendy people prefer the cafés north along Upper Street—but not so quiet as to give anyone ideas. I'd probably like it even more if I drank coffee. Then again, given how much people like to complain about Starbucks, maybe I wouldn't.

I'd already checked out the surroundings and the other customers, so when the woman walked into the shop downstairs I was free to focus on her. There are two ways of getting a look at someone with divination magic: You can look into the futures of you approaching them, or you can look into the futures of them approaching you. The first is better if you want to study them; the second is better if you want advance warning of what they're planning. I chose the first, and by the time the woman stepped onto the second floor I'd been watching her for nearly a minute.

She was good-looking—*really* good-looking, with gold hair and sculpted features that made me think of old English aristocracy. She wore a cream-coloured suit that probably cost more than my entire wardrobe, and everyone in the room turned to look as she passed. The three men forgot about their spreadsheets, and the two women put their chatter on hold, watching her with narrowed eyes. Her heels clicked to a stop as she looked down at me. "Alex Verus?"

"That's me," I said.

She sat opposite me, legs together. I felt the eyes of everyone in the room comparing the woman's outfit with my rumpled trousers and sweater. Now that she was on the same level I could see that it wasn't just the heels, she really was tall, almost as tall as me. She carried nothing but a small handbag. "Coffee?" I said.

She glanced at a slim gold watch. "I only have half an hour."

"Suits me." I leant back on the chair. "Why don't you tell me what you're after?"

"I need—"

I held up my hand. "I was hoping you might introduce yourself first."

There was a brief flash of irritation in her eyes, but it vanished quickly. "I'm Crystal."

I already knew her name. In fact, I'd gone out of my way to find out quite a bit about Crystal in the two days since she'd contacted me requesting a meeting. I knew she was a Light mage, one of the "nobility" with lots of connections. I knew she wasn't a player in Council politics, although she had friends there. I knew the type of magic she could use, where in England she was based, and even how old she was. What I didn't know was what she wanted me for, and that was what I'd come here to find out. "So what can I do for you?"

"I expect you know about the White Stone?"

"The tournament?"

Crystal nodded. "Isn't it due to start soon?" I said.

"The opening ceremony will be this Friday," Crystal said. "At Fountain Reach."

"Okay."

"Fountain Reach is my family home."

My eyebrows went up at that. "Okay."

"I want you to help manage the event," Crystal said.

"It's very important that everything goes smoothly."

"Manage how?"

"Providing additional protection. A diviner would be perfect for that."

"Right," I said. I've run into this a lot lately. People hear about my background and assume I must be a battle-mage. Now it's true that I'm a mage and it's true that I've fought battles and it's even true that I've fought battle-mages, but that doesn't make me a battle-mage myself. "I'm not really a bodyguard."

"I'm not expecting you to serve as a battle-mage," Crystal said. "You'd be more of a . . . security consultant. Your role would be to warn me of any anticipated problems."

"What sort of problems?"

"We're expecting over a hundred mages for the tournament. Initiates and journeymen, including a number of Dark representatives." Crystal clasped her hands. "There'll be competition. It's possible some of the participants will carry grudges off the piste."

It sounded like a recipe for trouble. "And stopping them will be . . ."

"There'll be Council battle-mages present. We're well aware of the potential for trouble. There will be sufficient security. We just need to make sure the security is in the right place at the right time."

"You haven't received any warnings or threats?"

"Nothing like that. There's been no suggestion of trouble so far, and we'd like your help to make sure it stays that way."

I thought about it. I've usually steered clear of Light tournaments in the past; my teachers thought they were a waste of time and on the whole I agreed with them. But if initiates were there, that changed my feelings a bit. Trying to protect adult mages is a thankless task, but apprentices are another story. "What exactly would you be expecting me to do?"

"Just to keep an eye on the guests. Possibly some investigation if anything comes up. We're particularly concerned about keeping the younger apprentices safe, so we'd been hoping you could help with that."

I started to nod—and stopped.

Crystal looked at me. "Is something wrong?"

I kept still for a second, then smiled at her. "No. Not at all. You mentioned investigation work?"

"Obviously, some mages are more likely to make trouble than others. We don't have anybody we're especially suspicious of, but it's likely things will crop up to turn our attention to someone. When they do, it would be very helpful if you could find things out for us about them. Their background, connections, that sort of thing."

"I assume the place is staffed?"

"Oh yes, the servants will handle all that. You'd be considered one of the guests."

"And you said the opening ceremony was on Friday. The guests will be arriving on what, the same day?"

"Exactly." Crystal was relaxed now; the interview was going well. "We're expecting the first guests by the morning, although of course the sooner you can arrive the better."

"And regarding payment?" I thought about cash, as soon as possible.

"Future service, as usual. Though if you'd prefer something more tangible that's perfectly acceptable."

"When could you arrange payment by?"

"Immediately, of course."

"Well." I smiled at Crystal. "That settles that."

"Excellent. Then you'll be able to come?"

"No."

The smile vanished from Crystal's face. "I'm sorry?"

"Well, I'm afraid there are a couple of problems." I leant forward casually. "The first issue is that I've had a lot of approaches like yours over the past few months. And while they all looked good on the surface, the last couple of times I've said yes they've turned out to be . . . well, let's just say I don't feel like a repeat performance."

"If you have a prior engagement I'm sure we—"

"No, we couldn't. Because the second problem is that you've been reading my thoughts ever since you sat down."

Crystal went very still. "I'm afraid I don't follow," she said at last.

"Oh, you were very subtle," I said. "I'd guess most mages wouldn't even notice."

Crystal didn't move, and I saw the futures whirl. Flight, combat, threats. "Relax," I said. "If I was going to start a fight I wouldn't have told you about it."

The futures kept shifting a moment longer, then settled. "I'm sorry," Crystal said. She brushed back her hair, looking remorseful. "I shouldn't, I know. I was just so worried you'd say no." She met my eyes, entreating. "We need someone as skilled as you. Please, won't you help?"

I looked back at Crystal for a long second. "No," I said at last. "I won't. Good-bye, Crystal."

Again the smile vanished from Crystal's face, and this time it didn't come back. She watched me without expression for a long moment, then rose in a single motion and stalked away, heels clicking on the floor.

I'd known Crystal was a mind mage, but even so I hadn't noticed her spell. Active mind magic like suggestion is easy to spot if you know what to look for, but a mage who's good with passive senses, reading the thoughts that others broadcast, is much harder to catch. The only thing that had tipped me off was that Crystal had been too neat. In a real conversation no one tells you *exactly* what you want to hear.

That last reaction had made me wonder, too. In between her magic and her looks, it occurred to me that Crystal probably wasn't very used to not getting her own way. I'd better be careful around her if we met again.

I noticed suddenly that everyone in the shop was watching me. For a moment I wondered why, then smiled to myself as I realised what it must have looked like. I left my drink on the table and ran the gauntlet of stares as I walked down to the ground floor and out into the London streets.

I never used to get offers like these. A year ago I could go weeks at a time without seeing another mage. In magical society I was an unknown, and all in all that was how I liked it.

It's hard to say what changed. I used to think it was because of that business with the fateweaver, but looking back, I get the feeling it was more to do with me. Maybe I was just tired of being alone. Whatever it was, I got involved in the magical world again and started getting myself a reputation.

Although not necessarily a *good* reputation. I got the fateweaver against some stiff competition, making a couple of very powerful enemies in the process, one of which came back to bite me five months later. A Light battle-mage named Belthas was trying to get sole ownership of a very nasty ritual, and when I tried to stop him it came down to a fight. When the dust settled, Belthas was gone.

That was the point at which other mages started to take notice. Belthas had been good—*really* good, one of the most dangerous battle-mages in the country—and all of a sudden a lot of people were paying attention to me. After all, if I'd been able to defeat someone like Belthas, I'd be a useful tool to have on their side. And if I *wasn't* on their side . . . well, they might have to consider doing something about that.

All of a sudden, I had to play politics. Take a job, and I'd be associated with whoever I worked for. Turn one down, and I'd risk causing offence. Not all the job offers were nice, either. More than one Dark mage figured that since I'd knocked off one Light mage I might be willing to do a few more, and let me tell you, those kinds of people do *not* take rejection well.

But I'm not completely new to politics, either. My apprenticeship was to a Dark mage named Richard Drakh, in an environment where trust was suicide and competition was quite literally a matter of life and death. It's left me with some major issues with relationships, but as a primer on power and manipulation it's hard to beat. Crystal hadn't been the first to try to take advantage of me—and she hadn't been the first to get a surprise.

But right now I didn't feel like dealing with that. I put Crystal out of my mind and went to go find my apprentice.

　　　　　ı ı ı ı ı ı ı ı ı

Mages don't have a single base of operations—there's no central headquarters or anything like that. Instead the Council owns a selection of properties around England that they make use of on a rotating basis. This one was an old gym in Islington, a blocky building of fading red bricks tucked away down a backstreet. The man at the front desk glanced up as I walked in and gave me a nod. "Hey, Mr. Verus. Looking for the students?"

"Yep. And the guy waiting for me."

"Oh. Uh, I'm not supposed to talk about—"

"Yeah, I know. Thanks." I opened the door, closed it

behind me, and looked at the man leaning against the corridor wall. "You know, for someone who's not a diviner, you seem to know an awful lot about where to find me."

Talisid is middle-aged with a receding hairline, and every time I've seen him he always seems to be wearing the same nondescript-looking suit. If you added a pair of glasses he'd look like a maths teacher, or maybe an accountant. He doesn't look like much at first glance, but there's something in his eyes that suggests he might be more than he seems.

I've never known exactly what to make of Talisid. He's involved with a high-up faction of the Council, but what game they're playing I don't know. "Verus," Talisid said with a nod. "Do you have a minute?"

I began walking towards the doors at the end of the hall. Talisid fell in beside me. "Since you're here," I said, "I'm guessing I'm either in trouble or about to get that way."

Talisid shook his head. "Has anybody ever told you you're a remarkably cynical person?"

"I like to think of it as learning from experience."

"I've never forced you to accept a job."

"I know."

The doors opened into a stairwell. Narrow rays of sun were streaming down through slit windows of frosted glass, catching motes of dust floating in the air. They lit us up as we climbed, placing us in alternating light and shadow. "Okay," I said. "Hit me."

"The task I'd like your help with is likely to be difficult and dangerous," Talisid said. "It's also covered by strict Council secrecy. You may not tell anyone the details, or even that you're working for us."

I looked over my shoulder with a frown. "Why all the secrecy?"

"You'll understand once you hear the details. Whether

to take the assignment is up to you, but confidentiality is not."

I thought for a second. "What about Luna?"

"The Council would prefer to limit the number of people in the know as far as possible," Talisid said. "However, due to the . . . nature of the problem I believe your apprentice might be of some help." Talisid paused. "She would also be in greater danger."

We reached the top floor and stopped at the doors to the hall. "I'll be down the corridor," Talisid said. "Once you've decided, come speak to me."

"Not coming in?"

Talisid shook his head. "The fewer people that know of my involvement, the better. I'll see you in twenty minutes."

I watched Talisid go with a frown. I've done jobs for Talisid before, and while they'd generally been successful, they hadn't been safe. In fact, they'd been decidedly unsafe. If he was calling the job "difficult and dangerous" . . . I turned and pushed the doors open.

The top hall had once been a boxing gym. Chains hung from the ceiling, but the heavy bags had been removed and so had the ring at the centre. Mats covered the floor and light trickled in from windows high above. Two blocky ceramic constructions were set up at either end of the hall, ten feet tall and looking exactly like a pair of giant tuning forks.

Inside the room were five students and one teacher. Three of the students were against the far wall: a small round-faced Asian girl, a blond-haired boy with glasses, and an Indian boy with dark skin and the khaki turban of a Sikh who was keeping a noticeable distance from the first two. All looked about twenty or so. I didn't know their names but had seen them around enough times to recognise them as seniors in the apprentice program.

The next girl I knew a little better. She was tall and slim, with black hair that brushed her shoulders, and her name was Anne. And standing close to her (but not too close) was Luna, my apprentice.

The last person in the room was the teacher. He was just under thirty, well dressed and affluent-looking with short dark hair and olive-tinted skin, and he stopped what he'd been saying as I walked in. Five sets of interested eyes turned in my direction, following the teacher's gaze.

"Hi, Lyle," I said. "Didn't know you'd taken up teaching."

Lyle hesitated. "Er—"

I waved a hand. "Don't let me interrupt. Go right ahead." I found a spot on the wall and leant against it.

"Um," Lyle looked from me to the students. "Er. The thing—Well, as I—yes." He floundered, obviously off his groove. Lyle's never been good with surprises. I watched with eyebrows raised and an expression of mild enquiry. I didn't feel like making it easy for him.

Lyle was one of the first Light mages I met when Richard Drakh introduced me into magical society. We'd both been teenagers then, but Lyle had a few years of experience on me: His talent had developed earlier than mine and he'd had time to learn the ins and outs of the social game. I'd been a Dark apprentice and there'd never been any question but that Lyle would try for the Council, but all the same we became friends. We were both the type to rely on cleverness rather than strength, and our types of magic complemented each other nicely. Unfortunately, our goals turned out to be less compatible.

At the time I was still feeling my way, unsure of what I wanted to be. Lyle on the other hand knew exactly what he wanted: status, advancement, prestige, a position in the Council bureaucracy from which he could work his way upwards. And when I lost Richard's favour and with it any standing I might have had, Lyle had to choose between me and his ambitions. Supporting me would have cost him. So when I showed up, alone and desperate, Lyle's response was to pretend I wasn't there. Under mage law the master-apprentice relationship is sacred. An apprentice is their master's responsibility, no one else's. I'd defied Richard, fled from him, and it was Richard's right to do with me as he pleased. The Light mages knew that Richard would come to collect his runaway and so they shut me out . . . and waited for him to finish things.

But something happened then that the Light and the Dark mages did not expect. When Richard sent Tobruk to kill me—the cruellest and most powerful of his four apprentices—it was Tobruk who died. And in the aftermath, instead of coming to take vengeance Richard vanished, along with his last two apprentices, Rachel and Shireen. I was left alive, safe . . . and alone.

Technically, under mage law, I hadn't done anything wrong. It's not illegal for an apprentice to successfully defend themselves against their master; it's just so bloody rare no one's ever bothered to pass a law against it. But I'd broken tradition older than law. An apprentice is supposed to obey their master for good or ill, and no other mage would take me on—after all, if I'd rebelled against one master, I might rebel against another. Besides, no one was quite sure what had happened to Richard. He might be gone for good—or he might suddenly reappear, in which case nobody wanted to be anywhere near me when he did. So once again, other mages distanced themselves from me and waited.

They waited and waited, and kept waiting so long they forgot all about me, by which time I was glad to let them do it. I started to make a new life for myself. I travelled, had some adventures. As a result of one of them I inherited a shop, a little business in the side streets of Camden Town. I'd been planning to run it only a few months, but as the months turned into years I realised I enjoyed what it brought me. The shop and the flat above it became my residence, then my home. I made new friends. Gradually I began to remember what it was like to be happy again.

And then one day Lyle walked into my shop and brought me back into the mage world with its politics and its alliances and its dangers. This time I was prepared. And this time, to my surprise, I found I liked it.

I snapped out of my reverie. Lyle was talking and seemed to have regained his confidence, though it was obvious that he'd prefer it if I wasn't here. "—remember that in a duel, you're representing both your master and the Council," Lyle was saying. "Now, I know some of you have done this before, but it's very important that your form is exactly right. Let's go through the basic greetings one more time . . . Yes?"

The one who had raised her hand was Luna. "Um," Luna said. "Could you explain how these duels work?"

Lyle blinked at her. "What do you mean?"

Luna looked around to see that everyone else was watching her. "Well . . ." She seemed to choose her words carefully. "You've explained about the selection process. And the rituals and the salutes, and the withdrawal at the end. What about the part in the middle?"

"What part?"

"Um . . . the actual duel."

"Well, it depends, I suppose." Lyle looked confused. "Styles change and all that. Personally, I find the performance is more important."

"We're supposed to be practising for the tournament today," the Sikh boy said. He sounded unfriendly.

"Oh." Lyle looked around. "Well, um . . . yes, maybe a practice match then." Lyle glanced quickly over Luna, then pointed to the other two girls. "Natasha and, um, Anne. Why don't you go first."

The round-faced girl, Natasha, looked at Anne in antic-ipation. Anne bowed her head slightly to Lyle. "I'm sorry, but I can't."

Natasha made a rude noise and the boy with glasses rolled his eyes. "Oh God, not this again."

"Er . . ." Lyle looked taken aback. "Is there some medical reason—"

"No, she's fine," Natasha chipped in. "She just won't do it."

"Anne?" Lyle said. "Is there a reason?"

"I'm sorry," Anne said again. She had a soft, quiet voice. "I don't mean to cause any trouble."

"It's nothing to do with trouble," Lyle said with a frown. "Unless you or your master can give a good reason, you're required to participate."

Anne didn't answer. "All right then," Lyle said, gesturing to the centre of the hall. "Off you go."

No response. "Anne?" Lyle said irritably. "Did you hear me?"

Anne stood silently, looking back at Lyle. "This is an order," Lyle declared, pointing to the mats. "Get over there and participate."

Anne still didn't move and Lyle was left standing with one arm outstretched. He looked vaguely ridiculous and everyone else in the room was watching him. Lyle hesitated, then lowered his arm quickly. "Anne, will you do as you're told, please?" It was probably supposed to sound authorita-tive, but it came out more like a pleading.

Anne shook her head mutely. "Oh, this is such crap," Natasha said angrily. "How come she gets to do this?"

"Just do the duel already," the other boy said.

"Yes, er . . ." Lyle said. "I need to impress upon you the seriousness of this. Refusing a direct order from an authorised teacher is—"

"Why don't you guys ever do anything about her?" Natasha demanded. "She always does this and you always let her get away with it."

"Leave her alone," Luna said.

"You stay out of this."

"What makes it your business?" Luna said. "You want a duel so badly, try me."

"I don't have to—" Natasha started saying angrily. The boy with glasses started to talk over her, and both Luna and the Sikh boy started talking over him, raised voices making a clamour.

"Quiet," Lyle said. "QUIET!" Gradually, he was obeyed. The five students fell silent, glowering at each other.

"As I was saying," Lyle began, then looked at Anne and trailed off. Anne hadn't moved. Her stance wasn't confrontational, but she was looking at Lyle with a sort of quietly polite expression. Lyle looked at Luna, then at Natasha.

It was easy to read Lyle's thoughts. He wanted to force Anne to do as she was told, but he couldn't think of any way to make her do it. The alternative was to let Luna step into her place, and he didn't want to do that either, in case that ticked me off. In the end Lyle did what Lyle always does: pass the buck. "Er," he said, looking up at me. "If your apprentice doesn't mind . . ."

I nodded at Luna. "Ask her."

"Er," Lyle said again. "Right. Well. Natasha and, er, Luna. Take your focuses."

Natasha was whispering something to the boy with glasses. I walked towards Luna, aiming to meet her by the table in the corner, but Anne got there first. "You didn't have to do that," Anne said quietly.

Anne is tall and slender, only a few inches shorter than me, with dark hair framing a face the shape of a downwards-pointed triangle. She looks about twenty-two, Luna's age, which is on the old side for an apprentice—most graduate to journeyman by twenty-one or so. Her eyes are an odd red-brown colour, set at an angle that gives her a slightly catlike look, and there's a stillness to her movements. She's striking, but she has a quiet unobtrusive manner that tends to make her fade into the background.

Luna looks very different. She's average height, with wavy brown hair worn up in bunches and a fair complexion inherited from both her Italian father and her English mother. She'd blend into a crowd, if she'd ever willingly step into one, which she wouldn't. She used to always have a distant look, but these days she feels more animated, connected to the world. As Anne spoke, Luna gave her a quick glance and moved automatically away. "Don't worry about it."

"I don't want you to get in trouble because of me."

Luna shrugged. "She was getting on my nerves anyway."

Anne had been standing with her back to me, but as I came up to them she turned and dipped her head slightly. "Hello, Mr. Verus."

"He hates it when people call him that," Luna said without looking up. "Just call him Alex."

Anne looked between me and Luna. "Ah . . ."

A sharp voice spoke from a little distance away. "Anne."

I looked up to see the Sikh boy frowning at us. He made a quick beckoning motion to Anne. "I'm sorry," Anne said. "Could you excuse me a second?"

I watched Anne walk away. "Very polite, isn't she?" I said once she was out of earshot.

"She's always like that," Luna said absently. "Okay, help me out here. I have no idea how to use these."

The Sikh boy was talking to Anne under his breath, making quick hand movements. He kept his face turned away, but from his stance he looked tense. I watched a second, then shook my head and turned back to Luna. "All right. How much has Lyle taught you?"

"A lot of stuff about how to bow and curtsèy."

"Square one then." I nodded to the giant tuning forks at either end of the hall. "Those ceramic things are azimuth duelling focuses. When they're activated, they maintain a conversion field around the person they're targeted on. The conversion field takes any external magical energy that tries to penetrate it and transforms it into light. Basically, it's a wide-spectrum shield. If a magical attack hits you, there's a flash and nothing happens. The flash is used for scoring. One flash, one point."

Luna nodded. "Okay."

"That covers defence. But some mages can't do direct magical attacks." I gestured to the table. "That's where the focus weapons come in. They act as conductors. You channel your magic through them. Hit the other guy with one and it'll trigger the conversion field."

The table Luna had been looking at held what looked like training weapons. There wasn't a great selection and they had a worn, chipped look; the kind of things I'd sell at a deep discount. Luna hesitated, then picked out a sword made out of some kind of pale wood. As she touched it the silver mist of her curse flowed around it, soaking in.

Luna's an adept, not a mage. Adepts are the next step down on the magical pyramid from mages, and the best way to think of them is as mages who can only cast one spell. That doesn't mean they're weak—in fact, since adepts spend so much time practising and refining their one spell, they tend to get really good with it—but they don't have the range and breadth of abilities that mages do. Luna's unusual for an adept in that her magic doesn't come from within, but from without: Her spell is actually a curse, passed down from daughter to daughter. It brings good luck to her, and bad luck to everyone else, which can range from "paper cut" to "struck by lightning," depending on how careful she is and how close you get.

Usually a curse like that just keeps working on its subject forever, but in this case something unusual happened. The curse has grown up with Luna, woven into her so that it can't be removed—but just as it's a part of her, she's a part of it, and over the last year she's started to learn to control it. She can't shut it off and she definitely can't let herself touch anyone, but she's gotten a lot better at guiding her curse away from people she doesn't want to hurt—not to mention sending it at people she does.

It's not actually forbidden for adepts to train as apprentices, but it's not customary either. So far it hasn't come up, partly because no one wants to be the first to get between a mage and their apprentice, and partly because Luna's area of magic is so poorly understood that not many mages can tell the difference between a chance mage and a chance adept anyway. It's probably going to cause trouble one of these days, but that's a worry for another time.

Luna studied the sword as her curse twined lazily around it. To my mage's sight Luna's curse looks like a silver-grey mist, shifting and changing, constantly seeping from her skin and soaking into everything around her. To living creatures that mist is poison, invisible and utterly lethal. I've seen people survive brushes from Luna's curse with nothing but a few bruises—and I've also seen a man die a violent death within seconds of touching her. That's why it's so dangerous—you can never predict what it'll do. "What do I do?" Luna asked.

"You're doing it," I said. "As long as you hold it, your magic'll keep it charged."

Luna looked down dubiously. "It doesn't look like . . ."

"Like anything's happening?"

"Yeah."

I smiled. "Focus items depend on who's using them. Your magic's subtle, so the effect's subtle."

"Is it okay to hit her with this?"

"The azimuth shield's enough to take most of the punch out of a magical strike. Don't go sitting on her, but a couple of hits won't do her any harm."

I became aware that the rest of the room had gone quiet, and looked up to see that everyone was waiting for us. Natasha was standing at one end of the azimuth piste. Unlike Luna, she wasn't wielding a weapon. "Luna?" Lyle said. "Are you ready?"

Luna nodded. "Ready." She walked out onto the piste. I saw Lyle concentrate, channelling his magic, and to my mage's sight the two focuses lit up with power, energy extending from them to weave a shield around the two girls. Luna flinched and glanced back as the effect touched her, and I saw the silver mist of her curse flicker and twist, merging with the shield. Natasha just looked bored. Anne and the two boys had spaced themselves along the wall.

"Er," Lyle said. "Let's say first to three. Ready and . . . go!"

Luna darted forward, sword raised, and blue light welled up around Natasha's hands.

ı ı ı ı ı ı ı ı ı

The bout was to three points. The score at the end was 3–0. Natasha and Luna fought two more bouts. The score at the end of each of those was 3–0, too.

It's not that Luna's clumsy or anything. And she's no stranger to fighting; there are fully qualified mages who've seen less combat than Luna has. But all the fights Luna and I have been through have been the nasty, lethal, anything-goes kind, where you stab the other guy in the back before he does the same to you. A duel is very different. It's not combat, it's a sport, with rules and regulations and a referee. Winning a duel and surviving a combat are very different things, and being good at one doesn't necessarily make you good at the other.

Luna's opponent, Natasha, wasn't especially strong or quick. But like all elemental mages she had the great advantage of range. While Luna had to run all the way up to Natasha to hit her, Natasha could just smack Luna off her feet with a water blast.

Which she did. Repeatedly.

When Lyle finally called the fight I waited at the table for Luna to get back. She was moving stiffly, but I could tell she was more angry than hurt. "Good job," I said as she reached me.

Luna gave me a look.

"I'm serious."

"That's your idea of a good job?"

"Everyone loses their first duel," I said. "What matters is you put up a fight."

"Did you know I'd lose that badly?"

"I didn't check."

Natasha was talking and laughing with the boy with

glasses, her hands moving in animation as she relived knocking Luna down. "All right," Lyle called. "Charles and Variam, why don't you go next?"

I looked at Luna. She was annoyed, obviously embarrassed about losing . . . and yet she looked better than I'd ever seen her. When she'd first walked into my shop a year and a half ago, she'd been silent and detached, never showing her feelings. Apprentice training isn't easy, but Luna was engaged now; she had a place in the world. "Come on," I said. "We've got a job offer."

I knew Lyle wouldn't question my taking Luna out of the class, and he didn't. As the door swung shut behind us, I got a look at the two boys, Charles and Variam, facing off against each other on the piste. From a glance into the future I knew this match was going to be a lot more eventful than the last one.

chapter 2

"Apprentices are going missing," Talisid said.

The little room at the end of the hall had been fitted out as an office of sorts, with an old computer on a cramped desk. Faded photographs of sports teams were mounted on the walls, and a window looked out onto the London rooftops. Talisid was behind the desk while Luna sat quietly on a table in the opposite corner. She'd agreed to Talisid's demand for secrecy and now was listening with her ears pricked up.

"Since when?" I said.

"You know there's always been a certain washout rate in the apprentice program," Talisid said. "Some give up. Some fail their tests. Some—not many, but more than we'd like—defect to the Dark. And some have something happen to them. That last one's rare, thankfully. But a few weeks ago some mages noticed that there seemed to be more going missing than there should be. Well, we put someone on it, and we found a very disturbing pattern. Within the last three months we've had three apprentices vanish from the program. No sign that they quit or walked out or had an accident. They just disappeared."

"Just apprentices? No adult mages?"

"We think so, but it's hard to be sure. Journeymen and masters aren't accountable for their movements in the way apprentices are."

"Any pattern to the disappearances?"

"None that we can find."

"Any suspects?"

"Well." Talisid looked at me. "There's the obvious, isn't there?"

I was silent. Luna looked from Talisid to me. "Um . . . ?" she said after a moment.

"Dark mages," I said. "They've been on a recruitment drive." I looked at Talisid. "You think they're headhunting."

"Or Harvesting," Talisid said.

There was a silence. "Even the Council wouldn't stand for that," I said at last.

"No," Talisid said.

"It'd start another war."

"Yes. But there's no proof."

We stood quietly for a moment before I shook my head. "Why the secrecy?"

Both Luna and Talisid looked at me. "It's not enough," I said. "Okay, this'll cause trouble. But any mage who put in the work could learn it. In fact, it sounds like lots of them know about it already. And if they do, they can figure out the same things I just did. Why is it so important to keep this quiet?"

Talisid looked back at me for a moment. "If you wanted

to find a missing apprentice," he said at last, "how would you do it?"

"If I had the resources of the Council?" I thought about it and shrugged. "Locator spells and detective work. Then I'd get a time mage and ask him to scry back to the missing person's last known location."

Talisid nodded. "We've done all those things."

"It didn't work?"

"It didn't work."

"Shrouds?"

"Yes. And something else. In every case, the missing apprentice disappeared somewhere where they couldn't be traced. No witnesses, no physical evidence. And once they vanished, they didn't come back." Talisid's eyes were grim. "Every disappearance was neat. Too neat. If these were simple kidnappings, we should have picked up some trace by now. Another apprentice, a witness, something overheard . . . by simple law of averages there should have been *something*. But we haven't found a thing. It's as if every missing apprentice has simply vanished into thin air." Talisid shook his head slowly. "I don't believe it's luck. I think they're receiving information from an inside source. Someone with close access to the Light apprentice program is providing information on where apprentices can be found and how they can be caught alone."

The office was quiet. Outside, a flash of white showed against the rooftops; a tortoiseshell cat. It stalked out from behind a chimney stack, stretched lazily, braced itself on the edge of the roof, and jumped down out of sight to a balcony below.

"You don't know whom to trust," I said at last.

Talisid nodded.

"But you trust me?"

"You aren't directly associated with the Council," Talisid said. "Besides, I think it . . . unlikely that you'd be responsible for something like this." He looked steadily at me. "There is another issue. If we accuse someone without evidence, it will not only cause enormous discord but also put those responsible on their guard. We have to be sure and we have to have proof."

I thought for a second, then shook my head. "So no leads, I can't ask for help from other Light mages, and even if I do find out who's responsible it's useless unless I can prove it. You don't ask for much, do you?"

"I warned you it was difficult."

"No kidding. You're at least going to give us copies of your research, right?"

"A little better than that." Talisid handed me a thick brown folder. "I can put you in touch with the one who wrote them." He smiled slightly. "I believe you know him?"

I opened the folder, flipped to the name at the bottom, and laughed. "Okay. So I get some help after all."

"Let's hope it's enough." Talisid's smile was gone again as he rose to his feet. "I'm afraid everything I've tried so far has brought me up against a blank wall. So I hope you succeed, because if not, I don't know when these disappearances will stop." He nodded to us. "Verus, Luna. Good luck."

⁏⁏⁏⁏⁏⁏⁏⁏⁏

By the time we got back to the hall the excitement of Charles and Variam's duel was over. Everything set on fire had been extinguished, the furniture was only smouldering, and Lyle was reading the riot act to Charles and Variam. "—absolutely unacceptable," he was saying. "Absolutely unacceptable! You could have killed each other, not to mention everyone else! A duel is a formal test of skill, not some crude brawl. You're supposed to be upholding the traditions of the Council—"

"What happened?" Luna whispered.

"I get the feeling Charles and Variam don't like each other very much," I murmured.

"And another thing—" Lyle caught sight of us and cut off. An expression of frustration crossed his face and he threw up his hands. "Go on! Class is over! You're dismissed!"

The apprentices dispersed, grabbing coats and packing bags. "So where do we start?" Luna said.

"We go back to the shop," I said. "First thing is to work through the material Talisid gave us."

The short wooden sword focus Luna had been using was still by her bag. She picked it up with a grimace and returned it to the table. "I hate that thing," she said as she came back. "It felt wrong."

"Wrong how?"

"Like the wrong size. Scratchy. It felt like my magic was fighting it the whole way."

"Mm." I looked at Luna, thinking. "Maybe it's time we got you a focus weapon."

"Please not that one."

I shook my head. "Not if your magic reacted that badly. Try a few others."

The focuses on the table were all swords or sticks, and Luna started picking each one up and taking a few practice swings. As she did I focused on her with my mage's sight and realised that Luna was right: Her magic *was* fighting the weapons. Each time it was drawn immediately to the weapon and soaked in, but instead of channelling through the focus it seemed to be attacking the alien object, trying to destroy it. "Huh," I said at last.

"They don't feel right," Luna said again.

"They're not." I tapped my fingers. "Maybe a sword's the wrong kind of weapon for you. I'll have a think about it."

I was concentrating on Luna and didn't notice that someone had approached until they were right next to me. I'd half-expected Lyle, but as I looked up I got a surprise. It was the girl Luna had been fighting, Natasha. "Hi!" Natasha said to Luna. "Are you okay?"

Luna looked up at her, then away again quickly. "I'm fine."

"Oh good. Listen, I just wanted to warn you. You really don't want to be hanging around her."

"Who?"

"Her," Natasha whispered. She tilted her head towards Anne and Variam, at the other end of the room. "Anne."

"Why?"

"Well, you know where's she's from, right?"

Luna looked blankly at Natasha.

"Oh God, you don't know!" Natasha covered her mouth with both hands, then looked at Luna with wide eyes. "You really haven't heard?"

"Heard what?"

"You *really* should be more careful." Natasha shook her head. "I can't believe you didn't find out."

Luna was silent. Natasha waited a little longer and then unbent, dropping her voice and leaning closer. "She was taught by a Dark mage," Natasha whispered. "Her and that other boy, Variam. They were both apprentices to him. And do you know what they did next?"

Luna didn't answer. "They started working for a *mon-*

ster," Natasha whispered. "A demon. That's where they're going now. Nobody knows what it is."

"If nobody knows what it is, how do you know it's a monster?"

Natasha looked at Luna in annoyance. "I'm *serious.* You've seen how she is. She's really rude to all the tutors and she won't do as they say. And it's a really bad idea to hang around her."

Luna met Natasha's gaze in silence. "You know," she said at last, "they say the same thing about me."

Natasha stared back at Luna, then shrugged. "Well, don't say I didn't warn you." She turned to where I'd been standing quietly, and made a good pretence of only just noticing me. "Oh, hi, Mage Verus. Bye!"

Luna watched Natasha go and shook her head. "I really hate her."

I made a noncommittal noise. Personally, I sympathised with Luna. Natasha's speech had sounded like pure trouble-stirring to me, and she'd carefully timed it so I'd hear it too. But it left me uneasy all the same.

Lyle and Charles had vanished while we were talking, and Natasha was on her way out. Anne and Variam were talking under their breath. The way they were standing made me think they didn't want to be overheard and as we approached I glanced through the futures in which I sneaked up on them, trying to eavesdrop. In most I was spotted, but in one I was able to catch a few words. "—sure it's him?" Variam was saying quietly.

"Yes," Anne said. "He just left—"

Variam saw me and made a quick gesture to Anne, and the futures of their conversation vanished abruptly as the two of them turned to watch us leave. Anne gave Luna a smile and a wave. "See you tomorrow."

"See you!" Luna said. Variam said nothing and his eyes tracked us as we left, suspicious and wary.

⁝⁝⁝⁝⁝⁝⁝⁝⁝

Luna was silent as we left the building, and stayed silent as she unlocked her bike from the railings and we started back towards my shop. The walk from Islington to Camden is a nice one, and despite the winter season the sun was shining with enough warmth to make it a pleasant journey.

We settled into a walking pace, both of us on the pavement with Luna wheeling her bike in between. "You met Anne three months ago, right?" I said. "At the acceptance ceremony."

Luna nodded. "How much do you know about them?" I said. "Her and Variam, I mean."

"She doesn't talk about herself much." Luna's voice was doubtful, and I knew it was bothering her too. "And Variam never talks at all. I thought he just didn't like me, but he's the same with everyone."

"Do they always show up together?"

"Mostly. Anne used to come on her own, but these days they're always together. Variam never lets her out of his sight. It's really hard to talk to her with him scowling all the time."

"Are they going out?"

"Anne said no." Luna frowned. "I can't figure Variam out though. He's always watching her but he doesn't act like he even likes her."

We walked a little way in silence. The air was crisp and clear, and cars buzzed past importantly. A cyclist overtook us, riding with her back straight, her front basket filled with shopping and making the bike rattle as it went past. "Do you think it's true?" Luna said.

I knew she was talking about what Natasha had said. "Allowing for exaggeration . . ." I shook my head. "I don't know. But there's *something* odd about those two."

"They could have started late, right?" Luna said. "Like me."

"From what I saw of Variam he's pretty damn good for a late starter."

Luna walked on, brow furrowed. "Does it matter?" she said. "If they were Dark apprentices before?"

"There are Dark mages and Dark mages," I said. "From what I hear some of them treat their apprentices okay. The others . . ." I shrugged. "One thing's for sure—it'd matter to the Council. It *would* explain why they're still apprentices. They'd have trouble finding anyone to sponsor them with a background like that."

"That was what happened to you, wasn't it?" Luna said. "You used to be a Dark apprentice, then got out."

I didn't answer. "Alex?" Luna said. "Could I ask you something?"

"I don't really want to—"

"What's the Council?"

I turned in surprise to see that Luna was looking straight at me, her blue eyes serious. The winter sun was shining down over the rooftops, picking out the waves in her light brown hair. "What do you mean?"

"I know there are people in charge and everything—" Luna stopped. "I mean, what are they—" She trailed off again and looked down at the pavement, frowning. "It's— Okay. When you first told me about the Light Council and the Dark mages I thought the Light mages were the good guys and the Dark mages were the bad guys. Then there was what happened with Griff." Luna's hand crept unconsciously to her right arm. "And Levistus and Belthas. But now I'm training with them. And we keep working for Talisid." Luna looked up at me. "Should I trust them or not?"

We walked in silence while I tried to figure out how to answer. "It's easier to understand Dark mages than Light mages," I said at last. "Dark mages are . . . honest, I guess. Bastards, but honest bastards. They say what they believe and they live it. Light mages are more complicated." I glanced at Luna. "You know how things were in the old times? Before the Light Council got formed?"

Luna shook her head.

"Okay. First thing to understand is that there were a lot more magical creatures back then. And I mean a *lot*. Think monster-of-the-week TV show. Except the heroes didn't win as much as they do on the TV shows, and when the monsters won a lot of people died. And sometimes the mages *were* the monsters. There were Dark mages around back then as well, and if half the stories are true they made modern Dark mages look *nice*.

"Well, the Light mages grew up in opposition to that. They believed they should use their powers to protect others. Not just mages, but normal people too. They wanted a world where human beings wouldn't have to live in fear of monsters. And that was what they worked for. Identifying the most dangerous magical creatures and learning their weaknesses. Tracking down the ones that fed off humans and destroying them. Guarding towns and cities. Stopping Dark mages from setting themselves up as tyrants. They kept doing it for hundreds of years."

"What happened?" Luna said.

"They won," I said simply.

Luna looked at me curiously. "I'll give you an example," I said. "Vampires."

"They're real?"

I nodded. "Not all the stories are true, but they get the basics right. Vampires were supernatural predators who fed off human life force by drinking their blood. They lived forever or until something killed them, and the older they got the stronger they got. They had powers related to mind magic—they could dominate their prey, make them willingly come back to be fed upon. And they could make more of themselves. One vampire could control a whole city, and they did. For a while they ruled most of the world.

"But then the mages got organised. It was one of only three times in history where the Light and Dark factions united. Even if they couldn't agree on anything else, they knew they didn't want to be vampire food. They smashed the vampire-controlled armies, and then they hunted the vampires down one by one and exterminated them. Not just some of them, all of them. They spent about a hundred years searching with a fine-tooth comb to make sure they got every last one." I shrugged. "There aren't any more vampires."

Luna was silent.

"The same thing happened to most of the really nasty monsters," I said. "Manticores, ogres, nightmares. The smart ones fled into other worlds or hid themselves away. The ones who didn't got hunted down. Mages had seen what it was like being prey and they didn't like it. They wanted to make sure humanity was at the top of the food chain. And that was what they did. And they did it so well that most people nowadays don't believe those creatures ever existed."

I fell silent and we walked to the sound of our footsteps on the pavement and the *click-click-click* of Luna's bike. "This is one of those stories that doesn't have a happy ending, isn't it?" Luna said at last.

"Well, there aren't monsters stalking the city every

night," I said. "But the Council—well, it sounds weird, but their problem was they succeeded. They wanted mages to protect normal humans from the magical world. But with the monsters gone, the biggest threat from the magical world was . . . mages.

"The Council's old purpose is pretty much gone these days. It's still the biggest power in magical society but nowadays people join it because they want to be in power, not because they believe in what it does. Every now and then a monster shows up and they get rid of it, but mostly they spend their time jockeying for position." I sighed. "I don't think they're actively evil. Not most of them, anyway. But they've made so many compromises you can't really count on them for anything. I don't know if there's anything they *do* believe in anymore. Stability, maybe. Keeping things the same."

Luna thought about it. "So does Talisid believe in the Council's old mission?"

"We'll see."

︱ ︱ ︱ ︱ ︱ ︱ ︱ ︱ ︱ ︱

My shop is in Camden, down a little side street and in the middle of a tangle of bridges and railway lines. It makes a small profit, though it'd make a lot more if I actually kept regular hours instead of hanging up the *CLOSED* sign every time I've got something else to do.

Inside the shop is quiet and cool, wide windows letting in lots of light from the street outside and a faint herbal smell in the air. Standing shelves hold just about every faux-magic item you can think of, from crystal balls to exotic powders, while a small unlabelled roped-off area to one side holds the stuff that really *is* magical. It's not designed for high turnover, but all in all I prefer it that way.

I ate lunch with Luna and then she had to leave; she had another class with a different set of apprentices in Kilburn. I waved as she cycled off, then headed up to my flat to get started on the report Talisid had given me. My flat is just above my shop, with a nice view out over the Camden rooftops. I settled into my chair and started reading.

I've never had any formal training as an investigator but I've had a fair bit of practice, enough to figure out the basics of what works and what doesn't. To be honest, I don't actually think I'm all that good at it. Other people tend to assume I am and I don't go out of my way to correct them, but the way I generally find things out is by cheating and using my divination magic. But divination doesn't help with a written report, and so I wasn't really expecting to find anything in Talisid's folder that other people hadn't spotted already. What I wanted was a feel for the facts.

I got one, and it wasn't pretty. Since the beginning of autumn a total of three members of the Light apprentice program had vanished without a trace. The earliest disappearance had been three months ago; the most recent was less than a fortnight old. It looked like Talisid was right; there wasn't any sign of this stopping. I picked up my phone and tapped one of the names in my address book. It rang five times before there was a click and a voice spoke from the other end. "Hello?"

"Hey, Sonder," I said. "Been reading your report."

"Alex!" Sonder said. "So Talisid *did* ask you to help? And you said yes?"

Sonder is a time mage, and it was him I'd been thinking of when I'd sketched out that plan to Talisid. It had been a surprise to find that Talisid had recruited him already, but thinking it over, maybe I should have expected it. Sonder may be young, but he's talented. He helped me out during the business with the fateweaver and again in the autumn against Belthas, and both times he made a real difference. But the real reason I like Sonder doesn't have anything to do with how good he is at seeing into the past—it's because he can be trusted. "Better we don't talk about it over the phone," I said. "Listen, I'm going to be another few hours getting up to speed on this report. Let's meet up tomorrow at nine and we'll put our heads together."

"Okay. Is Luna coming?"

"Yes, Luna's coming."

"Okay! See you then."

I shook my head and ended the call, smiling to myself. As I did, I noticed I had a message. It had arrived earlier, but I'd been absorbed in the report and hadn't noticed. I opened it.

What you're looking for is in Fountain Reach.

There was nothing else. Frowning, I checked the sender. It was an e-mail address from a free provider. The prefix on the address was a random string of letters and numbers.

Who had sent it?

Fountain Reach was the place Crystal had told me about this morning, but this seemed like a pretty weird way for her to entice me to take the job. Besides, we hadn't exactly parted on good terms.

What you're looking for . . . What I was looking for was the source of the disappearances. And within a few hours of starting to look, I had someone sending me an anonymous tip. How convenient.

It was a hell of a lot *too* convenient. This was way too easy. Maybe Talisid's right and I'm just cynical but I couldn't honestly believe that someone would just hand me the solution like that. It had to be a trick or a trap of some kind.

More worrying was the speed. Talisid had met me only hours ago and already someone seemed to know that I was involved. Had someone been spying on our meeting? Between the two of us Talisid and I should have been able to spot someone following us . . . maybe. Mages have a lot of ways of finding out information. But if their intelligence network was so good, why were they wasting it on such a clumsy trap?

I puzzled over it for an hour but couldn't find any answers. Outside the light faded from the sky, evening turning into a cold winter's night. I fixed myself some dinner and tried to finish off the report, but my mind kept drifting back to the message. I caught myself wondering how long it would take to make the journey to Fountain Reach, and pushed the thought firmly away. I had enough to worry about without going looking for trouble. But the idea nagged at me all the same.

I'd been vaguely expecting Luna back and had been keeping an eye on the possible futures all evening. When I saw that the bell was going to ring I put the folder down in relief, then I checked a second time and stopped. There *was* a girl about to arrive at my door—but it wasn't Luna.

I sat frowning for a moment, then locked the folder away in a drawer. I tucked a few items into my pockets and went downstairs.

My shop feels eerie after dark. The street is a quiet one, and while the background hum of the city never stops, the nearby shops empty out completely after closing hours. Inside the shelves stood silent, their contents making strange shapes in the darkness. The front of the shop was cast in a yellow glow from the streetlights, and their light passed through the windows to fall upon the wands in their display cases and glint off the metal blades in the shadows against the wall. Under the shop counter is a hidden shelf. I reached in and took out a narrow-bladed dagger, then stood alone in the darkness and waited.

Five minutes passed.

From out in the street came the throaty growl of a car engine. It grew louder and there was the crunching of tyres as it pulled in, then the engine died away to a purr and stopped. A car door opened and shut and footsteps approached, coming to a halt just outside. A moment later, from back in the hall, the bell rang.

I waited twenty seconds—about long enough for someone to stop whatever they were doing and come downstairs—then opened the door.

The girl standing outside was Anne. She'd changed clothes since the lesson and was wearing a long-sleeved pullover and thin trousers, both in shades of grey and brown that faded into the night. They looked good on her, but again I got that odd feeling that she was trying to blend into the background. "Good evening, Mr. Verus."

"Just Alex is fine," I said. Behind Anne was the car she'd arrived in. It was a sedan, big and sleek, and its lines gleamed silver in the streetlights with a winged *B* ornament at the front of the hood. There was a man behind the wheel. It was hard to make him out in the darkness, but I had an impression of a hunched figure and two unfriendly eyes. "Did you want Luna?"

"Ah . . . no. Thank you." Anne hesitated. "I'm here to give you an invitation."

I blinked. "To what?"

"Tiger's Palace," Anne said. "There's a gathering tomorrow evening at eight o'clock."

I'd never heard of Tiger's Palace. "Who's inviting me?"

"Lord Jagadev," Anne said. "He owns the club."

"Okay," I was still a little puzzled. "What sort of gathering?"

"Other mages are going to be there," Anne said. "I don't think it's for a special occasion."

Neither the place nor the name rang any bells, but that wasn't surprising. I'm pretty much an outsider to mage society, and I don't get invited to many parties. Which raised an obvious question. "Look," I said. "I don't mean to be rude. But why is this 'Lord Jagadev' inviting me?"

"I don't actually know," Anne said. She sounded honest. "He gave me a list of people to invite but he didn't tell me why."

"Do you always do what he tells you?"

Something flickered across Anne's face and she seemed to draw back a little. "What answer should I give him?"

I looked at Anne for a long moment. I couldn't sense any deception from her but my instincts were telling me something strange was going on. Mage parties are dangerous at the best of times. If I showed up, there was no telling what I'd be getting into.

On the other hand mage parties are also a mine of information and I hate missing opportunities to find things out. Besides, one of the things I've learnt over the past year is that if trouble's on its way it's a lot better to go do something about it than to sit around and wait. "Tell him I'll be there," I said.

"I will."

We stood in silence for a moment. "Do you want to come inside?" I said suddenly. As soon as the words were out I wanted to kick myself. It was a *really* inappropriate question to ask another mage's apprentice, especially a girl three-quarters my age.

"I'm sorry," Anne said. "There's another invitation I have to deliver in Archway."

"Okay," I said. "Uh, have a safe trip."

"See you tomorrow." Anne gave a small smile and walked back to the car. As she did I caught a flash of movement from the front seat; the man inside was putting away something that looked like a phone. Anne climbed in, the door snicked shut, and the engine started up with a growl that made me think of a big animal. I watched the car roll smoothly down the street, signal at the T junction, and pull away out of sight.

I closed and locked the door. Thoughtfully I took the dagger from where I'd been holding it behind the door and returned it to its sheath before going back up to my study.

Inviting Anne in had been a weird thing to do and as I climbed the stairs I wondered why I'd done it. I remembered the last image, Anne climbing into the dark car while that hunched shape waited behind the wheel, and felt a stir of disquiet.

My street was dark and still again, and the shop was empty. The distant *thump, thump, thump* of club music drifted over the rooftops, but there was no movement outside. I stood flipping the sheathed dagger absentmindedly between my fingers, frowning at nothing. Outside my window, lights shone from the blocks of flats across the canal.

I felt uneasy. I live alone and I should be used to the quiet of my part of Camden after sunset. But tonight something about the silence had me on edge.

It wasn't as if anything that had just happened was all that extraordinary. I do get invited to mage social events *sometimes*. Not often, but it happens. And sending an apprentice out to deliver invitations in person wasn't unusual . . . okay, it *was* unusual, but it wasn't unheard of. It must have just felt strange to me because I'd been off the social circuit so long.

I told myself that, but the uneasy feeling didn't go away.

I don't get these feelings often and when I do I've learnt to pay attention to them. I did a scan of the immediate futures, looking for danger, and found nothing. I spread my search further, looking for anything that might threaten or attack me.

Still nothing.

I tried half a dozen more ways of looking for danger and came up blank every time. Finally I tried something different. I looked into the future to see what would happen if I sat in my bedroom and did absolutely nothing.

One uneventful hour, two uneventful hours, four uneventful hours—then activity. In the early hours of the morning people were going to come to my door. Not ordinary people—mages. They'd want to talk to me, and they were . . .

I frowned. They were Council Keepers.

That was strange.

Keepers are the primary enforcement arm of the Council, kind of a mix between police and an internal affairs division. There are a lot of reasons for Keepers to come looking for a mage and very few of them are good. As I looked into the future the encounter didn't look hostile, but it didn't look friendly either. I wished I could see exactly what they were saying, but as I tried to focus on the distant strands the images blurred and shifted. It's hard to predict something as fluid as conversation. I can do it easily if it's only a few seconds ahead, but trying to do it a few *hours* ahead is almost impossible. I tried to focus on a single strand and pin it down.

The Keepers were asking me questions. They were suspicious. I tried to hear what the questions were about or why they were asking them, but couldn't pick up any details.

I shifted my focus to the beginning of the conversation. That was better. Now the Keepers were saying the same things in each future with only minor differences, the things they'd decided to say before my answers took them in other directions. I suddenly realised what the scene reminded me of: two police officers interviewing a suspect.

I strained my mental lens to its limit, trying to get the exact words. By concentrating and piecing together bits from parallel futures, I was just able to make out fragments.

"—where were—"

"—did you do—"

"—any contact . . . after—"

I shook my head in frustration. Useless. In every one of the futures, my future self seemed to ask the same questions. I focused on the answers the Keepers gave in return.

"—enquiries—"

"—was here—"

"—last . . . see her alive—"

I stopped dead. The futures I'd traced so carefully shattered, fading into darkness.

I stood motionless for ten seconds, then ran for the door.

chapter 3

As I ran down the street I skimmed through futures and searched the traffic, then changed direction to cut left down an alley that led into Camden Road. I ran straight out between parked cars into the middle of the main road. Horns blared as cars screeched to a halt.

A man wound down his window behind me and started shouting. His accent was so thick I couldn't actually understand what he was saying, but he didn't sound happy. I pulled open the door of the black cab in front of me with the yellow *TAXI* light above its window. "Archway," I said before the driver could open his mouth. "I'll pay you double if you get us there in five minutes. Triple if you make it in less."

"All right, mate," the driver said comfortably. "Not a problem."

The taxi pulled around the car in front of us, the angry

driver still shouting from his window, and we accelerated away north.

॥ ॥ ॥ ॥ ॥

No one knows the London streets better than a London cabbie. At this hour with the crowds and traffic it would have taken me at least ten minutes to make the drive from Camden to Archway. The cabbie did it in less than half that.

Archway is an odd place even by London standards. A network of concrete shops surround the Underground station, out of which rises the squat ugly brown shape of Archway Tower. Two roads fork away northwest: On one is the sprawl of the Whittington Hospital while the other passes under Suicide Bridge. "There you go, mate," the cabbie said as we reached the station. "Which street?"

I stared out the window, concentrating. We were at the junction around the old Archway Tavern, the ancient building forming an island amidst the A-roads. I looked up the hill to see the high arch of Suicide Bridge, marking the boundary between inner and outer London. I pointed to the right of the bridge, northeast. "That way."

As soon as we left the main road the streets narrowed and emptied. Cars were parked everywhere, making it hard for the cab to move, and minutes passed with agonising slowness as I scanned through futures, watching myself explore different directions in an expanding web.

A tangle of futures flashed; combat, danger. "Stop!" I opened the door before the taxi had stopped moving and shoved a handful of notes at the driver. "Keep the change."

The taxi had brought me to a housing estate. A long three-storey block of flats loomed above, walkways running along the top two floors with doors at regular intervals. An old decayed children's playground was laid out in the courtyard in front, the swings rusted and the animal figures vandalised. The base of the block of flats was shadowed, blending into a small cramped garden. High walls shut off the view to the street and only a handful of lights shone in the darkness. It wasn't late but the place had a dead feel to it. I moved at a fast walk, heading farther in. Behind, I heard the rumble of the taxi's engine fade away into the noise of the city.

From the shadows at the base of the flats ahead came a sharp metallic *clack*.

I broke into a run. The sound came again, twice, echoing around the brick walls: *clack-clack*. I passed under the building, reached the pillars that were blocking my view, and looked around the edge.

The housing estate was a big long construction of dark brick. There were two ways in: a pair of double doors leading into a stairwell, and a small lift. To one side was the car park; to the other was a fenced-off area of trees and grass. A single fluorescent light was mounted on the wall, casting a flickering glow over the scene in front of me.

Three men were standing near the wall. They wore dark clothes and ski masks and carried handguns fitted with the unmistakable long metal cylinders of sound suppressors. Two had their attention fixed on the person by the lift, while the third faced the other way, his gun pointed downwards in both hands as he scanned for movement. I was out of his line of sight, but not by much.

Anne was next to the lift, slumped against the wall, and as I watched she slid down to crumple onto her side. "Check her," the man in the middle said. He had a gruff voice and sounded English.

"Gone," the one closest to Anne said. He still had his gun pointed more or less towards her.

"Make sure."

"Three in the body. She's gone."

"Make sure."

"Fuck that," the shooter said. "You heard the guy, I'm not getting that close."

The red digital number above the lift had been changing from 2, to 1, to G. Now the doors grated open as a mechanical female voice recited, "Ground floor." The two men's guns were pointed into the lift before the doors had finished moving, but it was empty. White light shone from inside.

The man at the middle looked away from the lift to the shooter. "I said *make sure*."

The other man shrugged, then levelled his gun at Anne from less than ten feet away and started pulling the trigger.

I was already moving, but I wasn't fast enough. By the time I'd gotten the little marble out of my pocket the gun had gone *clack* three more times. The suppressor muffled the shot so that the loudest noise was the metallic sound of the action cycling and the *thud* of bullets chewing through flesh. The man shot Anne a final time as I threw the marble, and the man watching their backs had only time to flinch before it shattered against the wall.

The marble was a one-shot—effectively a single spell with an activation trigger. This particular one was a condenser spell, and as the crystal shell holding the magic in stasis broke, mist rushed out to blanket the area in fog. The cloud was only about forty feet across and it wouldn't last long, but for a minute or two anyone in that area was blind.

Except me. As I plunged into the cloud I flicked through the futures ahead of me, and by seeing the ones in which I ran into the men I knew where they were. The one at the back was the most alert and so I bypassed him, staying outside his field of vision. The man in the middle who'd been giving the orders was turned away, his gun blindly searching for threats, and it was simple to put two punches into the spot just below his floating ribs. He staggered, turning towards me and spreading his legs into a shooting stance, and I kicked him hard in the crotch and brought my fist up into his face. He went down.

I kept moving, getting to where the shooter had been standing over Anne, but he'd moved. I could hear his voice somewhere off to my right, calling to the man at the back. For the moment the men were confused, scrambling to figure out who was attacking them, but it wouldn't last. Anne was lying huddled and still at my feet and to my right was the glow from the lift, filtering through the mist.

Then Anne took a ragged breath.

I looked down at her for one second before my reflexes kicked in. I knelt, got my arms under her, and lifted her up. Anne cried out in pain as I did, and the men's voices suddenly fell silent. I knew what was coming and hauled Anne into the lift.

Clack-clack-clack went the silenced guns, along with a *crunch* as bullets tore into the brickwork where I'd been standing. I hit the button inside the lift marked *2*. With my arms holding Anne I couldn't reach the button without jolting her as well, and she cried out again. "Doors closing," the mechanical voice said loudly.

The men outside heard that and knew what it meant. I felt them shift their aim to track the sound and I stepped right. *Clack-clack* went the guns, followed by a *spannng!* as a bullet ricocheted around the metal interior of the lift, missing me once, twice, three times before dropping to the floor. The lift doors ground shut and I felt the shudder as it accelerated upwards.

I had a few spare seconds to look over Anne, and as I did

my heart sank. There were a half dozen holes in her pullover and around them the grey wool was turning reddish black. My shirt was already wet with her blood and she was sprawled in my arms with her head back, her breath slow and rattling. I don't know much about first aid, but she looked bad.

The lift decelerated and came to a stop. There was a wait that felt like an hour but could only have been two or three seconds, then the doors ground open. "Second floor," the recording said clearly. "Please mind the step."

Whoever had designed the block of flats had obviously worked to a clear set of priorities. Unfortunately, while *cost*, *size*, and *low-maintenance* had made it to the top of the list, *aesthetics*, *good escape routes*, and *shelter from gunfire* hadn't. The lift came out at one end of a walkway with a concrete balustrade and a railing. Twenty flats were spaced evenly along the walkway, and at the far end was another lift. The walkway was a dead straight line with no place to hide and thirty feet below was the concrete of the car park. I'd never make it past all twenty flats and to the other lift before the men behind caught us. And if I went back down I'd run into them even faster. Unless I could fly, there were no other ways out.

Well, if we couldn't get out, we'd have to get in.

I moved quickly along the walkway from door to door, scanning the futures. Flat 301—locked. Flat 302—locked. Flat 303—double locked. Flat 304—I stopped and flipped the mat to reveal a key. *There's always one.*

From the stairs behind came the sound of pounding feet, and I hissed between my teeth. These guys were fast. I set Anne down as gently as I could and moved back to the stairs. The entry to the stairwell was a swing door with no handles that opened both ways. The walkway was narrow and I knew that the landing behind the door would be narrow too. I braced myself against the railing, listened to the feet pounding up the stairs towards me, and just as the man on the other side reached the top of the stairs I stamp-kicked the door as hard as I could.

My foot encountered the door from one side just as the man reached it from the other, and there was a judder and a satisfying *crunch* as the door was introduced to the man's face. The door came off better in the exchange. The man staggered away, the door began to swing back towards me, and I kicked the door again.

This time the man didn't have any momentum to keep him upright and the door smacked him off the top of the flight of stairs. I had one glimpse of him going down the stairs in a whirl of arms and legs, the second man's face turned upwards, eyes startled as he saw what was about to hit him, then the door swung back towards me and I darted back to where I'd left Anne.

I could hear shouts from the stairwell but I knew I'd bought myself a few more seconds. The key turned in the lock and I carried Anne inside, gritting my teeth as she made an animal sound of pain. Those bullets had torn her up inside. If we kept moving I'd be killing her just as surely as those men.

The flat was scattered with dirty clothes and bits of audio equipment, but it was empty. I kicked the door shut, muffling the noises from outside, then carried Anne into the bedroom and set her down on the bed as gently as I could. Her skin had gone an ashen colour and the whole front of her body was soaked with blood.

Anne should be dead. She'd been shot in the body seven times and even if I don't know anything about gunshot wounds I know that's not something you're supposed to walk away from. But she wasn't dead yet and that gave me a bit of hope. Whatever had kept her alive this long, maybe it could last a little longer.

As I looked at Anne I realised there was some kind of magic working around her, something subtle and hard to see. But I didn't have time to take a closer look and Anne was too far gone to hear anything I could say, so I left her there and went up the carpeted stairs.

The flat had two levels, and the bedroom on the upper storey had a window that looked down onto the walkway from which I'd entered. I pressed myself against the wall, and as I did I saw the men through the glass, coming out from the stairwell. They were moving more cautiously this time, their guns up and scanning the length of the walkway. The first one looked to be moving stiffly from where I'd hit him, and the second had a bloody nose, but it wasn't slowing them down much. They looked at the empty walkway and conferred.

I'd known as soon as I saw the walkway that the only place to hide had been in one of the flats. Unfortunately, it looked like the men had figured that out too. As I watched they seemed to come to a decision and moved to the first flat along, 301. One covered the walkway while another worked on the lock. The door opened and they disappeared inside.

They were searching the flats.

Crap.

What should I do?

I could use a gate stone. In my left pocket I had what I call my GTFO stone, a gate-magic focus that's keyed to a safe house in Wales. Gate stones aren't fast, but I was pretty sure I could make it out in time.

But I couldn't bring Anne with me. My magic can't affect

the physical world without a focus, and even *with* a focus I'm terribly weak. A few months ago I'd tried to take the body of a humanoid construct through a gate stone portal, and the body had ended up in three pieces. That hadn't mattered for the construct. It would matter a lot for Anne.

As I looked through the futures I saw that the men would take no more than two minutes to search each flat. The men were three flats away. Two minutes times three meant that I had six minutes to come up with something.

So far I'd been hoping that if I put the men off balance and stung them enough they'd pull back to regroup. As I kept watching I saw that it wasn't going to work. These guys were too tough and too committed. They were planning to kill both me and Anne and the longer this went on the better the odds that they'd manage it.

Below, the men came out of 301 and moved to 302. Again they went to work on the door, and again they slipped inside.

I was running out of time.

The man they'd left outside would spot me if I went out the front. What about the back? I moved downstairs, through the glass door at the back that read *FULLY AIR CONDITIONED*, and out onto the balcony.

The balconies at the back of the flats were a forest of satellite dishes and TV aerials, facing south onto the lights of London. Each balcony was identical, a rectangular hollow of brickwork sticking out into space, one for each flat. I closed the door softly behind me and ducked down behind the balustrade of the balcony of flat 304. A moment later, I heard a creak and movement as one of the gunmen opened the door to the balcony two flats down, in number 302. He glanced quickly around and withdrew back into the flat.

They were being careful. One man outside to make sure I couldn't sneak out; two men inside covering each other as they searched room to room. I could try to hide but it would be risky. They were ready for someone ahead of them.

But they weren't ready for someone *behind* them . . .

The plan flashed through my head in an instant and I spent a precious minute checking for flaws, searching through the futures in which I tried it. As I did I realised there was blood in all of them. No matter what I did, in the next five minutes someone was going to die.

Well, I'd just have to make sure that someone wasn't me. As I made the decision I felt my mental gears shift. I stayed crouched, hidden in the shadows of the balcony of flat 304, and waited.

There was another creak, closer this time, as the door to the balcony of flat 303 opened next to me. Footsteps sounded, soft on the stone, as the man scanned left and right. He was less than ten feet away but the lip of the balcony hid me from his view. He saw nothing, turned, disappeared inside.

As soon as he was gone I stood and pulled myself up onto the balcony lip before stepping out onto the railing. A cold wind brushed my hair and I took a hold of the drainpipe between the balconies. The gap between was only a few feet. To my right I could see the glow of the night city; the white-yellow cluster of the West End and the double strobe of Canary Wharf in the far distance. I took a deep breath, then before I could think too much about the drop to the darkness below I sprang across. My foot slipped on the opposite railing and my heart lurched, then my clutching hand on the drainpipe steadied me and I dropped down into the balcony of flat 303.

It was only a small change of position. But now instead of being in an area the men hadn't searched, I was in an area they *had* searched and thought was safe. The man had left the balcony door open, which made my job easy. I slipped inside into the living room and pressed myself against the wall. From above I could hear the sounds of the men going through the upper floor.

I've always had an aggressive side but oddly enough I've never been comfortable with fights. One of my martial arts instructors once told me that the strongest attitude to battle, and the only truly strong mental stance, is to face your opponent with a smile and say "Go on, hit me with your best shot! I can take it!" I've never been able to do that. Human opponents scare me too much. When I was a child, the bullies I faced were always bigger and stronger than me. Then I awakened to my magic and found to my dismay that nothing had changed. The weakest of elemental mages could swat me like a fly, and I could never, ever face a battle-mage in open combat and live. For the longest time I thought that made me a coward.

But gradually I learnt there were other ways to fight. I'm no good as a duellist or a warrior. But I'm very good as an ambush predator. Stealth and surprise are natural to me, and if I'm a coward I'm a dangerous one.

The men above finished their search and came back downstairs. They didn't give the living room a second glance; they'd already searched there. As the first man passed by I drew my dagger but didn't attack. Predators take the hindmost. The second man passed, turning down the corridor towards the front door, his back to me.

I came out behind the man, and my left arm snaked across his throat to drag him off balance as my right hand drove the dagger up into his lower back. He made a funny choking sound and I stabbed him twice more.

The man in the doorway turned back and his eyes went wide as he saw me killing his friend. He brought his gun up

and sighted. The man I was holding was struggling, trying
to get away, and I let him pull me a little way around to give
his friend a clear shot.

The man in the doorway advanced a step, steadied himself with his gun aimed two-handed at my body, and fired
twice: *clack-clack*.

You can't be faster than a bullet, but you can be faster
than the hands that guide it. Just as the gun fired I twisted
the man I was holding to bring him between me and the
gun. The bullets sank into flesh with a harsh double *thud*.
Slowed by the suppressor, the subsonic ammunition didn't
have the power to go all the way through his body. The man
I was holding jerked as the bullets hit him, and his muscles
convulsed. I left the knife sticking in his back and reached
over to close my right hand on his gun, then using his body
as a shield I aimed at the other man and started pulling the
trigger.

The gun went *clack-clack-clack*, the bullets making
louder sounds as they tore through walls and threw out
sprays of plaster. The other man dived for the kitchen and I
tried to track him but the hand clutched over the gun spoiled
my aim and he disappeared from sight. Before he could lean
out for another shot I backed into the living room, dragging
the dying man with me, feeling his struggles becoming
weaker as the lifeblood pumped from his body. I clawed
another condenser from my pocket and threw it into the hall;
it shattered and filled the flat with a gush of grey mist. I
ripped my dagger out, letting the body fall, and made it out
onto the balcony before any more gunfire came. The fog hid
the railing and the drop below but my magic guided me
across and back into flat 304.

Anne was still lying on the bed. The sheets were smeared
with drying blood, but the bleeding seemed to have stopped

for the moment and as I came back into the bedroom her eyes flickered open and tried to focus on me. "Anne," I said quietly. "Can you move?"

Anne's eyes were hazy with pain. "There are still two of them," I said. "I've slowed them down but in a few minutes they'll be coming after us. Can you make it out of the building?"

Anne drew in a ragged breath. "Holding . . . together." Her skin was paler than it should have been, and I had the feeling she'd lost a lot of blood. "Can't move. Break apart . . ."

I tried to work out what Anne was saying, then I looked into the futures in which I carried her away and my heart sank as I understood. She'd managed to stabilise herself, but it was taking all she had to do it. Another journey would tear the wounds back open. I might be able to lose the men but Anne would be dead before we got anywhere safe.

I could stay and fight, make a last stand in flat 304, but the odds didn't look good. I knew that the last two men were still coming and it wouldn't take them long to figure out where we had to be. I might be able to take two armed men—maybe—but I couldn't protect Anne at the same time.

For a moment I hesitated. I can make snap decisions when it comes to my own life, but risking someone else's is harder. Then I shook my head and pulled out my GTFO stone. It had been a river rock once, worn smooth by flowing water, and I'd carved a rune into either side. "Do you know how to use gate stones?" I asked.

Anne gave a tiny nod.

"It'll get us somewhere safe," I said. "But I'm not strong enough to make a gate for both of us. I need your help."

Anne's eyes met mine, and I could see she was afraid.

Activating a focus is no danger for a healthy mage. But in her condition . . .

There was a *thump* of movement from the flat next door, and Anne closed her eyes and nodded. As gently as I could, I slid one arm beneath her legs and the other beneath her back, then placed my gate stone in her hand, our fingers interlaced over it. Her skin felt cold. I concentrated, then spoke words in the old tongue, channelling my will through the focus.

Gate magic is easy for elemental mages and hard to impossible for everyone else. It works by creating a similarity between two points in space, briefly linking them across a two-dimensional portal. A gate stone is an item which is metaphysically tied to a specific location. You can use it to gate to a place you haven't seen, or make a gate when you otherwise wouldn't be able to use gate magic at all.

As I focused a flickering oval began to form in the air, waxing and waning. I concentrated, pushing with my will, and the oval solidified into a shape five feet high and two feet wide, big enough for a child to step through or a man to squeeze through. Beyond was a dark room, cold and unlit.

Then Anne's fingers tightened over mine and I felt a surge of power run through into the focus. The edges of the gate portal shifted in colour from a translucent grey to a soft leaf green and the portal doubled in size, stretching from floor to ceiling.

From out on the balcony I heard the *thud* of someone landing from a jump. The gunmen were following and we were out of time. I lifted Anne off the bed and rushed for the portal.

This is the dangerous part of a gate spell: maintaining

your mental concentration on holding both ends of the spell while also doing the physical work of stepping through. If you mess it up the gate closes while you're halfway through, with results I'll leave to your imagination. Anne cried out again as I lifted her, and the power coming from her dimmed. The portal shrank, and for one terrifying moment I was heading for the gate too fast to stop but too slow to make it through. Then Anne recovered, a final surge of power threw the gate out to full size, and we were through. My foot came down on tiles.

As soon as we'd made it the energy pouring through from Anne shut off. The green light flickered and died and the gate winked out behind us, casting the room into pitch-darkness. I couldn't see, but with my divination magic I don't need to. I picked out the route through the kitchen in which we'd landed, noticing the futures in which I stumbled over chairs and avoiding them, and guided us blind to the corridor and into the bedroom beyond. I set Anne down on the bed as carefully as I could, then flicked on the light switch. We'd come into a plain room with a deserted guesthouse sort of feel, and the light that made it through the window splashed upon trees and grass before fading into the vast black emptiness of an unlit valley. The only sound was the soft *shhhhh* of a river outside. We were in the country.

I moved through the house, switching on the heat and lights, before returning to Anne. Lying on the bed she looked very small and very still, her black hair spread out on the pillow like a fan. I looked into the future to see what would happen if I left her and with a horrible sinking sensation realised it had all been for nothing.

Maybe it had been the extra effort of the gate stone; maybe it had been the final shock of moving her that last time, tearing her wounds back open. But whatever reserve

Anne had been drawing on to keep herself alive, it had been used up. She was dying. I stood over Anne, looking down at her still form, and felt helpless. With my divination magic there's so much I can find, so much I can do—but there was nothing I could do about this.

As if she could feel my gaze, Anne's eyes flickered open. Her breaths were shallow and she had to try twice to speak. "Need . . ."

I crouched next to her. "Need what?"

Reddish-brown eyes looked into mine. There was fear there, and desperation. "Take my . . . hand."

Anne raised her hand off the bed. I reached for it—

And my precognition screamed a warning. Instantly I sprang back, coming to my feet in the centre of the room, tense and balanced, ready to flee.

Anne's arm was still reaching out towards me, trembling slightly, then her strength failed and it fell to hang off the side of the bed. Her head was turned towards me and I caught a flash of something that made me stop. Pain, yes, but more than anything she looked ashamed.

"Can't . . ." Anne's soft voice was quick and ragged. "Nothing left. Please . . ."

I stared at Anne and saw the choice branching ahead of me. If I stayed where I was Anne's breaths would come slower and her words would become fainter and soon, in only a few minutes, those red-brown eyes would close and she would die.

But if I took her hand . . .

If I took her hand I'd be struck down by some kind of magical attack, something I'd never seen before. It would be fast as lightning and there wouldn't be a thing I could do to stop it. In the futures I saw myself crumpling, then blackness.

"Alex . . ." Anne said softly, and her eyes were pleading. "Please . . ."

Every instinct I had was shouting to stay away. It wasn't as if Anne were my apprentice. I wasn't responsible for her and it wasn't my fault she was hurt. And she'd just tried to . . . actually I didn't know *what* she'd tried to do. My divination magic can only see what my own senses would perceive, and all I could see down that path was darkness. For all I knew taking her hand would mean we'd both end up dead.

It wasn't my problem. No one would blame me for leaving her.

I looked at Anne, seeing the slim dying body, the fear and shame and desperate hope in her eyes, and walked forward. I had to fight myself to do it; my danger sense was screaming at me with every step. I reached down and took Anne's hand from where it hung limp.

There was a green flash and the strength in every part of my body vanished at once. My hearing cut out, my vision went black, and I couldn't see or sense or feel. I never felt myself hit the floor.

chapter 4

I woke up very slowly.

I felt awful. My muscles were like water and my head was dizzy. I felt like I'd caught a fever, starved for two weeks, then gotten the worst hangover of my life to top it off. As soon as I realised how bad I felt my first reaction was to try to go back to sleep.

I stayed like that for a while, drifting in and out of consciousness. What finally pushed me awake was realising how hungry I was. I opened my eyes.

It was morning and bright sunlight was streaming through the window. There was something odd about the quiet, and it took me a moment to realise what was missing: the background hum of the city. I wasn't in London anymore.

I was in a guest room with plain white walls and I was lying in a bed. I was still wearing my clothes but my shoes had been taken off, and looking to one side I could see that the contents of my pockets had been neatly stacked on a bedside table. The room was familiar, as was the sound of the river outside, and a moment later I realised where I was: my safe house in Wales. I just wasn't sure how I'd got here.

Then I remembered. Anne; the taxi; the battle and the gate. I tried to pull myself up and failed. My muscles were ridiculously weak; I couldn't even sit upright. My body felt different too, lighter.

Footsteps sounded from the corridor and I looked up to see Anne's head poking around the door. She vanished and reappeared a second later holding a tray.

Anything I'd been planning to say went right out of my head as soon as I smelt the food. My stomach growled and I realised I wasn't just hungry, I was ravenous. "Um," Anne said. "I think you should eat—"

I didn't quite grab it out of her hands but I came close. The food was oatmeal and fairly bland, not that I cared. Anne went back to the kitchen and got a second bowl, which lasted about as long as the first.

As I was starting on the third bowl I felt the stirrings of a spell and glanced up to see Anne reaching out towards me. As I looked at her she stopped. "May I?"

"As long as it's not whatever you hit me with last night."

Anne flinched as if I'd slapped her. I shook my head. "Sorry, didn't mean it like that. Go ahead."

Anne placed her hand against my shoulder. A faint green glow, the colour of new leaves in spring, welled up around her hand to soak into me. I could feel it spreading through my body but I couldn't tell what it was doing.

As I ate I studied Anne out of the corner of my eye. She was wearing a white T-shirt that left her long arms bare, and her skin was a healthy colour again. The bloodstains and bullet holes in the T-shirt were very obvious but she moved without any trace of pain or stiffness. In fact she looked a hell of a lot better than I felt.

I finished up the third bowl. Now that I'd taken the edge off my hunger, it was a little easier to think. Anne was still working her spell through the touch of her hand, and I could feel a faint tingle within my body. "What are you doing?"

"Ah . . ." Anne said in her soft voice. "I'm rebuilding your reserves."

"How?"

"Your body converts food into energy," Anne said. "I'm . . . speeding that up. You'll feel better soon."

"Okay," I said. "Look, don't take this the wrong way, but unless my memory's going you stopped seven bullets with your chest last night while I only got a few bruises. So could you explain why you're looking the picture of health when I can't even get out of bed?"

Anne made as if to speak, then went out of the room, coming back with another two bowls. She put them on the table and sat on a chair, not meeting my eyes.

I started on the next bowl. "You're not very used to talking about this stuff, are you?"

"Sorry."

"Well, if you want to eat too and don't fancy oatmeal, there should be something in the kitchen."

"I don't think it's there."

"It's in the cupboard under the sink."

"I know."

"What's wrong?"

"I . . . already ate it."

"You can't have eaten all of it. There was three days' worth."

Anne looked embarrassed.

"Wait, seriously?"

"Sorry," Anne said again.

I looked at Anne's slim figure in disbelief. "Where do you put it all?"

"I used too much last night." Anne brushed her hair back, looking down at the floor. "I burnt all my reserves. Muscle and fat. It took . . . quite a lot to rebuild them."

I looked at Anne a moment longer. "You're a life mage."

Anne nodded.

"That was how you survived those injuries," I said. "You were repairing the damage from the bullets."

"But it's hard," Anne said. "When I heal someone else, some of the energy comes from me and some comes from them. When I heal myself I can't . . ." She trailed off.

I stared at her for a second, and then it clicked. "Was that what you did to me? You took energy from my body and used it to keep yourself alive?"

Anne nodded again. She didn't meet my eyes.

Well, that explained why I felt so terrible. I'd never been life-drained before and I shivered a little as I remembered the feeling. Having the strength drained out of every part of your body at once is a uniquely nasty experience.

Anne still had her eyes downcast, and I realised suddenly that she felt ashamed. "Ah, relax," I said. "Don't beat yourself up over it."

Anne looked up in surprise. "You're not . . . ?"

"Well, I feel like crap," I said. "But all in all, I'd rather feel like crap than have you dead. Be a bit of a waste after I went to all that effort. Just try and take a bit less next time, okay?"

"I'm sorry," Anne said again. "I was—"

"I'm kidding," I said. "And you can stop worrying, I'm not going to report you to the Council."

I saw Anne relax a bit. Life-draining is outlawed by the

Council—it's too close to the forbidden technique of Harvesting—and in her position she'd be in serious trouble if accused. "Thank you."

"So I'm guessing this is why I'm so hungry?"

Anne nodded. "Your body stores short-term and long-term energy. I . . . took most of it. You've been burning body fat all night." Anne hesitated. "You, um, might find you're a bit lighter."

I lifted the covers and looked down at myself. "Huh. You know, you could make a lot of money in the weight-loss business."

"Everyone says that." Anne sounded faintly exasperated. "You're supposed to have *some* fat."

I noticed with mild surprise that I'd eaten the last two bowls of oatmeal without realising it. "You can read bodies, right?"

Anne nodded.

"How am I doing?"

"You're fine," Anne said at once. "You'll need to eat about three times as much as normal for a while but your body will tell you that. Just be careful for a day or two while your energy reserves build up again. But you could get up now if you wanted."

I suited the action to the word. My legs felt a little wobbly and there was a lingering weakness in my limbs, but I was feeling better and managed to stay on my feet. My phone was on the table, and looking at it I saw that it was past ten. "Ah hell," I said as I remembered my appointment with Sonder. "I'm supposed to be somewhere."

"Wait!" Anne said in alarm. "You can't use a gate stone already. You need to—"

"I'm all right," I said. "I just need to make a call."

⁚⁚⁚⁚⁚⁚⁚⁚⁚⁚

Once I was in the corridor and out of sight I took out my phone and saw that I had four missed calls. As I did, I saw that my hand was shaking. I leant against the wall and closed my eyes. It wasn't the physical drain that was getting to me, not really. I've been hurt before and I'm used to it. It was the memory of last night.

Killing with a knife is much more personal than with a gun. A gun is detached, clinical. Aim, squeeze the trigger, see the puff of red. Even looking down at the body afterwards it doesn't really feel like you did it. A knife is different. You feel the impact as the blade goes in, the warmth of the blood on your hands, the struggles of the man you're holding. It's harder to shut out.

I didn't try. Instead I ran through the events of last night, deliberately replaying the battle in the flat step by step. One after another I thought about the choices I could have taken and the other ways the battle could have ended. I thought about the men killing Anne or killing me and compared that to my memory of stabbing the man in the back. If I had to do it all over again, would I make the same choice?

Yes. I would. As I decided that, the memory loosened a little. It wasn't any easier, but facing it, understanding it, made it bearable. I stayed there for another few minutes, then once I was calm again I tapped a stored number on my phone.

The phone rang once and was picked up on the second ring. "Alex?"

It was Luna's voice, anxious and hopeful, and hearing it pulled me the rest of the way back to the world of the living. Suddenly I was awake again. "It's me."

"You're okay?"

"I'm fine."

I heard Luna sigh in relief. "It's him, he's okay," she called to someone else, then came back to the receiver. "Where have you *been*?"

"Long story."

"I called last night and I thought you were just asleep. Then I met Sonder this morning and he hadn't heard anything either! We've been worried sick."

"Sorry," I said. "I got held up."

"Don't scare me like that. I was afraid you'd been kidnapped again or something."

"No, I—Wait, what do you mean 'again'?"

"You know, like with Morden."

"That happened *once*."

"And the time with Belthas."

"I got caught that time because I was going after you."

"No you weren't. Anyway, what about—"

There was the sound of someone else clearing their throat. "Oh, right," Luna said. "Where are you?"

"Wales."

"Wales?"

"Wales."

"Why are you in Wales?"

"Three men tried to kill Anne last night. There was a fight and we evac'd to the safe house. Has anyone come after you or Sonder?"

"Tried to kill—? No, no one's come after us. Alex, what have you been doing?"

"Good." The weariness in my limbs wasn't going away and I realised Anne had been right. I didn't have the strength to use a gate stone yet. "Listen, I'm going to be laid up for a few hours. I want you to work with Sonder on those reports. Get as familiar with the information as you can."

"Are you going to be here?"

"No, I'm going to be following up on something else. Have you got any classes today?"

"Just one. It finishes at five."

"Good. When you're done go to Arachne's and ask her to fit you a dress. Ask her to find me something too while you're at it. I'll meet you there, but I might be late."

"You're finally getting a better wardrobe?"

"No, we're going to a party."

"Oh," Luna said. "Something *really* dangerous."

"As long as I don't have to arm-wrestle you to make you go this time. Now put Sonder on, I need to ask him something."

"Say please."

"Just do it."

"Sonder!" Luna called. "Alex wants to talk to you. He says he's got a date tonight and wants some advice on what to wear."

I rolled my eyes. When Luna took the formal oath of apprenticeship, she swore to obey me "without question." Luna's way of getting around this has been to follow orders to the letter but add some creative misinterpretation. I heard the clunking of the phone being put down and picked up, then Sonder's voice. "Um, hello?"

"Ignore Luna," I said. "Listen, I need you to do me a favour."

"Oh," Sonder said. "Okay. Sure."

"Three assassins tried to kill me and Anne last night in Archway. I'll send you the address. I need you to look around and find out whatever you can about those men. One's dead but two got away and I need to find them. There'll be police lines so it might be difficult to get in, but do what you can."

There was a moment's silence. "Do you think there's a

connection?" Sonder said at last. "I mean . . . right after you were asked to do the—the other job. It's a bit of a coincidence."

"Yeah," I said. "It is."

"Do you think it's the same person?"

I frowned. "I don't know. What I really want to know is what linked them to me."

"That's why you want me to find out about those men?"

"Yeah."

"Okay, I'll try. And I'll take Luna through the files."

"Thanks. See you tonight."

ιιιιιιιιι

I found Anne in the kitchen washing up. There was a stack of plates on the dish rack, and I could see from the empty cupboard that she hadn't been exaggerating about how much she'd eaten. I guess every kind of magic has its quirks. I sat at the table, not letting myself show how much of a relief it was to get off my feet—I could feel my strength returning but slower than I was used to. "Okay," I said. "So who do you know who wants you dead?"

Anne turned to me, face troubled. She was drying her hands with a towel and it would have been a peaceful domestic scene but for the bloodstains on her clothes. "I don't know," she said. "I've tried to think of anyone but I can't."

"Offended any Dark mages lately? Made any new enemies?"

"I don't think so."

"What about that girl from duelling class?"

Anne looked surprised. "Natasha? She's just a bit nervous about me and Vari."

I thought it had seemed a bit more serious than that but kept my feelings to myself. Besides, I couldn't really see an apprentice sending gunmen. "Well, *someone* wants to get rid of you," I said. "And they weren't kidding around. Those men were no joke."

"I know," Anne said. She looked at me. "Thank you. Not just for coming to help. For afterwards."

I nodded.

"But . . ." Anne hesitated. "How did you know?"

"I'm a diviner," I said. "It's what I do."

As I said it, though, something nagged at my memory. When I'd told Sonder about the attack, he'd leapt to the conclusion that it had been aimed at me. It hadn't been, not directly: Anne had been the gunmen's target and they hadn't attacked me until I'd intervened. But maybe Sonder had been on to something. "You know," I said slowly, "you might not have been the only target last night."

"What do you mean?"

"You were meant to be the victim." I looked at Anne. "I was meant to be the suspect."

Anne looked puzzled, but it fit. If her assassination had gone as planned, I would have been the last mage to see her alive. The Council Keepers would have come asking questions. Everyone knew I'd been responsible for the deaths of two Light mages already. Having yet another vanish so soon after meeting me . . .

It probably wouldn't have been enough to get me arrested, not on its own. But I've got enemies on the Council, enemies who'd be more than willing to overlook the holes in the case and maybe fiddle a bit of evidence to help things along. Even if the charge didn't stick, it would have made it a lot harder for me to go snooping around.

I tried to explain that to Anne in my halting way but didn't do a good job. "They wouldn't have blamed you, though, would they?" she asked.

"Maybe," I said. "It'd be less effort than sending those gunmen."

"But you didn't do anything wrong."

I looked at Anne, watching me seriously out of those odd reddish eyes, and couldn't help but laugh. But it gave me an idea. "Have you called anyone yet to tell them you're okay?"

A shadow passed over Anne's face. "No."

Now why not? I thought curiously. *You obviously thought about it. But you didn't call Variam and you didn't call this Lord Jagadev, whoever he is.*

What *was* the story with Anne? There was no way she should still be an apprentice with the amount of power she'd displayed last night. And her lack of fear or panic was telling. She was used to danger, even if she didn't look it. She was a weird mixture altogether—grave and wary and oddly naive underneath it all.

I wanted to keep asking questions but held back. Some instinct told me that pressing Anne for information now would make her shy away. So instead I helped her with the dishes and wondered if there was anything edible left in the house. As it turned out, there was.

| | | | | | | | | |

The building was an old farmhouse at the very end of a Welsh valley. I'd rented it a few months back during one of my more paranoid moments, as a getaway in case someone attacked my London home. As a place to live it's a joke—it's fifteen miles from the nearest village, there aren't any phone lines, and it floods every spring. But if all you want is somewhere to hide, it's a good deal.

On Anne's advice I rested for several hours before trying to travel, and I spent the time talking to her. I sensed she was uncomfortable with talking about herself and her powers, so I didn't ask. Instead I settled for getting the details of how she'd been attacked last night.

It had been done very simply. While on her way to Archway Anne had received a text message, supposedly from Jagadev, directing her to go to a different address and send the car away once she arrived. Anne had obeyed. She'd noticed the men but hadn't spotted the guns, and as she pressed the button to call the lift they'd shot her in the back.

Anne hadn't recognised any of the men, and neither had I. They hadn't been carrying magic, which along with the guns suggested they were normals. But they hadn't been fazed by my mist effect either, and from the few words they'd exchanged over Anne's body they'd known getting too close to her could be dangerous, and *that* made me think they were at least clued in to the magical world. Maybe ex–Council security, or some Dark mage's private army. Either way, I'd know more once Sonder had had a chance to investigate.

It was two o'clock when we left the house. I locked it behind us, then slid the key under the door—I didn't need it to get back in. "Are you sure you don't want to catch a train or something?" Anne asked.

"There are some things I need to get done," I said, and gave Anne a glance. "Besides, I think you might attract a bit of attention."

Anne looked embarrassed. She'd gotten the blood off her skin and out of her hair and had even had a try at washing her clothes, but they still looked exactly as you'd expect clothes to look if their wearer had been shot repeatedly in the chest. "I couldn't find anything else to wear."

"Yeah, I didn't stock the place very well." I started walking towards the river, picking my way through patches of grass. "Let's get going."

The end of the valley was cold and had a desolate look. Thistles sprouted between the rocks and grass, patches of nettles grew around the outbuildings, and there were bramble thickets under the bare trees. But the air was clear and the hills rose green around us and the place had its own kind of quiet beauty, even if few would come to see it.

The gate stone I'd used to bring us here had been made out of a rock from the bank of the river I was standing beside now. Gate stones have a lot of drawbacks, but the biggest is that they're always one-way. They can only take you to a single location, set when you create the stone. So if you want to travel around using gate stones you have to take a selection with you—which means you risk losing them if anything goes wrong.

The gate stone I'd used was keyed to the kitchen of the farmhouse behind us. I've also got gate stones for the ravine outside Arachne's lair, the Great Court of the British Museum, a mountaintop in Scotland, and a fairly random selection of other places, none of which I'd brought with me today. I'd brought the gate stone to my shop, though, and it was this one I took out now. "Ready?" I asked Anne.

Anne nodded and stepped up next to me. She seemed to be watching me closely for some reason but I couldn't see why, so I shrugged it off and spoke the activation words. Again the air shimmered and formed into a translucent oval, and again it shifted colour to a leaf green as Anne's fingers closed over mine and she channelled her power into my spell. Anne's magic worked much more easily with gate stones than mine did, but that wasn't surprising—even if it can affect only living things, life magic can still change the physical world.

We came down into the little back room of my shop and the air went from winter in Wales to room temperature in

London. "Will you be okay making it home on your own?" I asked as I led Anne to the back door.

Anne nodded. "There's somewhere safe I can go."

"Good." I looked at Anne. "Can you do me a favour? Could you stay hidden until tonight?"

"I . . . suppose," Anne said hesitantly. "Why?"

"If I'm right, someone was trying to get rid of both of us," I said. "If I show up at the party without you, they may think you're dead after all. Maybe I can get them to tip their hand."

Anne thought about it, then nodded. "All right."

We both stood in the doorway, and I realised with a feeling of surprise that I liked this strange girl. "Be careful," I said.

"I will." Anne smiled. "See you tonight."

I watched Anne go, then went inside.

। । । । । । । । ।

I had a few hours before I needed to get ready for the party, and I'd already decided what to do with them. I was going to Fountain Reach.

Given that I'd been sure only the previous day that the message pointing me to Fountain Reach had been a trap, you're probably wondering why I'd changed my mind. It's a fair question, and to be honest I wasn't quite sure myself. I just had the vague feeling that I needed to do *something*, keep searching and looking around. With hindsight, I think the attack on Anne and me had made me suspect someone was moving against us, and I wanted to try to turn something up before they made their next move.

I made my preparations, choosing my equipment more carefully than I had for my hurried departure last night. I kept the gate stone for my shop; it would be useless for getting there but would speed up the journey back. A second gate stone keyed to Fountain Reach would have allowed me to travel back and forth at will, but I didn't have one. I took another pair of condensers as well as a handful of extra items picked with an eye towards trickery and concealment. Finally I took my mist cloak from my wardrobe. When it comes to stealth my mist cloak is far and away the best item I own, and I'd already decided that stealth was exactly what was needed.

As well as my mist cloak, there's something else I always used to bring with me on these sort of trips: a thin glass rod, designed to call an air elemental named Starbreeze. Starbreeze is scatterbrained and ridiculously unreliable, and she forgets anything you tell her almost before you've said it, but she can turn a person to air and carry them faster than a bullet. If I'd been able to call her, she could have whisked me across the length of England and dropped me next to Fountain Reach in the time it takes most people to check their e-mail.

Unfortunately I don't have the caller anymore. I blew it up in the autumn getting away from a bunch of enemies, and I haven't managed to contact Starbreeze since. I worry sometimes that I never will: Starbreeze might wonder eventually why I'm not talking to her and come looking for me to find out, but Starbreeze is immortal. It might take her ten or twenty years to even notice.

So in the absence of gates or elementals, I took the train.

The directions I'd found placed Crystal's family home in the Cotswolds, between Oxford and Gloucester. I got off at the nearest station and took a taxi most of the way before walking the final stretch on foot. I crested a rise and found myself looking across a small valley at Fountain Reach.

My first thought was that it was the weirdest-looking house I'd ever seen. Mages like unusual homes and I've seen some strange ones in my time, but this was the strangest. It looked as if it had been grown rather than built, extra wings and storeys added on one at a time, each in a different architectural style. The windows were irregular and didn't match, changing in height and design, and there were too many chimneys and too many gables. The mansion was blockier and more cubical than it should have been, rather than the extended oblong common to most country houses. The inner rooms must have had no natural light at all.

The mansion was isolated, but not terribly so. The hillside cut off the view of the nearby town and rail line but the sounds of activity drifted up through the trees. The slopes were forested and I left the access road to angle upwards through the woods and look down on Fountain Reach from above. The gardens were extensive and looked carefully tended, beautiful flowerbeds mixing with copses of exotic trees. Birds pecked on the lawn, their calls echoing through the leaves, and the winter sun was dipping in the western sky, casting a yellowish light over the scene and giving a perfect view across the countryside below.

It looked about as unsinister a place as could be imagined, enough to make me feel a bit foolish. I half-expected a coach to show up and a bunch of European tourists to go wandering across the lawn with their cameras or something.

But I was here and I might as well do the job I'd come for. I found a good vantage point beneath an ash tree and crouched down, concentrating on the futures of me exploring the mansion below.

The technique is called path-walking, and it was the same one I'd used the night before. Basically, instead of looking forward into your various futures, you isolate just *one* future and follow it through the choices ahead. I'd tried it during the train journey in an attempt to speed up any search of Fountain Reach but hadn't had much luck. Hopefully it'd be easier now that I was closer.

To my surprise it wasn't. I could trace out the futures down to the mansion but as soon as I entered the images became narrowed, fuzzy. I kept trying for ten minutes before giving up with a frown.

I'd seen this effect before. You got it when attempting to use divination magic within an area that had been warded against scrying—*heavily* warded against scrying. As I focused on the mansion with my mage's sight I realised that the walls were layered with overlapping shields of magical protection, so thick that from my position I couldn't see through them at all. They were messy, uneven, but extremely powerful.

Now why would a private residence in the middle of nowhere have such heavy defences?

The obvious answer: because they had something to hide.

I waited for sunset. English winter days are short and it wasn't even four o'clock before the sun began dipping behind the hills. As soon as the sun vanished the temperature dropped like a rock, but my cloak kept me from more than the odd shiver. I know from experience that it's actually harder to spot someone in twilight than nighttime—the eye has trouble adjusting from the light sky to the dark ground—so once the sky had faded to blue-grey I set off downhill.

The dark woods were filled with roots and traps for unwary feet but my divination magic guided me safely through. My breath was visible in the cold air and the stars shone down from above, Orion and Sirius glowing brightly in a clear sky. I vaulted the garden wall and stole across the lawn, just one more shadow in the evening gloom.

Fountain Reach was occupied—that had been obvious from the cars and vans—but having watched the place for an hour I was fairly sure that there wasn't much security and I didn't pick up any danger as I approached. I reached the back of the mansion and studied the wards.

The more I looked at them, the more puzzled I got. Like the house, the wards had an organic look, as if they'd been grown rather than constructed. The design was massively inefficient but the sheer volume of energy made them formidable all the same. There was a gate ward, of course, and shields against spatial and temporal scrying, but search as I might I couldn't discover any barrier to physical entry. Which was very strange—why would anyone expend so much energy on making a place impossible to view or gate into but do nothing to stop anyone from just walking in?

The divination ward worried me, though. It's almost impossible to shut down a diviner's magic completely but the wards were powerful enough to damp it, and as I looked into the futures of my entering I found that I could see much less further than normal. Futures thirty seconds away were fuzzy, and beyond that they degraded quickly into uselessness. My ability to see into the future is the only major edge I have. Having it even partially suppressed makes me very nervous.

But if I was careful thirty seconds ought to be enough. There were windows all along the ground floor and it took me no time at all to find one that had been left unlatched. I pushed it up and climbed inside, and into Fountain Reach.

chapter 5

The inside of Fountain Reach was quiet, distant voices muffled by the intervening walls. I'd come into some kind of sitting room and I moved to the door and listened. I could hear movement, but not close by.

From a legal point of view, what I was doing here was kind of a grey area. The Council comes down hard on anyone trespassing on Council property, but entering another mage's residence isn't specifically forbidden—what the Concord prohibits against other mages is "hostile action." On the other hand, *hostile* is a pretty vague word. Mages tend to be trigger-happy about home defence and if Crystal found me sneaking around her mansion she'd quite likely shoot on sight. She'd have to justify it to the Council afterwards, but if she claimed I'd been there to attack her she'd probably get away with it—especially if I was too dead to say otherwise.

That last possibility didn't appeal much, which was why

I'd brought my mist cloak. My mist cloak doesn't look very impressive—it's just a length of soft cloth, coloured a sort of neutral grey, well cut but nothing worth taking note of. But when worn it has a camouflaging effect, its colours shifting to match the background behind, making its wearer fade into the scenery like a chameleon. If you stay in the shadows and don't move, a mist cloak makes you damn near invisible.

More important, mist cloaks function against magical senses too. Mind mages like Crystal can sense the presence of other creatures by detecting their consciousness, "seeing" thoughts in the same way that you or I can see light. Without the mist cloak she'd spot me the instant I got close. With it I had a chance of staying hidden.

I stole into the corridor, senses alert. My ears and my magic told me that there were people to the left and right along the edge of the building. I went forward, deeper into the mansion.

Fountain Reach was a bizarre house, with corridors that twisted and changed in size and design. There was no logic to the layout: Staircases led into dead ends and windows looked into other rooms. There were people here—lots of people—but as I moved through the mansion I realised most were servants or caterers. The opening ceremony for the tournament was tomorrow and the staff were busy with preparations. The stealth probably hadn't been necessary; with all the activity I could have just walked in the front door. As I moved deeper into the mansion the sounds of activity became fainter and fainter until they were silent. I'd known the place was big but the winding corridors made it seem bigger; with no direct routes it took a long time to get anywhere.

I'd been aiming for the bedrooms but found myself walking into what was obviously the duelling hall. It looked as though it had been a ballroom once, with a wide parquet floor and a high ceiling, but azimuth focuses had been erected at either end of the room and tables and chairs had been set up for refreshments. Despite the lights scattered around the hall, the place had a gloomy feel. I searched the room quickly and found focus weapons, protective gear, and scattered papers. In fact, exactly what you'd expect to find.

I went through the documents and found what looked like a schedule. The opening ceremony would be tomorrow evening and the elimination rounds would take place during the two days after that, with the finals the day after. The focus of the tournament seemed to be on the apprentice competition. The journeyman division had only a few mages competing while dozens of apprentices were scheduled to duel, with places still open.

Which told me . . .

. . . nothing useful at all. I straightened up from the papers, suddenly annoyed with myself. What was I *doing* here? I was taking risks sneaking into a place I really shouldn't be in, and for what? To find out information that wasn't a secret in the first place.

I could stick around and keep searching. But the mansion was huge, and with my ability to search through futures degraded I could look for days and not find anything. I turned and walked out.

I followed the corridors back, twisting and turning, until I came to a T junction. Had I come from the left or the right? I tried the left and it led me to a four-way intersection. I followed it down a flight of stairs that I thought was familiar, but it led into a hall lined with paintings that I was sure I hadn't seen before. I retraced my steps to the intersection but all the corridors looked identical. I picked one and it led me to a T junction, but the passages onwards didn't look familiar either.

I stopped, irritated. This was ridiculous. How could I be getting lost inside a *house*?

Usually, as long as my magic is working, I can always find my way home. All I have to do is search through the futures and look for the one in which I make it out. But with my divination range cut down, I couldn't see far enough— and since I'm so used to never getting lost I hadn't thought to memorise the route on the way in. It was a rookie mistake and it was embarrassing. I started down the corridor, trying to find my way to a window or some sort of landmark.

As I did I realised it had been a long time since I'd heard any movement. The house was quiet—*really* quiet. I stopped and listened but couldn't hear any activity at all.

The corridor I'd reached felt much older than the outer parts of the house. The furniture was dark and shabby, there were cracks in the plaster, and a fine layer of dust covered the tables.

And suddenly my precognition flared.

My divination magic might have been dulled, but my reactions weren't. In a flash I was hidden in a doorway, the hood of my mist cloak concealing my face, fading into the background against the shadows of the dimly lit corridor.

The house was silent. I held myself perfectly still. Only my eyes moved, flicking up and down the length of the corridor. I couldn't see or sense anything. But my magic was telling me that something very, very bad was going to happen if I moved even an inch from where I was standing now. One minute passed, two minutes, five. My feet itched but I didn't let myself move. I scanned for enemies using every trick I knew and came up blank.

And all of a sudden the threat was gone. I checked and

rechecked the futures and found nothing. I held still another five minutes, then moved quickly and quietly away down the corridor, holding my breath until I was safely out of sight.

Although I kept a tight grip on it, I was shaken. I hadn't been able to make out what the danger was but I was absolutely sure that *something* would have happened to me if I'd moved. Usually my magic shows me the outcome of bad choices in gruesome detail. I've always thought it's one of the nastiest bits of being a diviner but now I was finding that knowing something was after you without knowing *what* was actually worse.

As I moved I tried to figure out just what the hell had happened there. I'd sensed danger in the short-term future but the immediate future had shown nothing but an empty corridor. If something had been about to attack me, why hadn't I seen any trace of it?

I didn't know, but I wasn't staying around to find out. I reached an intersection and scanned ahead. I still didn't know which was the way out but I wasn't looking for that anymore: All I was focused on was evading the invisible threat behind me. One of the routes gave me a stirring of unease and I took the other, moving as fast as I could. I was concentrating on scanning for the whatever-it-was rather than looking for rooms or people, and so I didn't notice that I'd made my way back to the duelling hall until I came through the doorway.

The hall wasn't empty this time. There was a young man standing by one of the tables, going through the papers. He was tall and thin, dressed in black with a whiplike quickness to his movements. It had been eight months since I'd seen him but I remembered him very well. His name was Onyx, and the last time we'd met he'd been trying to kill me.

As I stopped in the doorway Onyx's head snapped up towards me. For a second we stared at each other.

Onyx cast a spell and I leapt back as blades of force slashed in an X pattern through the space I'd been in a second ago. Another blade hissed over my head as I rolled left into the corridor, coming to my feet in a run.

There was a wall between Onyx and me now, and I sprinted down the corridor before he could regain a line of sight. Looking ahead I saw that he wasn't chasing me, he was going to—

Crap! I threw myself flat, skidding on the carpet, and as I did splinters and plaster exploded all around me as Onyx sent a lethal spray of force blades tearing through the building. They were at waist height and he'd fired them straight from the duelling hall, cutting across the corridor and through the wall on both sides.

As he did, a bolt of agony went through my head, a mental shriek of pain and fury. It was so powerful it blanked my thoughts for an instant, making my vision grey out.

When I came to I was curled on the floor, my hands over my ears. I staggered to my feet and kept moving, trying to shake off the fuzziness inside my head. My hearing was still working and I could hear distant shouts from ahead of me, and I knew that we'd stirred up trouble, but the noise was enough to orient me and suddenly I knew more or less where I was going. I couldn't sense Onyx or the other presence anymore, and I kept moving. As I reached the corridor leading to the outer rooms, a group of people went hurrying past. I waited in the shadows for them to get out of sight, then slipped into the room from which I'd entered and dropped out the window.

As I left the walls of the mansion my vision of the futures ahead of me cleared, and my heart lifted as I could see properly again. I ran out across the garden under the starlight, my feet quiet on the grass. Looking back through the cold night air I could see the windows of Fountain Reach lit up. Distant shouts echoed through the walls, but I couldn't hear any sounds of battle.

I made it out of the garden and started back up the forested slope in the darkness. I could have activated my gate stone, but I wanted to put a safe distance between me and any pursuers before I did anything to reveal my presence. As I scanned ahead through the futures, though, I saw that I wasn't alone in the woods. Someone was ahead of me in the same vantage point I'd used earlier. Maybe they'd had the same idea as me.

I was tempted to just bug out, but I'd had time to recover from my scare. Now that my magic was working properly again I had my confidence back. I altered course towards the person above, and as I did I thought about Onyx.

Onyx is the Chosen of a powerful Dark mage named Morden. Morden was one of the two major players competing for the fateweaver back in April; he coerced me and a small cabal of Dark mages to go get it for him and sent Onyx along to ensure our cooperation. It turned out that Onyx's idea of cooperation involved him leaving with the fateweaver and everyone else not leaving at all. I got hold of the fateweaver before Onyx did and we had a frank exchange of views.

It ended up with Onyx on the floor and bleeding, barely escaping with his life. Unfortunately I'd only won because of the fateweaver, and the price tag on those powers turned out to be a hell of a lot higher than I was willing to pay. The fateweaver was gone but Onyx was still around, and that was bad news because Onyx was one of the deadliest battle-mages I'd ever had the misfortune to run up against. I wondered if he held a grudge against me for humiliating him like that. I had the feeling the answer was a definite *yes*.

The person waiting at the viewpoint near the top of the hill was a girl, nineteen or so. She was just a shadow in the darkness, but by looking into the futures in which I switched on my light I recognised her as one of Morden's slaves. I had to think for a minute before I remembered her name: Lisa. I hadn't really expected to see her again. Slaves to Dark mages have a high turnover rate. I let myself fade into the shadows and waited.

Onyx arrived five minutes later. He was obviously trying to be quiet but I had the impression he didn't spend much time in the woods and it wasn't hard to hear him coming. Unlike me his magic didn't give him any way to see in the dark and he'd resorted to some kind of black-light spell that cast a murky glow. I felt Lisa go tense as she saw him.

"Who did you see?" Onyx said as he walked up into the clearing.

"N-nobody."

"Verus was in there." Onyx was young, but his voice was flat and cold and sent a chill down my spine. "When did he go in?"

"I don't know—"

The blow didn't look powerful but it was augmented with force and took Lisa off her feet. Onyx had already turned away and was staring down at Fountain Reach. There was a sort of casual indifference to the whole thing. Onyx had been annoyed and Lisa had been in front of him, so he'd hit her. He didn't care whether it had been her fault and in fact he seemed already to have forgotten that she was there. Lisa stayed on the ground for a while, cringing, then pulled herself upright.

Onyx shook his head and turned away. The darkness shrouded his face but his body language looked frustrated. Magic flared around him as he opened a black gateway; he stepped through and Lisa hurried through after him without needing to be told. The gateway closed and I was left alone on the hillside.

I watched thoughtfully for a moment, then turned to make my way home.

᠁

"But what was Onyx doing there?" Sonder asked an hour and a half later.

Arachne's cave is wide and oval-shaped, hidden under Hampstead Heath and hollowed out of stone that's been worn smooth by the passage of hundreds of years. Clothes cover the furniture and every inch of the walls, turning the cave into a riot of green and blue and yellow and red. There are small changing rooms to one side and at the far end a tunnel leads down into darkness.

Sonder was sitting on the edge of one of the chairs, his clothes rumpled from a day spent indoors. He has messy black hair, a pair of glasses, and a way of peering at whatever he's reading that makes it look like he's completely oblivious to everything else, which is usually true. He's twenty-one but looks like a first-year university student. He still had his arms full of papers, and the reports he'd been reading were spread out over a pile of coats on the table in front of him. He pushed his glasses up automatically as he waited for my answer.

"I don't know," I said from my sofa. I was more tired than I should have been; the escape from Fountain Reach had taken a lot out of me and I obviously hadn't fully recovered from Anne's spell yet. "But I'm pretty sure he wasn't supposed to be there either."

"Do you think it's him?" Luna called. She was hidden behind the curtain of one of the changing rooms. "Him and Morden, I mean."

"They're vicious enough," I said. "But it seems like an odd thing for him to do."

"Onyx?" I could feel Luna shudder. "He'd do *anything*."

"Anything Morden tells him to. Don't forget that."

"We know they take slaves," Luna said. "Like that girl Lisa. Maybe that's where the apprentices are going."

"There's no way Morden would take that kind of risk," I said. "The reason he got involved in the hunt for the fate-weaver was because he wanted to become Council representative of the Dark mages. If he kept them as slaves it'd get out sooner or later, and as soon as that happened he'd lose any chance he ever had of getting that position."

"But what if—Oh, Arachne, could you have a look?"

"Of course, dear," Arachne said from her perch in the corner. She was working on something in vivid green. "Come right out."

Arachne is a weaver, the best I know, and everything in her lair is her own work. She's been making clothes since before I was born—probably since before my great-great-grandparents were born. She trades the clothes to mages and adepts in return for services and information, but honestly, I think she'd be just as happy to give them away. Arachne's a maker, and for her creating is its own reward.

She's also a giant spider, which bothers most people, although these days I hardly notice. Arachne had been working on the cloth in front of her with her four front legs, but now she turned her eight opaque eyes upwards as Luna stepped out from behind the curtain wearing a rose-coloured dress with a square neckline and ruffles. "What do you think?" Luna said doubtfully.

Sonder looked up as soon as Luna started to come out, and now he stared. "Um," he said at last. "It's, uh, good. Really good."

"Definitely not," Arachne said firmly, clicking her mandibles. "Not for where you're going. We'll save that one for the summer."

Luna disappeared behind the curtain. "What did you and Luna turn up?" I asked Sonder.

Sonder was still staring after Luna. *"Sonder!"* I said more loudly.

Sonder jumped. "What?"

"The disappearances," I said. "You know, what you and Luna were looking at all day?"

"Right," Sonder said. "Okay." He pushed his glasses up and started going through his papers again. "Where did you want to start?"

"With the victims," I said. From the changing room came the rustle of clothes, and from the corner the quick *flick-flick-flick* of Arachne's needle. "Who were they?"

"Well, um," Sonder said. "The first is Caroline Montroyd. She was apprenticed to an air mage in London but she lived with her parents in Watford. She left her master's sanctum one night and never came home. Her parents called the police, but they didn't find anything and the police think she ran away. She'd been having arguments with her father and mother and talking about leaving, and at first everyone thought that was what had happened, but . . ."

"But it's a bit of a coincidence," I said with a nod. "Go on."

"The second one's name is Chaven," Sonder said. He was beginning to focus again now. "Force mage, supposed to be a really good duellist, was actually one of the favourites for the White Stone. He'd mostly dropped out of university but he was still staying in the halls of residence for London Metropolitan. We don't know for sure when he disappeared. The doorman said he saw him go in one night, and he didn't show up for classes the next day. No one saw him leave.

"Then there's Ness," Sonder said, and he looked suddenly uncomfortable. "Vanessa, I mean. I . . . actually know her. She used to come to one of the classes I was teaching. Well, not really teaching, but the mage who was supposed to be doing it wasn't there, and . . . um. Anyway. She lived alone in a flat. She made it home one night and no one ever saw her again."

"Then how the hell did she vanish?" I said in annoyance. "Did someone kick the door down or what?"

"Nothing like that," Sonder said. "The door was locked. Nothing was broken. Although . . . Well, I was talking to the neighbours and the woman from the flat next door said she thought Ness had had a visitor after midnight. She heard a bell and voices."

"What kind of voices?"

"She didn't remember."

"Okay. So what did *you* see?"

Sonder is a time mage. It's got a few similarities to my own style of magic, but the things he can do with it are very different. For one thing, he can actually affect space and time directly, although it's not what he specialises in. What Sonder is really good at is *history*: looking back and seeing what happened. You'd think that would make solving mysteries pretty easy and it does, at least when you're dealing with normals. But in the magical world the abilities of time mages are well known and other mages take precautions against them.

"I couldn't find Caroline," Sonder said. "I traced her into

the Underground but then there were the crowds and the interference, and . . . Anyway. Chaven was a bit easier. I got a look at the halls, and he was definitely there in his room with some friends. Then he went to bed, and . . . nothing. Greyed out. Someone used a shroud effect over that temporal area. The same with Ness. I traced it and the whole route back to the entrance was concealed."

Shrouds are magical items that block scrying, especially the temporal kind that Sonder does. They're not cheap and they're generally only used by people who are very serious about keeping their activities a secret. I thought for a minute. "What about cameras?"

"Which ones?"

"Halls of residence have security cameras," I said. "So do most blocks of flats. And they store the records. If you saw the shroud effect, then you can narrow down what time you need to be looking at."

"Yes, but they wouldn't have let me look at them." Sonder looked uncomfortable. "I wasn't even supposed to be there."

"But Talisid will know people who *could* look at them."

"Wouldn't they have tried them already?"

"Mages tend to assume magic's the solution to everything," I said with a smile. I'd fallen into that trap this afternoon. "It's worth a try."

Sonder thought about it, then nodded. "Okay." He paused. "Alex? What's going on here? I mean . . . apprentices going missing like this? And someone trying to kill Anne? Why would anyone want to *do* all this?"

"I don't know," I said slowly. "And that's the problem. I think if we understood *why* all this is happening, we'd be most of the way there. People don't do things just because. Someone has a damn good reason for disappearing all these apprentices and shooting Anne and blaming me. If we can figure out the reason, we'll know how to stop it."

"Oh," Sonder said. "What do you think's happened to them? Ness and the others."

I looked at Sonder for a moment. "Best guess?"

Sonder nodded.

"They're all dead."

Sonder flinched. "But—"

"You know what's going to happen to anyone caught doing this," I said quietly. "So if I were doing it, I'd do everything I could to make sure that didn't happen. Like tying off loose ends."

There was the rustle of a curtain and Sonder and I looked up as Luna stepped out again. She'd changed into a yellow-and-white dress with a vertical design that made me think of a flower. She looked more confident this time and as we watched she gave a little twirl. "What do you think?"

"It looks amazing," Sonder said. He was staring again.

"No," Arachne said.

"But I like this one," Luna said.

"Of course you do," Arachne said. "But it's all wrong for where you're going. Here." She shook out the outfit she'd been working on, making it shimmer in the light, and held it out to Luna with two of her legs. "Try this."

Luna looked disappointed but disappeared behind the curtain again. "Now," Arachne said. She'd been listening quietly as Sonder and I spoke, working on the dress, and now that it was finished she turned her full attention to me. "I think Sonder—Alex, have you lost weight?"

"I don't want to talk about it."

Arachne gave me a quick up-and-down glance, did the spider equivalent of rolling her eyes, and pulled out a pile of dark cloth. "I think Sonder asked the right question," she said as she started modifying it. "Why was Onyx there?"

"Because he's involved, I guess," I said. "Though I can't figure out how Fountain Reach fits into it."

"It seems to me there's a simple explanation for both," Arachne said. "What if Onyx was there for exactly the same reason as you?"

I started to answer, then stopped. "That . . . would explain a lot. He looked like he was searching around."

"And obviously wasn't expecting the meeting any more than you were."

"And if Morden or Onyx got the same tip-off I did, Onyx is the guy Morden would send . . ."

"Which suggests he wants to find out what's happening," Arachne finished. "You should be able to take advantage of that."

Sonder had been looking back and forth between us. "Umm . . ."

"Oh, something I wanted to ask." I pulled a folded paper from my pocket. "Arachne, could you do me a favour?"

"Of course."

"Could you make me something?"

Arachne took the paper with two of her legs and she unfolded it delicately, reading with half of her eyes and working with the others. "Hmm. Interesting."

I glanced at Luna's changing room. "I know it's not easy—"

"Oh, I'd be happy to. I've been turning over some ideas along those lines myself. Drop by tomorrow and I'll see what I have ready. Well then." She held out the black clothes to me with two of her legs. "Try it on."

"Oh, right."

"You didn't even think about it, did you?" Arachne said. "Honestly, if I weren't here I think you'd show up in shorts and a T-shirt."

"I don't wear shorts," I said over my shoulder as I headed to the changing room, pulling the curtain shut behind me. "By the way, do you know this guy who's hosting the party tonight?"

"Yes, and he's not a 'guy.' He's a rakshasa."

I'd been holding up the outfit to get its shape, but at that I looked up with a frown. "Really?" Sonder said from outside, sounding interested. "I thought since the treaty they all stayed in India?"

"Jagadev is older than the treaty," Arachne said. "Very old and very powerful. Why he came to these shores I do not know, but I first heard of his presence in this city back in the days of your empire. He sides neither with the Council nor with any of the Dark factions. The Tiger's Palace is his domain and within it his word is law."

"Have you ever met him?" Sonder asked.

"Once."

Sonder fell silent, which was a surprise. I'd expected him to keep asking questions but something in Arachne's manner must have made him think twice. "Alex?" Luna said from the next room over. "Why was Anne delivering invitations for him?"

"I'm not sure," I said, putting the shirt on.

"Isn't that the kind of thing apprentices do for their masters?"

"Yeah," I said. "Arachne? Do you know if Jagadev takes human apprentices?"

"There are rumours," Arachne said. "But I always had the impression that Jagadev's feelings towards humans were . . . not warm. Especially mages."

I had a sudden flashback to Natasha's words at the gym. I shook it off—just because a creature looks like a monster doesn't mean it is one—but it left me with an uneasy feeling. "Come on, Alex," Arachne said, interrupting my thoughts. "You've had more than enough time to try them on."

I wanted to tell Arachne she hadn't complained about Luna taking three times as long but held my tongue. I came out at exactly the same time Luna did.

The outfit Arachne had made for me was plainer than usual: coal-coloured trousers and a top, with a long jet-black coat. On the whole I liked it. It was light and flexible, and if I got into trouble it would allow me to move fast.

If my clothes were understated, Luna's were the opposite. She wore a narrow dress cut in such a way that she seemed to be wearing nothing else, the cloth following the lines of her body and emphasising her shape. The dress was a vivid emerald green, shimmering in the light. It was beautiful and eye-catching but there was something disturbing about the colour. It made me think of poison, like a venomous snake.

"Wow," Sonder said. He was staring again. "You look . . ."

"Perfect," Arachne said.

Luna looked uncomfortable. "I feel like the evil queen in Snow White."

"Where you're going that's exactly how you want to look." Arachne scuttled forward and peered down at me nearsightedly with her eight eyes, then settled back. "You'll do too."

Luna gave me a glance, then a curious look. "Hey, did you lose weight all of a sudden?"

"I *said* I don't want to talk about it. Arachne, you keep talking about 'where we're going.' What are we getting into?"

"Tiger's Palace?" Sonder said in surprise. "Haven't you ever been?"

"I'm not exactly high up on the social circuit, Sonder."

"Um," Sonder said, hesitantly. "But it's not—I mean—"

"What Sonder is trying to say," Arachne said, "is that given the reputation of Tiger's Palace, most people would expect you to fit right in."

"What reputation?"

Arachne made a clicking noise, her equivalent of a sigh. "You really should get out more. Tiger's Palace is a . . . meeting point, a place of exchange. There are no entry requirements but it's not a place for the vulnerable or the careless." Arachne glanced at Luna. "Apprentices don't typically go. If you do, make very sure not to look like prey."

Luna and I looked at each other for a second, then I turned back. "Sonder—"

"I know," Sonder said resignedly. "You want me to go research. I can do other things too, you know."

"You haven't got anything to prove," I said with a smile. "But if someone's targeting me—and it looks as if they are—then going there together will make you a target as well."

"You're still taking—" Sonder began, then stopped. "All right. Be careful."

"Good luck, both of you," Arachne said. "And Sonder is right. The information you're looking for may be there or it may not, but either way I suspect the people there won't react favourably to nosing around."

ⁱ ⁱ ⁱ ⁱ ⁱ ⁱ ⁱ ⁱ ⁱ

"No ribbon this time?" I asked Luna as we walked up the polished stone of the exit tunnel.

Luna shook her head. The last time we'd gone together

to a party like this Arachne had made her a one-shot that absorbed and neutralised Luna's curse, making her able to touch people without fear of hurting them, just for a little while.

"She'd do it if you asked," I said.

"I know," Luna said. "But . . . I know it's hard for her to make those."

"Is that the only reason?"

Luna walked in silence for a little while. "I don't want to get too used to it," she said at last.

I nodded. "I think that's the right choice."

Luna looked sharply at me. "Items can be taken away," I said. "You don't want to get too dependent on them. The only things that are really yours are your magic and your mind and your body."

We reached the entrance and Luna hung back as I activated the trigger to make the earth ahead of us part with a rumbling sound. Arachne's lair is on Hampstead Heath, hidden beneath a ravine in the deep woods where few people go. It had turned into a clear, cold night, bright stars shining down out of a winter sky, and both of us shivered as we came out into the open. The entrance to the lair closed behind us and we turned our feet towards the Tiger's Palace.

chapter 6

The Soho street was noisy, music from a dozen bars blending together into a confusing racket. Neon lights flashed through the shadows, making the dark stone and brickwork flicker red-blue-green. People appeared and disappeared in groups, emerging from doorways and vanishing into the gloom. Buildings went up and up into the darkness, fading into an orange sky, but the lights and crowds couldn't hide the chill of the winter air.

Luna and I were sheltering in a doorway, looking at the building opposite. It was blacked out, dark except for a neon sign blinking on the roof, and I looked at it for a moment before glancing sideways at Luna. Her face was lit up by the sign above, flickering from red to blue. "Think this is the place?"

"It's the right number," Luna said.

I looked into the future, searching for the consequences

of us entering that building. "So Anne's . . ." Luna said. "I mean, the guy we're meeting. He's a rakshasa?"

"Yeah."

"What's a rakshasa?"

"Creatures from India," I said. "Or maybe they were before India and the Indians just gave them the name. In their true form they're supposed to look like a cross between a human and a tiger." I paused. "Oh, and their hands are supposed to be backwards."

"Backwards?"

"Reversed. The palms are where the backs should be."

Luna thought about that for a second, then grimaced. "Creepy." She held up a hand before I could speak. "I know. Don't judge by appearances, right?"

"Well . . . maybe just this once it wouldn't be a bad idea." I leant against the cold stone, studying the building opposite. "I don't know much about rakshasas, but none of what I've heard is good. They were supposed to be . . . I guess the word would be *malevolent*. They loved power, especially over thinking creatures. They ruled India once, if the stories are true. They lived in palaces built by their slaves, lords of everything they could see."

"But that might not be true," Luna said. "I mean, the apprentices say stuff like that about *all* magical creatures. Even Arachne. I've heard them. And he's looking after Anne, right?"

"I admit I'm very curious as to what two apprentices like Anne and Variam would be doing with a rakshasa."

"Maybe there are things he can teach them."

"Oh, there would be," I said. "Rakshasas are powerful. The old stories say they were partly divine, not fully bound by the laws of the physical world. I don't know if it's true but everyone agrees they're master shapeshifters. They can change their appearance and form, give themselves abilities that shouldn't be possible."

Luna stood quietly for a second. "So . . . how well do they usually get on with mages?"

"Have a guess."

Luna sighed. "Badly."

I nodded. "For a long time there was a secret war across the Indian subcontinent. The rakshasas won most of the battles but there were never enough of them. Mages could replace their losses; rakshasas couldn't. In the end there was a treaty and both sides agreed to leave each other alone. But rakshasas are supposed to hold grudges like you wouldn't believe. This one, Jagadev, was probably alive for that war. Maybe alive for all the others before it. I doubt he's forgotten."

"Oh," Luna said. She paused. "And this is the guy whose home we're visiting."

"Yes."

"This is going to be one of those eventful nights, isn't it?"

I finished my search and pulled my attention back to the immediate future. "We're in the right place. Let's go."

। । । । । । । ।

Two drunks slumped in a doorway watched us blearily as we passed. I walked past without a glance as Luna skirted them more carefully. Concrete stairs and a railing led down to a basement level and an open door.

Inside was an anteroom with three security men. Heavy-duty pieces of work, layers of fat covering rubbery muscle, their faces all broken noses and scowls. I came to a stop in front of them. "I'm looking for Jagadev."

The one at the centre looked at me with shark's eyes, flat and cold. "Name?"

"Alex Verus."

He studied me a moment, then jerked his head towards a doorway.

The corridor beyond was old concrete, stained and ugly. "Alex—" Luna whispered.

"Cameras," I said under my breath.

Luna glanced up. Electric eyes were watching us from both ends of the hall. The door at the end was padded and looked soundproofed to me, but I could feel a vibration through my feet. I opened the door.

Noise washed over us, deafening, the pounding beat of music. We were looking down over a club floor crowded with hundreds of people dancing and moving. The room was huge and dimly lit, red and blue and green lights flickering and clashing, painting some of the room in primary colours and leaving other parts in shadow. There was a wide semicircular balcony above, but it was darkened and anything within was invisible against the flashing lights below. Everything was noise and motion.

Luna said something. "What?" I shouted over the music.

"This is supposed to be a palace?" Luna shouted.

I looked around, scanning the floor. It was too chaotic for divination to be much use, but as I focused I could sense something else. "It's the right place," I shouted back.

Luna looked at the crowd. "How do we get through?"

"Follow me."

We descended into the swirling crowd. Noise pounded around us, the harsh beat of industrial music, a singer chanting words that were lost in the throbbing of the bass. I could have pushed through but Luna couldn't, not without getting too close. "Hey!" I shouted over the music. "Move!" People turned and I got a lot of angry looks, but enough of a path opened for Luna to follow after. With my mage's sight I could see the silver mist of her curse swirling tightly around her, held in check by her willpower. The people around us fell back, and Luna and I became the centre of a small empty circle on the dance floor. The clubgoers were young, teens and twenties, wearing clothes that ranged from ragged T-shirts and jeans to goth outfits. Luna and I didn't exactly fit in but we didn't look out of place either. Arachne's good at what she does.

Thin beams of green light danced over us as we made it to the bar. I managed to catch the eye of the barman, a bad-tempered looking guy with greasy hair and a leather jacket. "I'm looking for Jagadev," I called. The music was a little quieter here—still enough to give you a headache, but it was more or less possible to talk.

The barman flicked a glance at me. "Never heard of him."

I studied the barman for a moment. "Bullshit."

The barman shrugged and turned to another customer. I looked around to see that the crowd was looking at us. Not everyone, not even most of them, but a good couple of dozen of the guys and girls had stopped dancing and turned to watch. "You know," I said to Luna, "I'm getting the feeling we're not all that welcome here."

"What . . ." Luna said, frowning as she looked at the crowd. "Who are they? There's something . . ."

"Adepts," I said. "You're feeling their magic."

"All of them?"

"Could be."

"Hey you," a voice with a Liverpool accent said from the side.

I turned. The man—boy, really—was twenty or so, with brown-tinted skin and rasta plaits. His hands were stuffed into the pockets of a leather jacket and he was scowling. I looked back at him. "What's up?"

"What are you doing?"

"I'm looking for someone," I said. "Maybe you can help us out."

"Think you took a wrong turn, mate," the boy said. "You're not supposed to be here."

I glanced around. "No, I'm pretty sure this is the place."

The boy's face darkened and he took a step forward, his fists coming out to hang by his sides. Without looking I could sense that a half circle had formed around us. The barman had made himself scarce. "Fook off, mage. Go back to your fancy restaurants."

I looked at him, then deliberately turned away to look at Luna. "There are two more of them in the crowd," I said quietly. "Short-haired brunette in white over my shoulder and the skinny shaven-headed kid with the hoodie to your left."

Luna's eyes flickered, and she nodded. "What are they going to do?"

"They'll come at our backs as soon as this guy kicks off. Watch yourself."

"Oi!" the boy with rasta plaits said angrily. "I'm talking to you!"

Luna's eyes went over my shoulder. "Um, Alex?"

"I know," I said absently. "Just trying to figure out what these guys can do."

Rasta Plaits grabbed my shoulder and spun me around. "I said—"

I moved with the spin and kicked him in the balls. Rasta Plaits's eyes bugged out and he staggered back; I hit him again in the gut and as he doubled over I hammered a fist down onto the back of his head, sending him sprawling.

"Alex!" Luna shouted.

I jumped left and something exploded into the bar, throwing out splinters. I looked up to see the shaven-headed kid.

He was wearing a dark hoodie that looked too big for him and he was holding two metal balls, one in each hand, each one about midway in size between a marble and a pool ball. I felt a surge of force magic as he flicked one at me.

It should have been a weak throw but the ball shot through the air as though it had been fired from a gun. No reflexes could have dodged it, but my precognition had told me where to go and I was already sliding aside as the ball flew over the bar and exploded a vodka bottle into a spray of liquid and broken glass. The kid jerked his wrist and another ball dropped from his sleeve into his hand, and then he twisted and threw two more, one after the other.

This time the second shot was aimed to catch me dodging the first and I had to drop and roll left. The balls whistled over my head and smashed splinters out of the bar. I came up, about to rush him, but he was already backpedalling out of range and as he did I caught a flash of danger on my precognition. "Luna, move!"

Luna obeyed instantly, jumping to one side, and the girl who'd been sneaking up behind her stumbled past as she missed. Before she could turn on Luna I was on her, pushing her back. I moved in for a grab—and pulled myself back just in time, skidding to a stop as I saw what would happen. One touch and I'd be writhing on the floor.

The girl saw me and gave me a catlike smile. She was dressed all in white, with a PVC jacket and leggings. She came at me, hands swinging with fingers curved into claws, and I jumped out of the way. I could feel the spell she was using, a malign form of life magic designed to wrack a body with pain. But just like Anne's magic, it needed her to touch me to work. As the girl advanced on me I looked into the future, gauging her reach, then as she came in with fingers extended I put a side kick into her body.

It connected with a solid *thud*. My legs were longer than her arms and she went flying back, but her fingers brushed my leg as she fell. Agony shot through me, my muscles cramping and spasming. I lost my breath in a gasp and fell awkwardly, but it was over in a second. I pulled myself to my feet, shaking my head muzzily. "Alex!" Luna called, moving towards me. "Are you—?"

Rasta Plaits came up behind Luna and hit her in the back. Luna's head jerked back as she went flying to hit the floor hard. All of a sudden I forgot about the pain in my leg. I was on the guy in two strides.

He swung and went over my head. I came up, let him miss with another punch so I could get into position, then hammered a blow into his side just below his rib cage. The floating ribs are one of the vulnerable points on the torso and I hit with enough force to break them.

It felt like hitting a wall. Pain shot up my arm and Rasta Plaits didn't even flinch. He just grinned at me, then grabbed me and threw me into a table.

People scattered as the table and I went over with a crash. I hit the floor hard but ingrained reflexes turned the fall into a roll and I was up on my feet in an instant. A wide space on the floor had cleared and as I looked around I saw that both Rasta Plaits and the girl were coming around the over-turned table towards me. The thrower was back too, manoeuvring around for a clear shot. Behind them I could see Luna pulling herself to her feet. For an instant there was a pause.

I looked slowly across the three of them. "You have no idea who you are fucking with."

Rasta Plaits and the girl laughed and jeered. I didn't listen to the words; I couldn't get both myself and Luna out and that meant they had to go down. I tuned out the voices and the music, focusing only on my opponents.

Rasta Plaits attacked, his swings powerful but clumsy, and I moved away and let the attacks breeze past. As I studied him I realised he was using earth magic to harden his body, toughening skin and flesh to the consistency of rock. Hitting him would just bruise my hands.

Rasta Plaits kept punching and I kept dodging. My movements were quick, economical, and I gave only minor glances to his blows to make sure they would miss. For all his power he didn't have much skill and he was tiring fast. The girl danced around, trying to get behind me. The skinny kid was looking for a throw but with the three of us so close he couldn't get a shot. I considered manoeuvring Rasta Plaits so that he would eat one of the skinny kid's projectiles and saw that it wouldn't work—his skin was so toughened he'd just shrug it off. But it gave me another idea.

A silver mist was clinging to Rasta Plaits, the residue of Luna's curse. I let him push me back towards the bar. The girl had disappeared from my view and I could sense her at my back. As Rasta Plaits bullied forward she came up behind me, aiming for my neck.

I caught Rasta Plaits's rush and spun him around just as the girl struck, and as I did I felt the flare of magic as Luna's curse took, bending chance. The girl's hand missed me by an inch and got Rasta Plaits in the chest, and with my mage's sight I saw the green-black ooze of the girl's spell leap into his body.

Rasta Plaits screamed, convulsing as he crashed to the floor, and the girl fell back, staring in shock. I was already moving away, striding towards the thrower. The skinny kid hesitated, then seeing me coming straight for him he threw at my chest. I sidestepped and the metal ball flew all the way into the wall fifty feet behind. I broke into a run. He flexed his wrists and two more balls dropped into his hands;

he threw once, twice, and I dodged both without breaking stride. He had just enough time to get out another set before I caught him by the wrist and pulled him off balance as my right hand slid my knife from its sheath. I dragged the kid up with his arm twisted behind his back and my knife under his chin.

The kid froze. I was standing behind him, holding him by one arm. He couldn't see the knife but could feel the cold metal against his neck, the point digging in under his jaw. The music cut off and the club was suddenly silent except for the rustle and chatter.

Rasta Plaits was whimpering on the floor. The girl was standing dead still, eyes flicking from me to the knife to the people around. I saw her glance at Luna, who'd gotten to her feet and was a little way to her side. "Don't," I told her. I forced the kid forward, feeling him trembling against me. All around, the crowd was silent. "Let's try this again. We're looking for Jagadev."

The girl looked from me to Luna, then pointed at a staircase beyond the crowd, leading up.

"Are we going to have any more trouble?"

The girl shook her head.

"How about you, kid?" I pushed the knife a little bit farther up into his jaw.

"No," the kid said in a strangled voice.

I looked between the two of them, then dropped the kid and walked away, resheathing my knife as I did. A path cleared for us in the crowd, this time without my having to do anything. Behind us I felt the girl rush to where Rasta Plaits had fallen. The kid slumped over a table, rubbing his neck, and I sensed him think about aiming another shot at my back . . . then decide against it. As we reached the stairs, the music started up again.

"You okay?" I asked Luna once we were out of sight.

"Bruises," Luna said, rubbing her back with a wince. "I'll be fine."

I smiled slightly. "I remember when you'd almost forgotten what it was like to be hurt."

"Yeah, *that* changed all right. Seriously, Alex, can't I ever get dressed up to go out with you without this happening?"

"It doesn't happen every time we have a night out."

"Name one time it hasn't."

"Um . . . your apprenticeship ceremony."

"Somebody tried to mug us on the way back across the Heath."

"Oh yeah."

"Who were those guys?"

"Adepts," I said. "Like you, I guess, but dumber." I shook my head. "This sort of crap is why adepts end up on the bottom of the food chain. They've got just enough power to make them feel tough, but not enough to stop themselves getting flattened when they pick a fight with the wrong guy."

Adepts are a lot more common than mages, ten times more common according to some estimates. Adepts and mages tend not to get on all that well, and to be honest that's mostly the mages' fault. Mage society is based on a hierarchy of magical power and adepts are second-class citizens at best. In most cases adepts choose to stay out of mage business completely and mages generally let them as long as they don't break any rules. "Do you think that's what this club is?" Luna asked. "A place for adepts?"

"Maybe," I said. "But that's not what's bothering me."

Luna looked at me, questioning. "What bothers me," I said, "is that none of the bouncers did anything to break up the fight."

The balcony at the top of the stairs was big, more like a

mezzanine floor, and it was shaped in a wide semicircle that followed the lines of the room. It was better furnished than the lower level, with sofas and low tables, and something about the acoustics made the music a little quieter. It had the feeling of a place to sit and talk and watch the view rather than the frenzy of the dance floor below. A couple of hard-looking security men watched us as we entered, not speaking, and glancing around I could see that they would have had a perfect view of our fight below. *Where were you, I wonder?*

I knew we needed to go right, but Luna slowed by the railing. "Alex," she said, nodding down at the crowd.

"Where?"

"The two by the bar," Luna said. "I recognise them."

I looked down and saw two men talking with the bartender. They seemed to be asking him questions, and as I watched he pointed towards the staircase we'd used. There was something familiar about them, and I felt as though I'd seen them before. They made me think of police for some reason . . . and that made me remember. "Great."

"They were asking about Anne," Luna said. "Do you know them?"

"Never met them," I said. "Not yet, anyway." They were the pair of Keepers who would have come to interrogate me had Anne been killed last night. I headed along the balcony. "Come on."

"Wait," Luna said as she hurried after me. "Why are they still asking about Anne? Didn't she come back to London with you?"

"Yeah," I said. "I . . . might have asked her not to show herself to anyone."

"Why not?"

"Figured I might learn something."

"What, by getting arrested?"

"It seemed like a good idea at the time, all right?"

The balcony was less crowded than the dance floor, and the people were better dressed—fewer T-shirts and jeans, more evening wear. We skirted a table where a group of girls were chatting and drinking. To one side was a darkened booth with two shapes. I was about to pass by, then something caught my eye. "Lyle?"

Lyle started and looked up. He was dressed in a dark coat and looked like he'd been trying to be inconspicuous. "Alex. Um—"

"What are you doing here?" I said in genuine surprise. It was about the last place I'd expect to find someone like Lyle.

"I, er—" Lyle drew himself up. "I'm afraid I can't discuss the matter."

I looked at Lyle's companion. She was hanging back in the shadows but something about her height and the carriage of her head jogged my memory. "Oh, I get it," I said. "Hey, Crystal." I looked at Lyle. "So she's looking for help for the tournament."

Lyle stiffened. "I've asked you before not to use your abilities for—"

"I don't need divination magic to guess what you're up to."

Crystal looked at me pointedly. "I'm sorry, but this is a private conversation."

"Really? What's it about?"

Crystal didn't react but I felt a flash of anger behind her eyes. "Alex," Lyle said uneasily. "Keepers are looking for you. Given your position, I'm not sure you should be—"

"Oh, I'm sure it'll work out," I said cheerfully. "See you later. Crystal."

We walked away. "You really like annoying him, don't you?" Luna said under her breath.

"Old history," I murmured. "I'll tell you about it some day." The crowd up here was scattered, thinner. I searched through it, looking ahead for danger, and my heart jumped. "Oh shit."

Luna sighed. "Now what?"

"Behind that pillar. Out of sight *now*!"

Luna didn't hesitate, and neither did I. As we ducked out of sight a tall, slim figure appeared through the crowd, stalking towards us. Onyx.

I stood behind the pillar. A couple of people gave us curious glances but nothing more. We were fewer than twenty feet from Onyx, but I'd dealt with him enough times to get a fairly good grasp of what he could and couldn't do. Onyx was a force mage and all his powers revolved around the direct use of momentum. He was fast as a cobra and utterly lethal in a fight, but not much good at being subtle. When it came to detecting and identifying people, he wasn't any better than a normal man.

Onyx passed us without a glance. I waited ten seconds, then led Luna out and headed in the direction he'd come from, keeping an eye out. I knew Onyx would be back. "Is there *anyone* here who likes us?" Luna said.

"Apparently not." Ahead, the balcony ended in a square doorway. "Tell you what, let's ask the guy who invited me."

"Why are all these people here?" Luna asked quietly.

"No idea." Through the doorway I could see a big open room. As we walked in I had the feeling we were getting into something we didn't understand.

chapter 7

The room at the end of the balcony was tall with dark walls and pillars, and it was set into the building in such a way that despite its size it didn't extend out over the dance floor. To the left was a view down into the club, but a layer of tinted glass had been installed that I knew would block line of sight from below. Guards were standing on either side of the entrance and more were spaced around the room, each looking about as friendly as the ones we'd seen on the way in. A square of four black leather sofas sat to one side of the room, giving a direct view over the crowd, and on the other side was a corridor leading deeper into the building, half hidden behind a bead curtain. Girls and men in flashy clothes were scattered around, laughing and chattering.

At the centre, reclining on one of the sofas, was Jagadev. The rakshasa was big and powerfully built, with thick arms and legs. He had the head and the striped orange-black fur of a tiger but was humanoid enough to wear clothes—a black suit with a red silk shirt and tie. He held a wineglass in one clawed paw. He didn't move, yet somehow he dominated the room, as though everybody there were oriented towards him and waiting to take their cue.

I walked straight towards Jagadev. Faces turned to watch as we approached, and I had the sudden strange feeling that I was at a court, the inhabitants watching us draw closer to the king on his throne. An Asian guy in sunglasses stepped in front of us, blocking our way.

I stopped and met his gaze. "Alex Verus."

The man glanced back towards Jagadev. Jagadev made no movement that I could see, but the man stepped away. I walked up and stood before him. The girls to either side eyed me appraisingly. The room was silent but for the pounding beat of the music below.

Jagadev made a small gesture with his free paw towards the sofa behind me.

"Hi," I said. "Sorry, was that an invitation to sit down? I'm not that familiar with the code."

"Sit," Jagadev said. His voice was a rumble, midway between a purr and a growl.

"Thanks." I sat and glanced around. "Interesting place you've got here." Without turning I could sense Luna's presence behind me; she'd taken up a position a safe distance from the other people in the room, not too far from the exit. Although I kept myself relaxed, I was very aware of how many people were surrounding us. There were thirteen other people in the room apart from us and Jagadev, of whom four or five were between us and the exit. If things went wrong this could get ugly fast.

Some things are much easier to predict than others. Machines and other inanimate objects are simple. When you flick a light switch, the light comes on. You can flick the switch a hundred times, and the light will go on the same way every time. Sure, there's a tiny chance something will go wrong—the bulb might blow out, there could be a power cut—but even those can be predicted fairly reliably if you know what you're doing.

Forecasting what a living creature will do is much harder. Free will is one of the points at which divination breaks down; if someone genuinely hasn't made a choice then no divination magic can see beyond it. You can see the branching futures, see the consequences of each, but the final decision is always theirs.

But while everyone has free will, one of the odd things you learn as a diviner is that not everyone actually *uses* it. A surprising number of people don't make choices, not most of the time anyway—they just react on predefined patterns until something happens to shake them out of it. A thoughtful person, though, someone who makes decisions based on what they hear and think and see—to a diviner's eyes they look totally different. By looking at the shape of someone's futures, I can actually make a pretty good guess at what kind of person they are. So as I spoke to Jagadev, only a part of my mind was in the present. Most of my attention was on what he was going to do.

The shape of Jagadev's actions was . . . odd. Normally I see a swirl of futures, changing and adapting to my own actions. Jagadev's futures weren't like that at all—they were impassive, still. In all the futures of all my words and actions, Jagadev sat like a statue, controlled and steady. I could sense a powerful intelligence behind that mask, but what and how much he would reveal I didn't know.

It all took only an instant, and as Jagadev spoke I snapped back to the present. "I have always been here."

"You've gone for a different setup than mages usually do."

Jagadev's eyes drifted past me, looking over my shoulder. "And yet," he murmured, "mages come."

I looked back, following Jagadev's gaze across the balcony towards the stairs up from the floor below. The two Keepers I'd seen earlier were visible across the gap, their outlines dim through the glass. They looked around, then moved towards where Lyle and Crystal had been sitting. "So," I said, turning back to Jagadev, "not that I'm not grateful for the invitation, but why did you ask me here?"

"Why did you assist my ward?"

"You mean Anne?" I shrugged. "I'm a diviner."

"That is the how," Jagadev said. "I wish to know why."

Behind me, across the balcony, I could feel the two mages talking to Lyle and Crystal. Without turning to look, I sensed Lyle point them in our direction. The men started towards us. "Would you prefer I hadn't?"

"Answer the question."

"Let's just say I don't like seeing apprentices getting killed." I tilted my head. "Not intending to interfere in your business, of course."

Jagadev held my gaze for a few moments. "You have my gratitude," he said at last.

He didn't *sound* grateful. But then I was getting the definite impression that Jagadev didn't show much of anything. "Quite a well-planned attack," I said. "Somebody wanted to make sure she didn't get back."

"Those responsible will be dealt with," Jagadev said. His voice was calm, but there was an undercurrent that gave me a chill.

"So I'm curious," I said. "What exactly is your relationship with Anne and Variam? You called Anne your ward?"

"That is not your concern."

"Fair enough." The two mages were heading towards us. "But seeing as I was able to provide some help, is there any chance you could tell me something about a related matter?"

Jagadev gave a single nod. "This wasn't the first attack on an apprentice," I said. "Others have been going missing. Know anything about it?"

From behind came the sound of voices. The other people in the room turned to look; I didn't. Instead I looked into the futures in which I did, seeing behind me without having to turn my head. The Council Keepers were right outside and the Asian guy in sunglasses was in the doorway blocking their way. One of the mages said something. I couldn't make out Sunglasses's reply, but I got the gist: *Lord Jagadev is busy.* The mage's answer was short and threatening, and it wasn't a request. Sunglasses folded his arms.

I felt the snap of a spell: air magic. Sunglasses hit the wall to my right with a *whump*, crumpling to the floor. I turned my head to look over the back of the sofa as the mages walked in.

There was a rustle of movement from around the room. I recognised the sound of metal against leather and saw the glint of a gun from under one man's coat. Everyone was focused on the two men, but if they were worried about being outnumbered and surrounded they didn't show it. "Mage Verus," the one on the left said. He was tall and lean, with a hard face, and he was the one who'd cast the spell. "We'd like to have a word."

"You were told to wait outside," Jagadev said softly.

"We have business with Verus," the tall mage said. "It's not your concern."

"You would force your way into my domain?" Jagadev

said. He didn't raise his voice, but there was something dangerous there and I could feel everyone in the room tense.

"It's not your domain, rakshasa," the mage said. "You stay here because we let you. Now tell your servants to stand down or come morning this place will be a slag heap."

The music from below had stopped and the room was quiet. A dozen pairs of eyes were locked on the mages and I could sense weapons readied. The two mages didn't seem to notice but I could feel the tension of spells poised to trigger. Jagadev was sitting absolutely still and showed no expression, but somehow I was sure that he was furiously angry. The seconds stretched out, ticking away.

Then Jagadev made a small gesture and the men around us drew back, fingers coming off triggers and muscles relaxing. I let out a soft breath, and I wasn't the only one. I gave Luna a quick glance; she'd withdrawn to a safe corner and I gave her a nod to stay there.

"Mage Verus," the Keeper said.

"That's me," I said.

"Come with us, please."

"I'm kind of in the middle of something," I said. "Could I come sort this out with you later?"

"No."

"Could I at least know what the problem is?"

"All right, Verus, if that's the way you want to play it," the Keeper said. "An apprentice named Anne Walker has been reported attacked and missing and you're on record as the last one to have seen her. Under Council authority, you're required to answer our questions as to why."

As the mage spoke I felt a stir of movement from across the room. Behind where Jagadev was sitting was a doorway leading into the club, covered by a bead curtain. "So Anne Walker's been reported missing?" I asked, raising my voice.

"That's what I said."

I pointed past Jagadev to the doorway. "Then who exactly is that?"

The timing was perfect. Anne had been listening from the shadows, and as every eye in the room turned towards her she took her cue and stepped out from behind the curtain. She hesitated a second under the weight of the stares, then walked forward to stand behind Jagadev, heels clicking on the floor.

Anne looked . . . different. In place of the clothes I'd seen her in before she was wearing an outfit of tight black leather, reflections from the lights of the club gleaming from it as she moved. It left her arms bare and showed off the tops of her breasts, and as she walked her hair brushed the skin of her shoulders. She still looked as if she wanted to avoid attention but it *really* wasn't working and if anything it actually made people stare more. The only one who didn't turn to look was Jagadev. He sat unmoving, his eyes fixed on the two mages.

"Anne Walker?" the first mage said at last. Anne nodded.

"I think you've got some explaining to do," the mage said. "This way, please."

Anne glanced at Jagadev, waiting for his nod, before going to them. The two mages turned and walked out, flanking her as the rest of the room watched them go.

ı ı ı ı ı ı ı ı ı

The Keepers were questioning Anne. I could just see them across the room on the far side of the balcony, through the tinted glass. In Jagadev's room—what I'd taken to thinking of as his court—the atmosphere had eased. The weapons had been put away, though none of the men carrying them had left.

"You have done me a favour, so I will return it," Jagadev said, and I turned back to him. He had his furred hands clasped over his chest and I checked idly to see if they were backwards. They weren't. I guess not all rumours are true. "I do not know who is responsible for the disappearances amongst your kind but I know where they will be. You will find them at the White Stone tournament at Fountain Reach."

I don't think I showed anything on my face but it was a near thing. "How do you know they'll be there?"

"That is my concern," Jagadev said. "Anne and Variam will be attending the tournament. I will have them assist you."

"Uh . . . thanks."

Jagadev nodded. "You may go."

I hesitated an instant, thinking of asking Jagadev more questions, but as I looked into the future I saw he wouldn't answer them. I rose, gave Jagadev a nod, and withdrew. Luna fell in by my side. The guy who'd been thrown into the wall had picked himself back up and watched stone-faced as we left. As we passed through the door I heard chatter start up from behind us.

I did a quick scan of the area as we emerged back onto the balcony and saw that we didn't have anyone hunting us down right at the moment. "Well," I said. "I guess that could have gone worse."

Luna was craning her neck to try to look at the other end of the balcony. "Do you think Anne's okay?"

"She's not a suspect," I said. I leant against the railing and frowned. "That's the third time in two days I've been pointed towards Fountain Reach."

"Are you going to go?"

I thought for a second and nodded. "Yeah. I don't know

what's going on but I know *something* is." I paused. "Of course, it'd help if I had a reason for being there."

"You do," Luna said, and then caught herself. "Oh, right. You can't tell anyone you're there to watch the apprentices, can you?"

"Nope. Of course, if *my* apprentice had a reason for attending . . ."

Luna looked back at me for a second. "You want me to enter the tournament, don't you?"

"It would make things simpler."

"After how well I did last time?"

"Good practice."

Luna sighed. "Oh, fine. I suppose it won't kill me."

"That's the spirit. So what did you think of our friend Jagadev?"

"He was . . ." Luna frowned. "Different. From what I was expecting, I mean. I guess I thought he'd be like Arachne."

"Do you think he was being honest with us?"

Luna thought for a second. "I'm not sure."

"Neither am I. He was very hard to read."

"He said Anne was his ward," Luna said. "Does that mean he's like Anne and Variam's master?"

"Magical creatures do sort of adopt apprentices sometimes."

"Then he's supposed to look after them, right?" Luna said. "So why's he sending them to the tournament if he thinks the thing that's making apprentices vanish is there? Shouldn't he be keeping them *away*?"

I nodded. "And there's something else. Back there Jagadev was acting as though the only reason he was seeing me was because I'd helped Anne. But he sent me that invitation *before* I helped Anne."

"So why did he invite you?"

"Good question." I glanced into the future. "Looks like Variam's here too."

"Where?"

"Far corner over your right shoulder. Don't turn and look."

Luna had already taken a glance. "Why's he scowling at us?"

"I've got the feeling Variam doesn't like us very much," I said. Like Anne Variam had dressed up, but his outfit was much less eye-catching: a dark shirt and pants, a black denim jacket, and a black turban instead of the khaki one. By looking into the future in which I met his gaze I could watch him without seeming to watch him, and just as Luna had said he was staring at us with a scowl.

"What's his problem?" Luna said.

"Maybe he's pissed off that I didn't let Anne get killed."

Luna gave me a look. "I'm kidding," I said. "Probably." I glanced along the balcony. "Those mages are about to finish with Anne. Why don't you go talk to her?"

"Okay," Luna said, and started to turn, then stopped with a suspicious look. "Wait, are you just trying to get me out of the way?"

"Yes."

Luna rolled her eyes and left. I watched her go, seeing her move unconsciously to keep a safe distance from the people in her path. Luna's control over her curse is much better now and to my sight it looks like a tight, dense layer of silver mist over her skin, but through force of habit she still won't get any closer to another person than she has to.

Someone cleared his throat from behind me. "Hi, Lyle," I said without turning around.

"Ah," Lyle said. "So, er . . ."

"No, I haven't been arrested."

"Well, I'm glad to hear it."

I thought about saying *Are you?* but held myself back. I turned to see Lyle looking awkward. He was wearing his usual suit and really didn't fit into a place like this. I wondered why he'd agreed to meet Crystal here. "You want to know the story, don't you?"

"Well—"

I sighed. "Oh, fine. That apprentice Anne was reported missing. I was the last to have seen her so those two came looking for me. Luckily Anne wasn't missing after all."

"Ah. What happened?"

"If you want to know the details, you'll have to ask her." Which was technically true: Lyle would have to ask her because I wasn't going to tell him.

"I see. Well, it's good everything turned out well."

"Just a sec," I said. "While you're here there's something I wanted to ask. What's the deal with Anne and Variam?"

"How do you mean?"

"They're a bit too good to be in the apprentice program. Why haven't they taken their journeyman tests?"

"Oh, I see." Lyle relaxed a little. "Well, mostly because they don't have a sponsor. Do you know their background?"

I shook my head and Lyle settled down on the railing next to me, comfortable now. Gossip is Lyle's element. "Well, both of them are in the apprentice program, but they didn't start that way. Originally they were apprentices to a Dark mage named Sagash."

She was taught by a Dark mage. Her and that other boy, Variam . . . They started working for a monster! I remembered Natasha's words from the gym yesterday. Maybe she *had* been telling the truth, even if it hadn't been for the right reasons.

"Anyway, there was trouble of some kind," Lyle continued.

"I don't know the details but it ended with the two of them leaving Sagash's service on bad terms. After it was clear that they weren't going back, we got in touch with them via a Light mage named Ebber. He'd had some previous contact with them while they were staying at Sagash's residence."

"And?"

"And they turned him down flat. According to Ebber they were quite hostile. He would have been more than willing to put them in touch with a master, but they were totally uncooperative."

"Huh," I said. "So instead they ended up with Jagadev."

Lyle shrugged. "Apparently no one else would have them." He glanced around. "On the subject, Alex . . . what exactly are you doing here?"

"Got an invitation."

Lyle frowned. "I'd avoid associating yourself too closely with Jagadev if I were you. He may have some influence amongst the Council, but he's still a nonhuman."

"I'll keep that in mind. So how did your chat with Crystal go?"

"I, er . . ." Lyle looked flustered. "I ought to be going."

I watched Lyle hurry off. I hadn't expected that last comment to be the one to chase him away. Maybe I'd hit a nerve.

Down below the night was in full swing, hundreds of people dancing to the thumping beat of the music. Looking down over the crowd and concentrating, I could sense flickers of magic. None were powerful but there were a lot of them. Was that what Jagadev had created here—a sort of haven for adepts? It made sense. Mages wouldn't let a creature like Jagadev move into their own territory, but adepts aren't something they concern themselves with.

Up here on the balcony the crowd was thinner. I didn't recognise most of the guests, but there were a few that I did, and they were generally people I didn't want to talk to. Crystal and Lyle were leaving but Onyx wasn't, and he was heading back towards me. I stepped out of his line of sight again, waited until he was past, then walked away in the opposite direction.

As I did, I saw Anne. She was leaning on the balcony railing and looking out over the crowd, and everybody else was giving her a wide berth. I couldn't see Luna. I considered it for maybe half a second before coming to lean on the railing next to Anne. "Don't take this the wrong way," I said, "but I think your normal clothes suit you better."

Anne gave me a glance and a half smile. She didn't seem surprised, as if she'd known I was there. "Lord Jagadev likes me to wear it for gatherings."

"And you do what Lord Jagadev tells you." I put the tiniest stress on the title.

Anne looked out over the crowd. "It's . . . difficult." She was silent for a moment. "I don't like everything he asks us to do. But there are worse things than having to dress up."

"Trust me, I understand *that* part." I paused. "Thanks for showing up when you did back there."

"It's no problem." Anne turned back to me. "Did you find out anything?"

I shook my head. "Looks like I'll be around to give you updates though."

Anne gave me an enquiring look.

"So what's Jagadev's end of the deal?" I said. "He uses his connections to keep the two of you in the apprentice program?"

Anne looked away again. "That's part of it," she said at last.

"And the other part?"

Anne hesitated, seemed about to speak.

"Anne," a voice said from behind us.

I turned to see Variam. "He wants you," Variam said, ignoring me.

Anne sighed. "All right." She looked at me. "I'm sorry, I have to go. I'll see you soon?"

I nodded. "Till then."

Anne left. Variam gave me a flat unfriendly look which I returned blandly, then he escorted her away, glancing over his shoulder to keep tabs on me.

I waited until they were out of sight, then followed. I was curious about why "Lord" Jagadev suddenly wanted to talk to Anne. Anne and Variam entered Jagadev's court a little way ahead of me. I wouldn't be able to follow them in without being noticed . . . but then, I didn't need to.

The technique is the same one I use for watching people, slightly modified. First you need to be close enough that you can reach them in only a few seconds. Then you look into the immediate future in which you approach. As I concentrated, in every future I was stopped before getting all the way up to where Anne and Jagadev were talking, sometimes at the door and sometimes a little farther in. But in some of those futures I'd catch a snatch of conversation, and by putting those futures together I could get the gist of what they were saying. It's a pretty crude method of eavesdropping—an air mage could just carry the words right to his ears—but it does have the advantage of being almost completely undetectable.

". . . and what has been happening there?" Jagadev was saying.

"Just duelling classes," Anne said.

"Which mages were present?"

"Today? I wasn't there, so I couldn't see, but . . . Lyle, I think, and an air mage I don't know. And there was—"

Some people passed through the door, breaking my link and disrupting the futures in which I was watching them. I turned away and waited for them to pass. When they were gone, Anne was speaking again. ". . . nothing serious, really."

"I did not ask if it was serious."

"Well . . . there's Natasha and her friend Yasmin. But it's just talk."

"What kind of talk?"

Anne sounded uncomfortable. "Little stuff. Talking about us to the mages, that kind of thing. It's nothing important . . ."

"What else do your classes discuss?"

I frowned. Jagadev wanted to know about Anne's classes? I kept listening and Jagadev kept asking Anne questions—the other apprentices, the teachers, everything. I pulled my vision back and looked at the rest of the room. This time, instead of looking to see how the people of Jagadev's court acted towards him, I looked at how they acted towards Anne.

And to my surprise I got the very definite impression they were scared of her. It was subtle; they didn't look at her directly or come too close. But the more I watched, the more sure I became that the people in that room were almost as afraid of Anne as they were of Jagadev. Maybe that outfit wasn't for decoration, but to make sure she was noticed.

All the same, it was odd. I'd always heard that life mages were supposed to be dangerous, but it was hard to think of Anne as a threat. She seemed too—

"Alex? *Alex!*"

I jerked back to the present to realise that Luna was talking to me. She'd come up next to me while I was distracted, and she looked tense. "We've got trouble. Onyx just met someone and he's coming this way."

I looked into the future to see how far Onyx was . . . and saw the person he was with. "Oh *shit*. Luna, get out of here."

"Where?"

"Anywhere these guys don't see you! Move!"

Luna moved. I scanned quickly through the futures, looking for a way to avoid the men heading towards me, and realised it wouldn't work. Giving Onyx the slip was one thing but the man with him had already spotted me. If I ran he wouldn't pursue . . . but it would let him know I was afraid of him. I hesitated for an instant, then walked forward to meet them just as they turned the corner to come face to face with me.

Onyx was on the left and his face darkened as he saw me, but it was the man half a step ahead of him that I was watching. He was average height with jet-black hair and the good looks and confidence of a man in his prime. Physically he looked thirty, but I was pretty sure he wasn't. "Ah, Verus," Morden said. "I was hoping we'd have the chance to chat."

Onyx didn't move but I could sense that he was coiled to strike and I tensed, watching the futures. If he attacked this close I would have to move very fast. Morden glanced sideways. "Onyx, I'm afraid I'll be late to our meeting with Jagadev. Why don't you go ahead and give him my apologies?"

Onyx looked at Morden with narrowed eyes. "Today, please," Morden said. Onyx gave me a last glare and obeyed. I moved slightly to keep him in sight as he stalked off.

"Well, then," Morden said. "Why don't we discuss how we can help each other?"

Everyone else who'd been standing nearby had scattered, which reinforced just how dangerous Morden was, not that I needed the reminder. The first time I met Morden he scared off three veteran Dark mages just by looking at them. The *second* time he subdued those same three Dark mages without breaking a sweat. He's very powerful and very ambitious, and quite frankly he scares the hell out of me.

But if I've learnt one thing about dealing with Dark mages it's that you don't show fear. "Sounds great," I said. "You can help by keeping yourself and your psychopathic Chosen as far away from me as you can."

Morden sighed. "Yes, I rather expected we'd have to work through this." He gestured along the balcony. "Shall we?"

"Shall we what?"

"Walk. Unless you'd prefer to include your apprentice in the conversation?"

I didn't let myself glance towards where Luna was hidden. I began walking in the direction Morden had pointed. The Dark mage fell in beside me. "So let's get this out of the way," Morden said.

"You kidnapped me, lied to me, and tried to kill me."

"I don't remember you describing it as a kidnapping. In fact as I recall, you thanked me."

"That was *before* you tried to press-gang me into a plan that was supposed to get me killed."

"The next point," Morden continued as if he hadn't heard. "Perhaps you could explain how I lied to you?"

"You said you wanted me as intelligence officer," I said. "You didn't mention the part where Onyx was planning to kill me as soon as we got inside."

"And?"

"What do you mean, 'and'?"

"Which part did you think I was lying about?"

"Oh, I don't know. How about the part where we were meant to survive?"

"I simply made you a job offer."

"And you forgot to mention that you'd told Onyx to take my head off?" I said. "What, did it slip your mind?"

"Actually, I didn't give Onyx specific instructions as to what to do with any of you," Morden said. "That was left to his discretion."

I gave Morden a look. "I'm disappointed, Verus," Morden said. "Don't you recall our last conversation?"

"Enlighten me."

"Dealing with Onyx was your responsibility," Morden said. "If you were unable to manage such a situation, you would have proved yourself unsuited for the role."

"Let me get this straight," I said. "You knew Onyx was going to try to kill me and you still seriously believed I'd be willing to work for you afterwards?"

"Hopefully."

I shook my head. "You Dark mages have *such* a screwed-up way of looking at the world, you know that? I was stupid enough to work for you once. I'm never doing it again."

"Never is a long time." Morden didn't seem troubled. "You may have reason to approach me sooner than you think."

"Whatever," I said. We were approaching the end of the balcony. "Are we done here?"

"Are you really doing so well investigating these disappearances alone that you can afford to pass up help?"

I stopped and turned to face Morden. "And what do you know about that?"

"Let me guess," Morden said. "You received an anonymous piece of information pointing you towards Fountain Reach. Am I correct?"

"And you're expecting me to believe that was why Onyx was there? Another tip-off?"

"Why did you think he was there?"

"Maybe because the two of you are the ones *causing* the disappearances."

"And what would I gain from that?"

"Fewer Light mages, more Dark ones?"

Morden sighed. "Light mages always think it's all about them. Tell me, Verus, what made you so certain it was only Light apprentices who were disappearing?"

I started to answer and then stopped.

"Onyx was in Fountain Reach for precisely the reason you were," Morden said. "The difference is that unlike you, we know the informant's identity."

"Who?"

"I believe you just implied you considered me a suspect," Morden said dryly. "Now you want information?"

I was silent.

"Onyx will be at the White Stone," Morden said. "Again, for much the same reasons as you. I believe the two of you could profit from cooperation but I won't force you."

I turned and started walking back towards Jagadev's room. "Sure you're not doing all this just to get back at me for stopping you from getting the fateweaver?"

"If that were my objective I would have killed you already," Morden said. "I would have thought you would have firsthand knowledge of why the fateweaver is of little value to me."

"Fine. So if you expect me and Onyx to help each other, are you at least going to tell him not to try and kill me again?"

"Honestly, Verus," Morden said. "Haven't you been listening at all? Your issues with Onyx are your own problem. I certainly won't do anything to protect you from the consequences of your own actions. Not without something in return."

We'd nearly returned to the point at which we'd started. "Well, interesting as this has been, I have business to attend to," Morden said. "I hope you and Onyx can work out your differences."

"Don't take this personally," I said, "but I hope I don't see you again."

"Are you going to stop involving yourself in matters of importance?" Morden asked. He paused a second, waiting for a reply, then smiled slightly. "I thought not. Good night."

Morden left without a backward glance. I stepped out of sight and stood thinking.

Luna peeked her head out from a doorway. "Alex?"

"It's safe," I said, and shook myself. "I think we've outstayed our welcome."

Luna followed without argument. Once she would have complained, but she's learnt a lot since then. "What did he want to talk about?"

"I'll tell you on the way home," I said. "Let's get out of here. Morden won't take a shot at us if he sees us again, but Onyx will."

chapter 8

I caught Luna up on what she'd missed, and we separated at Camden Town. She had classes the next day and we wouldn't see each other until we met at the White Stone opening in the evening. I headed home and crashed.

I woke up the next morning starving and light-headed. Obviously the effects of Anne's spell hadn't worn off. I had to eat everything in my flat and make a trip to the supermarket for a second breakfast before I was feeling human again.

Sonder rang just as I was finishing up. "Hey," I said into my phone, carrying the plates to the sink.

"Alex?" Sonder said. "Those men who were after you and Anne? I found them."

⊢⊢⊢⊢⊢⊢⊢⊢

The block of flats was in Stoke Newington, not close to where the attack had happened but not all that far either.

It was a border area between a run-down council estate and a nicer street of semidetached houses; the sort of area you'd find students, immigrants, and anyone who wanted a place with more-or-less affordable rent and not too high a crime rate. The flats were dark brick, spread wide, and three storeys high, and they were quiet. It was late morning and most of the people living here would be at work or school.

The weather had clouded over and a chill wind was gusting down the street. I ducked into a doorway next to Sonder, taking what meagre shelter we could from the cold. "Which flat?"

"Second floor, number three twenty-nine," Sonder said. He was shivering.

I concentrated and path-walked, watching my future self cross the street, make my way into the flats, and navigate to the door. I kicked the door down . . . and the future dissolved into a chaos of combat and gunfire. I pulled back, the future fading away instantly. "It's them."

"I told you."

"How did you find them?"

"How do you think? I followed the route here."

"Were they in a car?"

"Yes."

"And you traced them on foot—"

"Yes."

"I'm guessing it took a long time."

"Yes."

"All right," I said. "Thanks. I know it wasn't an easy job."

"I'm freezing," Sonder said. He was still shivering. "What are you going to do?"

I studied the block of flats. "I'm going to go in and have a chat."

"Then I'm coming too."

"Sonder—"

"You always try to leave me behind," Sonder said. "I've been doing this for five hours. I'm not turning around and going home."

I hesitated. It's not that Sonder's incompetent. Several times he's managed to accomplish things on his own that I think are pretty impressive. Just because he doesn't specialise in combat doesn't mean that he can't look after himself; he can react surprisingly fast and he knows some uses of time magic that are very useful in a tight spot. I'd rather have him at my side than most mages twice his age.

The problem is that Sonder is basically nice. He doesn't fight except in self-defence and he avoids hurting people whenever he can. I on the other hand am not nice. The reason there were two people in the flat ahead of us rather than three was because I'd stabbed the third one to death. And if necessary I was quite willing to do the same to the other two. Sonder would never think of doing something like that. I've never been sure whether that's a good thing or a bad thing, but I knew the difference in approach was likely to cause trouble.

But Sonder had earned the right to come along, and I could use the backup. "You don't come into the flat until I tell you it's clear," I said. "Got it?"

"Got it."

We crossed the street, cold wind whipping our clothes. A fine drizzle had started to fall, chilling my skin and damping my hair. The entrance to the flats was sealed with a security door; I studied the panel for a second and pressed the button for a first-floor flat. We waited for a second and the speaker buzzed. "Hello?" a female voice asked.

"Delivery for flat seventeen?" I said.

"Delivery?" the voice said doubtfully. "I thought they

said tomorrow . . . Just a second . . ." The door beeped as the unlock light came on and we ducked inside.

"Why didn't she ask why you weren't using the tradesman's bell?" Sonder asked as we started up the stairs.

"No idea."

The stairwell was concrete, and cold. We were on the first-floor landing when something pinged on my precognition. I stopped, Sonder doing the same, and in the silence I heard footsteps descending above us.

I moved quickly to the doors, pulling Sonder through them and letting them swing closed behind me. Sonder started to ask a question and I raised a hand for silence. The door had a small wired-glass window and I watched through it.

The echoing footsteps kept coming, muffled through the wood and concrete, and then through the window I saw a man descend into view wearing the uniform of a London policeman. Black vest, webbing belt, conical hat. He crossed the landing, his hand twisted oddly on the banister and his back to us, and disappeared from view without showing us his face. His footsteps faded away.

I waited a minute, then pushed the door open an inch. There was no sound from below. "What was he doing here?" Sonder asked uneasily.

"I'm not sure."

"Do you think he was here to see those guys?"

"Maybe," I said. Something about what we'd just seen was nagging at me. One lone policeman . . . "Sonder? Don't police usually go in pairs?"

Sonder sounded doubtful. "I'm not sure."

If it was just a routine enquiry . . . but if it was a murder investigation . . . "Come on," I said, going up the stairs two at a time. Sonder hurried after me.

I gave the second floor a quick visual check as we

emerged from the stairwell. No security cameras. I walked quickly and quietly to number 329 and looked into the immediate future of going through the door. No movement. I pulled out my tools. "Cover me," I said, going down on one knee. Sonder stood above me, looking nervously from side to side.

Being able to see the future helps with a lot of physical skills and lockpicking is one of them. You still need to know how to use the tools, but with my divination magic I can see at a glance if a lock's beatable and if so how. Conscious of how exposed we were, I worked fast.

After twenty seconds there was a *click* and the door swung open to reveal a plain corridor, open doorways leading into rooms ahead of me. I signalled to Sonder to stay back and slipped inside. I was already scanning the futures, looking for the flurry of combat I'd seen before. Nothing on the ground floor, nothing on the first floor—that didn't make sense, I should be seeing a fight. I checked again. Living room, bathroom, bedrooms—no combat. I wasn't in any danger at all.

"Alex?" Sonder whispered from behind me. I waved to him to stay back. There was something odd about the air in here, a strange smell. Coppery.

I switched from a focused scan to a wide one. Instead of looking only for combat, I looked into the futures of entering the rooms ahead of me just to see what would happen . . . and suddenly I knew what that smell was.

"I—" Sonder started to say.

"Stay there," I said harshly and walked forward.

The men who'd tried to kill Anne two nights ago were in the living room. One was sprawled across the sofa on his back, eyes staring sightlessly up at the ceiling. His throat had been torn open with such force that it had almost severed his head, and blood glistened over his fingers and in a gory spray around his body. The second man was sprawled against the wall, greyish intestines strewn around his shredded stomach. The rich scent of blood filled the air.

I stood quite still, not going any farther into the room. My eyes took in the details. Furniture overturned where the men had fallen, but nowhere else. Coffee mugs on the table with a TV remote. A thread of steam was rising from the coffee and the blood was still fresh.

Sonder was trying to get my attention from outside, but I wasn't listening. My heart was pounding from the adrenaline and I looked into the future of searching the bodies, being very careful not to move. Wallets, phones, keys—and weapons. Both had been carrying guns, but they hadn't taken them out. Their hands were empty.

I thought back over my movements. I hadn't stepped in the blood. Had I touched anything that could have left fingerprints? No, I'd been careful. But any second now someone could show up. We had to get out of here.

All the same, I hesitated. These two had been alive when I'd checked five minutes ago. Someone had been here between now and then.

The policeman. The one who'd been alone. I turned and walked out, brushing past Sonder. "Move."

"Wait, what—"

"We're leaving." I hurried downstairs, searching through the futures for signs of movement. There were people about in the flats, and I altered our course to make sure we wouldn't meet them. I did *not* want any witnesses placing us at the scene when this got reported to the police.

Once we'd made it back down to the entry area I breathed a little easier. I looked into the future for any sign of the policeman, searching for what we would find if we opened the door. Nothing but falling rain. "Alex?" Sonder asked. "What's going on?"

I turned to Sonder, about to ask him to help me find where the man had gone. Then suddenly I stopped as I realised what I was doing. Whoever or whatever this guy was, he'd just ripped apart two trained gunmen. Did I really want to chase after him?

A door opened in the stairwell above and that decided me. "Come on," I said, opening the door into the cold drizzle. "I'll explain once we're out of here."

ıııııııı

"Did you manage to identify the man?" Talisid asked. It was two hours later, and Talisid and I were sitting in a French restaurant in Holborn. The tables were widely spaced and Talisid had chosen one at the back where pillars made us hard to see from the street. The room had a high ceiling and was light and airy. The lunchtime crowd wasn't too heavy, and the buzz of conversation around us was low.

"No," I said.

"Didn't you say Sonder was with you?" Talisid said.

"And I could have asked him to look back to see what happened and maybe follow the guy. Yeah, I know. I didn't."

A waiter appeared next to us. "May I take your order, sirs?"

"*Moules à la marinière* followed by *poulet à la moutard et au miel*." Talisid handed him the menu. "And a glass of the house red, please."

I pointed at Talisid. "What he said."

The waiter bowed and vanished as quietly as he had come. "I assume you had a reason," Talisid said once the waiter was out of earshot.

"Three reasons. First, it was too dangerous. Sonder needs

time to scan a location and every second we stayed made it more likely we'd be reported at the scene. And if we did manage to find where that guy had gone and chase him, there's a good chance he would have tried to kill *us*. Second, it wouldn't have told us anything useful. I already know what happened. That guy came to the flat and killed everyone inside."

"And the third?"

"The third is they aren't the guys we're looking for," I said. "Those three men and the guy who hired them aren't the ones who've been disappearing those apprentices."

"How do you know?"

"Because Sonder was able to trace them."

Talisid thought for a second, then nodded. "No shroud."

"No shroud. And something else—that attack on Anne was *messy*. It would have left her body, bloodstains, witnesses, you name it. The disappearances you set me to investigate are the exact opposite. Neat and clean, no sign of a struggle." I shook my head. "Completely different MO."

"So where does that leave us?"

"Not very far," I said. "We still haven't found any trace of whoever's snatching these apprentices, but I wasn't expecting to get quick results anyway. They haven't lasted this long by being careless. I'm hoping we'll find out more in Fountain Reach."

"You think it's there?"

"I think an awful lot of people seem to *want* me to think it's there. If nothing else it's the biggest gathering of apprentices in the British Isles. Seems like a good place to keep an eye on."

Talisid nodded and handed me a sealed envelope. "Registration papers. Luna's been entered as a competitor."

"Thanks." I tucked the envelope away just as the food arrived.

Lunch occupied us both for a while. It was good. I tend to be pretty casual with the food I eat and it's rare for me to go out somewhere nice like this. "I had someone take a look at those halls of residence," Talisid said eventually. "There *were* security cameras but unfortunately they didn't show anything. The relevant sections of recording on all the cameras were blank."

I looked up at that. "Huh."

"It was a good idea," Talisid said. "Pity it didn't come to anything."

"Yes it did. It tells us a lot."

"How do you mean?"

"If those security cameras were wiped, that means there was something on them they didn't want us to see," I said. "If they'd just gated into their room or something they wouldn't have needed to mess with the recordings." An image was starting to form in my mind: a shadowy figure walking in the front door, heading up to the room, knocking . . .

"A mage, then?" Talisid said, breaking into my thoughts.

"I'm thinking that way," I said. "And something else. I saw Morden last night at Tiger's Palace and he told me Dark apprentices have been disappearing too."

Talisid frowned. "Really?"

"Do you know if it's true?"

"I'd heard some rumours, but I hadn't known how accurate they were. Unfortunately the Dark mages don't have a centralised organisation as we do. There's no one representative we could approach to ask questions."

"Who's the closest?"

Talisid raised his eyebrows. "Probably Morden."

"Do you think he's really trying to stop these attacks? To boost his reputation amongst Dark mages?"

Talisid thought for a second, fork in hand. "It matches

his past goals," he said at last. "But I'm not sure it's the whole story."

"What else, then?"

"Well, I was surprised at Morden being at the Tiger's Palace." Talisid finished his meal and set down his cutlery with a clink, interlacing his fingers. "Morden and Jagadev are . . . rivals, of sorts. The people you go to see if you want something that Light mages can't do or won't. They've been competing for years and I've always been under the impression there's bad feeling between them."

"So what?" I said. "You think the other reason Morden's doing this is because he thinks it'll hurt Jagadev?"

"That would be my guess." The waiter approached, about to ask if we'd like any dessert, but Talisid waved him off.

I thought about it for a second then shook my head in frustration. "But both Jagadev *and* Morden were pointing me towards Fountain Reach. If they want opposite things, how come they're sending me to the same place?"

"Good question," Talisid said. "Any idea where to start?"

I tapped a finger on the tablecloth, staring off into the distance with a frown. "I'm going to stick around Anne and Variam," I said at last. "I don't know what's going on with those two but I've got the feeling they're tied into this somehow. Especially Anne. If someone takes another shot at her I'm going to be around for it."

Talisid nodded and motioned the waiter over, taking out his wallet. "Good luck."

⁝ ⁝ ⁝ ⁝ ⁝

I spent a few hours settling affairs in London. First I packed. My flat has a huge selection of equipment, tools, focuses, one-shots, gear, weapons, and miscellaneous stuff I've picked up over the years, most of which I never use. It looks like junk, and to be fair it usually is, but it's worth keeping around for when I need something obscure, fast. That wouldn't be an option in Fountain Reach—I'd have what I brought with me and nothing more. In the end I left the specialist stuff behind and took a selection of the general-purpose items I use the most—condensers, forcewalls, and a couple of weapons. I hesitated over my mist cloak. I don't like to carry it unless I really need it—a lot of its effectiveness comes from the fact that most people don't know that I have it or what it can do—but in the end it was just too useful to leave at home.

Next I wrote a sign saying that the Arcana Emporium would be closed for renovations and hung it in the window. It felt like I'd been doing that a lot lately. Now that I thought about it, between jobs, trouble, and Luna's training, it'd been months since I'd put in a full week at the shop.

And after that I went to explain to Sonder that he wasn't coming.

"But I can help," Sonder said.

"I know," I said. "That's why I want you somewhere else."

We were standing in the daylight outside the station. "You're taking Luna," Sonder objected.

"Luna's protected. That's the whole point of her curse."

"I can take care of myself too," Sonder said. He had a wounded look, like a dog that had been told it wasn't going to be taken for a walk.

"Come on, Sonder," I said. "You think I don't know that? But every person we bring is an extra risk."

"What if you need to find out what happened in the mansion?"

"You won't be able to look into the past inside the walls anyway. Look, this job is investigation, not combat. What we need you for is research, and you can do that more effectively and with less risk from London. There's a good chance I'll need your help up there later, but not right now."

Sonder sighed, though he still didn't look happy. "What do you need?"

And finally I went to see Arachne.

 ı ı ı ı ı ı ı ı ı

Arachne's home is one of the very few places I feel safe, and as I walked down the tunnel to her cave I turned off my mental radar and let myself relax. I wanted to take the chance to rest: Once I left for Fountain Reach I had the feeling safety was going to be in short supply.

I found Arachne perched over a table, working on something with her four front legs. I dropped down on a sofa with a sigh. "Hey."

"Hello, Alex," Arachne said. She didn't stop working; Arachne never seems to have any trouble making something and carrying on a conversation at the same time. Either she's had so much practice that it's automatic, or she's just really good at multitasking. "How was last night?"

"Well, it wasn't boring. At least I got a good look at Jagadev's place."

"What did you think?"

I was silent for a moment. "Confusing," I said. "I've been to mage balls, but this was different. I'm not sure what was going on."

"Confusion is Jagadev's way," Arachne said. "Shadows and misdirection. Always he keeps his true aims concealed."

"Do you know why he'd gather so many adepts?" I asked. "Or what he'd be doing with two apprentices like Anne and Variam?"

"No," Arachne said.

I thought for a second. "Jagadev's powerful," I said. "And he's a magical creature who lives in London."

"Yes."

"He must have dealt with the same problems you've had."

"Yes."

I looked at Arachne. "But you've never allied with him."

Arachne didn't answer. I wanted to know more, but I didn't push. The only sound was the click and rustle of Arachne's tools.

"He offered exactly that," Arachne said at last. "A long time ago in your years, a short time in mine. He came here to propose an alliance, of information and assistance." She paused. "I refused."

I looked at her curiously. "Why?"

"Jagadev is a destroyer," Arachne said simply. "He holds a grudge against humans. What he seeks is not creation but revenge."

Arachne fell silent and I sat on the sofa frowning. If that was true, then what was going on between him and Anne and Variam?

"There," Arachne said, her voice becoming cheerful. "All done!"

I looked over in interest. Arachne had set her tools down and was holding something out to me. I honestly couldn't tell you how the tools work or what she'd been doing. By mage standards I'm an expert on magic items, but Arachne's on a completely different level and I don't understand even the most basic principles of how she can do what she does.

The item looked like a wand, fifteen inches long and slightly tapered so that one end was narrower than the other. A handle was built into the wider end and a small sphere was set at the base of the handle. It had the colour of alabaster or ivory but as I took it from Arachne its texture felt more like silk. "Huh," I said, turning it over curiously.

"Now be careful when you test it," Arachne said. "In fact, if I were you I'd make sure to be all the way out of line of sight."

"I will." I looked up. "Thanks, Arachne."

Arachne waved a leg. "Don't mention it. Just come back safely."

ı ı ı ı ı ı ı ı ı

Fountain Reach looked very different in the daylight. It was still cold but the sun had come out, taking off the worst of the chill. Puffy clouds floated in a blue sky, with the green hills as a backdrop.

The driveway was crowded with expensive-looking cars and two more pulled past us as we walked in, tyres crunching on the gravel. In the centre of the front courtyard was an elaborate fountain. Statues of young women poured a steady stream of water from a stone urn, while two phoenixes looked on. "What's that?" Luna asked curiously.

"Fountain of Youth," I said. "Old mage legend."

We followed other people into the entry hall, handed Luna's papers to one of the administrators, and set off into the mansion, up a flight of stairs and then down again. I checked my watch; the opening ceremony was supposed to be starting now. As we reached an intersection I could hear the buzz of activity from ahead of us but couldn't tell exactly where it was coming from. "Which way?" Luna asked.

"Good question." Fountain Reach's wards were doing their work and I couldn't effectively map out a route. I looked around for someone to ask directions from, but all of a sudden the corridors were empty. There was something weirdly deserted about the mansion. The ambient noise made it feel as though there were people all around you, but when you stopped to look you always seemed to be alone.

I picked a direction that I hoped was right and Luna followed. "What's up with this place?" Luna asked, echoing my own thoughts.

"Not a clue," I said. "It must have been built for something but I have no idea what."

We turned a corner and the distant murmurs grew louder. To the right I could see a set of double doors and make out a voice speaking from behind it. More by luck than judgement I'd led Luna back to the same duelling hall in which I'd run into Onyx.

The hall was packed. Close to two hundred men, women, and teenagers were scattered around and I recognised dozens of mages in the crowd. Most were Light, some were unaligned, and a handful were Dark, but for every mage I knew there were two more I didn't. Some wore ceremonial robes but most of the Light mages, especially those connected with the Council, wore formal business suits. The ones in robes and the ones in suits mixed freely, forming comfortable groups. Other mages . . . didn't. The ones wearing smart-casual streetwear or anything else unusual were scattered more to the edges of the crowd, away from the "power" groups, as did the ones who by their dress or manner obviously *weren't* mages.

The apprentices looked much like their masters. There was a little more variety in how they dressed but not much, and it was surprisingly easy to match the apprentice to the mage. I picked out Charles, the apprentice Variam had been matched against two days ago, as well as Luna's opponent, Natasha. Charles was wearing a blazer and standing next to a white-haired mage who looked exactly like an older copy of him, while Natasha was with another Asian girl. They looked as if they'd been talking but now were turned towards the stage at the end of the room. Following their gaze I saw Crystal on the stage, wearing an elegant-looking two-piece suit. She seemed to have just finished a speech, and now she was reading from a clipboard. "The first elimination round will begin at nine o'clock tomorrow morning," she said, her voice raised to carry over the sounds of the hall. "The draw is as follows. Michael Aran and Charles de Beaumont; Vaya Merrin and Traysia Lacann; Dominica Soria and Fay Wilder; Stephen Jasper and Victor Kraft . . ."

Luna was craning her neck looking around at everyone. "Do you think Anne and Variam are here?"

"Probably. Try and find them."

"Gunther Elkins and Henry Smith; Desmond Yates and Variam Singh . . ."

"There's his matchup," I said.

"There!" Luna said.

I looked where Luna was pointing and saw Anne and Variam behind the rows of chairs. Anne was talking to a younger girl and smiling, while Variam watched them both with a surly look and his arms folded. "Variam doesn't look happy," I said.

"Variam's never happy."

"Mikhail Baich and Zander Rhys; Natasha Babel and Samantha Vash . . ."

I hadn't stopped searching, and as I recognised one of the figures my heart sank. "Ah, crap."

"What's wrong?"

"We've got trouble. Wait two seconds, then look over your left shoulder. Under those paintings."

Luna obeyed and saw what I'd saw: a thin figure dressed in black leaning alone against the wall. She sighed. "So we get to deal with him too."

". . . and that concludes the pairings," Crystal finished. "All apprentices not named in those pairings will go through to the second round." She looked around. "Thank you all and good luck."

"Wait, did she say my name?" Luna said.

"No," I said. "Let's see if we can get out of here before Onyx starts something."

We started towards one of the exits, moving through the crowd. I recognised the odd mage, but not many; I don't go to these kind of events often. "Aren't I on the list?" Luna asked.

"It's single elimination. There are more than thirty-two entries but fewer than sixty-four, so not everyone is fighting in the first round. The others get—" I stopped with a sigh.

"Going somewhere?" Onyx asked, stepping out in front of us.

I watched Onyx carefully, keeping a close eye on the futures ahead. We were surrounded by the buzz and chatter of conversation and at least twenty people had a clear line of sight to us. I didn't seriously think Onyx would start something with this many witnesses but got myself ready anyway. "Onyx," I said. I glanced over at the wall he'd shredded yesterday, then back again. "Seems they've made repairs from your last visit."

"Going to tell them why *you* were here?" Onyx said. He was wearing a black coat and trousers, not modern but not in line with traditional mage gear either. He was smiling and might even have looked friendly if you weren't paying attention.

"Not just yet," I said. "Well, it's great Morden's sent you here to help but we're kind of busy. See you around and—"

"Not so fast," Onyx said, stepping closer. His eyes glittered as he watched me. "You haven't entered."

"The tournament? Not my thing."

"Scared?" Onyx asked softly.

"Are you going somewhere with this?"

Onyx stared at me for a second, then raised his voice. "Bear witness!" he shouted. "The mage Alex Verus has caused me loss and harm, and under the ancient code"—he locked eyes with me—"I demand satisfaction."

Conversation around us fell silent as everyone turned to watch. Looking into Onyx's eyes, I felt a nasty sinking feeling. "You're challenging me to an azimuth duel?"

Onyx gave a cold smile. "No. Old style. Three days from now, Verus. I'll be waiting." He turned and walked out.

Slowly the buzz of conversation started up again. Everyone on this side of the room was watching us and I could see people whispering. "Let's get out of here," I said to Luna.

I ran the gauntlet of stares out of the hall and into one of the corridors. Luna hurried after me. "What just happened?"

"Pretty much what it sounded like," I said, thinking hard. How the hell was I supposed to win a duel against someone like Onyx?

"What's an 'old style' duel?"

"Like an azimuth duel, but no shields."

"Wait, no shields? So if you get hit—?"

"They're done to first blood or to submission."

"He's not going to be doing it to first blood, is he?"

"I wouldn't bet on it," I said. We came to a four-way junction and I shook my head, putting Onyx out of my mind. The duel wasn't for three days and I'd cross that bridge when I came to it. "We need to find Anne and Variam."

"He didn't even accuse you of anything," Luna said. "He just said 'loss and harm.'"

"Probably he'll send that part in a formal letter." Anne and Variam had left the hall while we'd been dealing with Onyx, but I hadn't seen where they'd gone. I took a guess and headed down a corridor that I hoped would lead us into the bedroom wing, Luna following.

"And he can just do that?" Luna said. "Fight you in a duel and try to kill you without anyone stopping him?"

"Pretty much."

"This is such *bullshit*!" Luna said. "How can he just walk in here? What about what he did in the spring at the British Museum? *He* should be the one getting accused of stuff and having to defend himself!"

"There were never any formal charges made about that, remember?"

"He tried to *kill* us! Everyone knows he did it. We *saw* him!"

"And it's covered by Council secrecy."

"He tried to kill you yesterday!"

"Which I can't accuse him of without admitting that I was here when I wasn't supposed to be."

"And all those men he killed at the British Museum?"

"None of them were mages." I led Luna down a flight of stairs and through a sitting room. A pair of mages were standing talking; they glanced at us, and both Luna and I fell silent as we walked by. "Onyx is Morden's Chosen," I said quietly once we were out of earshot again. "Accusing Onyx would be the same as picking a fight with Morden. No one on the Council wants to do that."

"I can't believe this," Luna said. "How can the mage world be so screwed up? I go to classes and everything seems fine, but—Mages like Levistus and Griff and Belthas and Morden and Onyx, they do all this and everyone just pretends like nothing's happening!"

"Remember how I kept telling you it was dangerous to get involved in my world?" I said. "And how you never listened?"

Luna glowered down at the floor. We walked a little way in silence. "What are you going to do?" Luna asked.

"Wait for his formal challenge," I said. We'd come into a long corridor with no doors leading off it. It didn't look anything like bedrooms. "By the way, I think we're lost."

· · · · · · · · · ·

G etting unlost and finding our way to the bedroom wing took us twenty minutes and by the time we got there Anne and Variam were somewhere else. It took us the best part of an hour to find them and when we finally did some-one else had gotten there first.

Variam and Anne were in the dining hall, along with the girl who'd been talking to Anne earlier. Standing opposite them were three apprentices. Two I recognised as the ones I'd seen back in the duelling class: the blond-haired boy with glasses, Charles, and the round-faced girl, Natasha. There was another girl with them too; like Natasha she looked Pakistani or Bangladeshi. To a casual glance they seemed to be just talking, but there was something about the way they were standing that didn't look all that friendly. ". . . let you in here?" Natasha was saying.

"They let *you* in, didn't they?" Variam said.

"We're not Dark apprentices working for a monster," Natasha's friend said sweetly.

The younger girl I'd seen talking to Anne made a slight movement, trying to get behind Anne, but it only drew atten-tion. "Why are you with *them*?" Natasha's friend said. "Do you want us to report you to the Keepers? Go on, get lost."

The girl gave a frightened glance back at Anne and scur-ried away. I watched her vanish down a corridor.

"You didn't have to do that," Anne said quietly. She was

looking steadily at Natasha's friend, and for the first time I got the impression she might be angry.

"Oh, what are you going to do about it?" Natasha's friend said. "It's not like you even entered—"

"Hi, kids," I said, walking up to them.

Charles, Natasha, and Natasha's friend stopped abruptly and turned to me. "Hello, Mage Verus," Natasha said.

"Hi," I said. "Anne, Variam, could you come with me please?"

The other three looked satisfied. Variam's face darkened, but Anne stepped forward with a nod.

I led Anne and Variam back around the corner to where Luna was waiting. As soon as we were out of sight of Natasha and the others I shook my head. What was it about the apprentice program that made so many of the people in it act like they were still in high school?

"We didn't need your help," Variam said.

"I was under the impression," I said, "that Jagadev asked *you* to help *me*."

Variam scowled and looked away. "Hey, Anne," Luna said with a wave.

"Hi. Thanks for coming in, Alex."

"I said we didn't need it," Variam said. "Why are—?"

"Anne, did you enter?" Luna interrupted. "The tournament, I mean."

Anne shook her head. "No."

"You know, maybe if you'd actually fight once in a while I wouldn't have to keep chasing those idiots off," Variam said.

Luna looked from Variam to Anne. "You know why I don't fight duels," Anne said patiently.

"Maybe it's about time you started."

Luna glared at Variam. "Maybe you—"

"All right," I said, cutting off the argument before it could start. "I assume you two know why Luna and I are really here?"

"Yes," Anne said, just as Variam said "No."

I looked between the two of them.

"You're trying to find out what's happened to the apprentices who've been disappearing," Anne said.

"That's what Jagadev *thinks* they're doing," Variam said sharply. Anne looked at him in surprise.

"Well, Jagadev's right," I said.

"What's the plan?" Luna asked.

We'd gotten away from the noise and the chatter into a quiet corridor. Luna and Anne were already waiting for my answer and even Variam turned to watch me suspiciously.

"For now I want you to protect yourselves," I said. "Keep your eyes open and follow up on anything you see, but your priority is to *stay alive*. Onyx is here, and he's not the only one—something tried to attack me last time I was here and I don't know what it was but I don't want any of you running into it. And finally there's whoever or whatever's going after apprentices." I looked from Luna to Anne to Variam. "And all three of you qualify. So while you're here in this mansion, I don't want any of you going anywhere alone."

All three of them looked back at me, puzzled. "All of the disappearances that have happened so far had something in common," I said. "The apprentice was always on their own when they vanished. Anne, are you sharing a room with anyone?"

"Ah . . ." Anne said. "I was supposed to be, but—"

"You are now. Luna, you're moving in with her."

"I think we were supposed to be assigned rooms," Anne began.

"Just find one that no one's using and take it. If anyone

gives you any trouble, tell them it's on my orders and for them to come to me, but odds are they won't."

"Wait a minute," Variam said. "We don't need—"

"You aren't going to be keeping an eye on her *all* the time, Variam," I said. "Not unless you're going to follow her into the bathroom."

Variam scowled. "What about you?" I asked him.

"What?"

"Are you sharing a room?"

"Why do you care?"

"If you're not," I said mildly, "then I think you should start."

Variam looked me up and down. "Are you in charge of us?"

"What do you mean?"

"You're not our master," Variam said. "Is there some Council rule that we have to do what you say?"

I hesitated. "No, but—"

"Okay, then we're going," Variam said. He glanced at Anne. "Come on." He turned and walked away. Anne gave us both an apologetic look and followed.

I watched the two of them disappear down the corridor. "You know, that guy is beginning to get on my nerves."

"You think he gets on *your* nerves?" Luna said. "I have to take classes with him."

"I'm starting to sympathise." I shook my head. "Who was that apprentice Anne was talking to?"

"In the dining hall?" Luna shrugged. "I don't know her name. The younger apprentices really like Anne. They tell her everything." Luna looked at me. "You aren't sure what to do, are you?"

I always have trouble hiding things from Luna. "I think

we're in the right place," I said. "But we still don't know what to look for."

"Are you sure there's anything here?"

"No, but it's my best guess. Everyone's been pointing me to Fountain Reach. I don't know what's going on but I know there's something." I gave Luna a glance. "I want you to keep an eye on Anne. Stay with her if you can and if you can't then make sure she's not alone. Someone tried to kill her only a couple of days ago and I don't want to give them an easy shot."

"I will. You think she's in danger here? In the middle of everyone?"

I looked around at the walls of the mansion for a moment before answering. "Yeah, I think she is."

      ι ι ι ι ι ι ι ι ι

I was sick of getting lost and so I spent the time until dinner exploring the mansion, keeping to the populated parts and trying to build up a mental map. The more I explored the weirder the layout seemed and I made a note to find out what the story was behind this place. It felt as though it had been *designed* to be hard to navigate. There were plenty of mages around, some of whom I knew, but I avoided them.

After dinner I went looking for Luna and Anne's new room. I found it quickly and turning in to the corridor I saw the door open with their voices coming from inside. Luna was laughing—not something she used to do, but a sound I hear from her more often these days. I slowed, and as I did I saw that Variam was about to arrive from the other end of the corridor. I stepped back behind a corner and watching with my divination I saw Variam turn in to Luna and Anne's room. Luna and Anne's voices fell silent. Variam said something, his tone harsh and accusing; Luna answered. Variam gave her an angry reply; Luna gave him one back. Anne tried to intervene and Variam told her to be quiet.

I kept my distance. Footsteps sounded and Luna emerged from the room, turning towards me. She was walking fast and sounded angry. "Problems?" I said as she walked past.

Luna jumped and whirled. When she saw it was me she sighed. "Don't scare me like that."

"I told you not to go off alone," I said.

Luna covered her eyes. "Crap. Sorry, sorry. Variam just pissed me off . . ."

With my mage's sight I could see the silver mist of Luna's curse writhing around her, tendrils curling outward like angry snakes. Luna's curse is tied to her emotions; she can control it fairly well when she's calm but it's a really bad idea to be around when she's upset. "Well, might as well take advantage of it," I said. "Come on."

"Where are we going?" Luna asked as she fell into step a few paces to my side.

"When I get annoyed I find a workout helps," I said. "Let's see if it's the same with you."

⸺ ।।।।।।।। ⸺

The hall was much smaller than the one in which Crystal had read out the matchups, but it was just barely big enough for a set of azimuth duelling focuses, and it was empty except for us. "What's this place?" Luna asked.

"Practice room," I said. "Tomorrow you're going to be fighting in the tournament and you're going to need a weapon." As I spoke I reached into my coat and took out the wand Arachne had given me that afternoon. "I talked to Arachne and she came up with a design that she thought would fit." I held it out to Luna. "This is for you."

Luna looked at the wand curiously as I held it out to her by the tip. With its pearly colour and tapered design, it looked more like a decoration than a weapon. "Really?" Luna said. Hesitantly she reached out and took it by the handle. "Thanks."

As soon as Luna took it I stepped back. To my sight Luna's curse had been curling lazily around her, the silver mist pulsing softly. She'd pulled it back to take the wand from my hand, keeping the lethal stuff away from my skin, but she couldn't stop it from soaking into the item as soon as she touched it.

Luna's curse works on objects as well as people, although nowhere near as strongly. Usually I can tell if something belongs to Luna by looking for the silver aura. As her curse touched the focus, though, something different happened. Instead of sticking to it the mist was drawn in, being absorbed. "It's attuned to you," I said. "It draws in your curse and uses it."

"Okay," Luna said. She was holding the thing by the handle but still looked a little puzzled. "What does it, um, do?"

I was about to tell Luna to try it and see when I remembered Arachne's warning. "Wait a sec." I walked out of the room and into the corridor, then put my back to the wall and leant into the doorway so that the only part of me visible from inside the room was my head. "Try it now."

"Uh," Luna said. "Okay. So I'm supposed to—"

Luna's curse poured into the focus and it activated. A thin tendril of mist snaked from the tip, extending to ten or twenty feet long. All of a sudden Luna wasn't holding a wand but a whip, the thong made from the silver mist of her curse. To anyone who couldn't see Luna's curse it wouldn't have looked like anything at all, but I could see the whip curling around her. "Hey," Luna said curiously. "It's doing something, isn't it?" She lifted the handle to look at it, turning it back and forth.

The whip slashed outward, zigzagging across the room, its length amplifying the small movements of the handle. I ducked behind the door frame as the end of the tendril lashed into the corridor. "Okay, it's working!" I shouted through the doorway. "Turn it off!"

I felt the effect shut down and peeked my head cautiously around the corner. Luna was standing at the centre of what looked like a spiderweb of silvery lines. Glowing trails of invisible silver mist traced lines along the floor, walls, and ceiling. Luna was looking at the handle with new interest. "Invisible whip," she said. "Cool."

"Arachne based the design off an Australian stock whip," I said, walking back out. "The long handle's for balance, but since the whip's weightless it doesn't take any strength to use." I glanced around at the glowing lines on the walls. "On the downside, the whip's weightless and doesn't take any strength to use. We're going to have to work on your aim."

"It feels . . ." Luna said, frowning down at the focus. "Strange. Not in a bad way. Natural, I guess. Like it fits."

"Arachne designed it for you," I said. "The thong of the whip is formed from your curse. If you hit someone with this whip it's as if you'd touched them. It's just as subtle and just as lethal." I locked my eyes on Luna. "This is a weapon, not a toy. You can use it on an azimuth piste safely. But never use it anywhere else unless you're intending to kill whoever you point it at. I'm trusting you with this. Don't make me regret it."

Luna nodded. "I understand."

"Good." I walked to the end of the azimuth piste and activated the shield. "Let's give you some practice."

I worked with Luna late into the night, and she picked

up the basics of attack and defence *very* fast. Both the whip and her curse seemed eager to do their job, striking out at targets and protecting her in return. The problem was control—the whip didn't want to hit just one target, it wanted to hit everything, and only the azimuth shields kept me safe. By midnight we were both exhausted. I dropped Luna off at her room and checked that Anne was there before saying good night. I wanted to sleep, but this was a good chance to get a look at the deeper parts of Fountain Reach.

ı ı ı ı ı ı ı ı ı

The outer rooms of the mansion were busy despite the late hour. Apprentices were still up and chatting in each other's rooms, excited about their first night at the tournament, while their masters talked over drinks in the lounges. I prowled the corridors, a silent shadow in my mist cloak. My cloak doesn't make me invisible—good light or movement makes it possible for a watcher to spot me, and both together make it almost certain. But when I combine it with my divination magic, watching for the areas where people will look and avoiding them, there's not much that can find me if I don't want to be found.

As I went deeper, the background noise died away. It seemed most of the guests had been housed around the edges of the building, and as I walked the halls I could see why. There was something oppressive about the inner mansion— the ceilings felt too low, the architecture too alien. Most houses are designed as places to live and they're meant to be comfortable for the people who use them. Fountain Reach didn't feel like that. It was as though it had grown for its own reasons; the people inside were just trespassers. All around I could sense the thrum of the wards, limiting my vision, and it felt as though the mansion were looking for me.

Turning in to a corridor I heard a muffled voice from ahead of me. The corridor was old and crooked, the floor age-darkened wood. Animal heads were mounted on the wall, gazing down with dead eyes: deer, leopard, buffalo. I stood still and listened. The voice came again: a woman. It was coming from a door a little farther down. I moved forward, placing my feet softly on the bare planks.

As I drew closer I recognised the voice as Crystal's. She was arguing with someone, but for some reason I couldn't hear the other half of the conversation. ". . . take some time," Crystal was saying.

A pause, then Crystal spoke again. "The end of the tournament, obviously." Another pause. "That's impossible. You'll just have to wait."

It sounded like she was on the phone with someone. I sized up the corridor and decided to take the risk of getting in close. A stag's head was mounted above the door, antlers reaching almost to the ceiling, glass eyes staring at the opposite wall. I put my ear to the door and listened.

"No," Crystal said sharply. The door looked like it had been well crafted, but it was warped from long neglect and there were gaps between the planks that let sound through. "Absolutely not."

Silence, then Crystal again. "I don't care. It's too risky."

Something was odd: I could make out Crystal's voice clearly but I couldn't hear anything else. If she was on a phone or speaking into a headset I should be able to hear something, even just a buzz. I looked into the future in which I opened the door to peek inside.

The room within was a bedroom that looked like it had been abandoned for years. A four-poster bed was piled with dust, the hangings moth-eaten. Old and darkened pictures hung on the wall and Crystal was standing in front of one of them. The angle caught her in profile, showing off the beauty of her features and making her gold hair shine against the murky background. She was frowning, though, and she wasn't talking into a phone or headset. She seemed to be talking to the wall.

"The whole point of this plan was so we didn't have to keep picking at random," Crystal said. "There's virtually no chance we'd get someone who'd meet—"

Crystal cut off. Looking again into the immediate future, I saw she was staring at one of the pictures. "Then *wait*," she said abruptly. "We've been preparing for months and you'd risk it all for this?"

There was no answer but Crystal threw up her hands. She was acting as if there were someone right there talking to her. "I don't care! It's too dangerous."

I tried to figure out what was going on. Mind mages can communicate by telepathy but that didn't explain why Crystal was saying her half of the conversation out loud. She was speaking as though to someone in the same room. I tried looking into the future and focusing with my mage's sight, searching for someone cloaked or invisible, but all I could make out was the background noise of the wards.

Crystal had gone still all of a sudden. When she spoke, her voice was quiet. "Are you threatening me?"

Silence. I couldn't hear any movement; we were alone in this part of the mansion. "Remember our agreement," Crystal said. A pause, then she let out a long breath. "All right. But this is going to be the only one. Understand?" Whatever answer she got seemed to satisfy her. Footsteps sounded from the room, heading for the door.

Even forewarned, it was a near thing. I made it to the next door and slipped inside just as Crystal stepped out into the corridor. Holding the door shut, using my divination magic to watch Crystal, I saw her turn away and head down the corridor without a backward glance. The clack of her heels on the wooden floor grew quieter and quieter until there was silence.

I gave it three minutes just to be safe, then stepped out, looking after where Crystal had gone. I hadn't checked to see what her exact reaction would have been if she'd discovered me there but I was pretty sure it wouldn't have been positive. She'd been careless, letting me eavesdrop like that. Probably she'd assumed that no one would be able to sneak up on her without her sensing their thoughts, and to be fair, most of the time she'd be right. But it's never a good idea to rely too much on your magic, no matter how powerful it is. My mist cloak had kept me hidden and given me some interesting little snippets into the bargain. It seemed like Crystal had been making a deal with someone. But who?

I entered the room in which Crystal had been talking and gave it a quick once-over. Like all the inner rooms of Fountain Reach it was windowless: The only illumination was the glow of the electric lights. I couldn't sense any signs of life, in either the present or the future. It looked as though the room had been dead for years.

Crystal seemed to have been talking to one of the pictures, and I took a closer look. It was an old portrait done in oils, its gilt frame dusty. It showed a man in his late middle years, thin and stooped with sunken, commanding eyes. I studied the picture but found no magical aura, no special devices. The painting had no name or signature either. The man looked out of the portrait with a fixed stare, his gaze following me.

I searched a little longer but found nothing. Tired and weary, I finally retraced my steps to my room. I hung up my mist cloak, set a few basic safety measures, and was asleep almost as soon as my head hit the pillow.

chapter 9

It was cold, and the roof was made of bones. The carpet was soft under my bare feet but the ceiling above was ragged and gleamed pale in the shadows. The corridors were hushed, and the halls were silent as a tomb.

"You shouldn't be here," Anne said from next to me.

I looked at Anne. Her face was pale and her eyes haunted. "What are you afraid of?"

Anne shook her head. "He knows you've come."

A sound made me turn. A brown-skinned girl was standing there; she looked familiar, and wore a look of terrible grief. Slowly she turned and began walking away. "Wait!" I shouted. "Don't!"

She vanished into the darkness. I ran after her and found myself alone. A door stood before me; it looked smaller and older than the others. I pulled it open.

My feet came down with a squish in mud. Inside I saw

tall hedges, only a few feet away, with gaps between them that led into darkness. There should have been a night sky above but there wasn't. I could feel the walls around me. Ahead, the entrances stood alone and empty.

Looking into the darkness, I felt a wave of terror. There was something inside, something horrible, and if I went inside I would meet it face to face. I backed away, but the door and walls were the same. Everything was hidden. I was already inside and something was watching.

I spun, fighting back panic, trying to see where to go. The wall shook with a banging noise. "Alex!" it shouted at me. "Alex!"

"Leave me alone!" I shouted back.

"Alex! Alex!"

* * * * * * * * *

I came awake with a gasp. My precognition was screaming at me—*danger danger danger!*—and I rolled out of bed while still half asleep, grabbing for a weapon. I came down onto the floor on one knee, bleary-eyed, knife in my hand, looking left to right.

The knocking on my door came again. "Alex?"

I should know who it was, but my sleep-fogged mind couldn't process it. I looked around the room. The flash of danger on my precognition had gone. The room was safe. I looked at the alarms I'd set before going to bed: the chair under the door handle with glasses balanced on it and the ward stone that would have triggered if something hostile had appeared in the room. Nothing had changed. I was alone.

Knock-knock-knock went the door. "Alex? Are you there?"

"Coming," I said vaguely, looking around. Something

had woken . . . no, it had set off my . . . what had it been? The dream was fading and I couldn't remember. I shook my head and reached for my clothes.

I opened the door to see Anne standing in the hallway, dressed in a long-sleeved blouse and a purple skirt. Her hair was styled neatly around her shoulders, and she looked as though she'd gotten up early—or at least a lot earlier than me. "Hey," I said. I looked from left to right. "Where's everyone else?"

"Ah . . ." Anne said. "Luna's practising with Gabriel in one of the azimuth rooms, Variam's getting ready for his first match, and everyone else is in the hall waiting for the first round to start."

"You're on your own?" I glanced up and down the hall again. Somehow that bothered me.

"There's something wrong," Anne said. As I looked at her I realised that she looked worried. "Yasmin's gone missing."

"Yasmin?" I frowned. "Who—?"

Suddenly I remembered. The girl from yesterday, Natasha's friend, who'd been trying to bully Variam and Anne. An image flashed through my head of her face turning away, mud, and tall hedges. I put a hand to my head, feeling a sudden chill. "Alex?" Anne asked.

"Yeah," I said. "I'm fine." Suddenly the walls of the mansion felt oppressive. We were alone and I couldn't sense anyone in the present or the future but I couldn't shake the feeling of being watched. "Walk with me. We're going outside."

ı ı ı ı ı ı ı ı ı

As soon as I was out in the sunlight I felt better. It had turned into a clear, crisp winter's morning, a low sun shining from a cold sky. The gardens of Fountain Reach were all around us, well kept and beautiful. Away from the wards my divination magic was back to full strength and the creeping unease had gone. A few other people were out and about, elderly gardeners tending the plants and apprentices walking in the sun.

"She was supposed to have been back last night," Anne said. We were walking along one of the gravel paths, curving slowly around towards the back of the house. "Natasha woke up this morning and found she never got in."

"She was outside the mansion when she vanished?"

"I think the last anyone saw her was at the station."

"And no one's been able to get in touch with her since?"

"I don't think so."

It sounded familiar—too familiar. I knew the Keepers would be searching but my gut told me they'd have no more luck than with the previous ones. "The tournament's still going ahead?"

"I don't actually think most of the apprentices know that she's missing."

I gave Anne a look. "So how come you do?"

"Um . . ." Anne said. "I guess people just mentioned it?"

I had a feeling there was more to it than that but let it slide. I took a glance around. The fountain in the central driveway was visible over the hedges and people were in sight in the gardens. From outside, the mansion and everything around it looked normal, peaceful . . . but I couldn't shake the feeling that something was very wrong here.

"Jagadev sent you and Variam here," I said. "What did he tell you?"

"He told us to help you."

"But why *here*? What does he know about Fountain Reach that made him send us to it?"

Anne frowned. "Variam asked, but . . . I got the feeling it was something about the place, not the tournament."

"What about the place?"

"He wouldn't say."

I thought for a second, then nodded. "Okay, I need to do something dangerous. Can you give me a hand?"

Anne hesitated for a second. ". . . All right."

⁙⁙⁙⁙⁙⁙⁙⁙⁙

The corridors of the mansion were empty as we headed back. I could hear the buzz of voices from the direction of the central hall, followed by a roar. The first round of the tournament had begun. "He's this way," Anne said. "Um . . . there's something you should probably know. Morden and Jagadev don't get on very well."

"So I gathered," I said as we started down one of the corridors. "What's up with that?"

"I'm not sure. But Morden once asked me if I'd leave and be his apprentice."

I glanced sharply at Anne. "What did you say?"

"I said no," Anne said. She sounded very definite.

We walked a little way in silence. Through the walls I heard a muffled cheer from the duelling hall, along with someone shouting something. "You don't have to answer this if you don't want to," I said. "But what exactly is the deal you and Variam have with Jagadev?"

Anne sighed. "Everyone thinks it's something really crazy. They think we're being trained as his apprentices or we're bonded to him or we go out and murder people on his orders or something. No one ever believes me when I tell them the truth."

"What is it?"

"He gives us a place to stay," Anne said. "That's all, really."

We reached an intersection and turned left down a long hallway. We were moving deeper into the mansion, and the sounds of the crowd were fading behind us. "But if you're staying with him, you're part of his household," I said. "You might not be his apprentices but every mage is going to treat you as though you are."

Anne was silent. "That's it, isn't it?" I said. "It's for protection."

"Jagadev . . ." Anne hesitated. "Mages . . . know about him. As long as we're with him they won't want to cause us any trouble."

"Variam told you that, right?"

Anne glanced up at me, then back down at the floor.

"Was Variam the one who made the deal?"

Anne shook her head. "Jagadev came to us. It was when we were in London, after . . . He said he could make sure nobody else came after us."

"And what does he get?" I asked. "What do you do for him?"

"Little things. Deliver messages, be around for gatherings. He'll ask me for information but he won't ask us to do anything dangerous."

"Until now," I said dryly.

Anne was quiet for a moment. "Jagadev didn't make me come here," she said at last. "I . . ." She stopped and looked in the direction of the wall. "He's there."

I glanced into the immediate future and confirmed it. "Okay," I said and took a breath. "Let's do this." I walked through the doorway and into the next room. "Onyx," I said, raising my voice. "Hi."

Onyx moved like lightning. One moment he was standing facing the wall, the next he was turned towards me, slightly crouched, one hand extended towards my chest. A very faint hum sounded from his hand, and with my mage's sight I could see the outline of the blade of force ready to be thrown. Looking into the future, I could see it streaking from his fingers and tearing through my chest in a spray of gore. I held quite still.

Then Anne stepped out next to me. Onyx's eyes flicked to her but his hand didn't shift. "Not going to say hello?" I said. My heart was racing and it took an effort to keep my voice casual.

Onyx's eyes shifted between us but he didn't answer. Dressed in black, he stood out against the old, musty room. Bookshelves made it look as though it had once been a library, but most were empty and the carpet smelt of dust. "Relax," I said. I deliberately turned away from Onyx and walked to one of the shelves, taking Anne out of the line of fire. "I'm just here to talk."

Onyx's hand moved to track me, but he didn't turn away from Anne. "Brought some protection?" he said.

"Protection?"

Onyx tilted his head towards Anne and gave me a thin smile. "I'll kill her before she makes it three steps."

I sighed. "Would you please quit the bullshit?"

Onyx held my gaze for a second longer, then lowered his hand, the force blade dissipating. "Okay, I'll play. What do you want?"

"I figure you might be able to help me," I said.

"Go fuck yourself."

"Here's how it is. What Morden sent you here to do is the same thing I'm trying to do right now. Now I don't like you and you don't like me, but for today at least we're on the same side and this'll go a lot faster if we work together."

Onyx curled his lip. "And what are you going to do?"

"I find things out," I said. "It's what I do. You, on the other hand, break things and kill people. I can do things you can't. This is why mages cooperate."

"If I want something from you," Onyx said, "I'll take it."

"And that worked out so well for you last time, didn't it?"

Onyx stared at me. "Let's start small," I said. "You're thinking of cutting through that wall, right?"

Onyx's eyes flicked to the wall to his right before he could catch himself. "What's it to you?"

"It'll set off the same alarm you triggered the last time you trashed this place. The tournament might be keeping the other mages busy, but not *that* busy."

Onyx didn't answer but I saw the future of him carving through the wall with his force magic waver and vanish. I hadn't been able to see many details, but I'd seen enough to know that the reaction would have been instant: that same psychic scream that had come before. "My turn," I said. "If you're thinking of going digging, you're looking for something. What is it?"

Onyx stared at me a moment longer, then gave a tiny shrug. "Bodies."

I relaxed very slightly, though I didn't let myself show it. To my left I could feel Anne watching, keeping silent. "So Morden thinks the missing apprentices are here in Fountain Reach," I said. "Why?"

"You don't need to know."

"He didn't tell you, huh?"

Onyx stared at me again. He had a flat unblinking way of fixing his eyes on someone that was really creepy, like a predator picking out a target. "Why here?" I said.

"Sealed room."

"Then let me find a way in." I moved to the bookcases, studying them.

The wards over Fountain Reach damped all kinds of scrying magic, reducing the range at which I could use my divination. To a new diviner, they'd probably be crippling. But I'm not a new diviner and I hadn't wasted the free time I'd had since getting here. Since I couldn't see as far into the future, I put the energy I would have spent into searching a larger range of short-term futures instead, and as I looked at the bookshelves a thousand future copies of myself studied them in a thousand different ways. I stepped back. "That one."

Onyx gave me a look. "There's a way in behind it," I said, giving it a nod. "The bookcase isn't fixed to the floor. Move it sideways."

Onyx didn't react. "I know you can do it," I said. "I've seen force mages lift ten times that weight."

"You don't tell me what to do."

"Fine. *Please* could you help move that bookcase so we can see what's on the other side?"

Onyx looked as though he was trying to think of a reason to say no, but after a moment he grudgingly twitched a hand. With a creaking, scraping noise the ten-foot bookcase rose and pivoted in midair. Dust bloomed around us and books toppled and fell to the carpet with thumps but the bookcase didn't wobble, held by bands of force. As it twisted away, a door was revealed in the wall. It was faded and looked ancient. "It's locked," I said. "Give me a second and I'll—"

Onyx made a flicking motion and the door burst inwards with a crunch of splintering wood, leaving the lock still attached to the door frame. Beyond were stairs descending into darkness and a clattering sound echoed up to us as the bits of door went bouncing down the stairs to hit the bottom with a double *thud*. "Or you could just do that," I said.

Onyx walked forward and down, disappearing into the gloom.

I waited for Onyx's footsteps to fade away, then looked at Anne. "Might be safer if you stayed out here."

Anne thought for a second and shook her head. "I'd rather go with you."

* * * * * * * * *

The basement at the bottom of the stairs was pitch-dark and silent. The air was dead and foul-smelling; there was obviously no ventilation. I clicked on my torch and its bright white beam revealed benches, shelves, strange equipment. Beakers and boxes were piled around the room and an open doorway led farther in. There was no sign of Onyx.

"What is this place?" Anne whispered.

"Looks like an old lab," I whispered back. Something about the basement made me keep my voice down. I moved to one of the tables and studied the contents, then angled my torch downwards.

"Do you think anyone's here?" Anne whispered.

I moved the splash of light from my torch across the floor. The stone foundations were covered by a thick layer of dust, broken only by the two halves of the door. Onyx's footprints were clearly visible leading through the doorway and there were no others. "We're the first ones to set foot in this place for years."

"So this isn't where the apprentices have gone . . ." Anne said, half to herself. She moved to one of the pieces of equipment resting against the wall. It looked like a giant angled casket made in black iron with odd-shaped pieces protruding. "What are these things?"

"Research equipment," I said. The table held nothing but long-corroded items, and I moved to the shelves. "For magical experiments."

Anne was studying the casket. "I've never seen any that look like this."

"You would have sixty years ago." I focused on the immediate futures of myself searching the shelves and saw a cluster of futures around the right corner where I found something. I moved closer and narrowed it down to a cardboard box on the bottom shelf. "Standard doctrine in the first half of the twentieth century was to use wrought iron for lab gear."

Anne started towards me, then paused, looking towards the archway. "Onyx is coming back."

I opened the box to reveal a stack of dusty papers and notebooks. I lifted them out and gave them to Anne. "Here. Take these and wait upstairs."

"But—"

"I'll catch you up. Quickly."

Anne hesitated, then obeyed. I replaced the lid on the box and gave the room a final quick scan to see if I'd missed anything. A moment later I felt the presence behind me.

Onyx was standing in the doorway. His dark clothes faded into the blackness beyond and the only parts of him that caught the light were his hands and face, pale and still. The torchlight cast his face in shadow and I could see the glint of his eyes as he watched me, waiting.

"Find anything?" I asked.

Onyx said nothing, and something about his eyes and stance sent a chill through me. I was suddenly aware of how alone we were. Nobody else knew we were down here and all the mages were at the tournament. There was Anne and that was why I'd sent her upstairs, but . . .

"Why'd you leave it behind?" Onyx said.

"Leave what?"

"The fateweaver," Onyx said.

I looked at Onyx, deciding how to answer. He looked relaxed and still but I wasn't fooled; I could sense violence lurking in the futures ahead. "You think it should have been you, don't you?" I said.

Onyx stared at me. "You should know better," I said. "What you have is what you can take."

"And right now," Onyx said softly, "I can take anything from you I want."

"Tell me something, Onyx." I met the Dark mage's gaze. "If you had something as powerful as the fateweaver, would you give it up? Or would you make sure you could still use it?"

"You think I'm stupid?"

I just looked at him. I *had* given up the fateweaver. But I know how Dark mages think. Someone like Onyx would never give up that sort of power. And he'd never believe anyone else would do it either.

Onyx started to say something, then stopped. I felt the futures shift and swirl. "So?" I said. "What's it going to be?"

For a long moment Onyx was still, then the futures settled. "I'll see you tomorrow," he said.

I turned and climbed the stairs away from Onyx. My back itched all the way up.

٠٠٠٠٠٠٠٠٠

"Okay," I said into the phone. "No, it isn't . . . Yeah . . . Yeah . . . About ten . . . We're fine . . . I said we're *fine* . . . Look, just be there, okay? . . . Okay. See you then." I hung up.

"That was Sonder, right?" Luna asked.

It was afternoon and the sun was already setting, the short winter's day drawing to a close. Through the window, yellow-gold light painted the lawns and cast long shadows over the trees. Though I still wasn't comfortable in the mansion I was finding that staying in the edge rooms near windows made it easier—the connection to the outside made it feel less oppressive somehow. Anne was sitting cross-legged on the bed while Luna was a safe distance away at the table, the silver mist of her curse moving in lazy arcs around her.

"He's with a team of mages trying to find Yasmin," I said. "They traced her from here to the station and all the way to London, but they lost her in Kings Cross. There was a shroud. Sonder says he's sure it's the same one as before."

"Do they know where she is?" Anne asked. She looked worried.

"Still searching. How's it going?"

"Well, I have no idea what most of this stuff means," Luna said, dropping the folder she'd been holding. The table and bed were covered with the dusty papers we'd taken from the basement. Luna nodded to the bed. "Anne does though."

"Sorry?" Anne seemed to wake up. "Oh. Um . . . I think most of this is life magic research. He doesn't use the same words, but . . ."

"Research into what?"

"Longevity," Anne said. "Life extension."

I frowned. "Why would—?"

I stopped and looked at the door. Footsteps sounded from outside, followed by a knock. I motioned to Luna and Anne to stay where they were and went to open it.

Crystal was standing out in the corridor. She was wearing yet another expensive-looking business suit, this one a dark blue. Her eyes measured me up and down. "Verus."

"Hey there."

"I've received a formal challenge request against you from the Dark mage Onyx." Crystal handed me a slim folder. "Here are the particulars."

I raised an eyebrow, flipped the folder open, and skimmed the contents. "Details of offence . . ." I read aloud. "Damage of property . . . attempted theft of property . . . actual theft of property . . . assault upon his person . . . attempted murder . . . trespass . . ." I glanced up. "Don't remember doing the last one."

"He doesn't seem to like you," Crystal said.

"So I gather." I closed the folder. "You're overseeing the challenge?"

"This is my property," Crystal said coolly. "Do you have a formal reply?"

"I don't have to give one for twenty-four hours, do I?"

"No."

"Okay, it can wait till then."

Crystal frowned slightly. "You don't seem to be taking this very seriously."

"Oh, I am. How long have you lived here, by the way?"

"I don't see how that's relevant."

"Just wondering how you came to move in." I leant against the door, folding my arms.

Crystal studied me for a moment. "Perhaps I might be able to help you."

"That's always nice. How?"

"Onyx's challenge requires my approval to be recognised," Crystal said. She tapped her long nails on the sleeve of her coat. "It would be possible to . . . delay that approval."

"And what were you thinking of in exchange?"

"I would rather the two of you didn't use my house as a battlefield," Crystal said. "You and Onyx seem to get on poorly. It seems to me the best resolution would be for you to leave."

"Sorry. Don't want to miss the tournament."

"There are other tournaments." Crystal studied me. "I would suggest you think it over carefully. Fountain Reach can be . . . inhospitable to those not welcome here."

I returned Crystal's gaze, keeping my mind and expression blank. Crystal turned and walked away without looking back. I watched her go, not relaxing. Only when she was out of sight did I step back into my room and close the door behind me. I leant against the door and folded my arms, staring down at the floor with a frown.

"Alex?" Luna asked. "What's up?"

"Change of plan," I said. "Luna, Anne, I want you to go find out everything you can about Fountain Reach. Who lives here, its past history, what Crystal does here. Try to avoid drawing attention to yourselves if you can but you're apprentices; you can ask a lot of questions before anyone gets really suspicious."

"What about all this?" Luna asked, gesturing to the papers.

"I'll look through them."

"Aren't we going to look for Yasmin?" Anne asked.

"I'm going to be honest," I said. "I don't have any idea how to find Yasmin, not directly. We could go where she was last seen and help Sonder and the mages there try and find her. But I don't think we'd help much. Sonder's better at that kind of thing than I am. Also . . ." I frowned. "Maybe it's just me but I've got the feeling that's exactly what whoever took these apprentices is expecting us to do and that's exactly what they're prepared for. And so far they've done a really thorough job of cleaning up the evidence. But in the meantime a hell of a lot of people have been pointing us towards Fountain Reach and now Crystal's just shown that she wants me out of here. I'm going to start taking them seriously."

Luna and Anne shared a look. "All right," Luna said. "I think I'm supposed to have my first match this evening."

"I'll be there. Go ahead and practice but make sure neither of you goes off alone."

ı ı ı ı ı ı ı ı ı

Once Luna and Anne were gone, I turned my attention to the papers. I've never gone in for magical research, but I've been around mages who have. As Anne had said it was longevity research, which actually made it easier for me to follow—it's not the first time I've seen it.

Life extension tends to be popular amongst mages. Like all people with power, they want to stick around so they can continue using it. At the lower levels, it's not difficult, either—between modern health care and life magic, mages can expect a natural life span well into their nineties. Of course, the actual *practical* life expectancy of mages is a hell of a lot lower than that, due to other mages taking proactive measures to bring down the average, but that's the theory.

Once you get beyond a certain age though, longevity starts getting harder to pull off. The problem is that at a fundamental level humans just aren't designed to live forever. As you get older it becomes more and more difficult to keep a body and mind in working order, until every part is breaking down faster than you can repair it. But this doesn't stop mages from trying, and over the centuries they've tried a *lot* of ways.

From the notes it looked like the author had tried most of them. Some of the avenues were described in detail, others referred to only obliquely, but reading them I got the definite impression that they hadn't been a success. Most longevity spells are based on life magic and it didn't seem as though the mage who'd conducted the research had been able to use life magic at all. Instead he'd tried workarounds that had nearly all turned out to be failures. The more I read, the more I also got the impression that the notes were incomplete. There were references to experiments that didn't seem to have been recorded . . . maybe because they were the kind you don't want written down.

I finished the last stack of papers, thought a bit, then pulled out my phone and called Talisid. He answered after only a few rings. "Verus."

"Hey, Talisid. Who used to live in Fountain Reach before Crystal? Say about sixty years ago?"

"Sixty years?" I could picture Talisid frowning in thought. "The Aubuchons, I would have thought."

"Who were the Aubuchons?"

"An old mage dynasty. Fountain Reach was their family home. Although as I understand it, they tore it down and rebuilt it practically from the ground up."

"When did they move out?"

"Died out, not moved out. The last living member of the family disappeared back in the eighties."

"Huh." I thought for a second. "How did Crystal get it?"

"Oh, that was a couple of years ago. She claimed to be the closest surviving descendant of the Aubuchon family, not that anyone really cared. The place was on the market at the time and she just bought it and moved in."

"How did the White Stone end up being held here this year?"

"Crystal pushed for it. What are you getting at?"

"I'd just like to know a bit more about the place."

"There's absolutely no evidence that Fountain Reach is connected to the disappearances." Talisid's voice was firm. "I know you're not fond of the Council but we're not idiots. You think we'd agree to let Crystal house more than fifty apprentices in a place we weren't confident in?"

"You've checked it?"

"Every one of the disappearances was cross-checked against Fountain Reach before the decision was made to host the tournament there. In every case we found absolutely no connection. In fact, the conclusion reached was that the gate wards would make Fountain Reach one of the safest possible locations in England. It was the principal reason that it was chosen."

"What about Yasmin?"

"We've narrowed Yasmin's disappearance to Kings Cross in London. She might have been at Fountain Reach earlier that night but she wasn't there when she vanished."

"Unless she was taken back."

"Do you have any evidence that she was?"

I was silent for a moment. "No."

"Verus, are you sure you're in the right place?" Talisid sounded sceptical. "I didn't question your plan to go to Fountain Reach but the majority of the disappearances have been in London and they aren't stopping. We could use you here."

"You got me for this job because you trusted my judgement," I said. "No, I'm not sure. But it's my best guess."

Talisid sighed. "All right. If you want to keep following this lead, I'll dig up what I can find about the last people to live in Fountain Reach and pass it on. I hope it leads you somewhere."

So do I. "Thanks."

| | | | | | | | | |

Hours passed. I searched, but found nothing. There was an urgency to it now; I had the sense that I was running out of time. As seven o'clock drew near I went to the duelling hall.

The hall was packed with mages and apprentices: dozens of competitors and five times that number there to watch. To one side two apprentices were sparring with focus swords, the inactive weapons striking each other with a *clack-clack-clack*. An older mage was giving some sort of demonstration to a group of apprentices, an illusory duel painted in blue-white light playing out in the air between them, while the mages placed in charge strolled around importantly calling out names. The hall was filled with noise and energy and at the far end a board showed the list of matchups. The two duelling pistes had been cleared, and spectators had already started to gather around them.

Lyle appeared from the crowd as I crossed the hall, looking from side to side. I'd known he was at the tournament but it was the first time I'd seen him here. "Oh, Verus," he said. He seemed distracted. "Have you seen Crystal?"

"Not recently."

Lyle walked past. I gave him a curious glance and kept going.

Luna was standing alone in a corner. She was fiddling with her focus weapon, flipping the whip handle between her fingers without seeming aware of it, and she gave me a grateful look as she caught sight of me. "Who are you up against?" I asked.

Luna nodded past me. I followed her gaze to see a tall, strongly built, good-looking girl with blond hair tied up in a bun. She was carrying a slim staff about three feet long and she was listening and nodding to an unsmiling older woman who seemed to be giving her instructions. "Her name's Ekaterina."

I looked at Luna, saw the way she was standing. "Relax."

"What if I mess up?"

"It's just a match."

"*They* don't think it's just a match," Luna said. "Everyone takes this really seriously. And . . . That girl's going to be a mage, right? I'm just an adept. How am I supposed to fight something like that?"

"Mages are still human."

Luna gave a short laugh. "Easy for you to say."

"You've stood up to mages before."

"And every time I do it I get kicked around like a football."

"Hm." I studied Luna. "Might be time to change that. Back in a sec."

I crossed the floor towards Ekaterina and the woman. As soon as I got close they stopped their conversation and turned to watch me. "Hey there," I said.

"You are Verus," the woman said with a slight accent. She was maybe fifty, with a hard unsmiling face.

"Good to meet you." I picked up a focus weapon from a nearby table, a dagger, and spun it in my hand. "Looking forward to the match?"

The woman's eyes narrowed slightly, and Ekaterina stepped into a defensive stance. To my mage's sight light brown energy flared around her, and I saw the staff pulse slightly. I looked into the futures in which I attacked Ekaterina, seeing the outcomes.

"What do you want?" the woman asked. She was standing at the ready, watching me suspiciously.

"Just saying hello." I put the dagger back on the table and gave them a smile. "Nice to meet you."

I walked back to Luna. "Okay," I said once I was close enough. "Ekaterina's an earth mage. Remember that guy we ran into in Tiger's Palace?"

"Yes . . ."

"Same sort of thing. Augmentation to physical strength, defensive reinforcement of her body. If she lands a hit she'll probably knock you out so don't let her. You have two advantages. First, your whip gives you range—she can use ranged earth magic but she obviously isn't comfortable with it or she wouldn't be relying on that focus weapon. Second, all her defences are designed to counter physical attacks. She doesn't have an answer to your curse."

Luna had been staring at me. "Okay, so . . . I keep my distance and try and hit her?"

"You're going to have to get used to facing mages sooner or later," I said. "This is good practice. And I think you've got a good chance."

A stir of movement from the end of the room made me look around. People were gathering around one of the pistes. "What number are you?" I asked.

"Fifth," Luna said. "Variam's second."

I caught a glimpse of Variam through the crowd; he was alone, holding an oddly shaped sword, and seemed to be searching for someone. I slowed and Luna moved ahead of me, her attention on the match. I frowned; something was nagging at me.

I looked around the hall. It was crowded with people, and everyone was drifting in the direction of the second piste. All the attention was on the duel. Variam was about to start his match. Luna was busy with hers. And I should be busy with Luna's. All of us were busy, our attention somewhere . . .

. . . where was Anne?

I hesitated for only an instant. Luna was my apprentice and I wanted to be there to watch, but this might be important. I looked through the crowd, searching for Anne, but she wasn't there. I moved towards the edge of the room, catching a glimpse of her through the futures—

And suddenly Anne was right in front of me. While I'd been looking for her, she'd been looking for me. "Alex?" Anne said in her soft voice. "Can you help me with something?"

"What's happened?"

"There's someone who says he knows about the people who used to live here in Fountain Reach," Anne said. "He agreed to meet me but only if we do it right now."

I glanced back at the duelling hall. I could hear someone announcing the names for the first match but the crowds blocked my view of Luna. To one side I caught a glimpse of Crystal standing on a podium with arms folded, watching. "Let's go."

ı ı ı ı ı ı ı ı ı

"His name's Hobson," Anne explained as we threaded our way through the maze of Fountain Reach, searching for the way out. From behind I could hear the murmur of sound from the duelling hall, but the corridors were deserted. Everyone in the mansion was at the match. "He said he used to work here."

"How'd you find him?" I said.

"I didn't," Anne said simply. "Sonder did."

"Oh," I said. It made sense. Luna and I got to know Anne because Sonder asked her to second for Luna's apprenticeship ceremony. I was starting to figure out how Anne was so well informed—she just talked to everyone. "How?"

"I rang Sonder and asked if there was anyone I could talk to who knew about Fountain Reach," Anne said. "He called me with Hobson's number and I called Hobson." Anne hesitated. "He was . . . I think Hobson was nervous. He didn't want to talk at first, but at the end he said he'd come meet me at the motorway services."

"How are you getting there, by car?"

Anne nodded.

I remembered Jagadev's silver Bentley and the hunched figure I'd glimpsed behind the wheel. "Is that same guy driving you?"

Anne nodded again. "He's out there now."

We came into the entry hall. It was filled with long tables and side doors led off into reception areas and a coatroom. I thought about what to do. I could catch a lift in Jagadev's car but some instinct warned me against that. Besides, if Hobson was nervous he'd be more likely to talk to Anne if she was alone. "Wait five minutes, then have him go," I said. "I'll follow you to the meeting. Hopefully nothing'll happen, but I'll stay close in case it does."

Anne nodded and left. As soon as she was gone I headed into the coatroom. Most of the guests at the mansion had moved into their rooms but there were still a few dozen coats, bags, and jackets lying around. I scanned them quickly, then walked to one of the coats and pulled a set of keys out of one of the pockets before turning to leave.

Variam was standing in the doorway. He was carrying his focus sword in his right hand down by his side, and he was staring at me. "What are you doing?"

"Getting my car keys," I said. I walked towards the door. "Haven't you got a match?"

Variam moved to block my path. "Where's Anne?"

"Go ask her."

Variam narrowed his eyes and I felt magic stir around him. The sword in his right hand was broad and heavy-looking and I could sense he was ready to use it. "I don't have time for this," I said flatly. "Anne's going to talk to someone and I'm going to make sure she gets there safe. If you're not going to help, get out of my way." I brushed past Variam and headed for the door.

Futures of Variam attacking flickered ahead of me and I tensed, ready to dodge . . . and then he hurried after me. "I'm coming with you."

I really didn't want Variam along but I didn't have time to argue and having him start a fight now would cause a delay I couldn't afford. "Then follow me and shut up."

The front drive of Fountain Reach was dark, only the lights of the windows illuminating the rows of cars. The sun had long set, the sky was overcast and shadowed, and the countryside around us was pitch-black. To anyone else it would have felt like stepping from light into darkness but for me it was the opposite; as I crossed the threshold of Fountain Reach the oppressive blanket of the wards fell away and I could see clearly again.

It took me only a second to pick out Jagadev's Bentley, its engine off but the driver sitting in his seat, parked in a spot out of sight of the front door. I turned away and started down the rows of cars, letting my feet down quietly on the gravel. Variam followed behind. I could feel his gaze on me, close and suspicious, but he didn't speak. I held the keys in my hand and concentrated and the futures of me trying them in every car in the driveway unfolded before me. In one of them the key turned and I headed towards it, the other futures fading away.

Anne reappeared just as we reached the car, carrying a coat over one arm. She walked past us in the darkness and to the Bentley. The window rolled down and I saw her bend down to speak with the driver. The inside of the car lit up as Anne got into the backseat and the engine started with a growl, loud in the empty night. It pulled out of the driveway with a crunch of gravel, lights disappearing behind the hedge.

The instant it was out of sight I hit the button on the set of keys and pulled open the door of the car next to us. Lights illuminated a set of angled leather seats and a sleek-looking dashboard. As I slotted in the key the car's onboard electronics started up and the instruments and wheel lit up in pale blue. A gearshift dial rose up out of the centre console and the engine started with a muted purr.

Variam slid into the seat next to me, looking around incredulously. "This is your car?"

"I'm in it, aren't I?" I looked quickly through the futures and typed in a code to deactivate the alarm system, then took off the hand brake and turned the dial to first gear. The Jaguar rolled out smoothly in the direction the other car had gone.

"Jeez." Variam sat back in disgust. "You mages love to flash your money, don't you?"

"Put on your seatbelt."

chapter 10

'm only a mediocre driver. I never learnt to do it until I was past twenty, and what with relying on Starbreeze and gate magic so much for travel I haven't had much practice since then. Luckily my divination magic lets me cheat—when you know exactly what will and won't make you crash it's easy not to hit anything. It didn't make the ride any smoother, though.

We followed Anne through the winding country lanes, rushing through the darkness. I didn't turn on my lights, relying on my magic to keep to the lines of the road as well as to keep track of the smudge of light up ahead that was the Bentley. As we headed south, back roads turned into B-roads and then A-roads until we came out onto the great winding length of the M4.

Once we were on the motorway, tailing Anne's car became easier. Despite the darkness of the winter evening it wasn't late, and there were plenty of cars to give us cover. Under the harsh orange glow of the motorway lights I pulled in one car behind the Bentley and held distance. After only a few minutes a green sign flashed by that read *Services 1 mile*. The Bentley pulled into the left lane and began signalling, and I followed. A red-and-white *Little Chef* sign flashed by and was gone.

The services were contained in a single large building surrounded by banks of grass, a petrol station, and a huge car park. Light shone from the windows, the surrounding trees muting the glow and noise from the motorway. By the time I'd parked and turned off the engine, Anne had already left the Bentley and was walking towards the building. I scanned for danger, found nothing, and followed her, Variam trailing behind.

The inside of the building had the vaguely soulless feel that motorway service stations always seem to have. The floor was linoleum, the lights were too bright, and the shops sold snacks and drinks and travel gear at about three times their actual value. Everything smelt of plastic and disinfectant. "Where is she?" Variam asked.

I turned left into the cafeteria. It wasn't packed but it wasn't empty either, and there were just enough people to give us some cover. Mothers kept a watchful eye over children while truckers drank from mugs of tea. "Hey," Variam said. "I said—"

"To your right," I said, then blocked Variam as he turned to look. "*Don't* stare. Buy something and sit down."

Variam glowered but didn't argue. He'd at least had the sense to wrap his sword up in his jacket. I bought something at the counter without paying attention to what it was and found a corner seat shielded by a big plastic children's area. Only then did I look over.

Anne was sitting at a table on the far side of the cafeteria. The edge of the services was a huge plate-glass window looking out onto the car park, and Anne's table was right next to it, bright against the darkness. Sitting opposite Anne was a man with grey-white hair wearing a thick coat with the collar turned up to shield his face. I couldn't get a good look at him but he was talking to Anne.

"Who's she talking to?" Variam said.

"Apparently his name's Hobson." I scanned through the futures but couldn't see any danger. In every sequence of events the services was filled with nothing but the bustle of travellers.

"Why are you following Anne?" Variam said.

"I already told you."

"What are you getting out of it?"

I didn't bother answering. Anne and Hobson weren't far away and I could have used my magic to eavesdrop if I focused on it, but I didn't. Instead I kept my attention on a short-to-medium-range scan, watching for danger. If anything moved to threaten Anne I wanted to know about it.

We sat for a little while in silence. Around us, people came and went. "Why'd you help her?" Variam asked.

I didn't take my eyes off Anne. "When?"

"Three nights ago. With those men."

"What's your problem with me, Variam?"

"You're a mage."

"So are you."

Variam scowled. "You know what?" I said. "Fine. It's not like they're going to be finished any time soon. I'll tell you why I helped Anne if you tell me how the two of you ended up with Jagadev."

Variam was silent. "Fine," he said at last. "Why'd you help her?"

"Because she needed it."

Variam waited. "And?" he said when I didn't go on.

"That's it."

"Bullshit—"

"What were you expecting me to say?" I said. "Mages can look after themselves; apprentices can't."

Variam looked at me narrowly. "I don't believe you."

At the other side of the cafeteria Anne was still talking to Hobson. She was sitting opposite him, leaning slightly forward with hands clasped, listening attentively. As I watched she took out a pad of paper and started writing, pausing every few seconds to glance up. Hobson seemed to be doing most of the talking, but his hand movements were jerky and at intervals he'd look back over his shoulder. Watching his body language I could tell he was nervous, afraid of something, but there was no danger . . . yet. "Your turn," I said to Variam. I didn't take my attention off Anne and Hobson. "You and Anne used to be apprenticed to a Dark mage named Sagash, right?"

Variam stared at me. *"Apprenticed?"*

"Is that true?"

"Is that—?! I'd rip out my own liver before being apprentice to that bastard. You mages talk so much shit. If you knew—!"

"Knew what?"

"You know how we met Sagash?" Variam demanded. "He kidnapped Anne right out of school. Used gate magic to take her away to some huge freaky castle in the middle of nowhere. He wanted her as his apprentice and when she said no he tried to make her."

I looked at Variam, keeping quiet. "There was someone who said he could help," Variam said. "A 'Light' mage, or that was what he called himself, guy called Ebber. Know what that little weasel did? He went and talked things over with Sagash and decided it was all just fine. He said we were better off like that!" Variam stared past me. "She was in that place for months."

"Did you break her out?" I asked.

"No," Variam said reluctantly. He sounded as if he didn't like to admit it. "She did. But I helped her get away. And we gave that bastard Sagash something to think about before we left."

I looked over at Anne. She was writing on the pad, listening carefully to what Hobson said. "What did Ebber do?"

Variam gave a snort. "Oh, he was pissed. More upset about us running away than he was about Sagash kidnapping her. Would have taken us back if he could."

"And that was when Jagadev came to you," I said. "He offered you protection, told you that as long as you stayed with him mages like Sagash and Ebber wouldn't bother you. And you convinced Anne."

"Yeah, so?" Variam looked at me, challenging. "That's how it works in your world, right? If you're not with someone, some mage like you can just pick you off. Well, we're with him."

I met Variam's gaze. He looked angry and I was pretty sure he wasn't lying. He might be exaggerating . . . but unfortunately nothing in his story was even the slightest bit hard to believe. Dark mages *do* press-gang apprentices. They won't usually touch one under the protection of another mage, but a teenager new to their powers and alone and ignorant of the magical world is easy prey. And once you're in, leaving is not an option.

Under Council law, a Light apprentice can't be forced to take the oaths. But Dark mages have no such laws. And once a Dark mage has got their claws into someone, precious few

Light mages are willing to take the risks involved in rescuing them. Much easier to turn a blind eye and smooth things over—it's not worth risking the peace treaty for one apprentice, is it? And once you've gone that far, it's really not that big an extra step to give the Dark mages a little bit of quiet assistance. After all, contacts on the other side are very useful and if you don't help them get an apprentice back they're just going to go to someone else . . .

It's easy to hate all Light mages for the actions of a few, and I've fallen into that trap myself in the past. But the world's more complicated than that. "You know," I said, "just because some mages act like that doesn't mean they all do."

"Right," Variam said with a sneer. "All the *others* are bad but you're the good guy."

"Not exactly."

Variam shook his head. "You don't have a clue what it's like. None of you do."

"You might be surprised," I said mildly.

"Bullshit. You get invitations to parties, you get guys like Talisid showing up to offer you jobs. You're part of the club; you don't know how hard it is for us."

I started to answer, then paused. *So you know it was Talisid who gave me the job? Interesting.* "So why do you think I took the job?"

"You want the apprentices for yourselves, right? You don't care what happens to them. You only help them if they're yours."

"You and Anne aren't mine," I said.

"So?"

"If I only care about apprentices who are mine, what am I doing here?"

"How should I know?"

"I'm just trying to make you see the logic here," I said. "By your reasoning, if I treat you cruelly like Sagash, then that means I'm self-serving and don't care about you. But if I'm nice and try to help you, then that means I must have some evil hidden purpose which *also* means I'm self-serving and don't care about you. Is that about right?"

Variam just glowered. "Whatever."

"They're going," I said, looking up.

Hobson had left the table and was hurrying away. I watched him curiously. Up until I'd arrived at the services I'd been more than half-expecting a trap, if for no other reason than that I remembered very clearly what had happened the *last* time Anne had been driven somewhere alone in that Bentley. But Hobson's behaviour didn't fit with that. Acting scared and nervous, okay—but he'd asked Anne to come to a public place, somewhere that would be crowded even at this late hour. That was the kind of thing you'd do if *you* were worried about a trap.

But if Hobson wasn't involved himself, that meant . . .

Anne had risen and was just leaving via the services' front doors. "Come on," I said to Variam, and walked quickly after her.

I was halfway there when I felt something shift in the futures ahead. I took one glance at them and broke into a run. The automatic doors slid open in front of me as I ran out into the night.

Anne was halfway across the car park, a slim shadow against the dark lines of cars, just about to turn down one of the rows. "Anne!" I shouted from behind her.

Anne stopped, turned. I kept running towards her. I couldn't see her face, but I knew she was looking at me in surprise. "Alex?"

"Behind you!" I shouted.

Anne turned back just as the figure flicked into view behind her. Her eyes went wide and she jumped out of reach as the shape reached out, grasping.

A second later I slammed into it. The darkness hid the creature's features; it had the silhouette of a human but was heavier. We both went down and hit the tarmac and I rolled away fast, staying out of reach.

A second figure stepped out of the darkness right next to Anne, reaching for her neck. I'd seen it coming and aimed a kick from the ground that took out its knee. The second one hit the ground next to the first and I scrambled to my feet, backing away with Anne. "Variam!" I shouted. "They're constructs, destroy them!"

Both constructs were rising to their feet and in the futures ahead of us I could see the paths they would take, solid lines of light changing to match our actions but without choice or initiative of their own. One was still locked onto Anne; the other was heading for me. But it took them a few seconds to reach us and Variam got there first.

Mages of Variam's type are called fire mages, but that's not really what they do. Their real power is over heat: generating it, controlling it, moving it. It's true that most fire mages *do* use fire in their spells, but that's as much psychological as anything; fire is what they think of, so that's what they create. Variam's approach was a little different. Instead of creating bolts of fire or some kind of flamethrower, he just poured a ton of heat into the area right between the two constructs.

Fire magic's not subtle and it's not great at defence, but for sheer destructive power there's not much that can beat it. There was a hissing sound and a *thump* of superheated air, a backwash of heat making me cover my eyes. When I opened them again the constructs were gone. A five-foot circle of tarmac where they'd been standing was steaming, and the corners of two car fenders that had been in the blast were glowing a faint yellow and starting to droop.

"Where'd they go?" Variam said in surprise.

"I don't know." I looked around. I could see figures in the darkness of the car park but they were too far away, and as I concentrated I saw that they had the branching futures of humans. "I—Anne, move!"

Anne started and tried to jump away, but this time she wasn't quick enough. One of the constructs seized her from behind, and a second later the other did the same to me.

Constructs move, but they aren't alive—they're dead things animated by magic, created to fulfil a certain purpose. All constructs are built with a guidance program, and once a construct's been given a command it'll keep going until the task's completed. They're strong—stronger than any human—but that's not what makes them so dangerous. A construct can't feel pain or fear or boredom. They don't get hurt, they don't get tired, and most of all they *don't stop*. If you get away from one, it'll just keep coming. The only way to stop a construct is to completely destroy it, either by breaking the spell that animates it or by doing such massive damage to its body that it can't physically hold together anymore.

But for all their power, constructs have limits. They can't draw conclusions, they can't take initiative, and they can't use tactics or prediction or deception. You can't program a construct to outsmart an opponent; you can only make it stronger or tougher or faster.

The construct that had grabbed me from behind was trying to break my neck, and if I'd given it even the smallest chance it would have succeeded. But it wasn't the first time I'd had a construct try to kill me and I've learnt from painful experience what works and doesn't. As the construct reached for my neck I twisted to one side, pulling it off balance and levering its hand away. Someone who knew how to fight would have recognised the move and countered it, but the construct didn't understand the concept of leverage and just kept trying to pull me in and crush me. I went with the movement and turned it into a throw, slamming the construct to the tarmac. The twisting motion pulled the thing's grip loose and I jumped back again out of range.

I felt a surge of magic and looked back at Variam and Anne. The other construct was gone and Variam was standing against Anne with his sword out, staring into the darkness. "Variam!" I snapped.

Variam looked at me, confused. "I don't get it. I hit him but—"

The second construct pulled itself up and went for us again. Variam narrowed his eyes and stepped forward, orange-red light flickering about his upraised hand. A pulse of heat exploded with a hissing thump from the centre of the construct's chest, hot enough to ignite the air in a flash.

An instant before the spell hit, the construct vanished and we were alone in the darkness. "What the *hell*?" Variam said. "I hit him!"

Anne was looking around, and as she did her eyes widened. "Vari, Alex! It's over—!"

I threw one of my condensers to shatter against the tarmac and grabbed Variam and Anne. As the cloud of fog rushed out around us I dragged both of them to one side.

An instant later the two constructs reappeared in the fog cloud. I couldn't see them but with my divination I knew where they were. Their futures were static lines of light—without any sign of where we were they were just going to stand there until—

"Let go!" Variam said angrily.

"*Shh!*"

The lines of light changed direction as both constructs moved, converging on the sound. Their heavy footfalls were audible and Variam tensed and shut up as I pulled him to one side. Anne stayed quiet, trusting me to lead her. The constructs reached the point where the noise had come from, only five feet away—and stopped.

I kept leading Variam and Anne away and this time Variam thankfully kept his mouth shut. The constructs didn't move; without sensory input their simple programming couldn't predict our movements. We came out of the fog cloud into the night, and now that Anne and Variam could see me I put a finger to my lips, ushering them towards the car.

"What's—?" Variam said once we were fifty feet away.

"Gate magic," I said, keeping my voice low. "Short-range teleport." Looking back I could see the patch of mist, weirdly out of place in the car park. The constructs were still standing motionless inside it—then as I watched they vanished. "Crap." I broke into a run. "Come on!"

We piled into the car. I started the engine and the gearshift dial rose up with a whirr. "Where are they?" Variam asked Anne.

"I don't know! They're not alive, I can't—"

One of the constructs blinked into view just in front of the car. I'd had a second's warning and as it appeared I stomped on the accelerator. With a roar the Jaguar leapt forward, ramming the construct with a hollow *thump* and sending it flying. I braked instantly, throwing Variam and Anne into the back of the seats, and pulled out into the car park. The second construct appeared an instant later, grabbing for the door, but I swung the car away and it caught only air. A green *EXIT* sign flashed up in the headlights and I turned towards it, accelerating and putting a row of cars between us and the constructs.

The exit road was dark and led around the side of the services, past the petrol station and back towards the M4. Anne reached to touch my shoulder from the backseat and a soft green glow sprang up as I felt the energy of a spell flow through me. The adrenaline racing through my body levelled off, and my fatigue vanished as my reflexes sharpened. Suddenly I could see the road more clearly and correcting the car seemed easier. "Thanks." I pulled my phone out of my pocket one-handed and handed it over my shoulder to her. "Anne, find Sonder and call him. Variam, keep watch out the back. We haven't lost those things."

"They've got a car?" Variam asked. He was peering out the back window.

"They don't need one—"

Variam said something in an angry voice. I didn't know the language, but the meaning came across loud and clear and I glanced up at the mirror to see that two figures had appeared in the shadows behind, running after us. As I watched they vanished and reappeared closer, still running. "Hang on," I said, and put my foot down. The Jaguar's engine roared eagerly and carried us out onto the M4.

The motorway was flat and slightly curved, hills and trees visible to either side in the darkness. Lights shone down from above, casting everything in orange-yellow except for the pinpoint reflections of the cat's-eyes marking the lanes. It was late but the M4 is the major artery linking England and Wales and all three lanes were dotted with cars. I pulled from the left lane into the centre and then into the right. A few seconds later I saw the constructs burst out onto the motorway behind us, running along the hard shoulder before teleporting a few hundred feet forward, still running.

"Hello?" Anne said from behind me. "Sonder? Alex, I've got him!"

"Hold it here!" I swerved between the cars. The Jaguar was doing more than eighty miles per hour but in the mirror I could see that the constructs were still closing on us. They'd sprint for a couple of seconds, then blink forward, hit the ground running, and keep going. For all our speed, they were catching up fast.

Anne scrambled over the gearshift into the passenger seat and held the phone to my ear. "Sonder," I said, keeping one eye on the side mirror. "We're being chased by two teleporting constructs trying to kill us. Need some suggestions."

"Teleporting—Wait, you mean—?"

"Yes."

"Are they—?"

"Just vanishing and reappearing."

"Um." I could imagine Sonder pushing his glasses up. "You know, I think—"

I leapfrogged an Escort that was blocking the fast lane, pulled the Jaguar around a station wagon ahead of us, and slid back in again, ignoring the angry blare of horns. "Fast would be good."

"Screw this," Variam said. "Open the roof!"

I hit a button on the dashboard and the sunroof whirred back, filling the car with a rush of cold air. Variam pulled himself up, standing on the backseat, and turned towards where the constructs were running. Fire magic surged and I felt the pulse of a heat burst behind and to my left.

"Um," Sonder said over the phone. "Okay. Well, there was a fashion back in the early twentieth century for making constructs with an imbued spell. The idea was they'd be able to use their one spell in the same sort of way as an adept, but it eventually fell out of favour because—"

"*Sonder.* How do we kill them?"

Again I felt the pulse of Variam's heat spells and again I heard him swear. I risked a quick glance away from the road to the left but I couldn't see the constructs. We'd entered a band of heavier traffic that was forcing me to keep my speed down. "Well, theoretically—" Sonder began.

The two constructs blinked in on top of us, one after another. With my second's warning I was able to swerve away from the first. It appeared to our left at road level and grabbed for the car but missed.

The second appeared an instant later while I was still recovering from the swerve. It landed on the Jaguar's hood with a *thump*, blocking my view, and turned to face us.

Anne drew in her breath in a gasp. For the first time I got a clear look at the construct; it had the form of an adult man in cast-off clothing with a blank face and dead eyes. Ignoring Variam, it locked its eyes on Anne and raised a fist to punch through the windscreen.

I stomped on the brakes and the Jaguar slowed in a sudden screech of tyres. The construct clutched at the smooth hood, but there was nothing to grab and it went flying head over heels. It slammed into the motorway ahead of us, rolling over and over. From behind I heard another screech of brakes and I hit the accelerator again. The construct finished rolling, looked up to see the Jaguar about to run it down . . . and vanished in a blink as we shot through the space he'd been in.

"Did you get him?" Variam called.

"No. Did you?"

"No! Every time I'm close they just—"

Horns were blaring from behind. I'd lost sight of the constructs but I could see a traffic jam in the mirrors; it looked like cars were slowing down to avoid something. Anne put the phone back to my ear and I heard Sonder's voice. "—lex? Alex, are you there?"

"Sonder, we need some ideas," I said. "Every time we're about to hit these things they just gate out and I don't know how long we can keep dodging them."

"Um," Sonder said. "Well, theoretically it should take a lot of energy to keep running that spell. They shouldn't be as tough as normal constructs."

"That's great; how are we supposed to *hit* them?"

I caught a flash of movement in my right mirror. A figure was running along the right side of the motorway by the divider; as I watched it vanished and reappeared much closer. "Variam!" I called and pointed.

Variam pulled himself back up and I felt him aiming another fire spell. "Can you tell what their primary sensory input is?" Sonder asked.

"What?"

"Well, there has to be something that triggers their evasion routine. When they teleport away, is it based on visual data, auditory data, tactile—?"

"How in the name of all that is holy am I supposed to know that?"

"Um . . . You could try attacking them with methods that can only be detected by one type of sense. Then based on which ones they dodge you could—"

"Are you serious?"

Bursts of heat erupted in the path of the construct chasing us but it blinked away, getting closer each time. As it pulled level with our car I cut left into the middle lane, using the stream of traffic as a shield. I had to slow down to do it and for an instant the construct was roughly level with us, its head turned to look into the car as it ran. Variam focused his energy for another spell, aiming to blanket its area, and Sonder started saying something else over the phone.

The construct teleported into the car.

There was a chorus of screams, one of which might have been mine. Variam's spell went off, the car swerved, and there was one frantic moment in which the car was on course to smash right into the side of a container truck. I pulled it back as the construct's long arms came reaching around the passenger seat, grasping for Anne's throat. Anne ducked and the fingers latched onto her hair instead; she yelped as the construct started dragging her back.

Variam was still standing on the backseat, half out of the sunroof. He turned and stomped on the construct's arms. The first kick made it bend at an impossible angle; the second broke its grip. I tried to turn to help and nearly crashed the car; I couldn't fight and drive the Jaguar at the same time. As Variam kept kicking at the construct and it turned its attention to him I hit the speed control setting, grabbed Anne's hand, and put it on the wheel. "You're driving!" Anne's eyes were wide, but she pulled herself up, trying to watch the road ahead and the construct behind at the same time.

The construct got a grip on Variam's leg and broke it with a snap. Variam screamed as the construct started to pull him in. I twisted to reach over into the backseat and jammed both thumbs into the construct's eyes, trying to gouge them out. The construct couldn't feel pain, but it reacted to the loss of sight, letting go of Variam and grabbing me. Its grip was like steel and I was yanked over the gearshift. "Variam!" I shouted as the construct forced my hands away and its dead eyes turned to focus on me. One of its hands went for my throat and I tried desperately to force it away. "Use the sword!"

Variam was crumpled in the corner of the car, his leg bent at a horrible angle, but as the construct started to drag me in he fumbled out the flat-bladed sword and channelled his magic through it. The inside of the car flashed orange-yellow, and I felt a surge of heat as the blade lit up with fire and Variam drove it straight for the construct's body.

The construct vanished as the tip touched it. I fell onto the blade, felt it scorch through my clothes and into my arm, and pulled back with a gasp of pain. An instant later the heat cut off and Variam fell back against the edge of the car. My left arm was burnt but I gritted my teeth and scrambled back into the driver's seat, taking the wheel back from Anne. "Help Variam!"

Anne climbed back into the rear seat as I checked the futures. As I did my heart jumped—the other construct was about to do the exact same thing. In a few seconds it would appear ahead of us and in one more it would blink in right on top of Anne and Variam. I held my left hand back without taking my eyes off the road. "Sword!"

There was an instant's pause, then I felt the handle land in my palm. The blade was heavy and awkward to lift with only one hand. I kept my feet on the pedals and my right hand on the wheel and as the construct came into view ahead of us, I thrust the sword into the space the construct was going to teleport into.

The construct blinked in and out—somewhere else. I felt the gate magic redirect and instead of dropping into the passenger seat and onto the waiting sword the construct appeared five feet up, right on the Jaguar's roof. The rushing air snatched it instantly off its feet and it went flying over the sunroof to hit the motorway behind. In my mirror I caught a glimpse of it rolling over and over behind us, and then the Toyota that had been following us hit it square on with a soggy *thud*. The construct's head snapped back and it vanished under the wheels and was gone. From behind came the screech of brakes.

"Variam!" I called. "Are you okay?"

"Fine," Variam said through gritted teeth. I could feel Anne's healing magic working behind me but didn't turn to look.

"Anne, where's the phone?"

Anne sounded distracted. "I dropped it. Alex, I need to concentrate."

I dropped the sword and bent down to grab the phone instead, driving blind for a second. "Sonder?" I said, straightening up.

"Alex!" Sonder sounded relieved. "You're okay?"

"Not for long. These things are tearing us up." Wind roared through the sunroof and I could see a traffic jam developing behind us. The constructs hadn't reappeared but I knew they hadn't given up and I didn't think we'd survive another attack like the last one. "Ideas?"

"I don't know! Um . . . Have you managed to damage them?"

"Well, we hit them with a car a few times but it doesn't seem to have slowed them down much." A sign went by overhead indicating a turnoff, and I pulled into the left lane, driving right-handed.

"Okay, so they're not programmed to avoid physical impact?"

"No, they— Wait. When I was about to run that one over a minute ago, it *did* avoid it."

"So they do—Alex?"

I thought fast. I'd managed to hit one with the Jaguar

back in the car park. But when one had gated onto the hood, it had gated away again when I tried to run it down afterwards. But then that last one *hadn't* gated away before being run over by the Toyota behind me . . .

Time. The one that had landed on the hood had had longer. "Sonder. How much energy would it take to do one of these teleports?"

"Um, a lot. That was why they stopped building—"

"Could it teleport and then teleport again half a second later?"

"Um . . . I'm not sure. I don't think so. The construct's internal energy reserves should need at least a couple of seconds to recharge between—"

"Perfect."

"What? Alex? Hello?"

I dropped the phone onto the seat and pulled the car into the turnoff. It was a motorway layover, just a small enclave on the side of the road with a public bathroom, surrounded by woods. Nobody else was there. I brought the Jaguar to a stop and the engine died away with a fading growl. Outside on the M4 the cars swept past with a rush of air, the swooshing sound muffled through the car. "Anne," I said. "Can Variam walk?"

"I need more time." Turning around, I saw that Anne was bent over Variam, green light glowing around her hands as she held his broken leg. She was concentrating and didn't turn to look. "Give me a few minutes."

"Can't." I got out and pulled the passenger door open. Variam looked up distractedly and I held out a hand. "Grab on," I told him. "I'm carrying you."

"Wait!" Anne said. "He's—"

"We've got sixty seconds until those constructs catch up."

Variam's face was pale from shock but he gave me one

look and nodded. I reached down and picked Variam up with a heave; his fingers tightened on my arms and I knew it must have hurt, but he didn't make a sound. "Bring the sword," I told Anne as I hurried into the woods.

There was a small clearing just twenty feet into the trees. Bits of garbage were scattered around from previous visitors, and the glow of the motorway lights was muted. I set Variam down against an ash tree. "Your weapon," I told Variam. "Can you channel through it when you're not touching it?"

"I—yeah. Why?"

"When I call, do it." Anne made as if to go to Variam, but I turned and blocked her. "No."

Anne looked at me in frustration. "At least let me—"

"If you want to help him, keep your distance," I said quietly. "I need you to do something dangerous."

"What?"

"Bait." I looked steadily at her. "These things are after you. They only attack us when we get in their way, and their targeting resets every time they lose sight of us. I need you to stand next to me and not move until I tell you."

Anne looked from me to Variam, and I felt the two of them share a glance. Then Variam gave a small nod. I took the sword from Anne and walked to the centre of the clearing. The sword was oddly shaped and didn't look like any weapon I'd seen; the blade was wide and heavy, broadening slightly from the hilt to the tip before narrowing abruptly to a blunt point. I walked to the centre of the clearing and moved the sword from side to side, feeling the weight of the blade. "Designed for cutting, right?" I asked Variam absently.

"Yeah." I could hear the tension in Variam's voice.

Anne moved beside me. "Do you trust me?" I asked her quietly.

In the shadows it was hard to make out Anne's expression, but I could sense she was watching me. ". . . Yes."

"Don't move," I said. "When I press down on your shoulder, get out of the way as fast as you can."

Anne nodded. I took a stance in the middle of the clearing, most of my weight on my back leg with Variam's sword held down by my side, and rested my left hand on Anne's shoulder. She didn't tremble but held still. Ten feet away against the tree Variam watched, tense. The only light in the woods was the orange-yellow glow of the motorway lights, broken up with the shadows of the trees. There was no sound but the steady *swoosh* of the cars. The air was cold and smelt of exhaust smoke and dried leaves.

I closed my eyes.

The flicker of gate magic came right when it was supposed to. I pushed on Anne's shoulder but she was already moving, ducking down and away. As the construct blinked in, reaching out for where Anne had been a second ago, I called "Variam!" and thrust.

My plan back in the car had been to try to set up the constructs to teleport onto the sword. It hadn't worked; the gate spell the constructs were using had a fail-safe preventing them from teleporting directly onto something. But after they teleported there was a brief window in which they couldn't teleport again.

Variam channelled and the edges of the sword lit up with licks of orange flame just as I rammed the blade through the construct's torso. It jerked and staggered but I was already turning and as the second construct blinked into view next to us I got it with a kick to the body that knocked it over. Turning back to the first construct I forced it back, pushing it with the blade. I could feel the heat radiating as Variam poured fire magic through the sword and into the construct. Its clothes were smouldering around the wound and as I watched they caught fire. The construct tried to teleport away but couldn't and I kept pushing it back, feeling the sword go loose as the construct began to melt from the inside. The construct fell over backwards and I followed it down, took a two-handed grip on the sword, and dragged the blade out sideways. The construct kept trying to grab me, empty eyes locked onto mine, and I stabbed it again and again until heat melted its body and the scrubby grass and dirt it was lying on ignited.

I turned to see Variam with his hand raised towards Anne and the second construct gone. Anne was standing at the centre of the clearing again, looking around. "Get down!" I shouted and ran towards her, bringing the sword back for a swing.

Anne dropped instantly and the second construct blinked in behind her. I'd already started my slash and as I did I felt Variam's fire magic flare to an inferno. The sword flashed white-hot, the heat scorching my arm and hand, and it cut through the construct's neck like butter. The head and body ignited, falling in different directions, and the sword spun away and went into the earth with a hiss.

And suddenly the clearing was quiet. The light of Variam's fire magic blinked out and the only light was the glowing remnants of the two constructs. I shook my burnt right hand and gave Variam a look. "Ow."

"It's dead, isn't it?" Variam was still propped up against the tree and he looked very tired. "Anne, you okay?"

Anne nodded. "Let me have a look at you."

"After we get out of here," I said. "You can patch us up later." I couldn't hear any sirens yet, but after the mess we'd caused on the motorway I knew they wouldn't be far away.

Neither Anne nor Variam argued. We limped back to the

Jaguar, put Variam in, and drove away. As I did I realised
my phone was ringing, and I took it out. "Hey, Luna," I said
wearily. The aftereffects of the fight were starting to kick
in and it was suddenly hard to talk.

"Hey!" Luna sounded excited. "I've been trying to
call you!"

"Sorry. Something came up."

"I won the duel!"

"Good job." A sign passed by overhead and I began signalling to take the turn that would lead us off the motorway,
northwards back towards Fountain Reach. "Meet us outside
the mansion in half an hour. We've got some news too."

chapter 11

It was one hour later.

Anne, Variam, Luna, Sonder, and I were in the woods behind Fountain Reach, in a small clearing on the other side of the hill from the mansion itself. The winter night was only a few degrees above freezing but a small fire burned at the centre of the clearing, its heat forming a bubble of warm air that kept away the cold. The five of us were spaced around the fire, Luna a little farther away. Around us the forest was dark and quiet, the only sound the rustle of wind in the trees.

We'd assembled on the grounds of Fountain Reach before heading into the woods. Sonder had been the last to arrive, having had to make the journey up from London, and as soon as he'd shown up we'd gotten out of sight. The burns on my arm and hand were gone; Anne had healed them along with Variam's broken leg to the point where I couldn't even tell where I'd been hurt. Now everyone was looking at me. I'd led them out here and they were waiting for me to tell them what to do.

"Anne," I said. "Before we start—are we alone?"

Anne nodded. She was sitting on the thin grass with knees up and hands clasped on top of them. "Yes."

Luna looked at her curiously. "How do you know?"

"I can feel them."

"Who?"

"Anyone," Anne said in her soft voice. "Their body, their shape, whether they're hurt . . ."

"How much can you see?" Luna asked.

Anne looked at Luna. "You've got a bruise on the side of your left knee from where you fell a couple of hours ago fighting Ekaterina. And you pulled two of the muscles in your thigh a little."

Luna's eyes widened slightly and her hand went to her leg. "We don't have to worry about anyone sneaking up on us," I said.

"Who are you worried about?" Sonder asked. He'd taken off the parka that he'd worn here and was sitting on it.

"Before we get to that," I said, and I nodded to Anne. "Tell us what you found out from Hobson."

As Anne took out the pad she'd been writing on and began to look through it, reminding herself of the notes she'd written during her conversation, I studied her. The firelight flickered off Anne's dark hair and the lines of her face, leaving most of her body in shadow.

She didn't look like the sort of person who should be getting assassination attempts. But someone had just tried to have her killed for the second time in four days and I didn't know why. Usually when a mage is attacked it's because they're a threat, but Anne seemed like about the most unthreatening apprentice I could imagine. I had to be missing something.

"Okay," Anne began in her soft voice. "Hobson told me that he used to work for the family who lived there, the Aubuchons. He didn't . . . Well, he didn't *say* they were mages, but he knew some of it. Enough not to ask questions.

"The master of the house when Hobson started working there was Vitus Aubuchon. He was in his seventies and he was really concerned with his health. He'd always been sickly and he had a lot of doctors on call making house visits. When he wasn't with them he'd shut himself away in his private rooms. His wife had died a long time ago and the only other member of his family was his son. Hobson had the idea Vitus was an inventor, but"—Anne glanced at me—"I'm pretty sure it was magical research. Anyway, a few years went by. The research didn't seem to be going well and Vitus stopped seeing anyone.

"Then all of a sudden things changed. Vitus came out one day and ordered the house torn down. He kept the central rooms and the basements but the two wings got demolished. Then he started rebuilding. He had a set of plans he was working from and he'd come out every day to check that it was being done right, and he'd fire builders who didn't do it the way he told them. No one could figure out what he was doing. Fountain Reach used to have a little summerhouse that Vitus used with a hedgemaze around it, and he built right over it."

I stirred, something catching at my memory. "The reconstruction took two years," Anne continued. "On the day it was finished Vitus took a walk around Fountain Reach to do his final checks, then he went inside and Hobson says from that day on he never left the house again. But he started to act differently. Before he'd always kept Fountain Reach private, but from then on he started inviting groups to come and tour the mansion. He wrote to local councils and tourist agencies and made Fountain Reach open to the public.

"Things kept on that way for a long time, but then there were problems. Hobson and the other servants started overhearing arguments between Vitus and his son. They'd never gotten on all that well, but things got worse and worse as Vitus got older. And people stopped coming to Fountain Reach."

"Why?" I said.

"No one seems to know," Anne said. "But Hobson said there was a police investigation, although it was hushed up. Apparently a travel group had been to Fountain Reach and someone went missing."

Sonder frowned. "Wait. You mean—?"

"Keep going," I said.

"After that Vitus Aubuchon wouldn't see anyone at all, not even the servants," Anne said. "His son left the mansion, then one night when most of the servants were away he came back. Hobson was there and he said Vitus's son was drunk. He told Hobson and all of the others to get out of the house and never come back, then he went looking for his father.

"That was the last anyone saw of either of them. Hobson and the other servants woke up the next day and couldn't find Vitus or his son. When they searched the house they found fire damage in one of the inner rooms—it looked like somebody had tried to burn the house down during the night. The police were called in and searched the house from top to bottom. Months went by and the house was closed and they kept on searching but they never found either Vitus or his son. And Hobson never went back."

Anne fell silent. "Someone went missing in Fountain Reach?" Luna asked. "How long ago?"

"Thirty years ago," Anne said. "She was our age."

"Why was this Hobson guy telling you this stuff?" Variam asked.

"I'm not sure. He was . . . odd. He seemed really jumpy the whole time. And he never asked why I wanted to know."

"That's weird," Luna said curiously.

"No, it's not," Variam said. "He was bait for a trap."

Anne frowned. "I know it looks that way but I didn't get that feeling from him. He was nervous about something, but he didn't seem like he knew what was going on."

"But why would anyone want to kill you in the first place?" Sonder asked, echoing my thoughts from earlier.

"So she couldn't tell anyone what she knew," Variam said.

"Doesn't make sense," I said. "The constructs were after Anne, not Hobson. And whoever sent them had to know it would draw *more* attention to Hobson." The more I thought about it, the odder it seemed. Between the tip-offs and the attacks, it was as though someone *wanted* to point me towards Fountain Reach. But why?

I came out of my thoughts to realise Variam was arguing about something with Luna. "Sonder," I said, cutting them off. "Did you get anywhere in London?"

"What? Oh, the investigation. No. It's just like all the others. We can trace them up to the point where they disappear, but the shroud stops us from getting anything useful."

"What about the information I asked for?"

"What information?" Luna asked.

"About the Aubuchon dynasty," Sonder explained. "Well . . ." He pushed up his glasses and leant forward. "It matches with what Anne said, really. The Aubuchons were a hereditary magical line. They used to be very famous but they dwindled over the years like a lot of mage families. Vitus Aubuchon was the last."

"What about his son?" Luna asked.

"He was a normal. No magical talent. Apparently Vitus wasn't happy about that."

"The rebuilding of Fountain Reach," I said. "That was when those wards were put up, wasn't it?"

Sonder nodded. "That's something I *was* able to find out. The reason he was doing that rebuilding was to build the wards in with the house from the ground up. Basically all of Fountain Reach is one giant focus. Lots of people were curious because it seemed like such overkill. I mean, everyone has wards, but those ones are about five times as strong as they should be."

"Did they figure it out?"

"Not really. The best guess was that the wards were acting as the skeleton for an envelopment focus."

"What's that?" Luna asked.

"It's a large-scale focus that acts as a magnifying effect," Sonder said. "As long as you're within the area you can use the energy to power spells that are much more powerful than normal, or ones from a different type of magic than you should be able to use."

"If they're so good, why doesn't everyone use them?" Variam said.

"Well, an envelopment focus only works within the physical area it covers. And the spells that run it are unstable, so they need a lot of maintenance. Basically it makes you more powerful, but only as long as you stay in one place."

"Why didn't any other mage take Fountain Reach for himself after Vitus disappeared?" I said.

"They couldn't get the wards to work," Sonder said. "Vitus had attuned them to himself."

I nodded. "And if it had been built in with the physical design of the place, it would have been more trouble than it was worth to change it."

"If those mages couldn't get Fountain Reach to work for them, how did Crystal do it?" Luna asked.

"Guess she figured it out," Variam said.

Sonder frowned. "But the mages who investigated the wards after Vitus's disappearances were . . . Well, I actually know two of them and they know more about focus magic than almost anyone else in the country. If they couldn't reattune the wards I don't see how she could have."

"Who cares?" Variam said. "Maybe she just didn't bother."

"But that would have problems too. Even if they aren't directly designed to defend the location, living in a place where you don't have any control over the ward layout is—"

"Okay, look," Luna said. "What about that missing girl? It has to be the same thing, right?"

Anne and Sonder looked at each other. "I'm not sure," Sonder said. He looked troubled.

"I am," Luna said. "Alex, do you think if we went looking we'd find a bunch of other people going missing there?"

I thought about it for a second, then nodded. "Maybe not obviously . . . but yes."

"I don't know how they missed this," Sonder said. "Fountain Reach was investigated—"

"Fountain Reach was investigated for disappearances involving mages," I said. "But I'll bet you the Council never looked into what happened to *normal* people who went there."

"But it still doesn't make sense," Sonder objected. "It's the apprentice disappearances we're trying to solve, and there's still no connection—"

"About that." I got to my feet. "Come with me for a second. There's something I'd like you to check."

. . . .

Fountain Reach was a cluster of light against the winter darkness. Stars twinkled down from above, and from the mansion dozens of windows glowed. We were at the edge of the woods bordering the gardens and even across the lawn we could hear the chatter of voices through the thick walls. Everything else was black.

"What are we doing here?" Sonder asked, shivering. Away from the warmth of Variam's fire spells, his breath was a pale shadow in the cold air.

"What you just told us was useful," I said, "but it wasn't why I asked you to come down. When's your best guess on when Yasmin went missing?"

"About one o'clock this morning."

"I want you to look back into the past over the period immediately after that. Let's say a three-hour window."

"Look, even if it *was* here, you know the wards would stop any—"

"The wards prevent scrying inside the house," I said. "I want you to search the grounds *around* the house."

"For what?"

"Nothing," I said truthfully. "See what you find."

Sonder sighed and closed his eyes. Behind him Anne, Variam, and Luna were half hidden by the trees, though only Luna was shivering. "Do you want me to look around the front?" Sonder asked.

"No," I said. "The farther out of view the better."

Sonder fell silent. The only noise was the murmur of voices drifting across the gardens. I kept my arms folded against the chill, trying not to show how tense I was. Minutes passed and I forced myself to stay patient. I went over the reasoning in my mind, checking it for holes. It all hung together. Sonder ought to find . . .

"Huh," Sonder said, interrupting my thoughts. "That's funny."

"What?"

"There's an empty patch."

"A shroud?"

"Yeah. One-fifteen to one-eighteen."

"Okay," I said, making sure to keep my voice calm. "Is it the same shroud? The same as when—?"

"Yes," Sonder said. He was looking at me. "The same one that was used at Kings Cross and all the others."

"Now check the time the last apprentice disappeared," I said. "Vanessa. Same deal, the period immediately after she went missing."

It only took Sonder a minute this time. "It's the same," he said. I couldn't make out his expression, but he was looking at me. "Alex, this means—"

"Check them all."

⁙⁙⁙⁙⁙

It was the same with all of them. The disappearances of all the missing apprentices matched up with a period of shrouded time in the back of Fountain Reach. By tracing the exact activation of the shroud, Sonder was able to figure out that the person using it had come from the woods to a little-used side door set into the mansion, half hidden by the bushes. Backtracking, we found that all of the routes led back to one of a pair of clearings a few minutes into the trees, where they stopped.

"But where did they come from?" Luna asked once we'd withdrawn back to the campsite and had warmed up again.

"A gate spell," Sonder said. "It has to be."

"Why didn't they just gate into the mansion?" Variam said.

"They couldn't," I said. "The wards over Fountain Reach stop you from gating inside. But they don't stop you from gating nearby and walking in. It's how half the guests have been getting here."

We sat around the fire in silence for a minute. "This means it's Crystal, doesn't it?" Luna said at last.

"We don't have any proof of that," Sonder said.

"It's her house."

"Yes, but all we know is that someone used a shroud," Sonder argued. "I know it's suspicious but it's not enough to bring to the Council. Anyway, we don't have a motive."

"Harvesting," Variam said instantly.

I shook my head. "It was one of the first things I thought too, but it doesn't fit. Harvesting is incredibly dangerous. Even doing it once is likely to kill you. To do it over and over again you'd have to be suicidal, and Crystal isn't."

"But how could it be Crystal?" Anne asked.

"Why can't it be?" Luna said.

"That missing girl," Anne said. "She disappeared back when the house still belonged to Vitus Aubuchon, thirty years ago. Crystal is . . . thirty-four?"

"Thirty-five," I said.

"So Crystal *couldn't* have done it," Anne said. "She would have been five years old."

"So maybe that was some other mage," Variam said.

"Come on," Luna said. "Two different mages just *happen* to kidnap a victim of the same age at the same place?"

"What do you think?" Sonder asked me.

"It can't be a coincidence," I said. "But if I had to guess, I'd go with Luna. I think it's Crystal who's been doing this."

I looked around the four of them. "Something that's been bothering me from the start is how neat all these disappearances have been. The victims never seem to fight back—it's as if they just walk out the door. Well, maybe that's exactly what *has* been happening. A mind mage like Crystal can overwhelm someone fast, especially someone young and inexperienced. And it would explain why we've never had any witnesses. Wiping memories is well within her range."

"But what about the girl from thirty years ago?" Anne asked.

"Before I met Crystal I did some digging," I said. "She's never taken an apprentice or taught any classes. In fact, until this tournament she's never shown any interest in apprentices at all. I think it stems from when she came to Fountain Reach."

"Isn't it supposed to be her family home?" Sonder asked.

"Yeah, and I'm pretty sure she was lying. You heard Anne's story. If Crystal was really the heir to the Aubuchons, why didn't the house go to her when the last two members of the family died?" I shook my head. "I think Crystal found something here, something hidden. And whatever she found was the reason she bought the house and arranged this tournament."

"But why the tournament?" Sonder said.

"That's the bit I can't figure out," I said. "Because until now the kidnapper has gone to a whole lot of trouble to keep these disappearances away from here. Yasmin was right here on the grounds, but they waited to grab her until she was all the way away in London."

"Why?" Variam said.

"To draw attention away from Fountain Reach," I said. "But if that's the case, why hold the tournament?" I shook my head again. "There must be something they think is worth the risk . . ."

"What do you think's happened to the apprentices?" Anne asked.

"Nothing good."

We talked for another hour. Although everyone agreed Crystal was the most likely suspect, it was clear we didn't have enough to go before the Council. Sonder thought we should go to Talisid and report what we'd found. Variam didn't trust Talisid or anyone else from the Council and wanted to keep it a secret. Luna wanted to investigate more, and Anne stayed quiet and didn't volunteer an opinion either way.

"All right," I said once the conversation had started going in circles. "Here's what we're going to do. Sonder, I want you to go back to London and buy some video cameras. Tomorrow night we're going to set up surveillance on those two clearings that are being used to bring apprentices in here. It won't do anything to help the ones already gone, but it should give us some proof if they get used again. There're some other things I want you to check up on too; I'll tell you those later.

"Luna, Anne, Variam, I want you to stay around the tournament. Keep on listening, keep on digging. There's got to be some reason the White Stone is being held here and we need to know what it is. And while you're there, see if you can figure out where in the house those missing apprentices might have been taken. They came into Fountain Reach and they sure as hell didn't leave, so where are they?"

Luna nodded. "What about you?"

"I'm going to follow Crystal," I said. "I still think she's the one responsible for this and I'm going to shadow her. If I'm lucky she'll lead us to something that can let us know what's going on. While I'm doing that, I want the rest of you to stay away from her. Crystal's really good at reading surface thoughts and the last thing we want is for her to know we suspect her. Before we go I'll teach you a couple of mental exercises to help with that." I looked around. "One last thing. I know I've told you this before, but don't go anywhere alone as long as you're inside Fountain Reach."

"You just said all the disappearances were happening *outside* Fountain Reach," Luna pointed out.

I sighed. "Look, I don't have any good answers. I just know that the longer I stay in that place, the more it creeps me out. It feels like there's something in Fountain Reach and it's watching me. And I really don't like that we've got so many apprentices staying there." I straightened up. "All right, that's it. Any questions?"

There were plenty, and by the time everyone was satisfied it was long past midnight. Variam doused the fire and we made our way back to Fountain Reach. The mansion was going dark as the people inside withdrew for the night, the lights in the windows vanishing one by one. I dropped Anne and Luna at their room and Variam at his before going to bed.

|||||||||

The dream came again that night. I was walking the corridors of Fountain Reach, and I was alone. The mansion felt different, dead; the halls were darker, the rooms older. Fountain Reach had always felt alien, an unwelcome place to live, but this Fountain Reach was different: It was hard to imagine *anything* living here. An old crooked door appeared before me and I stepped through.

Mud squished under my shoes as I entered the hedges. The branches and leaves were shrivelled and dead from lack of light. As I turned the corners I started to hear whispers around me, lost voices at the edge of hearing. The hedges parted before me to reveal a small ancient building with a metal door.

The room inside was lined floor to ceiling with cold grey tiles. They might have been white once but now were cracked and darkened with age. A metal table stood in the centre of the room with straps down its length, battered and stained. There were pipes along the walls, and in one corner was an old metal bathtub. The room was silent but for a slow dripping sound from the corner: *plink . . . plink . . . plink.*

A wave of fear rose up inside me, but I forced myself to go closer. Dust and debris crunched under my feet as I moved. As I drew closer I saw that the bathtub was filled with some sort of liquid, dark and still. The scent was horrible, something ancient and sickening, and I stopped, afraid to go closer, listening to the drops falling: *plink . . . plink.*

Then I heard a soft sighing sound and felt breath on the back of my neck.

I came awake with a gasp, heart pounding in my chest. The weapon under my pillow was out and in my hand and I was scanning for danger before I knew I was doing it. Futures leapt out at me, lines of light in the darkness that represented threat, a sudden change—but as I looked closer I couldn't see anything happening. I came fully awake, searching for what it was—

—And it was gone. All of a sudden, the futures were blank and uneventful. I sat on my bed, checking and rechecking, and found nothing.

My room was dark, but looking through the window I could see that the eastern sky was starting to brighten. A thick bank of cloud had come in overnight and its underside was beginning to light up with streaks of red: Once the sun rose it would block out the rays entirely. I stared out the window, letting my breathing slow and my heartbeat steady. Only once I was calm again did I turn back to my room.

The clock beside my bed read seven thirty-five—I'd been asleep only a few hours. From the rooms around I could hear the sound of the mansion's inhabitants waking up for the second day of the tournament. My room was quiet and undisturbed, the alarms hadn't been tripped, and everything was where I'd left it. Yet though I couldn't put my finger on what it was something about it felt off, like the feeling you get when you walk into your house at the end of the day and know someone else is there.

I dressed, threw on my mist cloak, and went out to find the others. The halls of Fountain Reach were cold but stirring with activity as more people woke, lights coming on one by one. Variam was still asleep but Luna and Anne's room was empty and I went looking for them.

I found them in one of the practice halls, and they weren't alone. A raised voice was echoing through the open doorway; it was a girl, not quite shouting but close to it. Moving into the shadow of the doorway I saw Anne and Luna on one of the duelling pistes. They looked like they'd been in the middle of practice when they'd been interrupted by the two apprentices opposite them.

"What have you done with her?" the girl said. It was Natasha, the round-faced girl who'd been sniping at Anne and Luna before. Back then she'd had a smile on her face, but she wasn't smiling now.

"I haven't done anything," Anne said. She looked troubled.

Natasha clenched her fists. "You're lying!" Her voice was high-pitched, on the edge of breaking. "You were fighting with her before!"

"I wasn't fighting with her—" Anne began.

"We don't know where Yasmin is," Luna said at the same time. "The last we saw her she was with you."

"You're *lying*!"

"Tash, come on," the boy next to Natasha said. It was Charles, the same boy I'd seen with her before, and he looked uneasy.

"I know it was you," Natasha said. She stared straight at Anne, ignoring Charles. "I know what you've been doing. Give her back or I'll make sure everyone else knows too."

Anne looked unhappy but didn't answer. "You've got it all wrong," Luna said. "Look, we're trying to *find* the guys doing this, okay? We don't—"

"You too!" Natasha whirled on Luna. "You think you can help her? I'll get you as well!"

"Listen, you stupid—" Luna began.

"Okay," Charles said loudly. "We've got to go." He pulled Natasha away towards the door. Natasha didn't resist, but as Charles led her out of the hall she shot Luna and Anne a glare and there was hate in her eyes. Then she was gone and Anne and Luna were left alone.

I stayed silent in the doorway, scanning through the futures to see if anything was coming to threaten them. "Well, this is just great," Luna said. "Now she thinks *we* did it. What do you think she meant about what you've been doing?"

"I'm not sure," Anne said. But there had been a moment's hesitation there.

Luna didn't seem to notice. With a sigh she sat on a bench, the whip handle dangling from her hand. "This is impossible. Onyx wants to get Alex, someone wants to get you, Natasha wants to get both of us, and in two hours I'm supposed to win a duel against some apprentice who'll be way better than I am."

"You don't *have* to win," Anne said.

"Mm," Luna said. "I want to."

Anne looked at her curiously. "Why?"

"I don't know," Luna said. "I guess it's just . . . I keep feeling useless, you know? Like I'm always leaning on Alex. I mean, it's taken me this long just to get to where I *probably* won't hurt whoever I'm with."

"Alex and Sonder don't seem to think you're useless."

"I always wonder if they're just pretending." Luna rested her chin in her hands, the whip sticking out to one side. "Don't you ever feel like you need to *do* something?"

"No," Anne said simply.

Luna twisted to look at her. "Really?"

Anne shook her head.

"Why didn't you enter the tournament?" Luna asked. "Does your magic not work that way?"

"It's not that. I *can* . . ."

"Why don't you want to, then?"

"I don't like hurting people."

"I can think of a few I'd like to," Luna muttered. "Like Natasha."

"She did just lose her best friend."

"I'm not sure mages *have* friends."

"I'm a mage," Anne reminded her gently.

Luna sighed and straightened. "Sorry. Can we have one more try with the stance thing? I think I was getting it by the end."

No sign of danger was showing through the futures I could see, and it looked as though Natasha had gone. As Anne and Luna went back to the duelling piste I withdrew silently—I didn't want to disturb either of them and I knew Luna would be focused on her coming match.

Overhearing these sorts of conversations always gives

me a strange feeling, like looking through a window onto a view I don't usually see. My "adventures" with Luna tend to be so dangerous that I've got my work cut out just to keep us both alive, so it had never really occurred to me to wonder how she felt about it. It's been a long time since I was an apprentice, but I can still remember just how scary it can be to go up against an experienced mage—hell, it *still* scares me, which is why I do it as little as possible. But I had the feeling that trying to make her feel better was the wrong way to handle things. Luna might have come to the wrong conclusion—she'd never been useless—but she was right about needing to stand on her own feet. The best thing for her to do would be to learn to face up to mages herself.

Outside the sun had risen, and the mansion was coming fully awake. I didn't think Luna or Anne would be in any danger and so I went searching for Crystal. She wasn't in or near the main hall, so acting on a hunch I headed for the place where I'd eavesdropped on her the last time—that empty corridor towards the top of Fountain Reach where I'd heard Crystal talking to what had seemed like thin air.

She was right where I'd expected, but someone else had gotten there first. I heard the murmur of voices from all the way down the hall and quietly moved closer.

As I got within earshot I realised the man with Crystal was Lyle. "I'm just not sure it's possible," he was saying, and he sounded troubled. "I mean, it was a worry before, but now . . ."

"Fountain Reach is the safest place these apprentices can possibly be." Crystal's voice was cool. "You tested the wards yourself."

"Yes, but with this girl disappearing, what was her name—"

"Yasmin didn't disappear in Fountain Reach. Wasn't that what you told me?"

"Yes, but—"

"You reminded everyone to ensure that their apprentices didn't leave the mansion. It's hardly your fault if they chose to ignore you."

"But Sarissa *had* told her." Lyle sounded uneasy. "She kept saying Yasmin wouldn't have left the grounds—"

"Lyle," Crystal said. She moved closer, and through the futures I could see that she was resting a hand on his shoulder. "You worry too much."

"I supported the nomination of Fountain Reach to the Council. If it turns out . . ." Lyle hesitated. "The Council wouldn't be pleased."

Crystal sighed and I heard her move away. "Is the Council all you think about?"

Lyle was silent. I was one door down from Lyle and Crystal's room, my hand on the handle, ready to slip inside should they come out. They'd actually left the door to their room open, which seemed odd but made sense in a way. Between Lyle and Crystal, nothing thinking or feeling could get into the corridor without them noticing . . . unless that someone was wearing a mist cloak.

"Have you thought about that offer?" Lyle asked.

"Working for Levistus?"

"It's an important position."

"I'm sure it is." There was faint distaste in Crystal's voice.

"I could . . . make some recommendations. We could—"

"We could do what? Run the Council's errands for them? Do all the work and take all the risk for a few crumbs of reward?" Crystal shook her head slightly. "I never understood your focus on the Council."

"They're the most powerful mages in the country."

"I can think of a few Dark mages who might disagree."

"Dark mages aren't an institution. They're just anarchy."

"At least they provide some opportunity." Crystal walked to the window and glanced back at Lyle. "Oh, stop thinking that. I haven't turned to their side. But I'm not going to serve the Council either."

"You could rise—"

"To the top of that old boys' club?" Crystal's voice was cool and precise. "After decades of bowing and scraping and cutting deals and begging for favours? Then once I'm old and grey, I *could* rise? I think not."

Lyle was silent. "I know what you want to ask," Crystal said.

"Could we—?"

"No," Crystal said. "Not as long as your first loyalty is to the Council." She turned to Lyle. "But there are alternatives. You made me an offer, now let me make you one. What if I could offer you something better?"

Lyle sounded taken aback. "What do you mean?"

"A way to have what we want without depending on the Council."

"How—"

Crystal shook her head. "Not now." She walked past Lyle, towards the door. "I have a tournament to oversee. Think about it."

I'd seen Crystal coming and was inside the room with the door drawn to by the time she stepped out into the corridor. She turned and left, heels clicking on the wooden floor. Lyle followed a minute later.

Once they were gone I stepped out again, looking after them quizzically. Lyle and Crystal . . . Well, it was interesting, but I couldn't see how it was much use. Crystal's words were much more suspicious though. Whatever Crystal's "something better" was, I had a feeling it wasn't anything good.

〉〉〉〉〉〉〉〉〉

I'm always reluctant to take off my mist cloak. Invisibility is such a safe feeling and it's so tempting to stay there rather than make yourself vulnerable again. But it doesn't make your problems go away—all it does is delay them. I hid the cloak and sat down.

There was something I'd been putting off and I couldn't ignore it much longer. My formal reply to Onyx's challenge was due in a few hours; I'd been avoiding thinking about it in the hope that it'd go away. It hadn't, and I needed to figure out what to do.

My odds of winning a duel against someone like Onyx were basically zero. Duels are designed to be fair fights, and I'm very bad at fair fights. With no cover it would come down to strength against strength, and even the weakest elemental mage outclasses me several times over in terms of raw power. I might give Onyx a surprise or two but there was only one way it could end.

What if I went in expecting to lose? I couldn't beat Onyx, but losing a duel wouldn't kill me. It'd be humiliating and I wouldn't enjoy it, but I've had worse.

But while losing a duel wouldn't kill me, losing a duel to *Onyx* might. Traditional duels aren't supposed to be fatal but more than a few mages have died from "accidents" in the ring. Onyx would never get away with it, not in front of so many witnesses, but that wouldn't be much consolation to me. And I really didn't feel like trusting my life to Onyx's self-control.

I leant back with a sigh, staring at the ceiling. I hate

dealing with this stuff. So much of mage politics involves these no-win situations. I'm much happier hanging out with Luna and Arachne or minding my shop.

How would I deal with this if I *were* in my shop? If some random guy walked in off the street and challenged me to a duel, what would I do?

I'd tell him to get lost. Then if he tried to start a fight anyway, I'd make sure it wasn't a fair one.

Was there anything stopping me from just saying no? Now that I thought about it I didn't think there was. By custom a mage is supposed to answer a challenge, but there aren't any actual penalties for refusing. Traditional Light mages would see it as dishonourable, but the traditional Light mages don't like me anyway.

The real danger was that I'd appear weak. But elemental mages *already* think diviners are weak, and it works to my advantage as often as not. Besides, I couldn't see how declining the duel could do any more harm to my image than having Onyx publicly kick my ass.

I noticed that I was about to get a call. I took out my phone and hit the green button midway through the first ring. "Hey, Talisid."

"Glad I caught you," Talisid said. "There's been a development."

"What's up?"

"Two Keepers have been sent to Fountain Reach. Avenor and Travis."

I frowned. "What are they doing here?"

"They're assigned to the apprentice investigation, so if they're coming to you it's a safe bet they're following some lead." Talisid paused. "It seems you're starting to convince people that Fountain Reach may be the right place."

"Well, I don't know who convinced them but it wasn't me."

"You haven't spoken to them?"

"No. When did they leave?"

"An hour or two ago. I'd expect them to be at Fountain Reach by now."

"Um." It bothered me for some reason. It sounded as though someone had tipped them off. But who?

"Have you made any progress?"

"Yes, but not over the phone. Talk to Sonder; he's working on something from his end."

"I will. Oh, and next time you go for a drive, make a little less mess, will you?"

"Yes, Talisid, the next time I have a bunch of unkillable construct assassins after me I'll make it my number one priority to make sure you don't have too much mess to clean up afterwards."

"Glad to hear it." Talisid sounded amused. "I'll be in touch."

I hung up and went to the duelling hall.

chapter 12

Heads turned as I walked into the hall. Onyx was there and I didn't see any point in waiting for him to find me first. I walked towards the end of the hall, past the groups of apprentices and the mages turning to look at me.

Onyx watched me as I approached, arms folded. "You challenged me," I told him once I was close enough. I didn't keep my voice down and I could feel the mages around me listening. "Here's my answer. No."

Onyx's lip curled. "Not fighting?"

"I'm not fighting."

"The charges?"

"There are no charges," I said. "You have a problem, take it to the Council."

I'd been expecting Onyx to rage or threaten. He didn't do either. Instead he stared at me for a long moment before giving a very slight smile that didn't reach his eyes. Then he walked out.

Luna was waiting on the other side of the crowd. "You're okay?" she asked.

"I'm fine."

"Was that it? You just had to say no?"

It wasn't it. That smile worried me. If Onyx had been counting on my accepting the duel he should have reacted more. But that was my problem, not Luna's, and I didn't want to put anything else on her mind just now. "Pretty much," I said. "When's your match?"

"They're going to announce it," Luna said. She'd dressed in a black form-fitting outfit I'd never seen her wear before and she was spinning the whip handle between her fingers. To my mage's sight her curse spun about her, agitated.

I looked around. "Where's Variam?"

"What do you mean?"

"Isn't he a bit late?"

Luna looked at me in surprise. "He's not in the tournament."

"He got knocked out?"

"He forfeited. He didn't show up to last night's match; I guess he was with you and Anne. I thought you knew?"

I remembered how Variam had appeared suddenly last night. As soon as he'd seen that Anne was missing he must have come after us, abandoning his match without hesitation. I was getting the feeling that I was starting to understand what Variam really cared about. "Did you tell Variam we were working for Talisid?" I asked Luna.

"What? No."

"What about Anne?"

"No. Why?"

"I was wondering how he found out."

"Well, it wasn't from me. You *said* not to tell anyone."

I nodded. I could only think of four people who knew that it was Talisid who'd come to talk to me that day at the duelling class: me, Luna, Sonder, and Talisid himself. And I was pretty sure none of them had told Variam.

But there was someone at that duelling class who could have found out that Talisid was there *without* being told. And now that I thought about it, that might explain the message too . . .

A chime sounded from the podium and conversation across the hall fell silent. More than half of the apprentices competing in the White Stone had been knocked out by now, but the number of spectators had gone up if anything. There's a lot of prestige to these tournaments.

Crystal was standing on the podium. She'd tied up her gold hair in a professional-looking style and was dressed in yet another cream-coloured suit of a slightly different cut. I wondered if she had a rack of them somewhere. She was looking confident and as everyone turned to watch she gave them all a smile. "Good morning, everyone, and welcome to the second day of the White Stone. The third round will now begin. The first match is between"—Crystal's eyes travelled up—"Gunther Elkins and Michael Antigua."

Gunther was a tall, serious-looking boy with Germanic features and a blond ponytail, and he strode onto the piste to face Michael, who was a head shorter than him with light brown skin and dark hair and eyes. Two mages were standing at opposite ends of the hall behind the tuning-fork focuses, and as I watched they activated them. Thin walls of energy sprang to life along the edges of the piste and shield bubbles appeared around Gunther and Michael. Both were invisible to normal eyes and even to my mage's sight they were faint and translucent. These were the conversion fields of an azimuth duel; they radiated no energy, but under the monitoring of a skilled operator they could react instantly to any attack that struck them. There was no ceremony; the formalities had been done yesterday. The arbitrator, a white-haired mage in ceremonial robes, glanced at Gunther. "Ready?"

Gunther nodded.

"Ready?" he said to Michael.

Michael nodded.

"Fight."

Michael attacked, strikes of water magic hammering at Gunther's shield. Gunther parried the first strike, and the second. As Michael began another attack, Gunther slammed a blade of air through Michael's defences, so fast that Michael had no time to raise a shield of his own. I had just a glimpse of the razor-edged shard before it vanished in a flash of light, the conversion field disintegrating it an instant before it cut into Michael's flesh. It wouldn't have been fatal, but it would have hurt.

"Point, right," the arbitrator announced. "One-zero. Places."

Gunther and Michael returned to the starting lines. The first round had taken less than three seconds.

"Fight."

The duel continued and it quickly became obvious that Gunther was both swifter and more skilled than his opponent. By the end the score was 3–0 and Gunther shook hands with a surly-looking Michael. I glanced down to see that Luna looked nervous.

"Victor Kraft and Oscar Poulson," Crystal announced.

Both apprentices were using focus weapons this time. Victor wielded a longsword, which was sharp and dangerous-looking even without the trail of frost it left in his wake. Oscar held something more like a fencing épée. The épée was fast and so was Oscar, but not fast enough.

"Fay Wilder and Barbara Cartwright."

Barbara was a plain-faced stocky girl. She carried no weapon but relied instead on touch spells. Fay had curly hair and a ready smile, and she was an illusionist. Barbara's touch spells hit only phantoms of light and shadow, while Fay's small dagger found its mark reliably.

"Anne and Variam are here," I commented as Fay walked off the piste to be congratulated by a smiling man in expensive-looking clothes.

"How am I supposed to beat these guys?" Luna asked. She was biting her lip. "Did you see what she just did?"

"Relax."

"I couldn't even see where she was. How can—?"

"Relax," I said. "Focus on the one you *will* be fighting."

Crystal was still on the podium and her gaze was resting on Fay Wilder, just as she'd watched every other apprentice who'd stepped onto the piste. I narrowed my eyes. *Why are you watching them so closely?*

Crystal turned away and raised her voice. "Natasha Babel . . ." Her eyes came to rest on us. "And Luna Mancuso."

I felt Luna go stiff. "Go for it," I said.

"It's—"

"I know who it is. Kick her ass."

Natasha was already walking onto the piste. Luna stepped out a moment later. She'd tied her hair back in a ponytail instead of her usual bunches, and as she took her place to the right end she looked quick and agile, standing balanced on the balls of her feet. The conversion field flared up around the piste and bubble shields appeared around Luna and Natasha. "Ready?" the arbitrator asked Luna.

Luna nodded. She was keeping the handle of her whip hidden and I nodded approvingly to myself. As I watched, the silver mist of her curse spread and unfurled around her, tendrils snaking out to a distance of two or three yards and causing faint flickers as they brushed the edge of the piste. Luna's learnt over the past year to hold her curse in, but it's more powerful when she doesn't.

"Ready?" the arbitrator asked Natasha.

Natasha said something under her breath, not quite loud enough for me to hear. Luna frowned and Natasha gave her a thin smile. Just as in their first duel, Natasha carried no weapon. With her water magic she didn't need one.

"Are you ready?" the arbitrator repeated to Natasha, more loudly.

"Ready," Natasha said without taking her eyes off Luna.

"Fi—"

Natasha struck before the arbitrator had finished speaking, a lance of blue light stabbing at Luna's chest. Water mages can't manipulate the water in a human body—that's the domain of life magic—and they can't create water out of nowhere. But they can use the water vapour in the air to do pretty much anything water can do in much larger amounts, including hitting someone with the impact of a fire hose.

But Luna had started moving at the same time, and whether through foresight or the luck of her curse her sidestep took her far enough out of the way for the water lance to streak past. As she dodged, her right arm came up in an underarm swing and the whip came to life, its silvery length slashing upwards and straight into Natasha. The strand dissipated as it struck the bubble of Natasha's conversion field, becoming a flash of brilliant light that made me shut my eyes.

"Point, right," the arbitrator said. He was frowning, but neither Natasha nor Luna had *quite* jumped the gun.

"What was that?" Natasha demanded. "That's not fair!"

"Point, right," the arbitrator repeated more loudly. "One-zero." Luna brought the whip back, the strand of silver mist curling around her feet. I'd expected it to go for the spectators, but it didn't; it was pointed towards Natasha, coiled and ready. For Natasha's part, she looked taken aback. This obviously wasn't going the way she'd expected.

"Ready?" the arbitrator asked once everything was settled. I could hear murmurs from the crowd, people whispering in undertones. Luna's curse is *very* difficult to see; my mage's sight is better than most and even I can only spot it because I know exactly what to look for. To most of the mages here, it would have looked like Luna hit Natasha without doing anything.

"Fight!"

A spherical shield of flickering blue light sprang up around Natasha, the water magic combining magical energy and pressure to repel attacks. Luna's whip sprang out eagerly and the silver mist bit into the sphere, but the shield held. Luna pulled back and struck again, stepping forward as Natasha stepped back. Light sparked from Natasha's shield at the points of impact, silver-blue instead of the white flash of the conversion field. The whip was fast and responsive and it gathered itself for a new strike more quickly than any normal whip could do, but there was still a slight delay between each attack. Natasha timed it carefully, then as Luna was pulling back for another stroke she dropped her shield and sent a full-strength blast of water magic streaming down the piste. Luna was off-balance and didn't manage to dodge. The azimuth shield took the brunt of the attack with a brilliant flash, but it couldn't stop all the kinetic energy of the impact. Luna flew five feet before hitting the floor and slid and rolled for another ten.

"Point, left," the arbitrator said as another murmur went up around the hall. "One-all. Is right able to continue?"

Luna got to one knee, steadying herself and locking gazes with Natasha. There was a small cut on her lip. "Oh, I didn't hurt you, did I?" Natasha said, her eyes wide.

"You wish," Luna said.

"Places," the arbitrator said loudly.

Luna rose and walked to the starting lines. Her curse lashed and twisted around her, and it looked pissed off. Over the crowd I caught a glimpse of Anne and Variam watching closely. Anne looked worried. Variam just looked like he was enjoying the show.

"Ready?" the arbitrator said. "Fight!"

Both Luna and Natasha started more cautiously this time, neither wanting to risk an attack that might leave them open. Luna attacked first, her whip flicking out to glance off Natasha's shield. Natasha struck back but this time Luna's whip met the attack head on, slashing into the lance of water and erasing it in a flash of light before it could reach her. Natasha pulled away.

Luna began to advance. This time instead of big slow swings she kept the whip in front of her, slashing at Natasha with quick strikes that didn't leave her vulnerable. Natasha backed off as the whip cut into her shield, the impacts landing left and right and left again. Luna kept advancing, eyes narrowed in concentration, and it became obvious that Natasha didn't have an answer for the steady beat of attacks. Experienced battle-mages can shield and strike at the same time but Natasha didn't have the skill. Natasha kept backing away, flinching. Left, right, left—and then Luna changed the pattern. Instead of going back to the right she flipped the whip handle through a complex move and the whip reared up behind Natasha like a striking scorpion, stabbing through the back of her shield where it was weaker in a flash of brilliant white.

"Point, right. Two-one. Places."

Luna backed off. She was breathing hard but she looked satisfied. Natasha didn't.

"Match point," the arbitrator said. "Ready?"

Luna nodded.

"Ready?"

Natasha gave a tiny nod.

"Fi—"

Natasha struck with overwhelming force, sending a pillar of blue light at Luna with bone-crushing power. But Luna's curse saved her again, her sidestep taking her just far enough away. The whip licked out without Luna even swinging it and the silver strand hit Natasha squarely in the face. The conversion field couldn't stop it all this time and through the brilliant flash I saw a tendril of mist stroke Natasha's cheek, soaking into her.

"Point, right," the arbitrator said. "Match. Luna Mancuso wins three-one."

The crowd started to applaud. Natasha just stood there, staring at Luna. Luna's curse can't be felt when it hits. To Natasha it would have seemed as though Luna had won without even touching her. The mages at the back of the piste released their spell on the azimuth focuses and the shields winked out. Luna turned her back on Natasha and marched down the piste, holding the handle of her whip high in triumph. She looked for me in the crowd, grinning. "Alex!" she shouted over the applause. "Did you—?"

Behind, Natasha's face twisted in sudden rage.

"Luna!" I shouted.

Dark blue-green light streamed from Natasha's hand and this time there was no azimuth shield to stop it. Luna had started to turn and the movement took her partly out of the line of the spell but not quite far enough. It splashed across her side and lower back.

Luna hit the floor with a shriek. A second later the arbitrator grabbed Natasha, dragging her off the piste. I was running for Luna but as I reached the piste I checked myself. Luna was writhing on the floor in pain and her curse was active and uncontrolled, twisting and striking blindly. If I came any closer—

Then Anne was there and she didn't hesitate. She dropped to her knees beside Luna, pulling Luna over onto her front. Luna screamed again and as I saw her back I drew a breath in horror. Natasha's spell had eaten through Luna's clothes and skin, revealing red muscle and white bone. And as Anne touched her, Luna's curse jumped into her, tendrils wrapping around Anne and soaking through her skin. If Anne was aware of what Luna's curse was doing she didn't show it. She placed her hands on Luna's back at the edge of the horrible injury and concentrated.

Soft green light flared up, linking the two girls together. Luna arched her spine, but she wasn't screaming anymore. The blood soaking from the wound stopped flowing, and as I watched the ruined muscles began to regrow, interlacing and rebuilding themselves before my eyes. White bone disappeared beneath flesh and the flesh disappeared beneath a new layer of pale white skin. It was over in seconds. Where Luna's back had been a ruined mess, now it was bare and flawless. The only sign of the wound was the ragged hole in her clothes.

Anne tried to get to her feet, staggered, and nearly fell. Luna's curse was still streaming into her and I jumped in and drew her away out of range. Luna sat up on the floor, but she was obviously dazed and didn't know what was going on. The hall was filled with shouts and noise. I held Anne up and an instant later Variam was there, supporting her as well. I could see the silver mist of Luna's curse glowing around Anne—

—And with a snap it was gone. I whirled, going tense. I've seen Luna's curse triggering enough times to recognise it. Something was coming for Anne and I tried to watch in every direction at once, expecting danger any moment.

Seconds ticked by and nothing happened. Luna was trying to get to her feet. "Luna," I called. "*Luna!* We're getting out of here."

Luna wasn't in any state to argue. I was vaguely aware of people trying to talk to us but I didn't care; I needed to get Anne and Luna somewhere safe. Somehow we got out of the duelling hall and into the corridor, me leading while Variam brought up the rear. My shoulders itched as we hurried down the hall. I didn't know what was coming, but it was going to be bad.

Nothing came. We made it back to Anne and Luna's room without anything happening.

I shut the door and locked it as Luna collapsed on the bed. Anne was sitting leaning against the wall, eyes closed, and she actually looked more drained than Luna. "Variam," I said. "Will they be okay?"

"They'll be fine." But Variam was frowning. "Isn't it dangerous getting close to—"

"Yes," I said. I was still trying to make sense of it. Luna and her bed and her clothes glowed with silver mist, but Anne had nothing. The only way that could make sense was if the curse had already activated . . . but if it had, why wasn't anything happening?

"Be okay," Anne said drowsily. "Just a little while."

Now that Anne and Luna were out of danger I was torn between wanting to stay with them to make sure they were safe, and wanting to find Natasha and kill her. Wanting to keep them safe won. "What about Luna?" I asked Anne.

"It's weird," Anne said. She still sounded half-asleep. "What you said last night? Now *I* feel like someone's watching me . . ."

Something about the words gave me a chill, but it was hard to concentrate with Luna like this. "Is Luna going to be okay?"

"What? Oh." Anne shook herself and seemed to come awake. "Yes. She just needs a rest."

I looked over at Luna. She was sprawled on her bed with one hand resting on the pillow and she seemed to have fallen asleep. As I looked into the short-term future I began to calm down a little. It was hard to see far but I couldn't see anything catastrophic happening to anyone just yet.

"Um," Anne said. She sounded a little embarrassed. "I'm going to need something to eat."

"I'll get you something," I said. "Don't leave this room." I glanced at Variam. "Stay with them."

Variam nodded.

⠀⠀⠀⠀⠀⠀⠀ıııııııı

It took a little while to find the kitchens and talk the staff into getting me something. I kept getting distracted by thoughts of what Natasha had done, and every time I did I felt a wave of white-hot rage. I wanted to go after her but knew that in my current state it would be a really bad idea. From the noise and the lack of crowds I could tell that the tournament was still going on, and that pissed me off even more.

I got back to Anne and Luna's room and had just set down the tray to knock on the door when I stopped. The door was open.

I pushed the door open with my left hand, my right slipping inside my coat. Luna was alone in the room, sprawled on the bed right where I'd left her, the silver mist of her curse twining lazily around her body as she slept. Anne and Variam were gone.

What the hell?

I scanned the immediate futures but couldn't find anything. With the mansion's wards I couldn't see far enough to find out where they were. I leant back out into the corridor and saw a girl peeking out of a room two doors down. "Hey," I said. "Where did the apprentices in this room go?"

"I don't know . . ."

As I looked at the girl I recognised her. She was the same one I'd seen Anne talking to two days ago. "What's your name?"

"Celia." The girl came hesitantly out of her room, drawing a little closer. She was small, with blond hair and glasses. "Is Anne okay?"

"Where did she go?"

"They took her away."

"Who?"

"Two mages. They said they were from the Council?"

"Where did they take her?"

"I don't know. Variam went with her, he was shouting . . ."

My phone rang. I took one glance at who it was, then pointed to Luna and Anne's room. "I need you to help my apprentice. Stay in that room and keep an eye on her. Don't go near her, just make sure she's not left alone. Okay?"

Celia hesitated. "Okay."

As Celia disappeared into the room I took out my phone, hit the Talk button, and started walking. "Talisid, can you explain to me why two mages who sound a hell of a lot like Council Keepers just took Anne away for questioning?"

"You've heard, then." Talisid sounded troubled.

"No, I just like making lucky guesses. Of course I've heard." I reached an intersection and stopped to think. The Keepers would have taken over a room for interrogation. It wouldn't be in the bedroom wing, it would be somewhere quieter . . . I picked a direction and started walking again. "What the hell are they thinking?"

"I've been on the phone to the department. Apparently they've received some new information linking Anne Walker to the disappearances."

"That's ridiculous. Anne's one of the ones helping me. *What* information?"

"There was a tip-off from an apprentice—"

"Natasha. Jesus." I covered my eyes. "She doesn't have a clue what she's talking about. They're arresting her over apprentice gossip!"

"That wasn't all. How much do you know about this girl?"

"Why does it matter?" I took a glance down an empty corridor, searching through the immediate futures of opening the doors. Nothing was there and I kept going, navigating by the distant murmur of sound from the duelling hall.

"After they received the tip-off they did some investigation. And they found that Anne Walker knew or was in contact with all four missing apprentices."

"*Every* apprentice knows every other apprentice. It's not that big a community."

"There's more." Talisid didn't sound happy. "They found that in each case Anne had been in a position to learn where that apprentice would be just a day or two before their dis-appearance. And with the first victim, Caroline Montroyd, Anne seems to have been the *only* one who was told."

I stopped. "How?"

"We always knew there was someone feeding informa-tion from the inside. We may have found that someone."

I started walking again and quickened my pace. "It's circumstantial."

"Maybe it is. But I'm looking over the report right now and I assure you it's very suspicious. Especially concerning a subject who was a Dark apprentice."

"She wasn't a Dark apprentice," I said in frustration. "Her or Variam. They got kidnapped into it."

"How do you know?" Talisid asked.

"They told me."

"Has anyone else confirmed that story?"

"No . . ."

"I see."

"This doesn't make sense," I said. "Someone's been try-ing to kill Anne. She's the *target.*"

"Didn't you say you thought there were two groups doing this?" Talisid said. I started to answer but he carried on, cutting me off. "Look, it's not yet established that she's a willing accomplice. She could be being used as an informa-tion source without her knowledge."

I thought of how Anne always seemed to know what was going on amongst the apprentices. Luna's words: *The youn-ger apprentices really like Anne. They tell her everything.* Something uneasy twisted inside me.

I heard the sound of raised voices ahead. One of the voices was Variam's, and as I heard it something fell into place. "I've found them," I said. "I'll call you back."

Talisid sighed. "Please try not to do anything stupid."

"When have I ever done that?"

"I'll let you fill in the response to that yourself," Talisid said. "Good luck."

I switched off the phone and looked down the corridor. A mage was standing in front of a closed door, arms folded, and Variam was shouting at him. One or two heads were peeking out of doors to see what the noise was about, but the tournament was still running and most of the mansion's population was in the duelling hall.

I walked out around the corner. "You can't do this!" Variam was shouting. "You have to—"

"Variam," I said. "We need to talk."

Variam and the mage both turned to me. The mage was lean and tough-looking, his eyes impassive. "This one yours?" he asked me.

"Variam," I said again.

Variam shot the mage a glare, then stalked down the corridor towards me. "They've got Anne in that room," he said as we turned the corner. "They won't let me in—"

I opened a door to the left. It led into a small boxroom. Variam walked in and I closed the door behind us as Variam kept talking. "Look, you've got to do something. They think she—"

"Shut up," I said.

Variam stopped, turning to stare in surprise.

"I just got off the phone with Talisid," I said. "Remember Talisid? The guy who got me to investigate these disappearances?"

"Yeah." Variam still looked taken aback. "So wh—"

"How did you know that?"

"What?"

"How did you know I was working for Talisid?"

"Uh—you were talking about it, last—"

"Last night in the woods, yeah. But you knew before. You told me at the motorway services while Anne was having that chat with Hobson."

Variam hesitated. "You must have—"

"After I got home from that duelling class four days ago I got a message pointing me towards Fountain Reach," I said. "You know what really bothered me about that message? How *fast* it was. In fact, the more I thought about it, the more I started to think that the one who'd sent it must have been at the duelling class too. But even then there was a problem. Talisid hadn't shown himself to you or Lyle or Charles or Natasha or anyone else. All you guys saw was me and Luna leaving the room and then coming back. But that doesn't matter to Anne, does it? She can pick out a living person through a wall with no trouble at all. She would have known we were talking to Talisid. And she trusts you. She would have told you."

Variam didn't move. "So you sent me that message," I said. "And I think I know why. Talisid just told me that all four missing apprentices had a connection to Anne. I think you've known that for a long time and you've been terrified someone else will find out. That was why you sent me to Fountain Reach. You were trying to get me looking there instead of at her."

"I—" Variam stopped. "No, I didn't."

"You probably sent the same message to Onyx too," I said. "And nearly got me killed as a result, not that you seem to care. For all I know you spammed a dozen mages and we're just the ones who happened to pay attention. What I want to know is *why*. You didn't pick Fountain Reach out of a hat. What did you know about this place that made you send us here?"

"I don't know."

"You don't know what?"

Variam hesitated. "I don't know what you're talking about."

"Bullshit! Tell me what you know, *now*."

"Screw you," Variam said. He was starting to get angry again. "Why should I trust you?"

I stared at Variam for a second, then turned on my heel. "You're on your own."

"Hey!" Variam shouted.

I looked back at him. "Hey, *what*?"

"You're supposed to be helping Anne!"

"Helping Anne?" I let go of the doorknob and stalked towards Variam, looming over him to stare into his eyes. Variam drew back, startled. "You ungrateful little shit. Since we met I have done everything I possibly can to protect you and Anne and you have given me nothing but grief for it. It's because of me those assassins didn't kill Anne four days ago and it's because of me those constructs didn't kill *both* of you last night. I've risked my life to help you and I haven't asked for a thing in return except your cooperation. Now I find you've been trying to manipulate me from the start and you have the nerve to ask why *you* should trust *me*? You can't even do something as simple as watch over Luna while she's asleep and helpless. You've been right on the fence between asset and liability for a while now and you just took a dive down the liability side." I shook my head and turned back towards the door. "I'm done wasting time on you."

Variam caught my shoulder. "Wait!"

"For what? For you to spin me more bullshit?"

"I need your help," Variam said. It sounded like it was difficult for him to get the words out, but he managed. "To help Anne."

"I've been doing nothing *but* helping Anne."

"All right," Variam said. He looked nervous. "I'll tell you."

"The truth this time?"

Variam nodded.

"Fine," I said. "But listen closely, because I'm only going to say this once. If I catch you lying to me one more time I'm going to cut you loose for good. And Variam?" I leant in close. "I'm *very good* at knowing when people are lying to me."

Variam flinched slightly and I pulled back. "Why Fountain Reach?"

"Look, I wanted to tell you," Variam began. "I just couldn't see how it was any use."

"Where did you get the name?"

"Jagadev," Variam said. "I went to him, after Vanessa. He told me the disappearances were connected to Fountain Reach but he wouldn't say why."

"Did he say anything about how or who?"

Variam shook his head.

"How long have you known that it was something to do with Anne?"

"It's not! She's not doing anything, none of us are! It's just . . . I thought it was just a coincidence. I mean, there aren't *that* many apprentices. But when every one of them seemed to . . . I knew what they'd think. Everyone always thinks we're some kind of monsters. I knew they wouldn't listen to us."

"So you tried to push everyone away." I shook my head. "If you'd told me earlier I could have gone looking for an explanation. Now she's already been arrested and we're up against the clock. You've made this a hell of a lot more difficult."

"I'm sorry," Variam said. "I didn't know what to do."

I sighed and put a hand to my head, tapping my fingers against my forehead. "All right," I said. "All right. The Council can be assholes, but they're not incompetent. If those Keepers have arrested Anne it probably means there's real evidence against her. Do you think Anne's been helping kidnap these apprentices?"

"Of course not!"

"Neither do I. That means someone must be using Anne as an information source. We need to talk to her and find out all the people she's been speaking to. Then we can narrow down who it might be."

Variam perked up. "Yeah. Okay."

I started for the door and paused. "Oh, and it's about time you dropped the rebellious teenager act. We're about to talk to Keepers. Be polite."

Variam looked indignant. "But they—"

"I know what they did and I know how you feel about it. But all it'll do is make them more likely to say no. You're an adult; time to start acting like it."

Variam gave a reluctant nod.

⠀⠀⠀⠀⠀⠀⠀⠀ ׀ ׀ ׀ ׀ ׀ ׀ ׀ ׀ ׀

I was rehearsing speeches in my head as we came back around the corner, but as we came out into the corridor I frowned. The door that had been blocked by the Keeper was hanging open. Variam and I exchanged glances and walked in.

The guest room was small, with a single faded bed, and had no windows or doors except for the one we'd just come through. One of the Council Keepers was standing in a corner with his back to us talking into his mobile phone: ". . . hair black, eyes red-brown, early twenties, wearing a green skirt and jumper. Last seen fifteen minutes ago and . . ."

The other Keeper, the hard-looking one who'd been blocking the door, turned towards us with a frown. "Where's Anne?" I asked before he could get a word out.

"What are you doing here?"

"Looking for Anne. Where is she?"

"This is a restricted area," the Keeper began.

"I'm looking for the apprentice you were holding here," I said, keeping my voice even. "Given that she was in your custody, that makes you responsible for her under Council law. I am making a formal request to speak with her. Please."

The Keeper looked from me to Variam and hesitated. "You're going to have to come back—"

The second Keeper snapped his phone shut and turned towards us. "Verus," he said. He was older than his partner, with greying hair and sharp eyes. "What do you know about this?"

"At the moment, nothing," I said. I had to force myself to stay calm. "Would you happen to know where Anne Walker is?"

The Keeper studied me. "She appears to have fled."

I looked at him, then around at the bare room with its complete absence of other exits. Then I looked back at him. "You left her alone?"

"She used a gate spell," the older Keeper said.

"That's impossible."

"Apparently not."

"Anne can't use gate magic!" Variam burst out.

"What about the wards?" I said.

The Keeper looked at me with raised eyebrows. "That is an extremely good question."

"This doesn't make sense," I said. It took all I had to keep my voice level. "I couldn't get through these gate wards, and neither could you. Are you seriously telling me that you believe an apprentice found a way through a gate ward when two Council Keepers couldn't?"

"I know what a gate spell feels like, all right?" the younger Keeper said irritably. "And that's what I felt through that door. Crystal and her 'impenetrable' wards, my—"

"Look, Verus," the older Keeper said. "We're a little busy. Can you tell us where Anne Walker is?"

I was silent. "I don't know," I said at last.

"Then I'm sorry but we've got work to do." The Keeper walked past, taking out his phone again as he vanished into the corridor. The other followed, shooting me a suspicious look.

"Where is she?" Variam demanded. He was looking around the room as if he expected Anne to pop out of hiding.

"Give me a second," I said quietly. My head was whirling.

"She couldn't have gated out of here," Variam said. "She can't even use gate magic!"

"I know," I said. I felt as though I were on the verge of getting it. I just needed one more piece . . .

"Those Keepers must have taken her," Variam said.

"They didn't," I said absently.

"There couldn't have been a gate spell."

"That Keeper said there was."

"Then he was lying!"

"Maybe—" I began, and stopped.

"You can't get a gate spell through these wards," Variam repeated. "If she's not here it means—"

"Variam?" I said. "Why are these wards still working?"

"Huh?"

"Remember what Sonder said last night?" I said. "Wards like this take a lot of maintenance. Why haven't they run down?"

"Who cares?" Variam said. "I guess Crystal's fixing them."

"But Sonder said Vitus Aubuchon attuned them to himself," I said. "It would have been almost impossible for someone else to take control of Fountain Reach."

"Well, Crystal figured it out."

"Maybe she didn't," I said quietly.

Variam looked at me in confusion. "What?"

I didn't answer. A dozen images and thoughts were spinning through my head. A portrait on a wall. Notes on longevity magic, failed experiments on yellowing paper. Vitus Aubuchon, who had been sickly and aging and obsessed with his health. Sonder's words: *Basically all of Fountain Reach is one giant focus. As long as you're within it, you can use it to power spells . . .* Luna insisting that it couldn't be a coincidence, two victims of the same age at the same place. Crystal's scorn at working for the Council until she was "old and grey." Anne's last words: *Now I feel like someone's watching me . . .*

I pulled out my phone and dialled Talisid's number. It took Talisid a while to answer and when he did he sounded harassed. "Verus, I've got two other people—"

"One quick question," I said. "The Aubuchon family used to own Fountain Reach."

"Yes—"

"The last mage of the dynasty, Vitus Aubuchon," I said. "Do you know what type of mage he was?"

"He was a space mage. Spatial manipulation, gate magic, that sort of thing. Is this—?"

Something clicked. "That's all," I said, and hung up and turned back to Variam. "We need to get back to Luna."

"Do you know where Anne is?"

"No. But I think I know who took her."

· · · · · · · · ·

Luna was sitting up in bed by the time we got back to her room. She'd eaten everything I'd brought from the kitchens and was looking a lot healthier. I thanked Celia and sent her away, closing the door behind her before turning to Variam and Luna. I hadn't answered any of Variam's questions and both of them were watching me. "We don't have much time," I began, "so we're going to have to make this fast."

"Who took Anne?" Variam said.

"The same man who took that girl thirty years ago," I said. "And God only knows how many others. Vitus Aubuchon."

Variam frowned. "I thought he was—"

"Not dead," I said. "Disappeared, yes, but not dead. He was doing longevity research, looking for a way to prolong his life. I think he found one." I looked at Luna. "Remember what I told you about vampires? How they could live off humans by drinking their blood? There have always been rumours that before they were wiped out, some mages got vampires to teach them the trick."

Luna's eyes widened a little. "Wait, you mean . . . ?"

"Here's what I think happened," I said. "Vitus Aubuchon wanted to live forever. He couldn't use life magic, so he designed this house as a giant focus for a longevity spell. But it needed fuel. Human fuel, young people in the prime of their youth and strength. It worked for a long time but then something went wrong. For whatever reason normal children weren't enough anymore. So Vitus decided to start feeding off apprentices instead.

"And then Crystal came. I don't know how they met, but they made some sort of deal. Crystal would find apprentices, ones who were vulnerable and alone, and bring them here to Fountain Reach for Vitus to feed on . . ." I trailed off, remembering Crystal's words from two nights ago. *The entire point of this whole plan was so we didn't have to keep picking at random . . .* "Shit," I said quietly to myself.

"What?"

"That's why Crystal held the tournament here," I said. "They're not looking for just *any* apprentice. They're looking for the *right* apprentice. The point of the tournament was so that they could get a close-up view of all the apprentices using their magic. Anne hasn't healed anyone since getting here, has she?"

"No . . ." Variam said.

I nodded. "Not until now. Vitus saw her and that was it. As soon as she was alone he snatched her and unless we stop him he's going to do the same thing to her that he's done to everyone else."

"How do we get her back?" Variam said.

"I don't know."

"What?"

"I'm still working on that part."

"You just said we didn't have much time!"

"Vitus is a space mage. He could have taken Anne anywhere and I don't know where."

"Wait," Luna broke in. "Didn't Sonder say Vitus would have to stay inside the house?"

I nodded. "I don't think she's far, but—"

"So let's burn the house down," Variam said.

Luna looked at Variam in disbelief. "Are you nuts?"

"It'll flush him out, won't it?"

"It's not going to—"

"Actually," I said slowly, "I think that's not a bad idea." I turned towards the door. "Get ready for a fight. I'll explain along the way."

। । । । । । । । ।

I got my gear, Luna got her whip, and I led her and Variam upstairs through Fountain Reach. "The first time I came here, Onyx shredded a wall," I said. "When he did there was a scream. It was like some kind of defence system, but now I don't think it was. I think Vitus is linked to this house. Hurting it hurts him."

"So how does that help us find Anne?" Variam asked.

We turned down an old crooked corridor with animal heads lining the walls. "Wherever Vitus takes his victims, it's somewhere hidden," I said. "We won't find it, not in time. But if Vitus could bring Anne there, he could bring us there too."

The bedroom within looked just as it had the last two times I'd seen Crystal in it: old and dusty with a moth-eaten bed. The portrait on the wall stared down at us, sunken eyes looking out of a thin face. "What about everyone else?" Luna asked.

"You remember Anne's story from last night?" I said. "Someone tried to burn Fountain Reach before and something stopped them. I don't think Vitus can do anything in this part of the house, not directly. He has to take them somewhere else first."

Luna looked from me to Variam. I could tell she wasn't sure about the plan but didn't want to go back either. "Now?" Variam asked.

I nodded. "Do it."

Orange-red light flared up around Variam's hands and heat poured into the back of the room. The wallpaper blackened then ignited, flames licking up from the floor. Luna and I backed away towards the door.

I felt a pulse of magic and a mental chime: an alarm spell. "Keep going," I said, but Variam didn't need to be told. More heat went in. The old bedroom was dry as dust and the flames were spreading quickly, the carpet at the end catching fire and the bed smouldering as well. The temperature in the room was rising but Variam did something and it levelled out, the heat staying in the far end of the room. Smoke was starting to spread and I coughed.

In the distance I could hear shouts and running footsteps. "Is it working?" Luna called.

"No!" I tried to think about the last time I'd seen the house react violently. Onyx had ripped a hole through the corridor. "Go for the walls!"

Variam raised his hand and an orange-red beam sprang out. It carved into the walls as though they were butter and cut sideways, burning a gash through the bones and structure of Fountain Reach.

This time the response was instant. A scream knifed through my head, pain and fury and discord. I'd been ready and only flinched, but Luna and Variam both doubled over. Variam lost his grip on his spells; the beam winked out and the heat rushed in, scorching me. "Variam!" I shouted.

Variam recovered, forcing the temperature down. The whole far end of the room was a sheet of flame now, the bed blackening and crumbling in the inferno as the fire reached eagerly towards us. Flames were licking up around the edge of the painting, the man inside seeming to glare out at us. I could sense people coming down the corridor and I recognised Lyle and Crystal. Variam struck again, that beam of fire slicing into the walls, and this time I felt the wards around us waver as Variam's attack cut through one of the weblike strands that supported the spell around Fountain Reach.

The scream was louder, and this time there was only pain. The wards shifted, turned, and I felt the pull of a gate spell, space seeming to ripple and twist just as Lyle appeared in the doorway. The spell was centred around me and Variam and Luna but Lyle was caught too, dragged in from the edge. I caught one glimpse of Lyle's startled face, Luna and Variam turning towards me, the flames guttering and dying as their fuel was sucked away from them, then the four of us were drawn elsewhere and everything was gone.

chapter 13

And silence.

. . . I was in a small windowless room that smelt of dust. I spun, checking for danger, but the futures ahead of me were silent and still. I was alone.

There were no lights but somehow I could still see. The place was lit with a weird kind of shadowy illumination that wasn't light or darkness but something in between. I scanned but couldn't sense the presence of Luna and Variam or anyone else. I opened the door and stepped out into a corridor. Like the room it was lit up in the same strange half-light, and looking down the hall I could see old darkened tables and animal heads mounted on the walls.

I was in Fountain Reach . . . except I wasn't. The air was too still, the corridors too quiet. I'd never been comfortable in Fountain Reach, but this place felt utterly dead; it was hard to imagine *anything* living here. And yet at the same time it felt oddly familiar, as though I'd seen it before.

As I stood in the corridor I felt a weird shivering sensation. Just for an instant it felt as though there were someone else in the corridor walking straight through me—and then it was gone. I drew back, focusing my senses, and to my surprise found I could sense the presence of other people, very faintly. As I watched their shadowy outlines flitted through a wall and were gone.

I remembered the sense I'd had in Fountain Reach of something watching me, and realised that now I was doing the same thing. I was invisible to these people, as though I were hidden in the walls, peeking out through the cracks into the world of light and life.

This was where Vitus Aubuchon had gone. He'd created another place within Fountain Reach, a shadow reality where nobody else could go but from where he could look out . . . and draw people in. As I realised that, I noticed something else: My divination magic wasn't damped and fuzzy anymore. Experimentally I tried looking a few minutes into the future and found that I could. The wards only blocked the *other* Fountain Reach, not this one. Vitus had designed Fountain Reach to cloud the senses of anyone coming here, but he'd left it so that he could see clearly himself.

I scanned ahead through the futures, searching for movement. I found Luna first, some distance away but on the same floor. Variam was next, moving towards Luna, and Lyle was nearby too. The spell had scattered us, splitting us up around this other Fountain Reach. But as I looked further, something else caught my attention. There was someone who wasn't here yet . . . but she'd be arriving in the next couple of minutes and she was someone I did *not* want near Luna or Variam.

I turned away from Luna and began walking quickly down the corridor, searching through the futures in my head to narrow down the entry point. My footsteps echoed in the empty hallway, loud in the silence. The colours looked odd in this place, washed out and grey, and the air tasted dead and stale. I noticed my route would pass near a window and took a moment to look outside.

The view outside was . . . strange. Just like inside, everything was illuminated in a weird half-light, but there wasn't any ground. Where the grounds of Fountain Reach should have been was a greyish mist and the sky above was covered in dark cloud. Looking farther into the distance, both mist and cloud faded away within a few hundred feet, meeting in blackness. Somehow I had the feeling that getting out of here on foot wasn't an option.

Our new visitor would be arriving in only a couple of minutes, and I hurried down a narrow disused corridor towards the small door at the end. I reached the door, opened it, and paused. Behind the door was only a blank wall.

Interesting. I closed the door, stood behind it, and waited.

One minute later, I felt a tingle of magic and there was the sound of a key turning in a lock. The door swung open—but this time it opened into a small old room, which seemed to flame with brilliant colour. This was the real world, not the half-real copy I was in. A beautiful woman in a cream-coloured suit walked in quickly, letting the door swing shut behind her without looking back.

She sensed me before she'd gone two steps, but too late. Before she could turn I had my left hand tangled in her hair and pulling her head up while my right hand held a knife against her throat. "Crystal," I said into her ear. "Fancy meeting you here."

Crystal held quite still. Without moving the knife I took the item from her unresisting hand, then held it up where I could see it. It was a small iron key and it radiated magic. "A focus," I said. "So Vitus gave you a way to get in and out of this place on your own, huh?"

"I don't know what you're hoping to accomplish," Crystal said without turning her head, "but this is not a good way to go about it." Despite the knife to her throat, her voice was steady.

"First things first," I said, dropping the key into my pocket. "Please don't try any attacks. No matter how fast you think you are, I promise you you're not as fast as a muscle twitch. Now how about you lead me to where Vitus Aubuchon has been taking the kids?"

"I'm not quite sure what you're talking about."

I let myself think about the fact that if Crystal was going to be uncooperative it would be faster just to slit her throat and find Vitus's lair myself.

"Oh, *Vitus* Aubuchon," Crystal said hurriedly. "You're looking for his sanctum?"

"Yes I am. Start walking."

Crystal did. I matched pace with her, keeping the knife pressed against her throat and keeping my divination focused on the short-term chances of her trying anything. As long as I kept the knife there, they were very low. I'd spent enough time around Crystal to get a fairly good handle on her personality and I'd pegged her as the cautious type. I didn't think she'd try to attack on her own, not as long as she thought she could get out of this some other way. "What is this place?" I said.

"I don't actually know the details—"

I let myself think of cutting Crystal's throat again.

Crystal changed gears quickly. "—it's a shadow realm of Fountain Reach. It's a copy, slightly out of phase with reality. The wards link the copy with the original."

"And that key is a focus that lets you go between the two, right?"

". . . Yes. But it's not easy to use, you have to—"

"I'm sure I'll figure it out."

"Please don't tell Vitus I let you know any of this," Crystal said. She sounded afraid, fearful. "He'll kill me."

"Uh-huh."

"I'll help you. I'll take you to him. Is that all right?"

"That's great. Down these stairs?"

"Yes . . . Could you take the knife away?"

"I don't think so." I started down the stairs, keeping the knife to Crystal's throat.

"Look, I didn't have any choice," Crystal said anxiously. "He brought me here the first time. If I didn't help him he was going to—"

"He was going to do what?" I said. "Vitus can't do anything outside this house. In fact, I don't think he can even *leave* this house. So what exactly was stopping you from walking away as soon as you got out that first time?"

"There are—things he can do," Crystal said with a little catch in her voice. "You don't understand. He's—"

"Oh, spare me the bullshit," I said. "I'm not as gullible as Lyle. If you're going to lie at least make it interesting."

Crystal was silent for five seconds and when she spoke again the pretence of fear was gone from her voice; it was precise and cool. "I'm going to enjoy watching Vitus kill you."

"You know, that might be the first honest thing you've ever said to me." Following Crystal's lead, I turned down another hallway; we were descending towards the lower regions of Fountain Reach. "While we're on this truthful streak, why don't you tell me why you signed up with Vitus?"

"Why should I?"

"Because you're hoping to kill me before we leave, so where's the harm?"

"That's an interesting perspective."

"Okay, let's try another question. How long has Anne got before Vitus kills her?"

"That is the question, isn't it?" Crystal said calmly. "Let's just say that if I were you I wouldn't wait around."

A flash of anger went through me but I kept my voice level. "You're very funny."

Crystal suddenly came to a stop. We'd reached an intersection, corridors stretching away in all four directions into darkness. When Crystal spoke, her voice was suddenly high and frightened again. "No, please don't hurt me! I'll do whatever you say!"

I growled. "Stop that." I was watching Crystal's future actions closely and I could sense she was coiled, ready to strike. "I told you—"

The attack came from behind: a chaotic surge of fear and emotion and confusion that scrambled my thoughts. Crystal reacted instantly, ducking away from the knife as she struck at me with a wave of agony. But I'd had an instant's warning and I was already moving, my instincts sending me diving to one side around the corner and out of line of sight while my conscious mind struggled to catch up. The backwash of Crystal's spell sent pain up and down my nerves but a moment later I had my back pressed up against the wall.

"Lyle!" I heard Crystal gasp as I collected my thoughts. "You made it!"

Anger drove out the aftereffects of Lyle's spell. "Lyle,

you idiot!" I shouted around the corner. "What the hell are you doing?"

"Look, Alex," Lyle called back. "Just put the knife down and we can talk about this."

"Your psycho girlfriend is the one I need the knife to protect me from!" I shouted. "Along with all the apprentices she's—"

Crystal moved in fast. I saw her coming, knew she was about to attack, and turned and ran. I might have been able to take Crystal one on one, but not with Lyle helping her. I sprinted down the hallway and ducked into a side passage a moment before Crystal made it around the corner. Crystal tried to chase me, but I was faster than she was and those heels didn't do much to help her running speed. It didn't take long before she gave up and went back towards Lyle, whom I could dimly hear calling in the distance.

I slowed to a jog, searching through the futures ahead as I mapped out a route to meet up with Variam and Luna. All the time I'd been interrogating Crystal she must have been talking telepathically with Lyle, convincing him that I was the bad guy and that she needed his help and directing him in to intercept us. And she'd done it while keeping up a second conversation with me *and* while reading my thoughts, all at the same time. I'd underestimated her.

I intercepted Variam and Luna at a landing leading off into a T junction. "Variam, Luna," I called softly around the corner. "It's me."

"Alex?" Luna asked. She sounded relieved.

"Wait," Variam said sharply. "Come out where we can see you."

Luna was about to protest, but I stepped out with a shake of my head. "It's all right." I held my hands up for Variam to see; he was in the shadows around the corner, where he thought I couldn't see him. "Okay?"

Variam studied me suspiciously for a moment, then nodded. "It's him."

Luna, Variam, and I gathered on the landing and I gave them a quick once-over. "You two okay?"

"We're fine, we met up a couple of minutes ago," Luna said. "Are you all right?"

I led Luna and Variam in the direction they'd come from and as I did I caught them up on my brief encounter with Lyle and Crystal. "Lyle's working with her?" Luna said indignantly.

"Much as I'd love to blame this on him, probably not. I think Crystal's using him as a patsy."

"You're keeping tabs on them, right?"

I nodded. "We're about two minutes ahead of them. Crystal had to spin Lyle a story and it looks like it slowed them down."

"Is Anne okay?" Variam asked.

"I think so."

"What do you mean, you think so?"

"I think so."

"Is she alive or hurt or in trouble or what?"

"Look, Variam, I'm navigating us a path, monitoring Crystal, watching for danger, and talking to you guys all at the same time. I'm a little—"

Fountain Reach shook. It was only a slight tremor but it was enough to make us stop in our tracks. Dust trickled from the ceiling and somewhere in my head I felt the ripple of a psychic scream, scraping along my nerves and making my hair stand on end.

"What was *that*?" Luna said.

"Trouble," I said with a sinking heart. "Don't slow down!"

The corridor ahead came to an end in a crooked door. Variam shoved it open to reveal a wide, dark space. There was a ceiling above but it was cracked and bumpy. Skeletal bushes rose before us, long dead. I led us in and mud squelched under our feet; the floor was earth, not wood or stone. "Where are we?" Luna asked quietly, glancing from side to side.

"Hedgemaze," I said. I'd already mapped the route and led Variam and Luna through at a fast walk. "But Crystal called the whole place a 'shadow realm.'"

Variam looked over with a frown. "We're in a shadow realm?"

"You know what one is?"

"Yeah, but this isn't really the time," Variam said. "Someone else just came in, right?"

The hedgemaze must have been quite a sight once. Now it was a petrified ruin, the dead wood fading into the darkness as we wound our way towards the centre.

"Onyx," I said. I'd been searching ahead and the futures where we ran into him were very hard to miss.

"How did *he* get in?" Luna said.

"From the sound of it I think he figured out how we got here and did a repeat performance." Probably he'd shot up the house the same way Variam had. This wasn't looking good—I'd been ready to deal with Vitus, but not Crystal and Onyx as well.

"Are we going to get to Anne first?" Variam said.

"Yeah, but not by much." I glanced through the futures in which we turned back. Crystal was still pursuing with Lyle trailing after, Onyx was behind them both but catching up fast, and I still couldn't pick Vitus out of the tangle. "Okay, this is going to get messy real fast. Vitus is up ahead and he wants Anne, but he'll be going after us second. Crystal wants to silence us, make sure we don't get out to spread the story. Lyle probably has no idea what's going on, so he's sticking next to Crystal. And Onyx . . . my guess is he's here to kill *everyone*. Vitus, Crystal, me, and anyone who doesn't get out of the way fast enough."

"What's the plan?" Luna asked.

"There isn't one," I said.

Luna and Variam looked at each other. I realised they were waiting for me to tell them what to do and felt a flash of frustration. Couldn't they tell I was making this up as I went along?

But they were looking to me to lead them, and even if I didn't know what I was doing I had to act as though I did. I tried to think of what would put Luna and Variam at the least risk. "All right," I said. "I'll go in and get Anne. You two hold the entrance as long as you can, then fall back. If we get separated work your way out of the maze back to the top floor of the house to the long corridor where we entered. I'll meet you there and we can get out."

"I'm going with—" Variam started to say.

"No," I said instantly. "Look, if these guys all attack us at once we're finished. Our only chance is to hold them as far away as we can. If we can keep them busy with each other, we can get away in the confusion. Crystal's key will get us out if we can make it to the door."

A shape loomed out of the darkness ahead of us and a moment later the skeletal bushes opened up into a clearing. Before us was a small building, its foundations sunk into the ancient mud and its upper level reaching up into the shadows. We'd reached the centre of the hedgemaze.

There was only one way in: a crosshatched metal door, stiff from long disuse. "Hold this door until you're in danger and then get out," I said as I got to work on it. "Try to delay

Crystal long enough for Onyx to catch up, but if you can't, or once the fighting gets serious, run." The door scraped open and I turned to look at Luna and Variam. "Got it?"

Luna looked around nervously at the dead clearing. "Okay."

"Fine," Variam said. "But if you're not back in five minutes, I'm going after—"

"If I'm not back in five minutes it probably means Anne and I are both dead. In that case, get out. There's a second way out through the hedgemaze around the back."

Variam scowled. Luna was watching the clearing. There was maybe thirty feet of muddy ground between the edge of the hedgemaze and the building, and the air was ominously silent. With my divination I could sense Crystal hurrying closer with Onyx on her heels. If Luna and Variam hid inside the door they'd have some cover, but not much.

"Alex?" Luna said. The clearing was quiet, but I knew it wouldn't stay that way for long. "Hurry, okay?"

I walked into the darkness.

| | | | | | | | | | |

The inside of the building was cramped and decaying. Pieces of wall crunched under my feet and I had to turn sideways to squeeze through the single corridor, yet somehow as I picked my way through the debris I knew this little old building was the heart of Fountain Reach. All the space and luxury outside were just for show. The corridor bent around, then inward.

The room within was lined floor to ceiling with cracked grey tiles, and it stank. The air was heavy with a kind of sickly rich coppery smell that made me hold my breath. My foot slipped underneath me as I took the first step in, and I put my hand against the wall to steady myself. The tiles were cold. The place seemed to be darker than outside and only as my eyes adjusted did I start to make out the features of the room: the bathtub in the corner, the counters along one side, and the metal table in the centre. Lying on the metal table was a body.

As soon as I saw that I rushed to the table, my shoes skidding on the floor. The body on the table was Anne, and as I saw her my heart sank. Her head was hanging back off the edge of the table, and her throat had been messily cut open. "Oh no," I whispered under my breath. I touched Anne's skin to find that it was cool. I looked into the futures in which I put my ear to her chest and listened and couldn't find anything. I've seen people with cut throats and I knew Anne's wound had to be fatal, but I still clung to a sliver of hope. I'd seen her survive lethal wounds before. There were straps holding Anne to the table and I started pulling them open. "Come on," I whispered to myself. "Please don't be dead, please don't be dead . . ." The straps were sticky, but I was able to get them off. "Anne, if you can hear me, now would be—"

Anne sat up with a gasp and I nearly jumped out of my skin. She looked blindly from left to right in a panic and I caught her. "Easy! It's okay, you're safe."

Anne clutched at my arm. "Where is he?" Her voice was raspy but recovering and the ugly slash across her throat was healing as I watched, new skin growing across the wound with a flicker of green light.

"He's not here," I said, trying to sound reassuring. "We're . . ." I trailed off. Anne was staring past me and as I turned I saw that she was looking at the bathtub. Something flickered on my precognition and I suddenly realised what I'd slipped on earlier. The floor was covered in patches of that dark, sticky liquid and it was spread all over the room . . . and filling the bathtub. And it was there that the smell was coming from.

"Oh," I said quietly.

The liquid in the bathtub stirred, dark ripples spreading and lapping at the edge. Something broke the surface, rivulets of blood trickling from the head as it turned slowly to face us. For a moment it held itself motionless and then the rest of the creature rose slowly and steadily out of the bath, coming fully into view as streams of blood splashed off the shoulders to splatter on the floor. It was a human body, wasted and twisted and skin pale from lack of light, but with pieces missing. The muscles were spaced unevenly around the spindly frame, too strong in places and too weak in others, and the arms were longer than they should have been, hanging below the knees. For all that, though, it could almost have passed as a man except for the face. There were no eyes in the sockets, only a pair of gaping black voids. The mouth opened, toothless, to let loose a hissing, sighing breath.

The creature that had once been Vitus Aubuchon stared sightlessly at us.

I moved first, half-dragging Anne in a rush for the door, but fast as I was Vitus was faster. There was a weird twisting, warping sensation and suddenly Vitus was standing blocking the exit, his breath making a cloud in the air as I backpedalled frantically.

There was one other exit, a doorway leading deeper into the building. I made a snap decision and bolted for it. Anne had found her feet again and followed me, and as we ran I heard a weird rasping, grating sound from behind us. Vitus Aubuchon was laughing.

We burst into the next room only to skid to a halt, and as I looked around I felt my mouth go dry. The walls were lined with alcoves, each about three feet wide by three feet deep, and they were all filled with human remains. The older alcoves contained bones, neatly piled on top of each other with the skull placed on top, rows and rows of them each with the skulls grinning emptily outward. The newer bodies were . . . fresher. Most were desiccated and dark but the closest alcove, on the far right, contained what looked like the huddled form of a girl, black hair covering her face. But for an odd shapelessness she might have been alive. There were dozens of alcoves, hundreds. Most were full, but there was space for more—a lot more. At the far end was a furnace but otherwise there was nothing else in the room . . . including doors. We'd come to a dead end.

From behind I could hear the dragging feet of Vitus drawing closer. I searched frantically through the futures, trying to find a way Anne and I could get out safely. I didn't find one. It was getting harder and harder not to panic and I had to clamp down on my feelings as I tried to figure out what to do.

"Alex," Anne whispered, and I could hear the fear in her voice.

"Can you do anything to stop him?" I said.

Anne hesitated for just an instant, then I saw something flash across her face and she nodded. "If I get close."

I sized Anne up. She still looked wobbly on her feet, though at least she'd repaired the gaping wound to her throat. But while her eyes were afraid, they were steady. "Do it," I said. "I'll draw him in." *And let's pray it works.*

Anne drew back to the corner of the room nearest to the door; she was weaving some kind of spell about herself but it wasn't doing anything that I could see. A moment later a shadow fell over the doorway as Vitus Aubuchon stepped in.

I stood facing Vitus, weight on the balls of my feet, tense

and ready to jump. I was maybe thirty feet from him, between the alcoves filled with the bodies of those who'd died here in Fountain Reach. Anne was to Vitus's right, less than half the distance away, but his sightless eyes were locked on me. I looked back into those empty sockets and felt a thrill of pure terror.

The energies of a spell swirled around Vitus and I threw myself right. The space I'd been in warped and shrank, the air seeming to ripple. It looked like nothing but I'd seen what would have happened if that had caught me. I came to a stop next to the alcoves; Vitus's head turned to track me and the same spell flashed out again.

The blast radius was wider this time and I only just made it out. Two of the skeletons and an iron partition were caught in the spell and there was a crunching, snapping sound as they were crushed into fragments, the space around them crumpling like a paper bag. Splinters rattled on the floor as Vitus gave a hissing sound and advanced towards me.

Anne moved the instant Vitus's back was to her. Vitus was just about to cast a third spell when Anne's hand touched his shoulder.

And in that moment I finally understood why life mages are feared.

Anne ripped Vitus Aubuchon's life out of his body like tearing a page out of a notebook. It was over so fast I literally didn't see it. There was a green flash and then Vitus's body was toppling, dead before it hit the ground.

I looked down at Vitus, then up at Anne, eyes wide. Anne was staring down at Vitus's body. There was something in her eyes I'd never seen before and for just a moment I felt a chill, and then it was gone and she only looked pale and tired. "We should go," Anne said.

Vitus's body was starting to dissolve, the misshapen form

turning black and breaking away into ash and dust. I picked my way around it to meet up with Anne. "Why didn't he see you?"

"He can't see," Anne said. "He senses life, so I masked mine . . . We need to go!"

We hurried back into the room with the table and the bathtub, now silent and still once more. "That was what you were doing before?" I asked.

"I played dead." Anne's face looked drawn but at least she didn't seem hurt anymore. "After he . . ."

I gave the room a last glance, shuddered, and was about to leave when I stopped. There had been a stir of movement from the bathtub. As I watched, a ripple spread across the dark surface, followed by another. "Anne?" I asked carefully. "He's going to *stay* dead, right?"

Anne shook her head.

The ripples were increasing, and as I looked into the future I saw that in a few seconds something was going to break the surface. I ran for the door.

ꞏ ꞏ ꞏ ꞏ ꞏ ꞏ ꞏ ꞏ ꞏ ꞏ

"I thought you killed him!" I shouted to Anne as we ran down the corridor.

"It doesn't stick!" Anne shouted back. "Fountain Reach keeps him alive; it's what it was made to do. As long as he's in this house, he can't die!"

I swore under my breath. "So he can teleport, he can bend space, and he's immortal. Wonderful."

In the time we'd been inside the entrance to the building had become a battlefield. The doorway was open and ragged now, the door a pile of scrap metal, and Variam and Luna were crouched on either side with gashes torn in the walls around them. Outside, the dark hedgemaze was lit up with flickering orange light; several of the dead bushes were on fire. Both Variam and Luna turned towards us as we approached and Luna's eyes lit up. "Anne!"

"You're okay?" Variam demanded.

I grabbed Anne and pulled her to one side. An instant later a salvo of force blades came scything in from outside, carving through brick and metal. They cut through the outer wall, went over the heads of Luna and Variam and past me and Anne, cut through the inner wall on the other side, and kept right on going. Variam swore. "So I'm guessing Onyx is here," I said.

"So's Crystal!" Luna said. She sounded shaken, but she was holding steady. "It's crazy out there, I don't know who's fighting who—"

"Can't make it across that ground," Variam said. "We need to go back the way you came."

"That's worse!" Anne said.

"She's right," I said. "We'll be caught between them and Vitus." I pulled a condenser marble from my pocket. "Variam, when I give the word put a wall of fire down parallel to the front wall thirty feet out. Then run. Go right, head for the far side of the maze, and don't stop."

Variam nodded and from outside I heard the thunderclap of force magic. I leant out and threw the condenser through the doorway and out into the clearing, ahead and to the left. It shattered and mist sprang up. "Now!" I called to Variam.

Orange light wreathed Variam's hands, and with a roar a wall of fire flared into life, lighting up the dark hedgemaze in leaping flame. It cut halfway through the mist and ignited the dead wood of the maze to the left and right, blocking off vision. Luna was out the door first with the rest of us right behind her.

Heat pulsed from the wall of flame ahead. The comforting grey cloud of the mist hung to my left, inviting me to enter, but I'd told the others to go right and that was where I ran. Normally when I create these mist clouds I run into them, using my magic to pick out a path where others would be blind. But I'd done it a few too many times lately and I knew that was exactly what Onyx would be expecting. Onyx couldn't see through the wall of fire but he could see the mist cloud, and I heard the hiss as a spray of force blades cut through it. A moment later we'd put the building between us and Onyx, and as we ran back into the hedgemaze I felt the familiar warp-and-twist of Vitus's teleport spell. I couldn't see where Vitus landed and I didn't stop to check. We were back in the maze and safe . . . at least for now.

We hurried through the maze, my divination magic picking us out a path. From behind I could sense the flash of attack spells as the battle continued. "Who's winning?" Variam called from behind me.

"Don't care!"

"They're all still there," Anne called. "Vitus, Crystal, Lyle, and Onyx."

The door at the far end took us back into the mansion. The sounds of battle had faded into an eerie silence and once more Fountain Reach seemed to be watching and waiting. I led us towards the exit, abandoning stealth in favour of getting us out as fast as possible.

As I approached the door by which Crystal had entered, I felt a presence ahead of me. "Alex," Anne whispered. "It's—"

"Crystal," I said. "I know. You guys stay back."

"Screw that—" Variam began.

"You'll stay the hell back," I said sharply. "Crystal is not stupid. If she's there she's got something planned. You and Luna stay ready. Vitus is still around and we know he's after Anne."

Luna nodded. Variam looked frustrated but didn't argue. I walked around the corner.

The corridor was narrow and led to the same small door. Without the key in my pocket I knew that door would open onto nothing but a blank wall, but *with* that key it would take us out of here. Crystal was standing halfway down the corridor, blocking my path. The weird half-light of this place blended with the yellow shades of her hair and clothes, turning her into a pale figure in the shadows. She watched me silently. I could tell she was holding herself ready, but I didn't know for what.

I hesitated an instant, then started walking towards her. "Not bringing your friends?" Crystal asked softly.

I didn't answer. I'd closed half the distance to Crystal, my knife ready in its sheath. Crystal watched me take two more steps, then shrugged slightly. "As you like."

From behind me I felt a surge of magic as Vitus Aubuchon teleported into the middle of Anne, Variam, and Luna. And at the same instant Crystal drove into my mind with all her power, trying to seize control.

She was horribly strong. I'd been ready for her, but even so I was almost overwhelmed in those first few seconds. It felt like an enormous weight bearing down on my thoughts, crushing me. I staggered back but the pressure didn't let up; if anything it grew stronger. Desperately I tried to force Crystal away, stopping her from getting any further in.

Dimly I could sense that a furious battle was going on next to me. Vitus's horrible form was blocking the hallway: He'd trapped Anne in a prison of twisted space and was attacking Variam, trying to crush him. Variam was dodging from side to side, a snarl on his face, while Luna's whip curled around Vitus, the silver mist soaking in. But I couldn't spare any attention; if I took my concentration off Crystal for even a second I knew she'd have me. I could feel tendrils snaking into my thoughts, trying to seize control, and I pushed back with all of my might.

"Coming here was a very poor choice on your part," Crystal said calmly. She didn't even sound out of breath.

I didn't answer. I focused on trying to hold Crystal back, drive her out of my mind. It was unbelievably difficult, like trying to push a car uphill, and in a sudden flash of understanding I knew that this was how all those missing apprentices had been brought here. "Just so you know," Crystal said, "I'm going to make you kill Luna and Variam with your own hands." She tilted her head. "How does it feel to know that you've failed completely?"

I felt a flare of white-hot anger and threw myself at Crystal's mental pressure, hammering at it. And it shifted. It was only a tiny, tiny shift, but I'd managed to push Crystal back just a fraction and all of a sudden I knew she wasn't invulnerable. "I don't know," I managed to say. "You tell me."

I took a step forward. It felt like wading through deep water but the first one was the hardest. I took a second step and then a third, and with each one I shoved Crystal a little further back. I saw a flash of surprise in Crystal's eyes, followed by concentration. The mental pressure redoubled and my progress halted.

Crystal and I stared at each other across the corridor. Neither of us moved but we fought as surely as if we wrestled on the floor. "Vitus is going to kill them," Crystal said. "I hope you know that."

I could still hear the sounds of battle behind me but I didn't let myself think of whether Crystal was right. "You think you're the first mage to try to possess me?" I said. I took all my anger and all my fear for Luna and Anne and Variam and threw it at Crystal, forcing her back. I took a step forward. "You think you'll be the one to break my will? I've beaten a mind mage who was stronger than you'll ever be." Another push; another step. "I've had enchantresses bewitch me and elemental mages burn me. I've stood against one of the most powerful battle-mages in this country and watched him die. I've faced Light mages and Dark, constructs and assassins, elementals and dragons, and *I'm still here*." Another step. "You think you'll be the one to take me down? You think you're going to succeed when they couldn't?" Another step. "Not you. Not today!"

And I felt Crystal's domination spell shatter, the force of her will scattering away and leaving my mind clear. Crystal staggered back and I moved forward, my hand going to the hilt of my knife. "Lyle!" Crystal shouted. "Help!"

Lyle burst in from a side door and I swore. "No!" I shouted, stopping him just before he could launch an attack. "We're on the same side, damn it!"

"Put your weapon down, Alex!" Lyle shouted. He was standing near Crystal protectively, ready to strike.

"Lyle, I don't know what Crystal has been telling you but I promise you it's wrong. She's the one who's been bringing those apprentices here. It's her *house*, for God's sake! You seriously think she's just an innocent victim here?"

Lyle shifted uneasily and I knew that whatever story Crystal had spun, it hadn't convinced him completely. "Look, we're just trying to get out of here," Lyle said. Now that I got a better look at him I could see that he looked dishevelled and rattled but he didn't seem to be hurt. "You've got the key, right? Just give it to us. Please?" His tone was pleading.

Crystal was standing motionless but I knew she was speaking with Lyle, even if I couldn't hear her. I bit my lip in frustration. Crystal was right there . . . but if I made a move to attack, Lyle would too, and I couldn't fight them both. I couldn't hear the sounds of battle from behind anymore and that filled me with dread. I needed to get back there fast. "You want the key?" I said. "Take it." I pulled Crystal's key out of my pocket and threw it to Lyle.

Lyle caught it and stopped. He seemed to be at a loss. Crystal looked taken aback too; whatever she'd been expecting me to do, it hadn't been that. "What are you waiting for?" I asked Lyle. "Open it and go find the Keepers. Unless you want to stay here?"

The words broke Lyle's paralysis and he hurried past Crystal to the door, inserting the key. I felt a flash of magic as it turned in the lock and then the door opened, spilling a wash of brilliant light into the corridor. "Crystal!" Lyle called from the doorway.

"Come on, Crystal," I said. "Let's go see what the Keepers say."

Crystal looked at me, then darted for the door.

I sprang after her but Crystal had thought and acted in an instant and I hadn't had any warning. Crystal made it through the door and swung it closed behind her. I had just a fleeting image of Crystal's lips curling in a slight smile, then the door slammed shut, leaving me in darkness.

A second later my hand closed on the handle and I yanked the door open to see a blank wall. I felt for the keyhole and swore. Crystal had taken the key with her. I stood there, staring at the wall, then turned back to where I'd seen Luna and the others and ran.

। । । । । । ।

By the time I got there it was all over. Variam was propped up against the wall, blood on his clothes; his right arm had been horribly mangled and was hanging limp by his side. Anne was kneeling next to him, her face lit up by a soft green glow and filled with concentration as she worked her hands around Variam's injured shoulder. Luna was leaning against the other wall; her face was white and she was shaking. But Vitus Aubuchon's body was on the floor, blackened and decaying into nothingness.

"Are you okay?" I asked.

"Where's Crystal?" Variam said.

"Gone," I said. "She locked the door behind her."

Variam looked at me, then away. "Um," Luna said. "Is there another way out?"

"I don't know," I said. I was trying very hard to think.

"Alex, we can't survive another attack," Anne said. She didn't look up from where she was working on Variam, and her voice was calm.

I didn't know what to do but I knew we couldn't stay here. "We've got about five minutes until Vitus comes back," I said. "And Onyx is on his way too. Let's move."

With Anne supporting him Variam made it to his feet and we started walking. I picked a direction away from Onyx that I thought would give us the most cover. "Okay," I said. "If anyone has any ideas, now would be a good time."

Anne gave me a quick glance and shook her head. "Can we get out?" Luna asked.

"I'm not sure there *is* an out," I said.

"Gate magic," Variam said.

I looked at Variam. "Can you get out of a shadow realm with that?"

Variam gave a small nod. He was badly hurt and I could tell the adrenaline rush that had got him through the battle was wearing off; it was an effort for him to talk. "Harder, but yeah."

Luna looked at me. "That other place we went to from

the British Museum. Deleo got out of there with a gate, didn't she?"

"Your stone . . ." Anne said.

I thought quickly. Gate stones didn't work inside the real Fountain Reach; the wards blocked them. But the wards didn't cover *this* Fountain Reach. I wasn't sure it would work, but I couldn't think of a better plan. "Let's try it."

We came into what seemed like this Fountain Reach's copy of the duelling hall. It was higher and narrower than the one in our reality, with an arched ceiling and pillars along each wall. I picked out a side room that looked defensible and headed in.

Once we were inside Anne helped Variam down on a chair and I pulled the gate stone from my pocket. The focus was dark in the shadows, the rune barely visible. "Anne," I said, holding it out. "Do you think you can work it on your own?"

Anne looked at it for a second, then nodded. I placed it into her hand. "Get going. I'll buy you as much time as I can."

"Wait," Luna said. "What about you?"

"Don't worry about me. This is what I do. Just get that gate open."

Luna's eyes flashed. I knew she was scared but even so she wanted to fight. "I'm not leaving without—"

"That was an order, not a request," I said flatly. "Stay here."

"We won't leave without you," Anne said. She was clasping the stone in one hand and her eyes were steady.

I nodded and walked out into the duelling hall.

⁞⁞⁞⁞⁞⁞⁞

Onyx strode in one minute later. The darkness seemed to follow him as he moved, and his eyes were black slits. I knew he'd been fighting both Vitus and Crystal but he didn't look so much as scratched. His eyes flicked from left to right, coming to rest on me.

"Looks like you're getting your duel after all, Onyx," I said. I was standing on one of the pistes.

"Nowhere to run?" Onyx asked. He walked into the room and stopped, turned slightly side-on to me, his hands ready by his sides.

"You wanted a traditional duel," I said. "Bring it."

Onyx tilted his head and studied me for a moment.

I was moving before Onyx threw his spell and the force blade hit the spot where I'd been standing a moment ago. Chips of wood went skittering across the floor as I ducked behind a pillar. "Run and hide," Onyx said contemptuously, walking forward. He kicked one of the wooden splinters, sending it clattering into the corner. "What does Morden want with a coward like you?"

"Speaking of Morden," I said, taking care not to poke my head out, "didn't he tell you to work *with* me?"

Onyx just laughed. He started to circle the pillar at a leisurely speed, not taking his eyes off my hiding place. I moved to match him, keeping the pillar between us. "Aren't you supposed to be getting rid of Vitus?" I asked.

"Vitus isn't going anywhere," Onyx said. "I've been waiting for this."

"Yeah, I bet you have," I said. "Remember our chat in the basement? As soon I saw that look in your eyes I knew what you were planning. I've seen it before."

"Talk, talk, talk," Onyx said. He was circling to a position where if I kept trying to keep the pillar between me and him I'd come up against a table. "Let's see what you got."

Just before Onyx could trap me I moved sideways and back. A second later Onyx came around the edge to see nothing but empty space. "What I figured," Onyx said.

"You know," I said from behind a second pillar, "Morden's going to be quite upset if you miss Vitus because you were busy with me."

"Morden's not here," Onyx said, and I could tell he was smiling. He started walking towards my new hiding place, following the sound of my voice. "You're supposed to know everything, right? Know why I'm going to kill you?"

"Yeah, as a matter of fact I do."

"Yeah?" Onyx said. I could feel him lining up another spell. "Why?"

"Because you're a murderous, egocentric asshole," I said. "Because nobody beats you and walks away, even if you were the one who started the fight. You're too aggressive to quit and too stupid to call it even. You're just going to keep coming back over and over again until you're dead."

Onyx stopped, and I could tell he wasn't smiling anymore. "Okay," he said after a pause. "Enough talk."

The plane of force was about the size and shape of an industrial saw blade, and it went through the base of the pillar in a spray of debris. I'd already gone flat and felt the breeze of the thing as it cleared my hair by six inches or so. The second force blade went through the *top* of the pillar. Cut at both ends, the pillar toppled and hit the floor with a shattering crash as I rolled out of the way and came to my feet. Onyx came into view a second later . . . and I hit him in the face with a staff.

This version of Fountain Reach didn't have focus weapons, but I'd spotted the six-foot metal pole before Onyx had entered and I'd been letting him back me towards it. I didn't know what it was made of but it was light and strong. Onyx was caught off balance—he'd obviously been expecting me to keep running, not close in—and I hit him with enough power to crack his skull.

Unfortunately it didn't do the least bit of damage. The force shield around Onyx absorbed the blow effortlessly. It did make him flinch though, and the blast he'd been preparing went wide, tearing a chunk out of the wall. I pressed Onyx, striking again and again and pushing him out into the centre of the hall.

I felt the flicker of a spell and a swordlike plane of force appeared in Onyx's right hand. To normal eyes it would have been invisible but to my mage's sight it was a razor-thin line of smoky glass, and Onyx brought it around in a wide arc that would have ended somewhere in my rib cage. Letting that happen didn't strike me as a good idea so I knocked the force blade up and over my head before landing the end of the staff in Onyx's body, driving him back another step.

We fought in the shadows of the duelling hall, staff against sword. The inertial planes of the force magic made only a dull *clack-clack* against the metal pole and the loudest noise echoing around the dark room was our footsteps. The force weapon was sharp enough to cut the staff like paper but I kept parrying the flat of the blade, turning the edge away. As blow after blow got through Onyx's guard it became clear that in terms of skill I had the edge on him. Onyx was fast—very fast—but speed alone isn't a match for technique. The problem was that hitting him wasn't actually doing anything. The invisible shield of force around Onyx had enough raw inertia to stop anything short of high-level battle-magic or a military heavy weapon, and my staff couldn't even scratch it. It was Vitus Aubuchon all over again. I couldn't kill Onyx but he could kill me.

I could feel the stirrings of magic in the room behind me, life and fire weaving together, and I knew Anne and Variam were trying to use my gate stone. They'd done the smart thing and stayed hidden, and from a glance through the futures it looked like they were starting to get it to work—

But I'd taken my focus off Onyx for an instant, and against someone as deadly as the Dark Chosen that was simply too long. My next attack was a fraction too slow and Onyx was able to get his blade in the way and this time the force blade met the staff edge-on. There was a faint *shinnng!* as one foot of staff went whirring off into the darkness, my next strike fell short, and Onyx's blade flashed out at me.

I had my staff in place to parry, but it didn't do much good. Onyx's blade barely slowed down as it went through the metal and my backwards leap wasn't quite fast enough. I felt a sharp horizontal sting across my chest and upper arm, then I was out of range and Onyx was bringing up his other hand, ready to throw another spell at me.

I dropped into a crouch, holding still. Onyx had been about to hurl a force lance, but as he saw that I was ready he stopped, standing side-on with his left arm up, palm flat. His eyes were fixed on me with flat concentration and I knew what he was thinking. He was trying to figure out how he could get me with that spell without me dodging out of the way. "Try it," I said.

Onyx didn't answer and I knew he was through with words. My chest and arm hurt and I could feel blood trickling down my skin, but I could still move and right now that was all that mattered. "You know," I said, "before you go back to trying to hit me, there's something I need to tell you. Actually, two things."

Onyx's eyes tracked me, ready to release the spell. I knew he'd fire the instant I moved. "First thing is we've been fighting for a few minutes now," I said. "The second is that force magic of yours is really easy to detect from a distance."

Onyx frowned slightly.

Behind Onyx, Vitus Aubuchon teleported into the duelling hall.

Onyx spun snake-quick and the force lance flashed out, but it curved away from Vitus, its path distorting. From behind I felt the flare of a gate spell and I heard Luna's shout. "Alex!"

I turned and ran. I covered the distance in seconds and I had one last fleeting glimpse of Vitus, re-formed and whole again, those ghastly empty eye sockets locked on Onyx and one hand grasping towards him. The space around Onyx was warping, trying to compress inwards, and Onyx was crouched in a snarl, the force shield flickering and trying to maintain its shape as the two magics clashed. Then I was through the door. Where I'd left Anne and Luna and Variam an oval gateway was hanging in the air, its edges flickering green to match the light around Anne's hands. Variam was already through and within that oval I could see the natural darkness of our own world.

Luna and Anne had only been waiting for me and as they saw me they darted through the gate one after the other. I knew the gate was about to close and I put my head down and sprinted.

It was very, very close. Anne's grip on the spell faltered when I had ten feet to go and I turned the last three steps into a running jump. I went sailing through the gate, hit Anne along the way, and felt the spell snap behind me. We both went into the table and chairs in the middle of the room and hit the floor in a crash of furniture.

The light of the gate stone had extinguished with Anne's spell and we were left in pitch-darkness, the only sound the noises of everyone checking to make sure they were in one piece. But it was natural darkness, not the strange half-light of that other place, and while it was cold it was the fresh cold of winter. I could smell dust and spiderwebs but the air was clean.

Orange light flared, illuminating Variam's face as he held an orb of magelight above his head. He looked battered and weary but he was still in one piece and his eyes were alert as he looked around. In the glow we could see the tiles and table and chairs of the kitchen of my farmhouse in Wales. Outside was the darkness of a winter evening, and looking around I could see Luna and Anne. We were safe.

"Okay," Luna said, breaking the silence with a sigh. "I do *not* want to do that again."

"You and me both." I pulled myself to my feet, wincing, and gave Anne a hand up. "You okay?"

Anne looked at my hand in surprise for a second, then smiled and took it. "I'm okay." She brushed herself off, looking around. "I guess we're back again?"

"Is it over?" Luna asked.

"No one's going to follow us," I said. I'd been looking into the futures of our staying in the house and they were all blessedly quiet. "It's over."

"What about Vitus?" Variam asked. He'd propped himself up against the wall, his shattered arm still hanging limp.

"*You* are not worrying about Vitus," I said. "You're going to bed to let Anne work on you. And you're staying there until you've had a chance to rest."

Variam tried to look indignant. "I'm—"

"You're going to bed," Anne said firmly. "Right now."

Variam seemed about to argue, then looked at Anne and changed his mind. He allowed himself to be led off grumbling. Luna watched Anne and Variam go, then shook her head. "What's the order, oh master?"

"You can get a fire started," I said. "This place is bloody

freezing. And while you do that I'm going to try and figure out who I should tell this whole crazy story to first."

Luna opened up the stove and sniffed at it, sneezed, then looked dubiously at the basket of firewood. I'd just taken out my phone and was deciding which number to dial when I paused. "Ah, damn."

"What's wrong?" Luna asked.

I looked towards where Anne and Variam had vanished. "I just remembered I never restocked the kitchen."

chapter 14

Explaining the whole thing to the Council kept me busy for the next few days.

I was interviewed by the Keepers, then by Council reps, then by the masters in charge of the apprentice program, then by the Keepers again, then by some other guys whose names I can't remember, then by the Keepers one more time. After that I had to tell the whole story to each of them again, except slower and in more detail. After *that* I had to tell the whole story to each of them *again*, by which point I was about ready to chew my own arm off, or possibly someone else's. Luna got lucky and was let out sometime around the second day.

Anne and Variam got interviewed too, and their interviews were a lot less friendly than mine. Anne had it especially bad—it took a long time to convince the Keepers that she hadn't fled from custody and even then they didn't stop treating her as a suspect. I later found out that the only way Anne finally got them to accept her story was by submitting to a memory probe.

The rest of the tournament—unsurprisingly—was cancelled. A Council task force evacuated everyone from Fountain Reach and established a cordon around the mansion. Fortunately all the remaining apprentices got away safe. Unfortunately Crystal did too. She'd seen which way the wind was blowing and had given Lyle the slip within minutes of getting back to Fountain Reach, and by the time the order went out to bring her in for questioning she was long gone. Talisid had been giving me regular updates and on the third day he sent me a message with an invitation.

        | | | | | | | | |

The train that took Luna and me into the Cotswolds was the same one I'd taken for my first trip there, and as we alighted I looked around to see that the country station was deserted. The train pulled away from the platform, and as the rumble and clatter of the carriages faded into the distance everything became quiet. The town the station was built in was a small one and there wasn't much traffic.

I walked out of the station and onto the main road. "Aren't we taking a car?" Luna asked. She'd been quiet on the trip and was looking around at the green hills. It was less than an hour to sunset and the light was fading quickly.

"We're early," I said. "Might as well walk."

Luna looked resigned but didn't complain, and we turned towards Fountain Reach and settled into a steady pace. It had been a clear winter's day and the temperature dropped like a rock as the sun disappeared behind the western hills. The stars came out, bright and twinkling in the clear air, the Square of Pegasus hanging almost directly overhead while the stars of the Summer Triangle sank into the west.

We came up around Fountain Reach from over the back hillside. We bypassed the campsite where we'd gathered around a fire with Anne and Variam and Sonder a few nights ago, and descended towards the clearing where I'd seen Onyx and Lisa before that. The woods were going from shadowy to pitch-black, but neither Luna nor I slipped or fell.

As we approached the clearing I began to make out lights between the trees, and we emerged onto the grass to see that shielded lamps had been stuck into the grass around the clearing's edge. Two men were talking at the centre of the clearing: one I didn't know and one I did. As I watched they finished their conversation and one turned and walked away down the hill, disappearing into the darkness. The other turned to us with a nod. "Verus. Luna."

"Hey, Talisid," I said. In the dim light I could see he was still wearing his maths-teacher suit, looking faintly ridiculous in the winter forest. There was the crackle of static and Talisid raised a hand apologetically. "Just a moment." He took out a radio and spoke into it. "Receiving."

"Charges are set," a voice said from the radio speaker. "Everyone's accounted for."

"Did anyone enter the building?"

"No."

"Good," Talisid said. "You have full tactical command from this point. Proceed at your discretion."

"Roger that," the voice said. "Moving into final positions now."

Talisid clicked the radio off and returned it to his pocket. "So you decided not to go in," I said.

"The Council decided that the chances of a successful recovery from Vitus's shadow realm were too low to justify the risks of mounting an expedition." Talisid gave me a glance. "Based on your report it didn't sound as though there was any realistic likelihood of finding survivors."

I thought of the slaughterhouse in Vitus's sanctum, piles of bones stacked neatly in their alcoves. "No," I said.

We stood in the darkness on the hillside, looking down upon Fountain Reach. The mansion was dark, no lights showing from the windows. I couldn't see any activity but I knew people were moving in the grounds. "Any news on Crystal?" I said.

"Of a sort," Talisid said. "We haven't been able to pick up her trail, but we managed to find one of her hideouts and it turned out to be quite a source of information."

"About her and Vitus?"

"It seems Vitus had been practising his particular brand of life extension for some time," Talisid said with an expression of distaste. "Apparently his ritual absorbed his victims' life force through the medium of their blood—I'll spare you the details. Unfortunately for him, the ritual was providing diminishing returns. Each killing was extending his own life by a shorter time. So he recruited Crystal to ensure a steady supply."

"What did she get out of it?"

"Knowledge," Talisid said. "Vitus shared his research with her. It seems Crystal came to believe that the flaw in the ritual had been Vitus's choice of subjects. Crystal started preying on adepts, and when that didn't work she began kidnapping apprentice mages. According to Crystal's notes, she believed that if they found the right mage the ritual would grant perfect immortality, without the . . . flaws Vitus had developed."

"And when they saw Anne use her magic, they decided she was the right mage."

Talisid nodded. "Hopefully we'll never find out if they were correct."

"As long as Crystal's still out there we might," I said sharply. "Do you have any leads?"

"Unfortunately since she disappeared in Fountain Reach there's very little to go on. We've tried tracer spells but so far nothing."

"So she gets away clean."

"I think the masters and relatives of the apprentices she helped murder might have something to say about that," Talisid said dryly. "I know at least five mages who are currently bending their full resources towards tracking Crystal down and killing her."

I made a neutral sound.

"Not everything is your responsibility, Verus," Talisid said, and his voice was firm. "You found her. Others will take it from here."

I turned away, looking into the darkness. Again I remembered that great bare room with its scent of death, rows and rows of alcoves filled with the remains of human bodies. I wondered how many Crystal had led there to their deaths, how many Vitus had butchered on that blood-soaked table. And I wondered what would have happened if Vitus and Crystal *hadn't* decided that their ritual needed an apprentice. If they'd kept on killing normals and sensitives and adepts, as they'd done for so long before, would any of the Light mages have noticed? And if they had, how many would have cared?

"Um," Luna said hesitantly. She'd been silent until now, watching our conversation from a safe distance. "Is Anne going to be okay? With the Council, I mean."

"She's still under arrest," Talisid said, "but as far as I know there are no plans to press for a trial. The last I heard from Avenor he was coming around to the view that she hadn't knowingly cooperated with any of the kidnappings."

"Knowingly?" I said.

Talisid nodded. "They seem to have accepted your explanation as the most probable one."

Luna looked between us. "What explanation?"

"Crystal had access to Anne through the apprentice program," I said. "She could have read the information she needed out of Anne's mind."

"It doesn't account for every detail," Talisid said. "But given Crystal's obvious guilt I think the Keepers are eventually going to accept it."

"So they're going to let Anne go?" Luna asked.

"I can't give any guarantees, but that's what I would expect."

Luna looked relieved. "Looks like it's about to kick off," I said.

Talisid turned towards Fountain Reach. "So it is."

For a few seconds the hillside was still. Then from below the night lit up in a flash as explosives went off all around Fountain Reach. The mansion's outer walls simply disintegrated, coming down in a tumble of bricks and stone even as the echoes of the first blast came rumbling around the hills. The inner layers of the mansion were spared from the initial shockwave only to be caught in the spreading flames, fire engulfing the house far quicker than should be possible.

The blaze grew by leaps and bounds, licking higher and higher. From below I could sense fire magic working to enhance the flames and air magic pouring in pure oxygen to feed them. Sparks and embers went soaring into the night sky. Even from here I could feel a slight warmth; down below it must have been truly hellish.

The wards didn't stand a chance and I felt them shredding and dissolving as the structure they were tied to burned away. I wondered what it must be like for Vitus, hidden in that pocket dimension that had once been his fortress and had now become his tomb. If it had been a smaller fire he might have been able to extinguish it by transporting away the air or the burning material as he had before, but there was nothing in the world that could have extinguished this. All he could do was sit there and watch.

I don't know if Vitus came out. There was a minute or two during which the wards still held, even while all around them Fountain Reach burned with a single flame. Maybe somewhere in that time Vitus Aubuchon did emerge, leaving his sanctuary for one last time in a final desperate attempt to defend his home. If he did he died there, alone and unnoticed in the blaze. A moment later the internal structure of the mansion groaned and broke, and Fountain Reach collapsed in an enormous crash, throwing a storm of smoke and sparks into the sky as the wards that protected it and linked it to that other copy of itself flickered and died.

The mages below didn't stop. They kept the fire going as the ruins of Fountain Reach dwindled, burning the wreckage to splinters and the splinters to ash. They weren't here to find or confront Vitus, they were here to eliminate him, as efficiently and safely as possible. Only when there was nothing left but dust did they finally let the fire die.

Talisid and Luna and I looked down the hillside in silence. Where Fountain Reach had stood was an open patch of scorched ground, still glowing with heat. "I think we're done here," Talisid said. "Was there anything else?"

"No," I said.

"You did a very good job," Talisid said, giving a nod to Luna to include her. "Call me any time you need my assistance. Good night."

Talisid walked down into the forest and disappeared into the darkness between the trees. I gave the scorched patch one final glance, then turned away. "Come on," I said to Luna. "Time to go home."

 ı ı ı ı ı ı ı ıı

"R un through it for me one more time," I said.

"Again?" Luna said with a sigh.

It was a few hours later and we were standing outside a coffee shop in Soho. Now that we were back in London the winter night was a little bit warmer but much less clear, the fuzz of the city glow clouding the sky above. Neon lights shone from the buildings and scatterings of people moved past in twos and threes. "I'm going to stay here until you pick me up," Luna said in her *why-do-I-have-to-do-this?* voice.

"Or?"

"Or until it's been one and a half hours."

"And after that?"

"I go somewhere safe and call Sonder and Talisid and read them the message in this letter."

"And if I call you and tell you it's all clear?"

"Then I run like hell. Is this about that thing you had Sonder research for you?"

"Yes." I handed Luna the envelope. "If everything goes to plan I'll be back within an hour."

"Why can't I come?" Luna asked, accepting it. "I did last time."

"If you open that letter you'll know. Enjoy the coffee."

||||||||||

Tiger's Palace looked pretty much the same as when I'd last seen it. The shark-eyed bouncers let me pass, and the roar of music washed over me as I crossed the dance floor. I caught a glimpse of one of the kids who'd picked a fight with me and Luna. The instant he saw me his eyes went wide and he vanished into the crowd. I smiled to myself and walked up the stairs.

Jagadev's throne room was filled with a smaller entourage than last time, and Jagadev wasn't there. The Asian guy with sunglasses stopped me once again. If he was still bruised from the last visit, he didn't show it. When I said I was here to see Jagadev, he gave a curt "Follow me" and led me farther in. The bead curtain parted to reveal a small maze of corridors. I passed a couple of heavies with badly concealed guns under their jackets who gave me unfriendly looks before Sunglasses stopped in front of a door. "Inside."

I opened the door and walked in. It swung shut silently behind me.

Jagadev was there, and he was alone. The chamber was a dining room, wide and tall, with hangings of red and dark gold. Gold statuettes stood on tables, and curved swords and intricately woven tapestries hung on the walls. A fire blazed in the fireplace, its flickering light illuminating the long table at the centre, and at the middle of the table sat Jagadev. A meal was laid out before him but he sat with his clawed paws clasped and still. His dark eyes watched me opaquely as I approached the table and stopped.

Jagadev made a gesture towards the chair opposite him. "Sit."

"Thanks." I pulled out the chair. Jagadev's plate was piled

with some sort of meat I didn't recognise and his glass was filled with red wine, but both seemed untouched.

"You wished to speak to me," Jagadev said in his growling purr once I was seated.

"I did," I said. "First, I'd like to thank you for the pointer towards Fountain Reach. It was very accurate, as I'm sure you know."

I stopped. "Is that all?" Jagadev said.

"No," I said. "I think I might have figured out who's been trying to kill your ward Anne. I thought you might be interested."

"Speak."

"Thanks." I settled back in the wooden chair. "It interested me because once I looked back on it the first thing I noticed was just how much bad stuff has been happening to Anne over the last week. First there were those assassins in Archway, then there were those constructs at the motorway café, then she got arrested by the Council and could easily have gotten executed, and *then* she nearly got killed off by Vitus. When you think about it it's actually pretty surprising she's still alive."

Jagadev watched me silently. "So," I said. "I looked at Anne and tried to figure out why someone would want her dead so badly. And I really couldn't come up with a good explanation. Okay, Vitus was after her because she was an apprentice who was the right age. And the Council were after her because they thought she was Vitus's accomplice. But the assassins and the constructs didn't fit with that at all. So I tried to figure out who was behind those.

"The obvious person to blame was Crystal, because she was the one who kidnapped all the others. But if it was Crystal then she should have been trying to *kidnap* Anne, not *kill* her. And there was something else—the more I thought about it the more it seemed to me that neither of the attacks would have done Crystal or Vitus any favours. They wouldn't have led us away from Fountain Reach—if anything they would have done the exact opposite. If I'd been killed in the middle of investigating that place it would just have convinced the next few investigators that I was on the right track. So whoever was behind it, they weren't on Crystal and Vitus's side. But they weren't on Anne's side either, because they were trying to kill her. And they weren't on my side or Variam's side, because they could have killed us too, and they weren't on Morden or Onyx's side, because those guys wanted me alive, at least until they found Vitus. In fact, it didn't seem like they were on *anyone's* side, which didn't make any sense.

"So I decided I'd been going about this the wrong way. I threw out all my ideas and started from square one. And when I looked at it with a fresh eye the first thing that jumped out at me was that every time Anne had been in danger, your name seemed to crop up. That first time in Archway she'd gone there in your car with your driver. Same with the motorway services. Vitus trying to kill her wasn't your doing . . . but it *was* your doing that she was in Fountain Reach in the first place. And that's a bit odd, isn't it? Anne doesn't duel, so why send her to a duelling tournament when there's someone out there kidnapping apprentices? Especially when you knew that Fountain Reach was the place those kidnappings were coming from? And finally there was the Council arresting her. It didn't seem like that could be your fault . . . until I remembered that habit of yours of asking Anne about her classmates. The Keepers are probably going to decide that Crystal got that information out of Anne's mind, but they're not a hundred percent happy with that explanation and neither am I. Of course, if the information was getting passed on to Crystal by someone she *told* it to . . . well, then that would make Anne a perfect spy, wouldn't it? She'd be Crystal's accomplice without ever meeting her. But as long as she was alive, she'd be a link that could be traced back to you."

I stopped and waited. The only sound was the crackle of the fire. "Are you accusing me of attempting to kill my own ward?" Jagadev asked.

"It doesn't seem to make sense, does it?" I said. "After all, you pointed me towards Fountain Reach. It's almost as if you wanted to get rid of *everyone*. Anne and Variam and me and Vitus and Crystal and Onyx . . . and a whole lot of random apprentices in England."

Jagadev extended his hand to pick up his glass of wine and drank from it, his eyes not leaving mine. "Then there were those gunmen who went after Anne," I said "I always had the feeling they were killed to stop them from talking about their employer, but it was interesting *how* they were killed, wasn't it? Those weren't gunshot wounds, more like claws. Almost like a big cat."

Jagadev set the glass down. "Please come to the point."

"Sorry. Anyway, the problem was that I still couldn't figure out any reasonable motive. So I did some historical research. I eventually found what I was looking for but I had to go back a long way. All the way to 1865."

I felt Jagadev go still. "For Americans, that was the Thirteenth Amendment," I said. "For Indians, it was the British Raj. And for mages, it was the rakshasa wars. That was the year a group of British and Indian mages supported by an auxiliary force attacked the palace of a rakshasa named Lady Arati. Arati was killed, but the other rakshasa in the palace—her husband—escaped." I paused. "Just out of interest I tried to trace the family trees of the mages who carried out that attack. It was very difficult. Over the decades nearly all of them seem to have suffered mysterious deaths or just disappeared. In fact as far as I can tell, there are only two direct descendants of those mages alive today. Their names are Anne Walker and Variam Singh. And the name of the rakshasa that escaped that attack was Lord Jagadev."

Jagadev didn't move or speak. "Mages like the idea of immortality," I said. "But I don't think many of us understand what it would really mean. What would it be like to lose someone with whom you were going to live forever? What would you do about it?" I paused. "You could take revenge. It wouldn't be hard, with all that time to do it in. But in the end, no matter what you did, all the men and women who did the deed would be dead of old age if nothing else. So what then? What price to avenge the death of an immortal? Maybe going after the children of the ones who killed her, following the line down and down until every one of their descendants was gone. Or maybe going after *all* mages, manipulating events to cause the deaths of as many apprentices as possible, reducing the number of mages in the world one by one." I stopped and looked at Jagadev. "What do you think? When is it enough?"

The room was very quiet, and Jagadev was still. The futures weren't. Looking ahead I saw futures branching, the room erupting into a blur of violence. "Before you make any decisions," I said, "I should point out that there are people who know where I am. They've got copies of what we're discussing and they're under orders not to open them. Yet."

Jagadev and I sat and looked at each other. Ahead of me the futures flickered between two branches. In one, we continued to sit and look at each other. In the other . . . I'd come prepared, but even so I wasn't sure I would make it out of the room. I expect to be threatened in these sorts of meetings, but Jagadev wasn't going to make threats. If he started something it would be spectacular.

Gradually the futures of violence began to recede and finally winked out. Jagadev stayed silent for a full minute before speaking. "I hope you have some proof for your assertions."

"Anne and Variam's family history isn't difficult to check," I said.

"Nor does it prove anything."

"Not on its own," I agreed. "Of course, if those two were to suffer mysterious deaths as well you'd suddenly become a very likely suspect."

"What do you want?" Jagadev said.

"First, no more assassins in the night," I said. "Second, I want you to cut your ties with Anne and Variam. They go free and clear with no more plots against them."

"And if I do not?"

"Then I'll take everything I've told you and everything else I've found and publish it to every mage in the country," I said. "Right now there are a lot of mages looking for someone to blame for their missing apprentices. They'd *love* to have someone to vent their rage on."

"Again," Jagadev said. "You have no proof."

"They won't care," I said. "Not for a nonhuman."

"And you think they will listen to you, Alex Verus?" Jagadev said softly. "To one who betrayed his master, turned against his tradition, and is responsible for the deaths of so many other mages himself? One who holds himself apart from the Light Council and the Dark associations, with mortal enemies amongst both, and whose closest allies are adepts and nonhumans? They will accept your story on nothing but your word? I think not."

"Jagadev, let me tell you something about diviners,"

I said. "You're right that other mages don't like us very much. But do you know the real reason they don't want us around? It's not because they don't trust us to find out the truth. It's because they trust us all too well."

"Then let me tell you something about myself," Jagadev said. His voice stayed soft, but something about it sent a chill down my spine. "You are very far indeed from the first mage to threaten me. Do you think I hold this domain at the whim of your Council? I have resources you cannot conceive of. If you bring war to me, then let me assure you that the apprentices whose lives you seem to value so highly will be the first casualties."

We sat staring at each other for a long moment, then I broke the deadlock, leaning back in my chair. "That is the problem, isn't it? If you ever really decided to cut loose you could do a lot of damage. On the other hand, by publishing this information I could do *you* a lot of damage. And if it came to war you'd eventually lose. You know it and I know it. It wouldn't matter how many you killed. It'd be wolves pulling down a tiger. They'd bring you down by sheer weight of numbers." I met Jagadev's eyes. "So I guess what it comes down to is this. Is taking your revenge on two human apprentices more important to you than your own immortal life?"

"And what do you gain from this?" Jagadev asked.

"Does it matter?" I said. "Anne and Variam are a liability to you now. I'm going to be watching them and so will others, and if anything happens to them while they're supposed to be in your care we'll know it was you. Even if it wasn't."

I could have said more, but stopped. Some instinct told me that trying to persuade Jagadev further wasn't going to help. Instead I sat and waited, watching the futures whirl ahead of me. The fire crackled in the quiet room, throwing flickering light over Jagadev's orange-striped face and glinting off his opaque black eyes.

"Anne and Variam are banished from my domain," Jagadev said at last. "As are you. Should any of you set foot in this place again your lives are forfeit."

I nodded.

"Go," Jagadev said.

I did. My muscles were tensed all the way to the door; if Jagadev was going to try anything, now would be the time. Every step I half-expected to hear a sudden rush of movement behind me.

But Jagadev did nothing. I reached the door and took a last look back. The rakshasa was still watching me from the table, lit up in the firelight, the meal untasted before him. I studied him for a moment and then turned and left. The guards let me go.

ı ı ı ı ı ı ı ı

It was another clear winter's day. The temperature had been getting lower and lower until it was close to freezing, and according to the forecasts there might even be snow this weekend. But for today the skies were clear, and we were taking the opportunity to do some moving.

"That the last one?" I said as I came back out into the street and saw the solitary box by the van.

"Yep," Sonder said. "Is there anything else?"

"It's fine," I said. "Go ahead and take the van back. Thanks for the help."

"It's okay," Sonder said. "Uh, you know, I could probably find somewhere they could use. The Council has a few buildings that are pretty much always empty."

I shook my head. "You've done more than enough."

Sonder hesitated. "Have you told them about . . . ?"

"What you found out about Jagadev?" I asked. "No. And to be honest, I'm not sure I'm going to."

Sonder looked startled. "Really?"

I nodded. "But . . ." Sonder said. "It's the truth. I mean, I know it's not going to be fun for them to hear, but . . ."

"You did the research on Anne and Variam's family history," I said. "How much of an extended family do they have?"

Sonder thought for a moment. "I don't think they have much of one. Not in their generation anyway. Variam used to have—"

"Right. How many of those deaths do you think were from natural causes?"

Sonder paused. "Oh."

"And how do you think Variam in particular is going to react when he finds out?"

"Um. I guess he's not going to be happy."

"No," I said. "He's not."

We stood by the van in silence for a moment. "What are you going to do?" Sonder asked.

"Sooner or later they're going to have to know," I said. "But . . . I think I'm going to wait. At least until things quiet down."

"I guess," Sonder said. "Are we still on for dinner?"

"Sure. Drop by whenever you like."

As Sonder drove the van away I picked up the box and carried it back to the shop. As I did I noticed that a couple of customers were hovering around the front door. "Hi," one of them said as I fumbled for the handle. "Are you open?"

"Sure," I said, shouldering the door open. "Come in and—" I stopped as I realised no one was behind the counter.

"Do you work here?" the younger one said.

"Yeah." I put the box down and headed past the counter for the hall. "Wait just a sec and I'll find the sales manager."

I heard the argument from all the way down the stairs. "You are *not* leaving that crap all over my room," Luna was saying.

"It's where I'm staying, all right?" Variam said.

"I don't care where you stay but you're not staying here."

"You said this was a spare room!"

"I told *Anne* this was a spare room. I didn't say *you* could have it."

"This is such bullshit," Variam said. "You don't even live here."

"Yeah, well, sometimes classes run late and I sleep over, and I don't want to be picking your dirty clothes off the floor."

"My clothes aren't—"

"Hi," I said, sticking my head through the door of the spare room. "Is there a problem?"

"Variam wants my room," Luna said with a frown. She was standing in front of the camp bed with her arms folded.

"It's not your room—" Variam started.

"All right," I cut in. "Let me break it down for you guys. I have two rooms available, the living room and the spare. I don't care who sleeps where, but if you're a guest here you should be polite to your host, and if you're a host you should be trying to make your guest feel comfortable."

Luna and Variam looked at each other, then back at me. "Okay?" I said.

"Okay," Luna said.

"So who gets the room?" Variam said.

"You're over twenty years old," I said. "Sort it out your-selves. Oh, and Variam, the rest of your boxes are down-stairs, and Luna, you're supposed to be minding the shop."

Luna sighed and obeyed. Variam followed. As I left I heard them start arguing again.

I wandered into the living room to find the rest of the boxes in a pile, stacked neatly but unopened. I thought for a minute, then went out onto my balcony and climbed the ladder to the roof.

There's not much on the roof of my flat—a little parapet around the edge, one chimney, and that's it. It's bare and cold and there's no shelter, but I love coming up here all the same and it's because of the view. The edges of the roof go out just far enough that you can't look down into the street, but other than that there's no direction you can't see. As I climbed I could hear the sounds of the city all around us; the whistling of the wind on the rooftops, the creak of stone and metal from the buildings nearby, the low steady growl of traffic. Voices echoed up from the streets around, a train rumbled along one of the railway bridges in the middle distance, and far overhead an airliner drew a clear contrail of white across the blue sky. Millions of people, millions of stories, all blending into the sounds of London.

Anne was sitting on the parapet, looking southward over the skyline with her hands around her knees. She looked back as I crossed the roof. "Cold?" I asked.

Anne shook her head and I sat down next to her with a sigh. It really was a great view. "Are Luna and Vari okay?" Anne asked.

"Oh, they'll be fine. Just sorting out the pecking order."

"Thank you for letting us stay here," Anne said. "And . . . for everything else."

"Don't worry about it."

"When Vitus took me . . ." Anne said. She was staring down at the building opposite, and she had to stop and take a breath before she could go on. "I was so scared I couldn't think. I was lying on that table, trying to keep myself alive and hide my life so he couldn't find me. I didn't know if I could do it. The first time nearly killed me and I knew if Vitus came back to take any more of my blood I'd die. Then I felt you come in and Vari and Luna and . . ." She looked up at me, red-brown eyes serious. "I wasn't scared anymore. I knew you'd come."

I looked away. I always get uncomfortable when people are grateful to me—I'm never sure I really deserve it. "Eh. The only reason it was me was because I made Variam stay back and guard the entrance."

"Vari always fights," Anne said simply. "He always tries to protect me and I know he'll never give up. But I don't know if he'll be *okay*. Usually . . . I guess it's like I need to be responsible for everyone. And I don't mind or anything, but . . . It feels like I don't need to worry about that so much that when you're around. It's nice."

"You know, I've always wondered," I said. "What *is* the deal with you and Variam? How did you get to know each other?"

"Everyone asks that," Anne said with a slight smile. "We met because of another boy called Harbir. He was Variam's older brother and when things started happening at my school Harbir came to help. He was like that." Anne's smile faded. "But he was killed. I didn't know how to use my magic back then, but . . . I wish I'd been able to do something.

"After that Sagash kidnapped me and took me away. I was in his castle for a long time. Sagash was a Dark mage but he didn't have any other apprentices. He wanted me to become his Chosen, and when I said no he tried to make me." Anne was quiet for a moment. "It was . . . bad. Really bad. Back then I didn't know Vari well—we only met because he was Harbir's brother. He could have stayed at home and been safe. But he didn't. He came looking for me and he tracked Sagash down and in the end we were able to get away. I think he did it because of Harbir. One of the last things Harbir had been trying to do before he disappeared was protect me and . . . I guess Vari feels he kind of inherited the responsibility. He takes that kind of thing really seriously. He'd never let me get hurt, even if he doesn't like me all that much."

"Wait, what?"

"He doesn't hate me or anything," Anne said. "But I think it gets on his nerves the way I'm so quiet about things. He likes it when people stand up to him."

"So that's why he finally started listening to me."

"What do you mean?"

"Nothing."

Anne gave me a puzzled look, then shook it off. "Did everyone make it out from Vitus's sanctum okay? The Keepers wouldn't tell me."

"Crystal got away clean," I said. "Lyle too—he got out with Crystal and she left him behind. He wasn't hurt or anything, but last I heard he was in hot water. He was supposed to be keeping the apprentices in the White Stone safe and instead he ended up arranging them an all-expenses paid trip to Death Mansion."

"Are the Council going to blame him?"

I shook my head. "He didn't actually know what was going on, so no. Still, I don't think he's going to be getting any promotions for a while." It was an odd feeling. I've had a grudge against Lyle for the longest time, but now that things had gone wrong for him I found to my surprise that I wasn't especially happy about it. If he'd gotten in trouble because he'd finally taken advantage of the wrong person I probably would have laughed, but the way it looked to me was that it had been *Crystal* who'd taken advantage of *him*. Somehow that just made it sad.

"What about Onyx?" Anne asked. "Do you think he's . . . ?"

"I wish," I said with a snort. "I've seen him survive worse. I'm just glad he hasn't come back for a rematch yet."

We sat listening to the sounds of the city. The cold air bit at me and I knew I ought to go in soon, but I was reluctant to break the moment. "It feels strange," Anne said at last.

"What does?"

"Being away from Jagadev," Anne said. At some point she'd stopped tacking *Lord* onto his name. "It's the first time Vari and I have been all on our own."

"You're wondering what you should do," I said.

Anne nodded. "Well, for the short term you can both stay here," I said. "I might not have as much status as some, but as long as you're living under this roof you'll have some protection at least."

"Thank you."

"Don't get too grateful. I'll probably want you to help out around the place."

I saw Anne try to hide a smile. "But . . ." I said. "In the long run you and Variam are going to have to decide what to do next."

Anne seemed about to say something, hesitated.

"I can't take the two of you on as apprentices," I said. "I couldn't take on someone else and teach Luna as well. But even if I didn't have Luna, I *still* couldn't teach you properly. I only understand the basics of elemental and living magic, and you and Variam are way beyond anything I could show you. Both of you have more power right now than I'll ever have. You need a teacher who can use the same type of magic that you can."

A chill wind gusted over us, ruffling our hair. "Or you could try and make a go of it as independents," I said. "But that's got its own problems. You're going to be seen as rogues or runaways or both. If you can get enough support and pass the journeyman tests, then the Light Council will have to recognise you as adult mages. But that's not easy."

Anne sighed. "None of it is, is it?" She straightened. "Well, we've made it this far. We'll make do."

"You will," I said. "And you won't be on your own this time."

Anne looked at me and smiled. I got up and held my hand out to her. "Come on. Let's go help Variam unpack."

We went down out of the cold and towards the warmth and voices below.

From
BENEDICT JACKA

cursed
An Alex Verus Novel

Since his second sight made him infamous for defeating powerful Dark mages, Alex has been keeping his head down. But now he's discovered the resurgence of a forbidden ritual. Someone is harvesting the life force of magical creatures—destroying them in the process. And draining humans is next on the agenda. Hired to investigate, Alex realizes that not everyone on the Council wants him delving any deeper. Struggling to distinguish ally from enemy, he finds himself the target of those who would risk their own sanity for power . . .

Praise for the Alex Verus novels

"Harry Dresden would like Alex Verus tremendously—and be a little nervous around him. I just added Benedict Jacka to my must-read list."
    —Jim Butcher, #1 *New York Times* bestselling author

"Benedict Jacka writes a deft thrill ride of an urban fantasy—a stay-up-all-night read. Alex Verus is a very smart man surviving in a very dangerous world."
    —Patricia Briggs, #1 *New York Times* bestselling author

penguin.com
facebook.com/AceRocBooks
benedictjacka.co.uk